GW01276012

MERCURIUS

Novels by Patrick Harpur

THE SERPENT'S CIRCLE

THE RAPTURE

MERCURIUS

or, the Marriage of Heaven & Earth

Edited
with an introduction
by

PATRICK HARPUR

M
MACMILLAN
LONDON

Copyright © Patrick Harpur 1990

All rights reserved. No reproduction, copy or transmission
of this publication may be made without written permission.
No paragraph of this publication may be reproduced, copied
or transmitted save with written permission or in
accordance with the provisions of the Copyright Act 1956
(as amended). Any person who does any unauthorised act
in relation to this publication may be liable to criminal
prosecution and civil claims for damages.

First published 1990 by
MACMILLAN LONDON LIMITED
4 Little Essex Street London WC2R 3LF
and Basingstoke

Associated companies in Auckland, Delhi, Dublin, Gaborone,
Hamburg, Harare, Hong Kong, Johannesburg, Kuala Lumpur,
Lagos, Manzini, Melbourne, Mexico City, Nairobi, New York,
Singapore and Tokyo

A CIP catalogue record for this book is available from
the British Library

ISBN 0-333-43781-0

Typeset by Matrix, 21 Russell Street, London, WC2

Printed and bound in Great Britain by Billings Book Plan, Worcester

To Eileen,
wherever she may be

ACKNOWLEDGEMENTS

The author would like to thank the following for their kind permission to reprint extracts: Merlin Press for *Totemism* by Levi Strauss, Times Newspapers Ltd for David Hart's article of December 1985, Faber & Faber Ltd for *The Dyer's Hand* by W. H. Auden, Anthony Gibbs and Phillips Ltd for *The Dawn of Magic* by Louis Pauwels and Jacques Bergier, Cambridge University Press for *The Dawn of Magic* by John Michell, Grafton Publishers for *The Alchemists* by Sherwood Taylor, and C. W. Daniel and Co. for *Gold of a Thousand Mornings* by Armand Barbault.

The engravings are reproduced by permission of the trustees of the British Museum.

The publishers have made every effort to trace copyright holders. If we have inadvertently omitted to acknowledge anyone, we should be most grateful if this could be brought to our attention for correction.

CONTENTS

	Introduction	ix
1	Calcination	1
2	Solution	69
3	Separation	121
4	Conjunction	181
5	Putrefaction	237
6	Congelation	291
7	Sublimation	351
8	Projection	415
	Notes	425

Know this: I, Mercurius, have set down a full, true and infallible account of the Great Work. But I give you fair warning that unless you seek the true philosophical gold and not the gold of the vulgar, unless your heart is fixed with unbending intent on the true Stone of the Philosophers, unless you are steadfast in your quest, abiding by God's laws in all faith and humility and eschewing all vanity, conceit, falsehood, intemperance, pride, lust and faint-heartedness, *read no farther* lest I prove fatal to you . . .

INTRODUCTION

These disconcerting words opposite were written on the first sheet of paper I took from one of two plastic bags which had been left on the doorstep of my third-floor London flat, 7 April 1983. The person who left them was passed on the staircase by two of my next-door neighbours – the wife of a Scandinavian diplomat and her nine-year-old son. The former described my visitor as a tall woman with a handsome bony face, close-cropped auburn hair and dressed in a long dark coat. The boy, on the other hand, insisted that the person was a man. He was probably confused by the height, hair and clothing of the visitor who, I think it's safe to say, was a former girlfriend of mine called Eileen. She and I had been intimate over a brief but intense period the previous summer. One day, without warning, she left her flat, her job and her liaison with me and moved to the West of England. This I learnt from a cursory farewell note, with no indication of her exact whereabouts, which arrived shortly after her departure. I have not seen her since.

Eileen was indeed tall, without being willowy. I would say she was attractive rather than 'handsome', although her face did have good bones, including a fine straight nose, as well as startling bluey-green eyes. Her hair, I'd say, was more red than auburn, and she used to wear it long. We met – as she describes – through a common involvement in book-packaging (a form of popular publishing). She was thirty-three, a year older than I. We had been contemporaries at Cambridge University, where she read Archaeology and Anthropology, but we didn't know each other then.

The plastic bags were full of papers, as well as an irregular lump of softish rock which was mislaid during the course of my move out of the flat only a week or so later. The papers were written in two hands: one belonged to Eileen, the other to a country vicar who calls himself 'Smith'. Through my interest in the work of the Swiss psychologist C. G. Jung (1875–1961) – whose work I had discussed with Eileen more than once – I realised that Smith was a modern practitioner of alchemy and that his writing included an account of the alchemical *Magnum Opus* or Great Work. Eileen's writings begin as (unposted) letters to me, but, following her discovery of Smith's manuscript, they change into something like a commentary on this alchemical operation.

It may be partly because her letters are painful to me that I neglected the documents for so long. I certainly sifted through them from time to time, finding myself amazed, frustrated, baffled, excited by turns. I even began sorting them out, separating Smith's stuff from Eileen's because the two had been jumbled up. However, I only set about them in earnest after I had finished my novel, *The Rapture*. I was made uneasy by the noticeable influence which the writings had exerted on the book, without my being aware of it at the time of writing. Thus I was driven to try and lay the ghost to rest once and for all.

This was more easily decided than done. I had to do a fair amount of research into alchemy simply so that I could put the papers in the right order. Both sets are only scantily dated, and so I have preferred to omit dates altogether. However, it's fair to say that Smith's account covers a period from March to December, 1952 or 1953; Eileen's runs from the end of September 1982, to the beginning of April 1983.

Another difficulty I had was deciphering Smith's small, crabbed handwriting in faded black ink. In addition, at the start of his work, he kept his journal in a black notebook, separate from his 'laboratory notes' written on loose sheets of plain, high-quality paper. I had, so to speak, to fit these together. Fortunately, he abandons the notebook before very long so that the record of his alchemical progress and that of everyday events become a single account.

Eileen is more consistent, but scarcely more intelligible, as she dashed off reams of scrawled prose – letters, thoughts, daily occurrences alike – on the same loose pieces of A4 paper, some of which are torn in her haste to rip them off the pad. By the time I had sorted out her writings from Smith's, I realised that she probably mixed them up deliberately, wanting them to be read concurrently rather than serially; and so I have laid out their writings in alternating sections. The advantage of this arrangement – which Eileen, I think, intended – is that various of her acute alchemical analyses can be taken out of chronological order and placed nearer to those entries of Smith's on which they can cast much-needed light. Otherwise I have preserved as best I can the chronological order of events and philosophical reflections in both collections of papers.

In order to reduce the book to manageable proportions (both writers were almost maniacally prolific!) I have preferred on the whole to omit entire entries rather than to edit or cut them individually. The loss to Eileen's text is insignificant; the loss to Smith's, more serious. For, in removing the record of many trivial events that threaten to distort the outline of his *Magnum Opus*, I have also done violence to the very real impression he gives of being a hard-working, conscientious, essentially *good* pastor, who does not allow his occult activity to interfere with his parochial duties. In other words, the full text shows him to be far less eccentric and self-absorbed, far more kindly and concerned for the needy, than my truncated version suggests. I have also excised some of his less crucial alchemical entries because, as repetitions of various processes and 'circulations', they overload a text which is already, of necessity, too repetitious.

I was tempted, of course, to edit a number of Eileen's uncomplimentary references to myself – especially where, naturally, I think she's quite wrong. Needless to say, I resisted. But I would ask the reader to take her statements regarding our relationship with a pinch of salt.

In case the book proves offensive to anyone who appears in it, or to their relatives, I have changed all names (except, of course, those of the two writers) to those which, I trust, catch the flavour of the originals.

So much for the provenance and appearance of the book in its raw state. Now, a word about its content . . .

Until I read Jung, I knew nothing about alchemy except that its purpose was to make the Philosophers' Stone, which either transmutes base metal to gold or confers immortality, or both. In other words, I assumed that it was a primitive forerunner, riddled with superstition, of chemistry proper. Jung, however, shows that its *Magnum Opus* was more a psychological than a physical process – a quest for self-realisation under the guise of a chemical experiment. Although his writings on the subject are nearly as difficult as the alchemical recipes – complex agglomerations of psychology, theology, mythology, philosophy and chemistry – I was satisfied that he had cracked the problem. And, in the course of my reading, many misconceptions about the Art were dispelled. (For example, I learnt that no alchemist worth his salt was ever interested in making ordinary gold. He was interested only in making 'philosophical gold' – another name, presumably, for the Philosophers' Stone whose authenticity was *tested* by applying it to lead or tin, say, and seeing if it turned these metals to gold. Thus, gold was, as it were, a by-product of alchemy and not its main purpose.)

Now that I have edited these texts, I am less satisfied with Jung's explanation. Quite apart from the fact that he is not concerned (as he admits) with the practical side of alchemy, but only with its subjective effects, he often begs more questions than he answers. It begins to look as if alchemy is a larger and more profound phenomenon than psychology can embrace – a whole science of the soul, in fact, which has yet to be adequately realised. Even Jung is, in the end, prepared to concede that it entails a view of the world which belongs, not to the past, but to the future.

The alchemists disagreed on just about every aspect of the Great Work, except one: that it is impossible to succeed without the *secret*.

This usually came either through a revelation or, more often, through an alchemical master who already possessed it. For example, Elias Ashmole (1617–92), the famous English antiquarian, joyfully records in his diary for 13 May 1653, that William Backhous, 'lying sick in Fleet Street, over against St Dunstan's Church, and not knowing whether he should live or die, about eleven o'clock told me in syllables the true matter of the Philosopher's [*sic*] Stone, which he bequeathed to me as a legacy'. Whereupon it is said that Ashmole, who collected alchemical manuscripts and wrote freely about it, never again uttered a word on the subject.

'What was this secret?' asks F. Sherwood Taylor,* a former Director of London's Science Museum and author of many chemistry books. 'Of this we know nothing. That the alchemical works were unintelligible without it, no one will doubt who has read them; but what there was that, when told by one alchemist to another, could

---

* In *The Alchemists* (London, 1952; reissued 1976).

render them intelligible, we cannot guess. Yet that something was imparted in this way is quite certain.'

I believe that, on this contrary, we *can* guess the secret – and that all the information necessary for such a guess is contained in the texts presented here.

However, whether or not the secret is discovered (alchemical tradition forbids it to be broadcast, for very good reasons), I hope that the journey of discovery will be as worthwhile for the reader as it was for me. There's a great deal to divert us on the way. For instance, Smith's testimony is one of the very few extant accounts of actual alchemical practice. Moreover, in a series of 'meditations', he includes as clear and as incisive a description of alchemy's general principles and history as can be found anywhere. On a personal level, I was most affected by the suffering his Great Work entails, and by the deep conflicts it arouses in him both as a priest and as a man.

Eileen's is a different, but equally illuminating, story. Like us, she is confronted with the formidable task of having to make sense of the strange and paradoxical Work. She does a remarkable job. I always liked and admired Eileen, but I would never have guessed her capable of the sustained labour that an understanding of alchemy requires. It has to be, and clearly is for her, a labour of love. She is often confused, but just as often brilliant – and sometimes profound. I can vouch for the accuracy of her summary of Jung's psychology; I can applaud her application of it to the bizarre manuscript she unearths; but I could not have dreamt that she would be led to produce such a penetrating critique of Jung's work. Nor is this all. She has also pioneered an approach which, as far as I know, is entirely new: that is, to apply the principles of structural anthropology to the Work. Her results are truly enlightening. Whether she finally succeeds in unravelling the great secret, readers will judge for themselves.

The book is far from being all hard work – more than half the entries entertain us with the ordinary lives of the authors. As with all lives, these abound in lesser mysteries and questions which I have left unedited because I cannot be certain that they have no bearing on the book's main thrust. Will Robert, for instance, succeed in manufacturing the blue glass of Chartres? How did Pluto become disfigured? Under what circumstances did Nora become pregnant? What is the nature of Tim's vision in the graveyard – and where does he get his dresses? Why is Eileen frightened of her father's study? Is Mrs Zetterberg deranged or merely a satanist? Who was Smith's alchemical master? Will Nightingale Wood be axed? And so on. I had a lot of surprises when I tracked down the answers.

Lastly, something quite unexpected emerges from these writings taken as a whole: the sense that alchemy is the supreme expression of a world-view which, superior in many ways to our own, the book goes a long way towards reconstructing. More than that, the book can be seen as a plea, and a warning, not to neglect our deep-rooted spiritual heritage. At the very least, it is a unique and intriguing psychological case-history.

There are three kinds of notes in the text: brief insertions contained in square brackets, footnotes indicated by asterisks, and longer comments (often alchemists' biographical details), indicated by a number and placed at the end of the book. I have prefaced each of these more extensive notes with the phrase or sentence (in italics) to which the number in the text refers, to remind readers of the note's context.

There is no bibliography. Wherever I can, I cite the sources of quotations, authorship of books, etc. mentioned by Smith and Eileen (and myself) as and when they appear. Even if I could I wouldn't attempt to go into the history of alchemical scholarship. It's enough to say that scandalously few alchemical treatises have been translated and published. One or two can be found scattered in books or periodicals on alchemy, but serious research has to be conducted among the original (usually Latin) manuscripts in such august institutions as the British Library. Some fine collections exist, notably *Artis Auriferae* (2 vols, Basel, 1593), *Theatrum Chemicum* (vols 1–3, Ursel, 1602; vols 4–6, Strasbourg, 1613), Ashmole's *Theatrum Chemicum Britannicum* (London, 1652) and *Musaeum Hermeticum* (Frankfurt, 1678). This last collection has been edited and translated by A. E. Waite as *The Hermetic Museum Restored and Enlarged* (2 vols, London, 1893) and is still the standard source of alchemical treatises for non-Latin-readers.

The alchemical engravings which decorate the first pages of each stage of the book are taken from J. D. Mylius' *Philosophia Reformata* (Frankfurt, 1622).

ONE

Calcination

SMITH

Know this: I, Mercurius, have here set down a full, true and infallible account of the Great Work. But I give you fair warning that unless you seek the true philosophical gold and not the gold of the vulgar, unless your heart is fixed with unbending intent on the true Stone of the Philosophers, unless you are steadfast in your quest, abiding by God's laws in all faith and humility and eschewing all vanity, conceit, falsehood, intemperance, pride, lust and faint-heartedness, *read no farther* lest I prove fatal to you. For I am the watery venomous serpent who lies buried at the earth's centre; I am the fiery dragon who flies through the air. I am the one thing necessary for the whole Opus. I am the spirit of the metals, the fire which does not burn, the water which does not wet the hands. If you find the way to slay me you will find the philosophical mercury of the wise, even the White Stone beloved of the Philosophers. If you find the way to raise me up again, you will find the philosophical sulphur, that is, the Red Stone and Elixir of Life. Obey me and I will be your servant; free me and I will be your friend. Enslave me and I am a dangerous enemy; command me and I will make you mad; give me life and you will die.

So begins my translation of the manuscript which I carried away from my master's lodgings twenty years ago or more. It is rough and ready, I admit, and written with the same tremor that afflicts my hand whenever in the past I have pulled it from my desk drawer and glanced guiltily at its caveat. Today I do not thrust it away again out of sight (though rarely altogether out of mind).

What possessed me to free Mercurius from his Latin bonds into the vernacular? Does it mean that I intend to *proceed*? I hardly know myself. I thought I had done with our Philosophy. Yet, as Mercurius describes with fresh urgency the perils and rewards of the Magnum Opus [Great Work], a stupendous zest batters my heart as though I had recovered the last two decades.

Outside my window the light withdraws along the valley; the graveyard grows indistinct, the old yew is a knot of shadow; an old man, bent over, hurries home across the village green. I thought I had done with memories, as well; but now I find myself once again on the bridge beside my master. His face is dark, his skin leathery from years of suffering under Saturn in mean smoky rooms; his stooped ascetic frame, reflected in the Seine, wavers below him. He glares into the water as if it were withholding what he has searched so long for. His study of the Art was as profound as any man alive. He knew the *secret fire itself*. Yet he lacked the one thing needed to begin.

On the other hand, I who abandoned him after barely a year, I who least deserve grace, *I* have been vouchsafed – without effort or gratitude on my part – *that very thing* he squandered a fortune to find. I want to shout, 'Look! *Maître*! It's been *given* to me, take it, your search is over!' He stares into the water. He cannot hear me. But it's true, it's here, shivering under my hand – the most precious thing perhaps in all the world.

Is it his doleful memory that prompts me, *cries out* to me, to renew my hateful friendship – my loving enmity – with that strange godling Mercurius? Or is it –

I am seeing things. Lifting my eyes for a second, I saw (as if in answer to the above question!) a small woman, under five feet in height, wandering through the graveyard. Against the dull, still-wintering grass, against the granite headstones and the leafless grid of hedge, in front of the grey church, she glittered as incongruously as tinsel on a Christmas tree.

She wore a crimson evening gown, with long red satin gloves. The dying light caught on her gold earrings and golden lamé handbag. A black pill-box hat with a black veil attached hid her head and face. They gave her an air of mourning which contrasted bizarrely with the flashing brilliance of the red and gold. To see her drifting, exotic as a bird of paradise, among the graves at dusk, sent a cold shiver through me. But for her apparel, I could almost believe that she was Mrs B.'s infamous White Lady! Mesmerised, I watched her kneel briefly by a grave; but by the time I had started up and craned out of the window for a closer look, she was gone.

I wonder if such visions are to be a side-effect of my serendipity. Since my discovery, even familiar views have seemed more vivid, as if my eye-muscles have tightened up in order to pull the world into sharper focus. My hearing, too, has improved. My ears can detect Mrs B.'s righteous step in the hall, as she comes to light the lamps. As always, she will knock and enter in one movement, hoping to catch me in some unholy act. As always my face will be bland and calm. She will see me writing at my desk. Next to my hand she will see a crude unsightly lump of nothing-much, the great Chaos and priceless treasure of the Philosophers, which she will want to throw out before it 'soils' her carpet.

This is how the prima materia [prime, or first, matter] was disclosed to me.

Three inarticulate workmen arrive at the vicarage. They have been digging up the east end of St Catherine's for a week now at the behest of the Dean and his archons in the Close [that is, of the Cathedral]. This was something my predecessor initiated last autumn. He was, it seems, alarmed at the rate the church was sinking. (I'm not insensible to the metaphorical aptness of this event.) Indeed, a sizeable fissure has appeared at the base of the wall. The cause of the subsidence is a spring which, once localised about fifty yards from the church, has now gone underground and grown sufficiently unruly as to undermine the building's foundations. Water surges up whenever a hole deeper than about five feet is dug. The workmen began, for reasons inscrutable to me, just such a hole directly beneath the altar where, if they had but asked me, I could have told them that the bones of St Uncumber are reputedly laid. Sure enough, they struck an unmistakable grave. Uncertain as to how to proceed, they alerted me; and I, seeing the inevitability of the operation (though not the need for it), alerted the Close. I suggested that the grave be left in peace. But no, they wouldn't hear of it. I was enjoined to think of the opportunity for publicity the grave would afford. I thought about this, and suggested that it be left in peace.

The story of my church is not without interest. I researched it sporadically during the winter when, being still recently arrived here, I was left very much to my own devices. (The villagers dislike pushy vicars as much as I do. Janet tells me that, to be accepted, all I have to do is live here for sixty years – after which period they will freely address remarks about the weather to me.) It dates from the fourteenth century but its foundations are Saxon – part of the lower wall at the unhappy east end still exhibits the original flint. However, I have no doubt that, judging by the residual ditch around the site and the megalith embedded in the north wall, pagan worship took place here in the Iron Age or even earlier.

The fourteenth-century church was not dedicated to St Catherine. She was introduced in the early eighteenth century when the first patroness, St Uncumber, was denounced as, at best, unChristian and, at worst, a fraud. Sadly her very existence is disputed. A single miracle was supposed – rightly, in my opinion – to have earned her canonisation: she grew a beard to avoid the sexual attentions of her importunate husband.

There is also a legend, only recently recorded in writing, that 'sometime in the Dark Ages' a travelling family of dyers camped next to the spring which is now eroding my poor church. One of them, an old woman, went out late at night to prepare a dye at the spring. Her family frowned on this because they believed that the baneful influence of the new moon would spoil the dye. However, the old woman was feeble and slow at her work so she had to work after moonrise if her dye was to be ready for market. Whereupon the Blessed Virgin Mary appeared to her in a nimbus of bright light and imparted to her the secret of preparing Tyrian purple, a precious dye known to the Romans – for instance, it coloured the borders of senatorial togas – but the art of whose manufacture had since been lost.* The old woman gave the secret to her family, who went on to make a fortune from it; but she vowed to remain by the spring and dedicate her life to the BVM, drinking only spring water and eating only the Host, until such time as God was pleased to take her.

Far from dying of this meagre diet, the old woman flourished. The peasants who came to her with ailments and sick animals – she had quickly acquired the reputation of a healer – observed that she

---

* We now know that Tyrian purple was derived from a Mediterranean mollusc, *murex*.

was growing younger and stronger. By the time of her death she was said to have the appearance of 'a fine strong handsome youth'. (The wording suggests that she had become a man. However, no beard is mentioned!)

A variant of the story asserts that she did not in fact die, but was assumed to Heaven – like the Virgin herself – in a fiery circle of light (a Catherine wheel?). One sees how, over the centuries, legends intermingle in the popular mind.

At any rate the place by the spring where she lived – a soggy hollow still remains – became a shrine for pilgrims; and, eventually, it was commandeered by some monks (of an unknown order) who built a chapel nearby (presumably the Saxon church?) and a small monastery on whose site the vicarage now stands. The remains of its refectory, having subsided over the years, now form my cellar. Some people say that the monks carved out a number of secret passages which connect the vicarage to the church and to the natural network of passages which is supposed to underlie the surrounding fields and hills. They were used by the monks to escape from Henry VIII's men at the Dissolution of the Monasteries. Others say that there are no passages other than those created by the many-branched spring which works its way in a circuitous web towards the river. Only the other day Joan Thorpe's little dog, having gone missing for two days, reappeared dripping wet under the feet of a farm labourer, who had no hesitation in asserting that it had fallen down some hole into the watery maze underground and was lucky to have found a way out. The well which the monks sank in my cellar is credited with healing powers similar to those of the spring from whose waters it derives.

Anyway. His High Churchness the Dean arrived, as nearly in person as he's able, along with a genuine university archaeologist whose tweed suit bespoke immense *gravitas*. The handful of locals interested enough to attend the official grave-opening twittered with anticipation. Most were there in the hope of seeing something horrible. Mrs B.'s sister, Lydia Simmons, remarked in a small voice that she hoped to see the uncorrupted body of St Uncumber. Nobody listened to her. The Dean wanted the church cleared but since he would not do it himself and I would not do it for him – the villagers have more right to be there than we – we pressed on with the business of levering up the heavy flagstone which covered the grave. The archaeologist warned of noxious gases. Fresh twittering broke out, but no movement. The stone was lifted to reveal a tomb shored up by crumbling wood props. I did not expect to see the bones of St Uncumber, nor her uncorrupted body. Nor did I expect to see the unassumed remains of the old woman (or young man) who had seen the BVM. I *did* expect to see the dust of some revered monk, perhaps a former abbot, belonging to the old monastery.

In the event, none of these was in the grave. It was empty. Except for . . .

The workmen worked away carefully with their spades for a bit. There was nothing to see except rubble. The archaeologist lowered himself into the hole and grubbed about for a while, tossing up on to the church floor stuff which got in his way. The little crowd dispersed, disappointed. The Dean sloped off to Mrs B.'s tea.

It was the last thing he tossed up before climbing out and following the Dean. He treated it as if it were rubbish. He did not see, as indeed nobody saw, that *it was the prima materia of the Philosophers*. I knew it *at once*. I fell to my knees. How it came to be there – who knows? Did some wise monk, learned in the Sacred Art, bury it there? Did some earlier people place it there out of superstitious awe, like a relic? I don't know. I only know that I thank God I was there at that moment to see it, rescue it, to unlock its secret.

On this propitious day [26 March], the forty-second anniversary of my birth, I, Smith, will begin the Magnum Opus . . .

I woke this morning in a sweat of excitement and apprehension such as I have not experienced since my fourth birthday (it had been hinted that, were I good, I might receive a genuine cowboy's gun and holster!). I knew that I was going to make my vow to begin. I cannot vacillate any longer because I must initiate *Solutio* [Solution] before Sol enters the Bull [i.e. before the Sun enters Taurus].

I have managed to conceal my birthday from Mrs Beattie so at least I do not have her blandishments to contend with. However, she was as deeply suspicious of the packet and card among the morning post as I was intrigued. (And, I must say, slightly thrilled. I cannot remember receiving a present since '43, the year poor heart-broken father followed my mother into the grave as soon as he decently could.)

The packet contained a delightful edition of Aubrey's *Lives*, from 'your affectionate friend, Janet'. Her thoughtfulness is really most moving, even painful – it reminds me how I have never quite succeeded in forgetting my birthdays in recent years. In any case they never quite live up to my irrational expectations. (The gun turned out to be a child's toy; the holster was not even real leather.)

The card was from Robert. How on earth did *he* know? I recall letting the date drop (no doubt somewhat wistfully) to Janet, but never to him. It is most gratifying. It is also not without a certain irony since neither of these two well-wishers attend my church.

However, the point is, on this day of new beginnings, I intend to set down honestly and clearly everything that occurs in the laboratory so that future Philosophers might profit from my failure or, *Deo volente*, my success. I promise to open as much of the great secret as is not forbidden and in such a way that anyone who reads with the eyes of the spirit may find the Opus plainly disclosed.

The Philosophers are fond of insisting that nothing is achieved without constant meditation – which is nothing else, they tell us, than a *perpetual dialogue with one's own soul*. Although she may appear to speak in riddles, paradoxes and obscure images, she nevertheless throws direct light on whatever problems we are powerless to tease out on our own. Therefore I will record my meditations on the Opus and address them in part to all true Philosophers – but mostly to our Lady Alchymia whose moonlit image, like the poets' Muse, we hold before our mind's eye that she may exact dutiful service and mercifully oversee all our pains.

De auro

Maier says that the sun by its millions of revolutions spins gold into the earth.[1] Little by little the sun imprints its image on the earth, and that image is gold, as the sun is itself the image of God and the heart is the sun's image in man.

The first man to see gold glittering in the primeval streams or pulsing like life-blood in the veins of some common ore, knew it as a glimpse of the earth-spirit shining in the dark earth as the sun shines in the sky. When he found it soft and easy to work, yet immune to rust or corruption, he knew it was a material spirit, like coagulated light. He knew it was a symbol of immortality's gloriole, whose lustre later men mistook for temporal wealth.

In gold, Nature seems to confound herself; for even in its raw state gold already appears the product of some art, as different from its surrounding ore as the soul is from the body. The earth's gold is like a great shattered mirror whose every fragment reflects the sun. Thus the Philosophers are known as Earth's astronomers because they gaze into the unknown terrestrial regions, the infernal sulphurous depths, the abysmal mines where the chemical Treasure blazes like a cold star in the blackness, waiting to be raised up into warm sunlight.

All metals aspire to the condition of gold, and to this end (our philosophy asserts) they grow in the ground. This simply means that metals – like men – have a goal, or *telos*, an innate disposition to perfect themselves. They are determined in essence by the same principle or *seed* which is nourished in the world's womb and simmered in the furnace of the earth, until it grows into its highest state – gold.

In this doctrine, that all metals are imperfect stages of growth towards gold, we find a profound truth: that all Creation is groaning and travailing, striving for fulfilment. The aim of the Great Work is to achieve in a short time what it takes Nature millions of years to complete. In other words, the Philosopher duplicates the natural process in his glass and accelerates it. He extracts the seed of the metals and grows it (but because we say 'No generation without corruption,' the seed must be killed before the plant can live). The metallic seed is more perfect in gold but less easily extracted than from the less perfect metals, just as it is easier to grow a fruit tree from a root or cutting than from the seed in a ripe fruit. Thus gold rarely plays a part in the early stages of the Opus.

For my Hermetic egg I have decided, after long deliberation, upon a double pelican.

Mrs Beattie was more than usually skittish today. When she summoned me for what she calls high tea I was bewildered to find *two* places laid in the dining-room. I rigorously consulted my memory to discover when exactly I had invited her to eat with me, but I drew a blank. Her only contribution was to assure me that it is unhealthy to be so much on my own – especially, it seems, at meal-times. As One who has Lost a Husband, she knows Only Too Well what Loneliness can do to a Body. I shudder at the images she evokes.

Oddly, I cannot recall that she was supposed to have any kind of evening meal here. I rather thought we had agreed (or did I assume it?) that she would make mine and get hers at her sister's as usual. This arrangement clearly suited her while darkness fell early; but now, as the evenings grow lighter, so her fears of an encounter with the White Lady are allayed, and she finds herself able to stay later.

I put a good face on it. If she *is* to stay for high tea it would indeed be ridiculous to eat in separate rooms. Besides, after months of eating with the men in Italy, God knows I'm not fussy. They were a foul-mouthed lot, as filthy as the conditions, but not above arguing points of theology over cold rations while the rain filled up our boots and the enemy mortars sent a stream of shells whistling over our heads. Preferable anyway to the officers' mess where it is *de trop* to touch on religion at all, except in a clipped and *manly* way.

Preferable, as it turns out, to Mrs B.'s mortar-blasts of winsome banter and *bon mots*. I scarcely know how to counter them without gross incivility. If I lapse for a second from the fixed smile and kindly, wrinkled eyes of the institutionalised vicar, I am assumed to be *out of sorts*, as her brother-in-law – and my verger – Out-of-Sorts Simmons so often is. There is nothing for it then but to *jolly me along* or, *in extremis, take me out of myself*. Gossip, delivered in an arch stage-whisper, assists her in this duty.

I have warned her that I will not tolerate gossip. This is because I find it impossible not to listen to it. However, she persists. She calls it news – an elastic category which includes rumour, and (I suggest) invention. Mostly she seems simply to pick it up out of thin air as though the air itself were thick with possibilities, like radio waves, which congeal at certain points to come within range of human hearing. They may or may not become facts; but their existence points to a potential factuality so that, even if they are not true, we can very well believe they are.

I listen to her gossip partly because I am ashamed of being so out of touch with my parishioners. (I am ashamed of listening

– and also of pretending not to.) Mrs B. can sniff out a birth or death before the persons concerned know anything about it. She can see through walls. Today she tells me that Mrs Maltravers is seriously ill. She has 'taken the liberty' of popping over to Goose Farm with a small pot of nourishing minced meat. This accounts for the paucity of same on my plate. It's quite usual for her to be in and out of others' houses, tirelessly performing her good works, whether they like it or not – and the more so now that she has cast herself in the role of my honorary helpmeet; it is certainly not usual for her to visit Goose Farm. Mrs Maltravers is, according to her, a heathen and a trouble-maker. This alone would incline me in the old lady's favour. Unfortunately she avoids vicars, as I avoid Mrs B.'s devilled kidneys. I have seen her at a distance, coming out of a cottage where she had no doubt been dispensing the herbal cures that Mrs B. condemns as a danger to the village's health, but which the inhabitants seem to feel the benefit of. I hoped Mrs B. would use the word 'witchcraft' but she managed, with the help of her corsets, to hold it in.

I can sense a tinge of fear in Mrs B.'s voice when she speaks of Mrs Maltravers, whose forebears used to own the Manor before hard times forced them to sell to Caldwell. Now that she is ailing and defenceless, she no longer awes Mrs B. who feels free to encumber her with charity.

Her grandchildren, Mrs B. adds darkly, are 'running wild'. They live with their father, Able Seaman Thomas, in one of the hideous new houses on the far side of the village. The girl I have seen in church; the boy has lately returned from his aunt's. She looks after him, it seems, while Thomas, a widower, is at sea. The girl often stays with her grandmother and is now looking after her; or, as Mrs B. says, neglecting her. I must obviously keep an eye on the old woman and the children, and it is thanks to my indiscreet housekeeper that I know about them. Thanks to her, too, I know that Janet orders her silk underwear from London! Mrs B. could just about forgive her Catholicism – but the underwear goes too far.

Anyway. What I chiefly object to in Mrs Beattie's new position at the dining-table is her manner of eating. As her enormous jaw moves up and down, her mouth is stretched from side to side in a perpetual smile, exposing her long yellow teeth. These have spaces between them, through which partially chewed food is forced in the process of mastication. While chewing and smiling, she also talks, so that I'm obliged occasionally to glance towards her at a time when all my attention is required simply to get through enough of the wretched, over-stewed food on my plate to avoid offending her. It is all I can do not to invoke the White Lady who, if she frightens Mrs B. away, can only be a friend to me.

De prima materia

Concerning our prime matter, the first thing to be taken note of is that it shares many characteristics with the *ultima materia*, that is, the Philosophers' Stone itself. According to the beautiful description by the anonymous author of *Gloria Mundi* [*The Glory of the World*, 1526], each is 'familiar to all men, both young and old, is found in the country, in the village, in the town, in all things created by God; yet it is despised by all. Rich and poor handle it everyday. It is cast into the street by servant maids. Children play with it. Yet no one prizes it, though, next to the human soul, it is the most beautiful and the most precious thing upon earth and has the power to pull down kings and princes. Nevertheless, it is esteemed the vilest and meanest of earthly things'.

Now, owing to the literalism that afflicts all ages, poor deluded puffers* have always looked for the prima materia in common, preferably unhygienic, substances such as eggs, hair, nails and blood. Piss and dung (horse and human) have been popular candidates, and also worms and basilisks (subject to availability). It doesn't take much advancement in the Art to know that the mysterious matter is not to be found in filth of this kind.

It has a thousand names.** They include mercury, sulphur, gold, iron, lead, salt, earth, fire, water, air, dew, sky, cloud, sea, mother, moon, virgin, dragon or serpent. I call it Chaos because it is a microcosm of the original Chaos that obtained before Heaven was divided from Earth. The first great European chemist, Albertus

---

* A derogatory term for an ignorant alchemist, who is presumed to do little more than puff away at his fire with bellows.
** Martin Ruland's *Lexicon of Alchemy* (1622) lists over fifty synonyms for the prima materia.

Magnus [1200–80] calls it Mercurius. He is not referring to common quicksilver but rather to that spirit of the metals which we find still, more than four hundred years later, running through the works of the mighty Basil Valentine.[2] For him, the prima materia is an 'earth' inhabited by a spirit which is nourished by the stars and which nourishes in turn all the living things it shelters in its womb.

As so often, it is Sir George Ripley who is most explicit:[3] he distinguishes between the prima materia (which he calls 'our toade of the earth') and the Raw Stuff from which it is extracted in the form of a 'water'. As the principle underlying all matter, this 'water' can indeed be found everywhere, in gold or in dunghills. It is the 'treasure hard to attain' and, more particularly, the *secret fire* which must be released from our Chaos and made visible. God created this fire, the *Gloria Mundi* tells us, in the bowels of the earth, just as he created the fire of hell; and in it God himself glows with divine love.

A minute examination of our Chaos's surface revealed a faint vein or seam which, shaking in my boots, I began to chisel with all the care and trepidation of a diamond-cutter working on the Koh-i-Noor. The pile of tiny flakes grew steadily. The task required a degree of concentration to which I am utterly unused. I rested every five minutes, resuming when my eye was clear and my hand sure. The matter warmed under my palm as if responding to light after a long dark age in the earth.

When I had gently cracked it all the way round like an egg, I had to nerve myself for the single blow that would divide it into two parts of about two and three pounds respectively. I intended to start the Opus with the lighter of the two, storing the other away against an emergency.

As I raised the hammer to strike the decisive blow, I remembered Ripley's Vision of the prima materia as a 'Toad ful Ruddy' and I half-feared that such a toad, like the genius of the matter, might come hopping out at the moment of impact. However, I recollected that Exposition upon the vision by Philalethes, sanest of men:[4] 'the Toad is gold; so called, because it is an Earthly body, but most especially for the black stinking venomousness which this operation comes to in the first days of its preparation, before the whiteness appear; during the rule of Saturn, therefore, it is called the ruddy Toad.'* (In this Toad the great Cosmopolite detected 'the whole secret of the Philosophers'.)

The hammer fell; the break was clean! I marvel at the subtle striations which thread my prima materia like the veins and arteries of a living body – at which thought, I, of all people, could scarcely forbear weeping at the pains it will suffer in the long course of the Opus.

Placing my chosen portion in the mortar, I set to with the same iron pestle – 'it must be made of iron, my boy' – that my master let me take away as a keepsake. It has been, good God!, a paperweight all these years... There are more efficient methods nowadays of reducing a substance to fine powder but I am determined to adhere to the traditional paths of the Philosophers – except where they were, by their own admission, at a disadvantage. This is not to say that I abide by tradition for its own sake, but because innovation may be dangerous. One cannot foretell what may or may not be crucial to the success of the Opus.

For example, it is certain that the work must begin under the auspices of the Ram [i.e. Aries] whose fiery effluvia nurture the conception of the Opus; but the role of other astrological influences is less certain. Thus the reason for repeating one process or another, over and over again, is not only to extract wholly new properties from old substances, but also to ensure that at least one of the repetitions is subject to the correct (but unknown) planetary alignment or phase of the moon.

The Art would not be so wearisome if the conditions for its success were known, if its effects could be measured and its results repeated at will. But then it would not be the Art. Our conditions cannot be known in advance but are discovered on the way; all effects are unpredictable. No man can repeat another's Work any more than he can die on another's behalf.

Every soul who embarks on our Magistery does so alone, for the first and only time, with fear and trembling...

---

* *An Exposition upon Sir George Ripley's Vision written by Eirenaeus Philalethes, Anglus, Cosmopolita* (London, 1677) was one of a series of commentaries on Ripley's works published under the title *Ripley Reviv'd*. Ripley's original vision is to be found in his most famous treatise, popularly known as *The Twelve Gates*.

*

Reasonable attendance at matins. Congregations burgeon briefly towards spring and decline in summer. I cannot help noticing that mine is considerably older than the average age of the village. I suppose children have always shirked church, seeing only a building which smells a bit queer, like school during the holidays. But I'm afraid in case they get into the habit of not coming, afraid that their parents will no longer compel them to come because they, too, increasingly see only a pathetic sinking building. Why has the church moved to the periphery of the village where once it was its beating heart? It was once a place of wonders and visions but now, as if it has exhausted its ration of sanctity, it seems strangely empty, emptier even than elsewhere. How can I restore the *spirit* of the place? The answer is, I can't. The wind of the Holy Spirit bloweth where it listeth. It may be that, in this age, the spirit must be looked for outside the churches. Meanwhile I must do what I can to instil more vitality into my services while avoiding that dreadful empty enthusiasm which despairing vicars fall prey to.

At least I now recognise most of the faces. Caldwell and his whey-faced wife sit prominently in the Manor pew. Her nose runs. Every week she seems thinner and more faded as if her vital forces were being steadily drawn out of her by her robust and florid husband. His neck bulges over his collar, his thick arm lies negligently along the back of the pew. He makes no effort to disguise his lack of interest in the service. Next to him his son Bradley, making a rare appearance and plainly under sufferance, lolls insolently in his seat. Father and son have none of the landed gentry's natural arrogance. Rather, they have the wary, smug, challenging look of the *nouveaux riches* for whom there has never been a moment's doubt but that hard cash and brute force are the princes of this world. Caldwell has retired to the country having made his pile. If only he would be content to sit on it instead of becoming a 'gentleman farmer'. For, more farmer than gentleman, and less farmer than businessman, he is set on compelling his land to yield a profit even if it means tarmacadaming every inch of it into car parks. Meanwhile, Caldwell *fils* exercises what he imagines to be his *droit de seigneur*; and, when he oversteps the mark, father is ready, wallet in hand, to sugar over the unpleasantness.

I do not like to see the faces of Mr and Mrs Stebbins, sitting five rows behind. They have aged in the short time I have been here, become wrinkled and blank and collapsed-looking. Mrs B. has got wind of something. I've heard her say: 'Jenny Stebbins has been a long time staying with her cousin . . . ' It's only a matter of time before all is known. The Caldwells should not be able to look into their eyes, but instead it is the other way round. It's the prey who invariably feels shame, not the predator. The Stebbinses listen to my sermons who least need to; the Caldwells, who may profit from them, do not.

I grind the matter by hand, a little at a time, and only at times when I am relatively unsullied – no taint of thought, word or deed may be allowed to infect the subject at this first, vulnerable stage when it is being dismantled into its constituent elements. Mrs Beattie shall not be let near it.

But I *must* do as much as possible every day. Time is running out. If I miss the propitious season for *Solutio* I can kiss the Work goodbye until next year. At the same time I *cannot* hurry – if the matter isn't properly calcined, with proper reverence, the Work will be still-born. At this moment I could wish for an assistant, such as I was to my master. Better still, a *soror mystica* [mystic sister] who could share the burden, as the fair Perrenelle helped her husband, the peerless Nicholas Flamel.[5] I could almost wish that Annabelle – but this is folly. I have, and need, no one except Our Lady Alchymia who will, I pray, help me to make the marriage bed of mercury and sulphur where we'll share the *Elixir Vitae* [Elixir of Life]. I must be ready, I *will* be ready.

De nomine meo

The name I have chosen, Smith, is a philosophical name. There are good reasons why the Philosophers so often write under pseudonyms. Firstly, throughout the Art's long history they have been variously accused of counterfeiting gold, of practising the Black Arts and (in Christian countries) of heresy. It's wise not to draw attention to oneself.

Secondly, the Philosopher does not wish to be known because he is liable to be pestered for the Great Secret; and, thirdly, because he wants to work in the same way as he prays – in private, before God alone.

He often chooses the name of a famous adept – partly to lend his work authority and partly to stress the long tradition in which he is working. He also wishes to pay tribute to the sage whose name he borrows. Above all, a pseudonym prevents the intrusion of personality into writing which is less the product of one's own will than dictated by the Great Work itself. The true philosopher feels himself to be, and is, in an important sense, *anonymous*.

'Smith' signifies both the anonymity of the man-in-the-street and a metal-worker. It's the fate of such craftsmen to be set apart, whether they are humble village blacksmiths carrying the taint of the iron they work, or whether they are immortal like halt Hephaestus who fashioned the weapons of the gods in his volcanic forge – what philosopher has not woken at dead of night to hear the dactyls of his hammer knocking like kobolds in his heart, warning of the dangers of the fiery trade they share?

Smith is the name chosen for hotel registers by those who wish to be faceless. Smith signifies no one in particular. This is what I aspire to. The pagan age of heroes is gone. They were heroes because, by definition, they were what the mass of people could never become – exceptions, epic men. Since the advent of Christ, we are commanded to become precisely what everybody can become and in the same sense, namely, ourselves. Ourselves alone in the face of God. The individual who *accomplishes* himself will in no way appear heroic or exceptional because his achievement is inward and invisible. In fact it is an agreeable irony that the man whom this realised soul most closely resembles is the man-in-the-street, just another Smith . . .

If I had been better established in the parish would I have spoken to Stebbins as I did? The gravity of my first real pastoral duty rather panicked me. There were no preliminaries during which I might have considered the matter more deeply. He simply sat down in my study, lit his pipe and remarked:

'Our Jenny is three months' gone.' He stared into the distance; he might have been discussing a dog or a horse.

My first, absurd thought was that I should offer some condolence for the death of his daughter three months ago. Since the war I've been out of practice at recognising such directness. My second thought not only grasped that his unmarried daughter was with child but also, through the peculiar certainty of direct intuition, who the father was.

I had all but forgotten the occasion on my first day of active service, so to speak, when I was walking in Nightingale Wood, surveying the terrain. I came across a courting couple. I would have passed by, with eyes averted from a scene of natural and innocent romance; but the girl's face told me at once that she should not be there in the wood, alone with a young man. Bradley Caldwell was leaning against a tree, his arm slung proprietarily over the girl's shoulder, the hand hanging open. He embodied all the assurance of youth and wealth – tall, fashionably dressed, with long glossy hair swept back with studied negligence.

Both of them understood that I was the new vicar. The girl looked away, but Bradley rested his black eyes on me unwaveringly, just this side of insolence. The stern look I intended to give him changed, against my will, to a civil nod of greeting which he did not reciprocate. I should have stopped and said something – should have reported them to their parents. Instead I weakly preferred to believe that my original estimation of their innocence had been correct.

'She's going away,' said Stebbins. 'Mister Caldwell's seeing to it. Money and that.'

It was a statement, and yet he did not speak as one resigned to the inevitable. There was a question in the air. I didn't know how to answer him. Disguising lameness with firmness, I said:

'That's very fair of Caldwell. It's the best thing. It must be for the best.'

Did I imagine it, or did his face begin to collapse at that moment?

'She's off to her cousin's in Falmouth. She'll have it there. She wants it adopted. I wanted you to know the facts of the matter, like. There's bound to be talk.'

We shook hands like unwilling conspirators.

I have no aspirations for my account of the Magnum Opus. The great texts of our Philosophy have always been reviled or written off, mocked or misunderstood, by the Schoolmen and official scholars, the learned clergy and the scientists, the playwrights and the critics. Nowadays the texts are not only ignored but virtually unheard-of. Doubtless my own small contribution will suffer the same fate. It can't be helped. The world has always been intransigent, harder to convert than the metals. And, perhaps, after all, the Art has only ever been for those who have eyes to see.

Although very little is known about the immortal Philalethes, one thing is certain: he found the life of a Philosopher full of difficulty. In *An Open Entrance* he tells us:

> So long as the secret is possessed by a comparatively small number of philosophers, their lot is anything but a bright and happy one; surrounded as we are on every side by the cruel greed and the prying suspicion of the multitude, we are doomed, like Cain, to wander over the earth homeless and friendless. Not for us are the soothing influences of domestic happiness; not for us the delightful confidences of friendship. Men who covet our golden secret pursue us from place to place, and fear closes our lips, when love tempts us to open ourselves freely to a brother . . . even our kindness and charitable compassion are rewarded with black ingratitude . . . It was only a short time ago that, after visiting the plague-stricken haunts of a certain city, and restoring the sick to perfect health by means of my miraculous medicine, I found myself surrounded by a yelling mob, who demanded that I should give to them my Elixir of the Sages; and it was only by changing my dress and my name, by shaving off my beard and putting on a wig, that I was enabled to save my life . . .

There are two things the Philosopher must assiduously avoid: fame and scientists. The former exposes him to the sensation-seeking and greed of the ignorant; the latter – more dangerously – exposes him to the learned worshippers of those twin idols, Empiricism and Objectivity. The story of James Price is instructive. Born in 1752, he arrived two hundred years too late. He belonged to the great age of Elizabethan alchemy; instead he was thrown to the wolves of *scientism*. No doubt he was flattered at being elected to the Royal Society at the age of only twenty-nine, especially as, to the best of my knowledge, he had not yet published any work. It's always tempting for a young, solitary, brilliant Philosopher to accept what he thinks will be public recognition of his ideas and achievements. No doubt it was tactfully suggested by his fellow Fellows that he should publish as soon as possible. He was not a professional academic – he worked privately on his modest estate at Stoke, near Guildford, thanks to a decent inheritance. I suppose he thought that academics gave as little thought to their own professional advancement as he did; thought that they valued truth above their own academic standing . . . At any rate, he published his experiments in a pamphlet.

It is hopelessly 'unscientific'. He asserts, for instance, the 'old-fashioned' belief that the heavier metals such as gold, silver and mercury are variant forms of the same basic substance. (Conscious, perhaps, of his recent elevation, he does not dare extend this principle to all metals.) He does not specify his process, except to say that it is 'tedious and operose' – every Philosophical heart will go out to him – but he nevertheless obtains a 'white powder' able to transform mercury or silver to gold. (Naturally he does not specify the process. It is forbidden to do so. Not something his new colleagues would be sympathetic to.)

By July 1782, he had made about four grains of the red powder and about three times as much of the white.* He revealed nothing of their composition except, interestingly, that they contained arsenic. Over a period of three weeks he performed seven 'experiments' in front of some twenty witnesses, many of them being present on three or four separate occasions. The last one, for instance, was attended by two Lords, two Knights, three clergymen, a doctor and four Fellows of the Royal Society. The 'experiments' were of three kinds:

1. Fusing mercury, and transforming a small part of it into either silver or gold with the white and red powders respectively.

2. Fusing silver and by adding the red powder producing an alloy of eight parts silver to one of gold.

---

* The account of James Price's life given by Rupert Gould in *Enigmas* (my copy of the book was published in New York, 1965, but I think it was written much earlier, possibly around 1929) says that he produced sixteen grains of white powder and five of the red by May 1782.

3. Amalgamating mercury with either powder to produce small quantities of silver and gold.

All the equipment was brought by the witnesses and every stage of the projection performed by them, including the addition of the powders, in order to rule out trickery. The amount of gold obtained was not great, but found by the assayers to be very pure. (A detail which will interest, but not astound, Philosophers is that the mercury on which the powder had been projected showed no sign of evaporation, or even of boiling, although it was in a red-hot crucible.)

The experiments were reported in print. Naturally they caused a sensation. The usual charges of fraud were levelled at Price. He rebutted them calmly: the experiments had been carried out under strict laboratory conditions, and besides, why should a man of independent means, a high reputation and a recently acquired, official, academic position jeopardise all this for a few grains of gold?

The wolves began to howl. The Royal Society (under that old autocrat Sir Joseph Banks) demanded that Price divulge the composition of his powders. Of course Price could not do that, nor could he say why; he simply said he was unwilling to do so. Would he then be so good as to repeat the experiments? (An old scientific trick this – to repeat the experiments until you get the result you want. In this case, no result.) Unfortunately, Price could not do this, nor could he submit the powders for 'analysis', because his supply was now exhausted and it would cost him too much in time and danger to his health to make more.

His first mistake was to think that the world would accept scientific demonstrations of transmutation; his second was not to retire quickly into philosophical obscurity. Under appalling pressure to repeat his experiments or suffer the consequences, he promised to do his best and retired to his estate. He was young, he was attached to fame, he wanted to continue to enjoy the good opinion of those whom he imagined were his fellow scientists. Poor James. No one knows what he did during the last months of his life, although we can readily guess.

He is reputed to have tried to make more powder, and failed. Then, in July 1783, he invited the Royal Society to witness a repetition of his original experiments. Only three members came, so eager were they to arrive at the truth of the matter.

Price showed them into his laboratory and invited them to examine his equipment. Before they had finished doing so, Price collapsed. He was found to have poisoned himself with prussic acid. It was generally agreed that the balance of his mind had been upset by over-work, anxiety and public ridicule. And, having examined in retrospect his reasonable – and empirical – pamphlet, some scientists clearly saw evidence of insanity, while others saw only the fraudulence which he demonstrated in his 'alleged' transmutations.

To Goose Farm. I am determined to do my best for Mrs Maltravers whether she likes it or not. Especially now when I must guard against allowing my fascination for the Opus – Lord, I can still hardly believe it! – to interfere with my obligations.

The farmhouse is set back from the lane and quite high up on Grimm's Down, roughly level with Robert's chapel across the valley. It is smaller inside than it looks from without because of the thickness of the walls. The porch gives on to a narrow passage flanked by the two principal rooms – not unlike the vicarage's arrangement – which are low-ceilinged and somewhat dark despite the low windows.

Receiving no reply to my knock I peeped into the right-hand room. A tall pretty child was sitting on the window-seat, her bare legs and feet curled beneath her. She was immersed in a book. I was speechless for a second with the surprise of seeing her – and with the striking grace of her attitude which might almost have been posed against the piercing spring sunlight pouring through the oblong window. Then she looked up, her eyes still full of the book's images, and said, 'Yes?' Stupidly, I asked her what she was reading. In reply she quoted:

> 'Beauty is but a flower
> Which wrinkles will devour . . . '

Recognising Tom Nashe's poem ['In Time of Pestilence'] and being at a loss for other words, I took up the refrain.

> 'Brightness falls from her hair,
> Queens have died young and fair,
> Dust hath closed Helen's eye.
>   I am sick, I must die.
>   Lord, have mercy on us!'

She uncurled her long legs and stood up. We looked at each other in silence, perhaps embarrassed.

'Brightness falls from the *air*!' she said. 'What?' I said. 'You said "Brightness falls from her hair". It's "*the air*".' 'Of course. Stupid of me.' In truth I was unsettled. How could I have ruined what is probably my favourite line! 'I'll go and see if grandma feels like seeing you.' She returned a minute later. 'No, she doesn't.' She added 'sir' as an apologetic afterthought. I was amused by her matter-of-factness; vicars clearly don't afford her the usual discomfiture. I have seen her in church, of course, but not close to. Her eyebrows, being darker than her thick blonde hair, are rather fetching. So is her curious mouth – too big really and tilted up at one side, with a slightly bee-stung bottom lip.

She tells me her name is Nora. She is staying with her grandmother – as is her brother Timothy, who was not in evidence – to look after the old lady and also because her father is away at sea. Her mother, who died soon after (as a result of?) Timothy's birth, is buried in the graveyard. Nora was affronted when I suggested she was a trifle young for all this responsibility. 'I'm twenty,' she said, 'and when grandma dies, I'll look after Tim and Dad if necessary.' Surely she didn't think Mrs Maltravers was going to die? 'I *know* she is. She told me.' Nora is obviously set to become as singular as her grandmother. As I was leaving, she shyly blurted out, with touching sincerity, 'I don't care what grandma says about you, sir. Anyway, it's not personal. And I like your sermons.' I was much cheered by this, but I wonder now if she wasn't simply being polite or trying to compensate for Mrs Maltravers' hostility towards the Church.

EILEEN

Dear P.,

What am I *doing* in this God-forsaken dump? What's got into me? I don't *know* any more. I can't stop the tears running out of my face. I can't stop my nose running, I'm chilled to the marrow after the soaking I got on the way back from the pub, and even my change of clothes feels damp in this damp wreck of a house where none of the windows fit and there's no phone or electricity. Mr Salmon's sorting them out – I'll get to that – but meanwhile what am I going to *do*?

I found some old branches in the overgrown orchard and broke them up for a fire, but they're too sodden to do anything except smoke and spit while I huddle in front of them in all my jerseys drinking vile wine I bought from the pub to supplement my dwindling supply of tequila and Special Brew. The camp young barman with the Irish accent, jug ears and innocent face swore it was dry but in fact he gave me a revolting sweet quasi-Liebfraumilch – out of malice, probably, or else as part of some black initiation rite that all newcomers to this pig's bum of a village have to undergo, another quaint part of which is to order your drink in the midst of an ostentatious silence while five unshaven men around the bar stare at your breasts.

I would've liked to have stayed awhile in front of the (real) fire and to have drunk a pint or two and, eventually, to have exchanged a friendly word with a friendly native. But I chickened out and trudged back across the boggy village green to this creeper-ridden barn of a house. And here I am with the thought half-formed that I should describe all this in such a way as to *amuse* you, you bastard, even though at this moment I could kill you.

Later. Misery and sickly wine must have drawn a merciful veil of oblivion over me because I crashed out. It's now – I don't know.

My watch has conked out. From boredom perhaps. I guess three in the morning. That's what it feels like. I'm shivery and headachy, threaded on a ribbon of acid indigestion. Nothing a couple of Special Brews won't cure, if I can just hold them down.

I'm still damp. Probably from the mattress I dragged down from upstairs and put in front of the fizzled-out fire. My kidneys hurt. This room is beautiful. High and airy. It must've been a small library – rows of empty bookshelves line the wall opposite the tall black uncurtained windows. I hope no one is passing; they'll see my candles flickering in the dark and have a fit. The wind is blowing the rain against the glass like handfuls of gravel. It's like being in a ship at sea.

That's what I was dreaming just now. Of being at sea. I could hear the rhythmical slap of water in the bilges. I can still sense it – the movement of water underneath me – unless it's the ebb and flow of Special Brew in my arteries.

Oh P., I keep thinking it's you throwing pebbles at the window and not the rain. The front gate creaks – the whole house creaks, like a ship under strain – and every time it creaks my heart stops because I'm sure it's you who have found me somehow and have come to take me home. I can see your face just beyond the window; it's wearing your smile, the sweet sheepish one. You've seen the light! You want me back! You're so vivid it's frightening. Are you lying awake in bed thinking of me? You are, you must be – your presence is making the house creak, your thoughts are spattering the huge blind windows.

Drink works. Up to a point. It takes away your gift to me, the freezing iron spike in the abdomen – but only to replace it with a more generalised pain, numb pain, as though pain itself were the anaesthetic and I were paralysed inside it.

I know you're not outside. I know you never will be. I know time will bear me away from this brink just as it bore me to it. But how am I to kill time meanwhile?

Dear P.,

Slept fitfully until first light. The illusion of being all at sea, suspended over fathoms of black water, persisted. I schlepped across the cold hall, with its black and white stone floor, to the kitchen. It's in reasonable nick, large and dark with only one smallish window over the sink. But it's got a fridge and a lovely old long wooden table and, thank God, a *gas* stove on which I boiled up a gallon of tea.

I drank the tea in the library, sitting on the wide window-seat, too hung-over and shell-shocked and spaced-out to do anything but stare at the dismal graveyard being punished by the rain. Beyond the headstones there's a small church, pretty old, nothing much to look at, and shut up now. I could just make out the figure of a tattered woman walking towards it. I can't imagine who'd be up this early and out in this rain. Some old leech-gatherer or rat wife I expect. She disappeared behind the church. I waited for her to reappear on the other side, but she didn't. I began to think that my eyes were playing tricks. Everything outside is grey and green and smudged. It took me a long time to decide that the church, embedded among the graves, is in fact lop-sided, sunk down at one end as if it had pushed its head into the earth and gone to sleep. This must've happened years ago, or maybe not: my house has not yet been renamed the *Old* Vicarage, nor converted into a pair of bijou weekend residences.

You'd like it here, P. I thought that as soon as I saw it. I forgot that you're the one person I won't ever see here. You'd appreciate its leaky decrepitude, its rich exhibition of mould and fungi, its mixed architecture. Mr Salmon went pink and murmured that former tenants had found that the house had 'atmosphere'. Euphemism for ghosts, I bet. But, in spite of everything, it's not in the least spooky. Its atmosphere is decidedly benign.

Sorry about last night's outpourings. I'll do my best not to bleed all over the paper. It's just that, against all reason and contrary to your opinion, all things considered, on balance, with respect – I love you so much.

Dear P.,

I don't know where the day's gone. I can't seem to do anything. I'm all shot to bits and so tired that I keep forgetting you for whole minutes at a time. I go into a sort of limbo and then a guilty wave of remembrance comes over me as if it were sinful to forget you for a second.

All the same, I have had an extraordinary day. In between catatonic states and having you sweep over me, you scum-bag, all manner of flotsam came floating up from my wrecked heart; but, above all, my *soul* came – without my calling him – and now maybe, just *maybe* I can see a way out because this business of the soul has given me a bit of leverage on you and on my bloody life. I'll explain about my soul, if I can, because I want to and because I want you to understand – but first I must tell you about the cellar. I made a grisly discovery: I really am under threat from floods. I should have guessed when I saw how the whole area is reverting to water-meadow.

You see, this library and the two bedrooms above it are Victorian additions, slapped on to, and above, an older (sixteenth-century?) cottage. The hall, dining-room, kitchen (and the two bedrooms above) are Georgian, originally built on at right angles to the cottage. The latter is just a corridor now, and three small rooms – sculleries etc. – which are empty and crumbling. They've sunk to a lower level than the rest of the house so that when you go through the door set into the bookcases at the back of the library, you have to go down some steps to the former cottage's dark and narrow corridor, which ends in a blank wall. At the end on the left is a door which leads back to the hall, next to the main stairs; opposite is a low door I had to force open.

If I'd walked through it, it would have been curtains: the doorway opens on to a sheer drop into a large cellar. Its exact size is difficult to gauge in the pitch darkness. At the foot of the doorway there are two charred wooden struts set into the wall which suggest that there were once some wooden stairs. I fetched my torch and the step-ladder I'd noticed in the woodshed outside the kitchen door. The torchlight made very little impression on the darkness. There's a light-fitting hanging intact from the ceiling, but without a bulb.

I lowered the step-ladder into the cellar and lowered myself on to it. I'd put on my wellies, fully intending to wade about and see what could be done about the water which came up to the second rung. I couldn't take the plunge. I had the irrational fear that I would step in out of my depth. The water slapped against the walls, making a faint echo. Eerie. I stood, dithering, on the ladder, trying to make out what the shapes rising out of the water in the far corner were. I heard a plop. It gave me the creeps. Maybe the water's alive with something, some creature. Maybe there are rats, all white and pink-eyed like the legendary alligators in the New York sewers. Maybe there are – God forbid – sp*d*rs down there (remember the one with muscly legs in my bedroom, P.? I had to forcibly prevent you from calling the police) . . .

I scuttled back up the ladder and hauled myself up through the door. Something will have to be done. I'll have to get on to the Zetterberg – give her a chance to show exactly what sort of landlady she's going to be. Am I going to be able to stand it here?

All afternoon I wandered aimlessly around the house, unable to think straight or settle to anything, but full of anxiety about what I'm to do now. There's about one room's worth of serviceable furniture upstairs and I began to lug some of it into the smaller back bedroom and some of it downstairs to mitigate the blank accusing stare of the big empty bookshelves. I couldn't be bothered to stick at it. In the end I gave up and wandered from room to room, all jittery and so dry-mouthed I couldn't eat. Sometimes I cried, which, as you know, is simply not like me at all.

I have trouble believing I'm here. It has all happened so fast. It's as if another person were here. I watch her wandering, her hand touching things, trying to colonise the alien territory. There seems so little of me left. I said my name out loud a few times. I was devastated by the terrible feeling of dislocation it produced, a fearful claustrophobia at being trapped in this body and being stuck with this banal brain all my life. I came over all trembly and had to sit down, look out over the solid graveyard, get hold of myself.

Then, for the second time in a week, it happened. Like a rushing wind my soul was with me, pressing up against the back of my face. It was hair-raising, like losing all control, but also exhilarating – too mild a word – because I saw that he was the reason I was here as much as you or anything else; and, in the rush of his coming, I found myself for a split second in full ecstatic possession of the whole of myself, a simple person to whom the view outside was luminous, and sufficient for all my hunger and need.

I was forgetting, dear P., that you don't know how I found this place. In fact, you can't know anything except what Muriel [i.e. her flatmate] might have told you in the highly unlikely event that you've tried to contact me. Not that Mu knows anything.

That was the only way I could do it. Make the break. I mean, when I told you that I wanted never to see you again, I was lying. In fact I nearly came crawling round to your place the very next day instead of going to work. But I thought, 'Well, I'd better hold out for a day at least.' Then something weird and wonderful happened: *Weird and Wonderful* folded.* No doubt you've heard by now how the US publishers suddenly pulled out of the deal. After all those months on the book – to be left high and dry! As the contract hadn't been signed, it was either go on without them or cut our losses. But I think we – they – did the right thing by pulling the plug.

They were kind. Room on other books could be found for me. Not as editor, of course, but in some capacity or other. Thanks but no thanks. It all fitted into place. I have enough dough saved to last a year, providing I don't eat or set foot outside the front door. I saw my chance to shove off and be free free free. Oh the *relief*. How I'd secretly dreaded doing that idiotic book with its pre-digested bite-sized chunks of titillating prose on crackpot topics from A (Acupuncture, wonderful cures by) to Z (Zen masters, weird abilities of)!

Before fear of freedom could set in, I jumped into the car, hit the M4 and headed west. Without even collecting my toothbrush. The immediate plan was to visit Penny (whom I've spoken to you about) and to find a place to rent in a day or two. But Penny wasn't there; her cottage was all locked up. So I drove all the way to G— (by which time it was nearly midnight) and found a hotel I couldn't really afford and flopped into bed.

You know, P., in all this I was behaving a bit like someone who's had their arm severed, who carries it to the nearest hospital, who jokes with the doctors as they sew it back on – and only later succumbs to shock.

I treated myself – what the hell, in for a penny etc. – to an extravagant breakfast and concentrated on not thinking about anything in case I should think 'I'm never going to see P. again',

---

* Produced by a book-packaging company for which Eileen worked, *Weird and Wonderful* was to be a short illustrated 'encyclopedia' of quirky facts and phenomena. I had applied to this company for work as a freelance sub-editor and was assigned to this ill-fated project, on account of which I was introduced to Eileen (in a pub) by a mutual acquaintance in the company.

and I still felt pretty good at this stage – a bit manic, a bit hyped up – but pretty pleased with myself at being in a dozy little hotel in the West Country on a working day with the waiter wondering who I was. I *did* feel free, and sort of stripped for action.

I read the local newspaper. Houses for rent, it said. The Vicarage. I phoned the number. Just for a laugh really – I knew it'd cost at least £75 a week – but I *had* to keep going. I was zinging like a telegraph wire that's been hit by a stone and I knew that the moment I stopped zinging I'd plummet to earth where the foul fiend was waiting in the shadows to spring on to my back.

The man was v. nice and jokey. I went to see him. A solicitor, name of Mr Salmon! Fair hair, rosy cheeks, maroon waistcoat, permanently embarrassed, young i.e. twenty-eight going on sixty-five. He was cultivating an Olde Worlde charm which included plying me with elevenses (Bath bun and Earl Grey). He was agent for the Vicarage but didn't know too much about it because the affairs of the owner, Mrs Zetterberg would you believe, were handled by the senior partner who was in Florida at that moment. Mrs Z., he confided, was 'difficult'. She had apparently bought the Vicarage off the Church Commissioners at some point but was so fussy about her tenants that the house had been empty for as long as Mr Salmon had been working there, and that was five years at least. Before I could stop him he was on the blower to Mrs Z. to find out what the rent was.

He pulled a face at me over the receiver. His cheeks grew rosier. Mrs Zetterberg wanted a word with me.

The voice was formidable. Distant and cold. The accent was from somewhere between New England and Norway. I had the impression she was speaking from some isolated fjord. Her questions about my circumstances – about my *life* – were abrupt and impertinent; but I was too intimidated not to reply in full. Mr Salmon was so embarrassed that he had to disappear from my line of sight and rummage in the bottom drawer of his desk. Finally the voice asked me what I intended doing in the Vicarage. Write, I said wildly, write a book. The thought hadn't crossed my mind before. My fear was just beginning to turn into anger when the voice said I could have the place for £70 *a month*. To show I was no longer intimidated, I said I'd take it.

Mr Salmon and I were subdued after this, as though Mrs Z. were in the room. He remarked on the alleged 'atmosphere' of the house. I was still reeling from my rash commitment. Perhaps panic-stricken is the word. I thought the least I could do is look at the Vicarage before I called the whole thing off. Mr Salmon gave me the keys and kindly offered to arrange for electricity and phone.

The village is a fifteen-minute drive from the town. The house looked dauntingly large – 2 receps., 4 beds., etc. – but beautiful with its tall windows and Virginia creeper. I didn't even bother to go in. Instead I drove back to London, loaded the car with my worldly goods, stuffed a month's rent into Muriel's hand (she won't be sorry to see the back of me) and arrived back in the small hours.

And that's how you start a New Life . . .

Soul is what Mum called it. She was never overtly religious. She had some kind of private, rather woozy theology made from bits of Catholicism and bits of Madame Blavatsky.

She stood at the sink, outlined in the eternally grey Sunday light, dreamily slopping grey soapy water over some plates, looking out of the small window at our few blighted rose-bushes. I sat at the kitchen table, colouring a picture of giraffes. I was about five years old. I must've asked her a question – or did I dream this whole scene? – because I remember her talking in that special rhythmical faraway Irish voice that sometimes came over her when we were alone, but never of course when Dad was there. She talked about the soul.

From that moment on I conceived of the soul as a little man who lived deep inside me in an area of inner light. He was like a guardian angel – which I naturally knew about already – but on the inside and able to be summoned in times of need. I'm sure everyone has something like this, some similar notion, but they never examine it at all – I can barely do so now because it's so close that you don't see it. It's just the backdrop to life, like the way I picture numbers stretching away into infinity. They've always just been there.

Soon after this I heard, perhaps from Dad, about grey matter. I imagined the soul living at the end of a mass of involuted tubes, like miles of intestine, not necessarily in my head, but definitely inside my cavernous self. As I grew older, I was always dimly aware of my soul encased in golden light at the heart of the labyrinth. I realised, too, that he was not small in himself but because he was distant. Gradually I taught myself to hold my breath and blank out my mind and concentrate on that golden chamber where my soul patiently waited, until he'd suddenly come barrelling through the maze of tunnels lighting them up as he passed.

That's not quite right. I mean, that's how I picture it – but I also feel as if the labyrinth and the soul were one and the same, as the wave and the sea are one; and the labyrinth uncoils as the soul approaches until it's a shining channel straight to the heart of me. In another way, the process is a single movement of the unravelling soul which fills me from foot to head with light, brimming out of my eyes and mouth. From being small and remote he becomes in an instant very large and tall as if he had *stood up in me*, where the standing up is at the same time a rapid expanding.

I don't know what he looks like. I may have done once, when he was, if he was, my infancy's guardian angel. Over the years I couldn't help associating him with one set of features or another. Dad's mostly, I suppose. And lately, yours.

It takes energy to summon the soul. (Sorry to keep banging on about this, dear P., but it's all to do with why I'm here and, if I can just gush it out, we can both forget it. I have to clear the decks for action.) He only comes in moments of unusual longing and need, regardless of their objective importance. Like when I was baffled by maths homework. Exhausted and tearful, I'd beg for his help; and if my efforts had been great enough, he'd come like magic and make the answers to equations appear, as if of their own accord. It's the soul who works things out while we sleep so that what seemed impossible the night before is easy in the morning.

On my first day in a class with older girls, Susan Brinkman baited me and got others to do the same. Morning lessons passed in a blur of fear and rage and shame. I heard nothing except the pulse in my burning head; and I called on my soul over and over again in time to it, not knowing what I wanted. At lunchtime, Susan Brinkman broke her wrist in the playground. I was afraid to call on him again after that.

I managed without him – or, at least, without being aware of his direct intervention – until I was eighteen and so passionately in love with Philip Allegro that I stood on the landing of our old grey house, looking out of the window at the white rhododendrons, clutching the cold radiator, and sent some wild incoherent plea down towards my neglected soul. He came at once and so violently that I was nearly lifted off my feet. I was terrified of being taken over. I had to fix my whole mind on the radiator's hardness to stop myself being smitten beyond reach. At the same time, the rhododendrons smouldered in cold glory and I glimpsed there an inkling of a love a long way removed from my turbulent emotions towards Philip.

My soul's stirring now, but I dare not send for him. I'm still too frail to admit the force and fullness of that unbridled spurt, as he stands up inside me like a jet of molten gold.

SMITH

'Theophilus,'* said Robert instead of a greeting, and with his usual scowl, 'says that the French used little square stones in their melt to make blue glass.' He fussed around his kiln, not the modern one he uses for his stained glass commissions, but the primitive one he built himself. He hopes that by reproducing the materials and conditions of glass-making in the Middle Ages he will eventually hit upon the secret of the fabulous blue glass displayed in the rose-windows of Chartres cathedral.

'You see, padre, cobalt wasn't officially used as a colouring agent until the seventeenth century. But what if, *what if* the "little square stones" were *tesserae* – bits of mosaic, from Constantinople perhaps? The blue bits had cobalt in them. So, cobalt could have slipped into French glass by accident!'

This flow of speech does not, strictly speaking, run counter to his normal taciturnity because it is more like thinking aloud or, at best, addressed to his melt. If he throws in the odd 'padre' it is only to annoy me. He knows I dislike being reminded of my army years as much as he, who won't even be called by his surname, let alone 'sir' or 'Major' if he can help it. Yet our ease with each other stems in part from this common background – and in part from the sense of being 'new boys' together since he moved here only a matter of weeks before I.

He is younger than I am, a little over thirty I guess, although in many ways I think of him as older – perhaps because of his greying hair or because he was decorated in both North Africa and Italy. I am impressed by this, and also (I confess) by the two long scars, very white against his dark skin, which run in deep parallel grooves

---

* A German monk of the eleventh to twelfth century who wrote about glass-making.

from under his collar up to, and over, his jawbone. I don't know the origin of them any more than he knows of my own lesser, because non-physical, scars. I dare say there's a trace of hero-worship in my attitude towards him – if only because he resembles a *Boy's Own* hero of the dark, flinty-eyed and clipped voice variety. Apart from that, I like him very much. I would like him to meet Janet, whose exuberance is so infectious. He has been misanthropic but is beginning to show signs of thaw. He no longer barks like a dog at ramblers who stray too close to the chapel; he still tears at himself when absent-minded – picking at his skin, chewing his fingers – but he is no longer a soul in torment. His scowl which kept a whole curious village at bay for months is more habitual now than heartfelt. He is ready for her, I think, while she would appreciate his irony and his sudden, almost lyrical, bursts of passion for his glass-making. They would be good for each other.

I would have visited him more in the early days were his company not so congenial. Like me, he doesn't find it necessary or desirable to unburden himself; and his contempt for the clergy coupled with a staunch atheism ensures that he tolerates my presence for its own sake. However, it wouldn't do to have begun my duties in this parish by following my inclination and taking the easy, often indulgent, route of friendship.

'Of course cobalt is probably not the answer,' he said to his kiln. 'It makes a beautiful blue, a violet blue. A blue that's almost too pure. I need a warmer . . . *denser* blue that transmits some of the longer wavelengths of light. It's got to . . . hide the other colours of the spectrum inside it.'

Robert knows that I can more or less follow his train of thought. In the past we have discussed fluxes, for it is not only in glass-making that the melting-point has to be lowered and the ingredients fused. The Magnum Opus sometimes employs a flux to make the metals flow more easily but it's no more than a catalyst, to be avoided if possible. This does not stop many benighted chemists from elevating it to the secret fire itself, calling it 'Sophic Salt' or 'our mercury' and citing every kind of tartrate, nitrate and soda.

He gave me a cup of vile Camp [i.e. coffee essence] and I gave him my design for the pelican. While he studied it I looked out of the window. I could see Mrs Maltravers', Nightingale Wood above and the whole village stacked in the valley below. I don't know what mad Methodist chose this lonely site for his chapel nor can anyone recall a service ever having been held here. Robert bought it cheaply with the money his parents left him – enough to live on too, providing he supplements it here and there with glass sales.

Inside, the chapel is a single high-ceilinged room partitioned at the far end to make sleeping quarters. Thus the functions of studio, kitchen, drawing-room etc. all overlap – there's food on the work-table, armchairs pulled up to the kiln, jars of brilliant oxides on the draining-board, clothes drying in front of the fire, bits of glass everywhere and paintings hanging higgledy-piggledy, including some suspended from the roof-beam and turning slowly like mobiles. A disgraceful Bohemian place which, recalling Paris to me, makes me feel comfortable as nowhere else in the parish.

'It's a funny shape,' he remarked. 'Sort of *womanly*. Arms akimbo.[6] What's it for? Poteen?'

'Mind your own business.'

'I'm too busy at the moment. And I haven't blown any glass for ages,' he grumbled.

'It has to be top quality. Fire-resistant.'

We shook hands on it. He looked around for paper to write down my specifications, muttering that he could find nothing since the place had been 'tidied up'. I was surprised.

'The Thomas girl comes up to clean for me. Nora. You know? It was Tim's idea. Where *is* Tim? He was here a moment ago.' I told him I had met Nora but not Tim.

'So you've not met Tim?' he repeated, and laughed. 'He comes to give me the benefit of his advice on glass . . . '

I must meet Tim – meet the fellow who can make Robert laugh.

De ovo Hermetico

About my Hermetic egg I have little to say. For better or worse I have chosen the double pelican; but so much depends on Robert's skill in shaping it. It should be a *vas mirabile* [wonderful vessel]. If it cannot be completely round like the world, then it should be oval, like a hen's egg, so that Mercurius may move around it as his namesake describes an oval orbit about the sun. If it is not ovoid, then it should be shaped like a uterus for the gestation of the noble son of Sol and

Luna, the princely *lapis* [stone]. It must be *unum* [one thing]. As we say, 'One the matter, one the vessel, one the work.'

As to the size, Philalethes' advice is sound [in *The Marrow of Alchemy*]:

> So big thy glass let be, as may contain
> Four times at least as much as you enclose,
> For vacant space receives the dew and rain,
> Which falling down the body doth dispose
> To die and rot, and after to revive.

I have always been amused by the story of Johann Friedrich Böttger [1682 or 1685–1719] who suffered the typical fate of the overweening Philosopher – yet managed to extricate himself by his own ingenuity. As a young Berliner who worked as an apothecary's apprentice, he was sent by his busy master to attend a sick man called Lascaris. The latter was a mysterious fellow who claimed to be the Archimandrite of a convent on the island of Mytilena. He was supposed to have a vast reserve of the red transmuting powder – the Philosophers' Stone – which he distributed with unprecedented liberality. Naturally he gave young Böttger a healthy portion of it in return for helping him recover. (At this point Lascaris slips away from the story and out of sight.)

The astonishing transmutations that Böttger then began to perform brought him fame and wealth. No doubt his success went to his head, for he began to intimate that he possessed the secret of making the powder. (It's not clear to what extent Böttger can lay claim to the title of 'Philosopher'; he was, it seems, fairly proficient in the Art but nowhere near attaining the Stone.) At any rate he was summoned by the Prussian King, William I. Knowing the fate of Philosophers who fall foul of the powerful and mighty, and fearing the worst, Böttger fled to his uncle at Wittenburg and thence put himself under the protection of August II, Elector of Saxony. The latter, having witnessed one of the young man's impressive projections, immediately made him a Baron.

He lived extravagantly – until his powder ran out. He found himself deeply in debt. The Elector, hearing that he was about to flee once again, placed him under house arrest and provided him with the equipment he hoped was sufficient to make the Philosophers' Stone.

Böttger tried, and failed; but his knowledge of chemistry was such that he solved an altogether different, but extremely valuable problem: he discovered how to make the first European porcelain which had hitherto been imported at great expense from China. Böttger was restored to favour and to a life of over-indulgence which killed him at about the age of thirty-seven.

I took the early train to London and bought the following equipment: –

One American dual hot-plate with thermostatic control; 1 alembic (still, condenser and receiver); 3 heat-resistant flasks; 2 ditto retorts; an asbestos sheet, magnet, funnel, sieve, 1 box rubber bungs, 1 large magnifying glass, torch, 2 evaporating dishes, 6 storage jars. Also acids (sulphuric and nitric), iron pyrites, cream of tartar, nitre. All are to be sent on by train except the alembic which I carried with me to avoid breakage.

These purchases have taken a sizeable slice out of my stipend, but I account it as nothing when I think of the fortunes lost in pursuit of the Art in the past. The most painful feature of the old texts is the endless recital of lab accidents which have ruined the work of years. The two main causes of disaster were, firstly, the frequency with which the fire went out and, secondly, the routine breaking of stills, retorts and cucurbits. How I rejoice in my modern paraphernalia! I am not at the mercy of an apprentice or servant who might neglect the fire; nor am I faced with the problem, well-nigh insurmountable in the old days, of bringing a controlled heat to bear on our matter for months, even years at a time. In order to increase the heat gradually through each stage, as the Opus requires, the old Philosophers had a terrible time of it. They often had to resort to a whole series of athanors [furnaces] from manure boxes to *bain-maries*, to full-scale wood, charcoal or coal fires, open or closed, with or without bellows – and even then they had no means of knowing whether the temperature was correct since no practicable thermometer was available until the late seventeenth century! My 'fire', on the other hand, will deliver a steady gradient of heat, even in my absence, at whatever temperature I set.

The old equipment, too, was a nightmare. Needing to repeat certain operations a hundred times or more, the heart of many a Philosopher was broken at the same moment when, at the brink of success, some crude vessel or other cracked from overheating or shattered under pressure from the combustion within.

I evaded Mrs B.'s thinly veiled attempts to worm out of me my purpose in travelling to London! Later, unable to sleep for the plans and thoughts that buzzed inside my head, I went down to see what sort of state the cellar is in. I think it will do very well as my laboratory.

It is all stone, of course, being part of the original monastery, except for the wooden steps which lead down from the doorway. It is cool, dry and spacious. It even has a ventilation grille near the ceiling in the back wall which, because of my garden's slope, is above ground level at that point. Bang in the centre of the room is the round well, fed by the holy spring which now follows its own inscrutable course underground (to the discomfiture of my poor old church). I heaved open its great wooden lid and shone a torch down the shaft. It's beautifully constructed out of dry stone, except for the top three feet or so which are rather shoddily made out of ill-fitting, mortared stones as if someone had needed to extend it in a hurry. It is deep. I couldn't be sure if my torch beam reached as far as the water or not. I dropped a sherbet lemon down the shaft. There was a suitable pause before I was rewarded with a dull plop,

I started at once in a fit of eagerness to clear the place up. I'm partly compensating, I know, for the frustration I feel at the necessary slowness of calcination. I stacked all the furniture that's stored down there at the far end, save a table for my athanor, some handsome shelves for my other apparatus, an armchair, a small card-table which I'll use as a desk, a chair and a marvellous carved prie-dieu that will no doubt prove useful during my long vigil. Thus, too, I shall fulfil poor Khunrath's prescription for a laboratory that is also part oratory.* Prayer and praxis are simply the inside and the outside of the same thing.

The single light bulb above the wooden steps is the only source

---

* Heinrich Khunrath (?1560–1605) illustrated his Laboratorium-Oratorium in *The Amphitheatre of Eternal Wisdom* (1609) which contains a number of beautiful engravings. He is 'poor' presumably because he is thought to have been mentally unbalanced.

of electricity. I can take a wire across from the socket to run my athanor. For lighting I will use the oil lamps which I prefer to electricity in any case. Indeed, my master positively recommended the natural illumination of lamps and candles as better suited to a true perception of what takes place in the Hermetic vessel. The secret fire is shy, attracted to its common counterpart and repelled by the overbearing inquisition of a harsh, artificial glare.

I have been worrying about how to conduct my business in the cellar without interference from Mrs Beattie. One excellent thing is that I can unseal the door in my study which gives on to the back passage where the cellar door is. Thus I can go to and fro without having to cross the hall every time. The solution to the Beattie problem came to me over one of her curate's eggs this morning: with ringing voice I forbade her, on pain of light capital punishment, ever to go near the cellar. To our mutual surprise, she humbly agreed.

De calcinatione

The aim of calcination is to prepare our matter for dissolution and separation by which the elements are divided and rendered *philosophical*.

Nothing has caused more confusion in the Art than the question of *elements*. Thus it is well to remember that the prima materia, while always remaining One, is also – like the Stone – *quadratus* [square, four-fold].

(It's worth noting here that in the course of its long history our Philosophy underwent many modifications. It rejected new influences sparingly, always striving to accommodate previous theories of man and matter and to employ them all, at different levels, in the Opus. In this it resembles an oriental philosophy such as Hinduism which is able to embrace other creeds within its elastic boundaries – in contrast to the religions of Jew, Christian and Moslem which tend to reject and separate even as our Philosophy, hidden within them, accepts and reconciles.)

Following Aristotle (who had it from Plato and, before him, Empedocles) our Philosophy asserts that the world consists of earth, air, fire and water. It is a modern idiocy to suppose that we believe these to be the literal constituents of the world. Rather, the four elements point to the four-fold *principle* which organises all matter. As an analogy one may say that earth typifies the solid; water, the liquid; air, the gaseous; while fire, the most spiritual element, consists in the ethereal [i.e. ether-like] principle of combustibility.

The four elements arise from combinations of two pairs of attributes called *hot* and *cold*, *moist* and *dry*. Thus air is hot and moist; fire, hot and dry etc., viz.: –

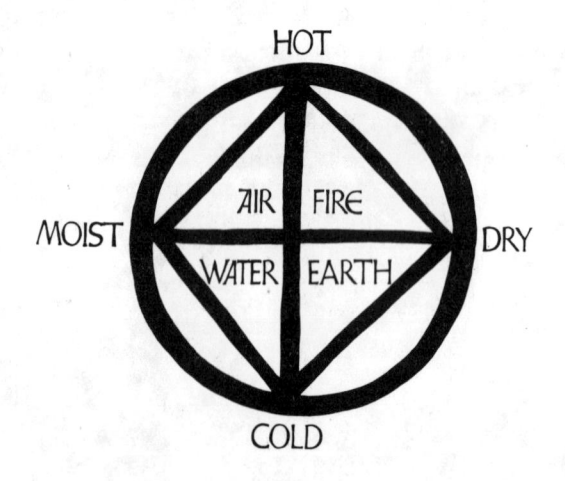

In one sense the Art consists solely of changing one element into another by the substitution of attributes. For example, to change earth into water, dryness is substituted for moistness; while water into air is an exchange of hot for cold.

However, Aristotle had an alternative theory of matter,* which seems to have formed the basis for the Arabs' refinement of the elements to two: henceforth *mercury* and *sulphur* became the twin principles of matter. Crucial to the Art was the description of the former as *volatile*, and of the latter as *fixed*.

To the Greek and Arabic theories, Europe added a third from that most profound and influential text, the Smaragdine Table.[7] Its

---

* Smith outlines this theory in the course of his tribute to Jabir, the great Arab alchemist, on p. 86

greatest contribution was to add a new spiritual dimension to the existing knowledge of matter, a dimension which emphasised the *vertical* antithesis – as Above, so Below – in contrast to the *horizontal* qualities, volatile and fixed. It also introduces us to the father and mother of the 'one thing': Sol and Luna [Sun and Moon]. This royal pair of elements corresponds to the Above as mercury and sulphur correspond to the Below, rather in the same way that sun and moon are said to correspond to gold and silver; or, we might say, Sol and Luna correspond to fire and water as mercury and sulphur correspond to air and earth.

At any rate the four-fold scheme which my own invaluable manuscript employs can be expressed like this:

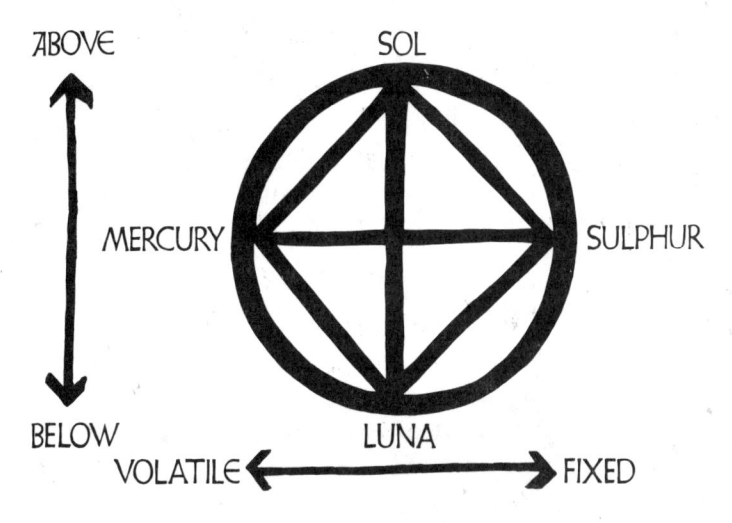

[Diagram: A circle containing a square inscribed with diagonals. Labels around the circle: ABOVE (top left, with upward arrow), SOL (top), MERCURY (left), SULPHUR (right), BELOW (bottom left, with downward arrow), LUNA (bottom), VOLATILE ← → FIXED (horizontal arrow beneath).]

The most obviously remarkable feature of my scheme is the absence of *salt*. Often believed by the ill-informed to be a fundamental principle of our Magistery, salt is of course a later accretion, brought in by von Hohenheim [i.e. Paracelsus] and his followers around the first half of the sixteenth century. Subsequently it became pretty much a standard ingredient of the Art – although, I suggest, mostly with those Philosophers who had already begun to abandon the laboratory in favour of a purely speculative chemistry.

The inclusion of salt was an attempt to reconcile the trinitarian thinking of Christianity with the Arabs' binary scheme. Since Christians held that all things, including the metals, possessed a body, soul and spirit, it was natural for Christian chemists to invoke a corresponding trinity of elements (mercury, sulphur and salt) which also reflected on Earth the heavenly Trinity of Father, Son and Holy Ghost. What they did not understand was that our Philosophy is itself a way of redressing the Christian imbalance and completing its trinities. Our Art, so to speak, squares the circle of the three-fold.

So, whereas I happily agree that matter, like man, has a body, soul and spirit, I would add that spirit is in reality a double entity so that matter (like man) is in truth organised according to a four-fold or (more accurately) *double binary scheme* – but I must take care not to say too much.

What promised to be another interminable parish meeting suddenly caught fire during 'any other business' when our chairman mentioned *en passant* that he intends to do away with Nightingale Wood. Silence among the rest of us. Never before has it been brought home to us with such force that we are all fundamentally cowed by Caldwell.

At length, Janet, bless her, with whom I exchanged a single eloquent horrified glance, spoke up. Her protest was characteristically from the heart: it didn't seem *right* to cut down all those lovely trees. General murmurs of concurrence. Caldwell pushed his chair back and sank his thick red neck further down into his collar. He sighed, world-weary but, at the same time, determined to be patient.

'For the first time in the history of our people' – portentous pause – 'there are more tractors than horses working the land.' He smacked his lips as if personally responsible for this technological advance. Indeed this statistic seemed to settle the argument for him. Tractors and trees are natural enemies, ergo the trees must come down. We must continue the wartime practice of putting as much land under the plough as possible; we must 'capitalise' on it. If we do not, we jeopardise *progress*.

Naturally we all fell respectfully silent at the invocation of that great idol. Any argument against Progress is in extremely bad taste. I tried to think how I might present to Caldwell the criminal folly of his proposal, but I could come up with nothing that might carry weight with him. The argument against destroying the wood is as self-evident as its trees – the beautiful old English hollies, oaks, thorns and apples and the more recent beeches and copper beeches, elms and ashes. Every sort of flora and fauna find sanctuary there, from bluebells (which are just beginning now in massed profusion) to badgers and lovers. I felt the helplessness of the Stebbinses of this world who can only watch without hope as their daughters are defiled and paid off. They take the money because they are powerless and, not to do so, pointless. But it gives no comfort; it only strengthens their belief in their own weakness in the face of people like the Caldwells; and their faces wrinkle and collapse, like lungs. I said: 'Do you have the right?' Timidity made me sound more challenging than I intended. His eyes bulged briefly with anger before he turned on me with the special pitying look he reserves for men of the cloth whom he assumes to be unworldly (my experience of the Dean and his cohorts is that they are quite the reverse).

'The wood belongs to me, you see, Vicar?' He spoke slowly as if addressing a retarded child.

'What about the right of way through the wood?'

I saw at once by the pleased way his head bridled that I had fallen into his trap.

'In point of fact' – looking round the table at all of us and tapping his index finger on the table for emphasis – 'the right of way goes *round* the wood on the west side. Everyone who walks *in* the wood is, in fact, trespassing. However, I shall not be taking legal action against those who walk in the wood while it is still there.' The others actually smiled at this. I think it is his *relish* of the situation which I find most offensive. He pushes what meagre charity remains to me to its limits. 'Naturally,' he went on, 'I shan't interfere with the authentic right of way,' and he added with a sly twinkle, 'Heaven forbid.' The others smiled even more cravenly at this, except Janet who went red and said loudly, 'I think it's a bestial thing to do.'

'We must face harsh realities, Janet,' he said kindly, as if that meant something. He lifted his hands in a helpless gesture to indicate that he was only obeying the will of higher powers, such as the Laws of Economics and Progress in Agriculture. He sighed. He alone, it seemed, was able and willing to face up to Unpalatable Facts and make Necessary Sacrifices.

The meeting was over. It was a rout. But the war has only begun. The wood will not come down because I cannot believe that the village will stand by while Caldwell reaches into its breast and tears out its heart.

Today I visited Mrs Crowther whose three youngest are down with whooping cough. The poor woman is at her wits' end, having no time to fetch the necessary medicine and no cash to buy provisions. She is too loyal to say where her money goes, but it's no secret that Crowther likes more than a flutter on the horses. I wish all immediate problems were as easily solved as hers. I set off for the vicarage to get my bicycle. The thought of the long ride into town was disheartening but I could not afford both the bus fare and the things she needed – as it was, I had to find the money out of the minimum sum Mrs B. demands for housekeeping.

Janet pulled up beside me in her natty little sports car. It does one good to see her – so energetic, so healthy somehow and full of life. She normally leaves her mass of chestnut hair loose, but in the open car she ties it back with a daring bandanna. Sometimes we walk together, making an incongruous couple – I, with my deliberate, self-conscious gait and dark uniform, she, swinging along beside me, chattering away, her outstanding figure encased in gay dresses that are perhaps more close-fitting than is usual in these parts. Today she wore a pair of slacks which would make Mrs B. sniff and look the other way. Mrs B. does not approve of my seeing Janet whom as a Catholic she suspects of being in league with the Devil. Mrs B.'s distrust of Catholics comes from nowhere, as far as I can tell, except her own innately low church soul. Janet, in her turn, does excellent and cruel impersonations of Mrs B. meeting the Pope, who offers her his ring to be kissed. (Today she mentioned Mrs B.'s husband who, as everybody knows except me, *ran off with a land girl*! Now I come to think of it, I can't say that Mrs B. ever actually *lied* to me – but she definitely led me to *believe* she was widowed.)

She offered me a lift into town. Despite, or because of, the quickening of my pulse, I hesitated. It crossed my mind that it was not exactly *seemly* for a man in my position to be seen so much about with Janet, especially in a *sports* car. As if guessing my thought, she laughed. I was ashamed. In her very nature Janet cannot help cutting a dash; but she does so without a trace of immodesty. She is unconscious of the effect of her beauty. Joyfully I jumped into the car, feeling pleasantly *doggy* and, I realised with dismay, more like a man and less like a member of the third sex exclusive to clergymen than I had felt for a long time.

The roar of the engine and wind in the open-topped car made conversation difficult. I shouted the news of the children's whooping cough. Janet shouted back: 'That's one trouble I'll never have to put up with!' I was shocked by the grief and bitterness in her voice. I hadn't thought to wonder why she has no children. She is certainly of an age – a year or two older than Robert, I think, about thirty-four – when she should think seriously about it, if she intends to have them. She is very fond of children, I know. Perhaps her husband is the stumbling-block. Farrar is a lot older than she (even older than I) and not an easy man to live with, I suspect. He appears to make more money than I knew solicitors could, and he spends a lot of it in the Green Man. I confess that he is one reason why I don't go to the pub as much as I would like – he has a way of latching on to you and boring you to death. I dare say he is better at home, as who would not be with a wife like his? At least Janet does not complain of him. She married him when she was very young but does not seem to mind a much older man as a husband – unless the absence of children is a bone of contention. Feebly I said 'I'm so sorry' in reply to her remark; but the wind carried the words away and I couldn't bring myself to repeat them in a shout.

Tea with Lydia Simmons in an atmosphere of faded gentility and refinement. She is a kind soul with a look of perpetual anxiety. It is painful to watch the intensity of her concentration as she plays the harmonium on Sundays. It is remarkable how she grows thinner as Mrs B. grows fatter, like a cuckoo in the nest. No two sisters could be less alike. Their father left all his money to Lydia, the elder of the two, so that Simmons, who is reckoned 'frail', fortunately has no need of getting a living. This gives him a lot of time for misty-eyed piety. He carries à Kempis around with him.* Mrs B. accounts him a 'saint'. I would that he were less of a saint and more of a verger. I sense that Lydia is of the same opinion – I once quoted to her a pithy Yiddish proverb: 'A man who's too good for this world is no good for

---

* Presumably *The Imitation of Christ*.

his wife.' She shook with a laughter that was not, I thought, without a hint of hysteria.

I am sitting in front of Mrs Beattie's fire, in her parlour next to the kitchen. She has gone home since it is long after dark and I have crept down, like a guilty Prometheus, to steal her fire before it expires in the grate; for my study is expensive to heat, and I can better withstand the chilliness than poor Mrs B. who must have her fire.

I dined on a stew made from scrag-end of wildebeest. Mrs B. is not in her nature a cook. She has not the art of selecting the ingredients in the right proportions and conjoining them steadily by the proper application of fire. Her stew was instructive, a stark reminder of the care required in that greater cuisine, the cooking of metals. The Philosopher will no more *isolate* his elements than isolate the spice from the stew; rather he will *separate*, but only that he may the better unite. Unlike Mrs B. who bangs the pot on to the flames and scorches it for an hour regardless, he will temper the outer, manifest fire with the hidden fire within, and by continual vigilance allow the 'stew' itself to teach him what degree of heat is wanted.

Before taking up these writing materials, I took a turn with the pestle for a while. The mortar is full of wonders! I did not grind hard but stroked the matter steadily. A thousand subtle hues flickered in response to the firelight as the matter warmed to my touch. I sense I'm getting to *know* it. The first springlike hint of *viriditas* [greenness] has begun to tint the shiny earth and from time to time there's the quick sparkle and wink of a nobler metal.

Mrs B.'s fire sends its golden shoots up the dark chimney. I am like the first man to whom the gods gave fire for protection against the ravening beasts and evil spirits that roared and twittered outside his enchanted circle of light and heat. Did he, as I do now, watch his own thoughts leaping and disporting themselves in the flames like salamanders and, watching, hearing the hiss and crack, dimly divine his own future? I must make friends with fire: any day now, my calcination complete, I begin the first crucial stage of the Magnum Opus when – oh, *Deo volente* – Mercurius will leap like a flame from the precious prima materia.

Robert once described to me the wonder with which he, as a child, fired his first clay pot. The oxidation of vegetable matter or minerals mixed up in the unrefined clay caused the pot to magically change colour from grey to orange, to red, to purple. In that simple transformation I saw a metaphor for the transformation of clay-footed man into a rainbow-winged creature.

De Ígne

Master fire and you master the *Magnum Opus* which is begotten as it ends – in fire.

All metals contain seeds which, kindled into life by fire, grow into purest gold.

Our Stone (that is no stone!) is a species of fixed fire. Ripley calls it an invisible fire made visible. Being of the nature of fire, fire cannot burn or consume it.

Dying is learning to walk in the living fire, head high like Shadrach, Meshach and Abednego.

Neglect the fire and it roasts like the bonfires of hell; heed it, and it nourishes like the light of heaven.

Mrs B. unusually silent at tea, bar the sound of her jaws as they zealously processed her food. However, I was not to escape entirely.

'That woman,' she suddenly announced, 'is an ungrateful 'eathen.' She must indeed have been in an extremity of passion to drop an aitch.

'That woman . . . ?'

'Mrs Maltravers! Said she wouldn't 'ave me in the 'ouse. You'd think she'd want all the friends she could get, being nearly passed on an' that. Well, *I* won't go where I'm not wanted I'm sure.' And so on. I thought of the old lady, on her death-bed by all accounts, banning Mrs B. from the premises, and my heart lifted.

To Goose Farm. It's curiosity more than compassion which drives me to pester Mrs Maltravers.

Nora was on her knees in the small front garden, weeding primroses. She did not hear me come up and so, absurdly, I hesitated to speak because I knew it would startle her. I watched her at work. She has long brown fingers. I called her name softly. She looked around without surprise and, recognising me, stumbled forward. When she raised her face again it was flushed, and I noticed that her eyes are so blue that they give off a clear blue light.

Mrs M. sent down her regards and an enquiry after my health. She was not well enough to receive me, however. 'It's not just you,' Nora tried to assure me. 'She doesn't see anybody, not even Doctor Sparrow, unless she wants some pain-killers. But she's quite happy.' I decided to try again in a few days' time. It's not my experience that people have a great desire to see clergymen as they approach death, but you never know.

De aqua

I refer not to ordinary water but to the indispensable philosophical water. It has as many names as the prima materia, but we need not concern ourselves with them. Our water is the substance of the whole work. So much so, that in the *Fons Chymicae Veritatis* [*Fountain of Chemical Truth*], Philalethes identifies 'our vessel' with 'our water'; and 'when we speak of fire, again understand water; and when we discuss the furnace, we mean nothing that is different or distinct from water'.

Our water is unique, penetrating and dissolving. It can burn like the sharpest vinegar or revivify like the waters of the Nile as they flood the parched land. It is the material of the lapis itself, for which reason it is called the Red Tincture; for metals can be turned to gold by the action of this water spreading through them like a dye. Yet Philalethes reminds us in his extraordinary *Introitus* that 'in our water fire is sought'; and this is why our water 'does not wet the hands'.

'*Aqua Philosophorum est ignis*' ['The water of the Philosophers is fire'].

At evensong I preached on the lilies of the field. I couldn't resist one or two indirect swipes at Caldwell, who toils and spins too much. I regret this. A pulpit is no place from which to muster support for the cause of Nightingale Wood. (But I don't regret it as much as I should.) Anyway, Caldwell sat entirely unperturbed in his pew. He does tend to listen these days, in case I threaten him with insurrection, but I am obviously too subtle or, more likely, too mealy-mouthed to put even a puff of wind up him. I note that Bradley is absent again.

Simmons hovered, hangdog, after the service. The heart sank. He tried to help me divest but I drew the line at that. He is a verger not a valet. He is 'out of sorts' again. His soul troubles him. I had stayed up all last night, working (and praying); I fasted all day – a long one, with three services and two sermons here, and two services and one sermon at Upper D— . I was dog-tired. But his soul is unique and precious in the eyes of God; and besides he works hard at his church chores and keeps the graveyard neat. I suggested he might like to come back for a sherry. His long face lit up; he moistened his swollen red lips. I knew I was in for a lengthy session.

Like Lydia and Mrs B., Simmons is in his fifties. They all live together in a kind of menopausal gloom. More than once he has coyly let it be known to me, in his refined nasal way, that he, too, had once felt called to the priesthood. Alas 'it was not to be' – although *why* not he doesn't say. Tonight he spoke of *The Imitation of Christ* in a sentimental way, like a lovesick schoolgirl. I felt increasingly queasy. He feels very close to Our Saviour at times but his wife is too worldly and cannot understand him; he is grateful that 'God has seen fit' to bring Mrs B. into his (i.e. Lydia's) house. She is 'a tower of strength'.

He wished me to pray with him for the forgiveness of his sins. I agreed to this but declined to kneel with him on the floor. He began to call on 'Jesus', like some Pentecostalist, in a moaning sort of way. I think it is the familiarity towards the Son of God which most repels me.

The poor fellow is addicted to his milksop mysticism. If I am too robust with him his lip trembles, his round fervent eyes blur. I listened to his nasal complaining voice for a long time. Apparently we are 'two of a kind' . . . 'cut out for Higher Things' etc. I could not decently bundle him out until 2 a.m., heaping as I did so words of encouragement on to his narrow head.

I prayed until I could no longer keep my eyes open and then I did an hour or so at the mortar. To my surprise and joy I found the work easy and light, the matter yielding under the pestle. My dark thoughts flew away. I forget how blessed I am. I resolved to exercise more patience and charity, especially towards Simmons and Mrs B. who are a daily reproach to my incapacity for love.

I dreamt that I was gazing down a black shaft like that of my well, up which something was crawling towards me. Its legs knocked with a hollow sound on the walls. I could not move. I woke into 'the fell of dark not day'.* There was a hammering on the door. I stumbled downstairs. Young Nora stood there. 'Grandma's asking for you,' she announced calmly. She turned on her heel and disappeared into the cold night.

I pulled on clothes and, not risking my lightless bicycle, ran to Goose Farm. All the lights were on as if in celebration of some festival; but only Dr Sparrow was there, puffing at his pipe in the parlour. 'Too late I'm afraid, Vicar. She's gone.' I could not take this in immediately. 'Dead, Vicar.' I thought that there must be some mistake. I explained that she had asked for me. 'Yes. That's true,' he admitted. Then, seeing my distress, he added: 'But don't worry. She wasn't upset or anything. No death-bed confession. She just said, "I'd like a chat with that priest now. The hag told me about him. I like the sound of him." Nora nipped off at once to get you, but . . . ' I took the hag to be Mrs Beattie.

Sparrow told me to go away. It was getting on for morning and he would stay with Nora who had gone up to sit with her grandma. Her grandma's body. She was composed, he said, even cheerful. Her grandmother and she had prepared for the former's death together. They had agreed on the existence of a benign afterlife. They would meet there later on. Sparrow told me this in a studiedly neutral way.

I went out and examined the stars. On such a clear night they cram the sky right down to the rooftops, surrounding the world with silver filaments, quickening the metals in the ground. I managed a reasonably sincere prayer for the soul of Mrs Maltravers. I was sorry to have missed her. I liked the sound of her.

Caldwell wants to install streetlamps around the village green. He will ensure, if he can, that none of us ever sees the stars again.

---

* Smith is quoting from a poem by Gerard Manley Hopkins.

*

Today I played truant from my duties to go walking with Janet in Nightingale Wood. My excuse was that it might be the last time I would be able to see the famous bluebells which carpet the ground so thickly that the trees seem rooted in a hazy, almost ultra-violet sea. Neither of us mentioned Caldwell's plans.

I suggested we visit Robert for tea, taking the long route around the valley by following the curve of Grimm's Down. Janet was doubtful but I egged her on. I judged Robert to be ready for more exciting visitors than the Thomas children and the odd vicar; and, besides, I could no longer wait to see my pelican which Robert had promised for today.

It never occurred to me that my two friends would not take to each other; but in fact the visit was a disaster.

When we arrived, Robert was lying fast asleep on the floor among his pots and flasks. Janet's laugh woke him and in a flash he was on his feet, frowning and ready to spring at our throats. I attempted to introduce Janet. They both said, 'We've already met,' at the same time. I was put out – neither of them had mentioned their mutual acquaintance to me, nor that they so obviously disliked each other.

Robert cleared a space on his paint-bespattered table and, pointing to two chairs, set about making us tea. He dropped and broke one of his cups; when he offered us a slice of fly-blown Battenberg cake, his hand shook. He was scrupulously polite but spoke only when necessary. I was as irritated with him as he was probably furious with me. I tried to draw him out on the subject of his glass, so that Janet would see him in his best light, but he answered me shortly and never once addressed Janet whose cool amused gaze clearly disconcerted him.

At the same time she either looked bored or addressed rather crass remarks to me. I desperately wanted Robert to see Janet, not as she appeared, but as I knew her to be underneath the brittle smartness – a person one can open one's heart to and read in her sea-grey eyes understanding, empathy, approval. We sat there, stilted and uncomfortable, until I could bear it no longer. I could have smacked them both. As we left Robert shoved a cardboard box packed with newspaper into my arms. I thanked him. I knew what it was.

It stands before me now, beautifully executed, perfectly symmetrical: the Egg in which my Philosophy is to be hatched – on which the success of my venture along the left-hand path depends.

Predictably, the workmen cannot solve the problem of my church's subsidence. Experts have come to stare into the long trench stretching from the altar to the east wall. They scratch their heads. They go away again. Water seeps into the trench. They are filling it in tomorrow – a prelude to forgetting about it. I'm glad. I don't want the building messed about. It has served the site well for centuries. If it is time for it to sink back into Nature, well, let it. The Church against whom the gates of hell shall not prevail was never made of ordinary stone.

'One book opens another,' the Philosophers tell us truly. There is no understanding of the Art without long and anxious study of those texts in which the angelic keys to our Philosophy are concealed. However, to the uninitiated eye, the bogus recipes of some imbecile puffer can appear as wise as the works of the Bridlington Canon [i.e. Ripley].

Even when the masters have been weeded out from among the charlatans, it is still no easy matter to interpret their words. It has been said that no adept has ever described the whole operation of the Red Stone, but that each describes some portion of it so that one must put the Magnum Opus together from a number of different sources. On this subject I have no fixed opinion. I have elected to abide by my master's advice: by all means study and study again in diverse texts, but always return to a single one in which one can have faith. My guiding light is the one he set great store by. It is (he said) simple, direct and, above all, it contains the Work in its entirety except for the preliminary calcination which may be taken as read.

I am inclined to believe, from internal evidence, that it is not an ancient text but rather a product of the late – and arguably greatest – flowering of our Philosophy in the latter part of the sixteenth century. At any rate, it was clearly written by an adept who received it from, or ascribed it to, Mercurius himself. There are no endless perorations or deliberate obfuscations to impress or put off the reader. Instead, it is modest and brief.

My manuscript is divided into three parts. Firstly there is the prologue in which Mercurius describes himself and issues his warning [see p. 3]. Secondly there's a description of the Regimen of the Moon by which the White Stone is accomplished; and thirdly we have the Regimen of the Sun which culminates in the creation of the Red Stone – that is, the Tincture, *Filius* [Son] or *lapis philosophorum* [Philosophers' Stone].

The second part – the point at which the praxis begins – can be translated as follows:

(Mercurius says) Know this: that my Science is accomplished in easy stages of which there are but two, namely the *Regimen of Luna* and the *Regimen of Sol*.

To begin the Regimen of Luna, acquaint yourself with the winged and wingless *dragon*, with the *virgin queen* whom it holds in thrall, and with the *king* who alone can slay it. Above all, find the secret fire which binds them together with hidden affinities (*cum correspondentiis occultis*) and by which they must be divided, and you have *the whole secret* of our Magistery.

It is necessary to join the Above with the Below, and the Below with the Above, which conjunction the Philosophers call *Heaven*. Then will the White Stone of the Wise appear.

To which end, dissolve our calcined matter in our sea. Repeat as often as is necessary to loosen the beautiful *Luna* from the fiery embrace of the *dragon* who lies coiled in the *chaos* beneath the sea. Maintain the matter at the first degree of fire for seven days and seven nights. Allow the winged dragon to fly up into the Above and *drip his venom* on to our body. When it is exhausted you will see *the rising of Sol*, who will draw his sister out of the depths. As he hurls his bright spears into the dragon who gave birth to him *before time began*, observe the creature's death throes and how they make the sea seethe and boil, dividing the water from the land, which is to say, our clear *volatile mercury* from our earthy *fixed sulphur*. Now, as Ripley says, 'Turn the Wheele óf Alchymy . . .'

Circulate for a month, day and night *without cease*, and there will appear, slowly spreading through our body and permeating every pore, that *blackness* we call *mortification*. Weep as the *noble Sol* is eclipsed by the sea. Let him sink down and be devoured by the dragon. Let him remain in *the belly of the dragon* three nights, suffering ordeals by fire. At the same time Luna will rise; not in bright refulgence but in darkness as sinister as the horned new moon. Let her spread her wings *as black as the raven's*, yet veil her mourning face from the conjunction of Rex and Regina [i.e. King and Queen] who, being interpreted, are *the body and soul of our matter*. When these two are joined in the mercurial fountain and burned by the sulphurous fires of Gehenna, you will see the *Rebis* [Two-Thing] in whom the seed of *our Stone* is conceived.

Increase the heat to the second or third degree until you observe the wheel turning *full circle*. Thus, as Luna descends to her zenith [*sic*] her tears purify and raise up Sol. For *these tears* are dry white water which some call a *salt*; and so they cleanse the body to whiteness but also *consume* it until its blackness is burnt to white ash. But mark well that the *Albedo* [whiteness] is only true and pure if it is presaged by the *cauda pavonis* [Peacock's tail]; for when you see the thousand colours appearing you know that the holy marriage of Sol and Luna is at hand, which resembles *a star set in Heaven*. Here dwells the White Stone whose touch transmutes basest metal to purest silver. The Stone is volatile through its mercurial nature for it is I [Mercurius] who joins Sol and Luna; yet it is fixed by virtue of its body of white sulphur.

Only when this body is exalted from its earthly state can the Red Stone of the Philosophers come into being. And so I turn to the second and final operation, the Regimen of Sol. [The Regimen of Sol is transcribed by Eileen. See p. 146]

Dismal day. Relentless rain leaking from grey skies, seeping down our necks as we stood in the graveyard to see Mrs Maltravers buried. She gave no instructions about the disposal of her body so, *faute de mieux*, the good old Church of England stood in despite her earthly distaste for it.

Hers is only the latest in a long line of burials. They have been the mainstay of my brief spell here. The village seems to be dying on its feet. No one comes to replace the dead. Even the river which once powered our derelict mill has swerved away over the years and now silts up in Upper D—, leaving us poor Lower D—s to our own devices.

The funeral attracted a huge turn-out. Mrs M. was either popular or else she still exerts some strange sway over the people from beyond the grave. Her son-in-law was chief mourner, although by rights it should have been his daughter, who stood very straight and pale beside him. Thomas's ship, I was told, does not sail until the day after tomorrow, and so he was able to dash up from Southampton later on the day of her death. He is a small, swarthy, Welsh-looking fellow with powerful arms and shoulders but disproportionately short legs. Nora must have inherited her mother's legs as well as the thick honey-coloured hair; but the straight dark eyebrows are her father's. So, I realised with a shock, are her eyes which are not in the least blue as I had seen them (maybe by virtue of association with her blonde hair), but brown and close together so that father and daughter both appeared to be staring at some unattainable horizon.

I searched the vicinity eagerly for a glimpse of Tim. But he either cared too little for his grandmother or too much, because he was not, as usual, in evidence.

Prominent at the edge of the grave was Out-of-Sorts Simmons, wearing his hair well greased and parted down the middle in the old-fashioned manner. His narrow face was further pinched by an expression at once lugubrious and self-important as if her death would not be complete without him. He held an umbrella to protect Mrs B.'s best hat which squatted like a malign purple familiar on her righteous head. She seemed to be struggling against her tears, and even swayed slightly such that for one long sickening moment I thought she might rest her great tragic head on Simmons's weedy shoulder. I savoured again the memory of how the old lady, with words alone, had ejected Mrs B. from Goose Farm. (The latter, incidentally, was sold cheaply some time ago to Caldwell on condition that she could stay there while she lived. It now reverts to him and will in turn be let to his estate manager. Janet tells me that the Maltravers once owned all the land hereabouts, including the Manor; but, having fallen on hard times, they were reduced to Goose Farm where the family name has now expired along with its last owner.)

The men were lowering the coffin into the hole when suddenly the hush was sawed in half by the roar of a motor-cycle. On the green a group of youths was clustered around Bradley Caldwell who, sitting astride his new machine, ostentatiously revved it. Startled, one of the coffin men let the slippery rope run too quickly and the box tilted and dropped with unseemly speed. I tried to raise my voice above the cacophony of the motor-bike but the perennially moving words of the burial service – 'cut down like grass . . . Earth to earth, ashes to ashes' – were all but lost in the din. It ceased just as the coffin hit the bottom of the grave with, horrors, an audible splash. The prolonged rain had caused our unpredictable spring to rise up around the church, filling the grave with a good six inches of water. I was troubled by a brief vision of the dead bursting out of their sodden coffins all around us, their bodies washed clean of sin and flesh, eddying out of the darkness and, skinny and grinning, rising up on that unholy tide towards the light.

The spell of solemnity was broken; the burial teetered on the edge of farce. I finished as best I could. As I left the dispersing group of mourners I thought I saw young Caldwell turn in his saddle and, with one leg cocked on the petrol tank, follow me with his black eyes all the way back to the vicarage.

EILEEN

By eight o'clock this evening I was about ready to jack it in. Whatever bracing effect I'd got out of solitude had given way to abject loneliness. I pushed off to the Green Man – give it a last chance, Eileen, why not? – and found myself looking at it through your eyes, P., and half-fantasising that you were with me, down in the country for a smutty weekend . . .

Six months ago I would have turned up my nose at the horse-brasses and plum Dralon. Dad drilled me from an early age in matters of taste. I still recoil at 'toilet' when lavatory is meant. Now I don't give a fart about Taste, thanks to you. I'm certain Dad's fastidiousness has shortened his life. Besides, the pub has the essentials – cosy lighting, fire, etc. – and the locals obviously like it regardless of what ideas snotty townies like me have about how country pubs should be.

The camp barman greeted me like an old friend. It cheered me up. He's Brendan from Co. Kerry. He asked me how I'd enjoyed the wine. I mentioned that it had not been quite as dry as he'd promised. He screamed.

'Well, slash me wrists, I never thought you'd notice. There's not a dry wine in the house at all.' Then, unrepentant, he looked studiedly into the distance while pointing at his light blue pullover.

'What d'you think of the *cashmere*?'

'Very nice.'

'Nice? *Nice*? It's only *gorgeous*. Cost me an arm and a leg. I'm not lending it to *you*.'

Things were looking up. I sipped a pint of the strongest beer *you've* ever tasted and was just wondering whether I'd risk a shepherd's pie when this great clot of a bloke with tattoos on biceps the size of melons lights up his Old Holborn. The smoke wafts me like a magic carpet back to the room where you sit, puffing merrily away on your miserable little roll-ups and writing your miserable little book in short jerky bursts while I watch you from the sofa, pretending to read Kierkegaard's Greatest Hits just to please you . . .

I got out of the Green Man sharpish and went mopping and mowing across the muddy Green with the rain sizzling down, damn you.

We met in a pub, remember? I was with Piers the art gallery man for whom I suppose – though you didn't know it – I was trying to drum up some romantic feelings. I might have managed it too if you hadn't whispered (when he slid out of his round for the second time), 'Bet you 50p he tucks his shirt *and* his cardie into his underpants.' That said it all, really.

I dreamt that you were in bed with me and all I had to do was to stretch out my hand to feel your warmth. I couldn't move a muscle. Waking was a nightmare. A descent into my groaning wreck of a body. I tell you this because I want you to feel bad about it. I want you to have *your* share of pain. Have you any idea how callous you are? Of course not. You only see what suits you.

The rain took a breather. I walked out to get my bearings. The village is picturesque, only just on the right side of cute, its thatched cottages alleviated by the odd Georgian house and the small but beautiful Manor, Queen Anne I guess, opposite the Green Man – all spaced artistically around the Green. Fortunately the village shop is an eyesore. Built in early Tesco style, it boasts some fine neo-Safeway features, such as a luminous orange blaze of cut-price posters. Its brickwork is in Public Lavatory bile-yellow, the same colour as the housing estate which stretches from the south-west end of the village to almost as far as the main road to town.

Whereas the village is full of older people, the estate is a cheery place, designed for youth. As the high wind blew puffballs of cloud across a blue wash of sky, young mums in colourful loose-fitting clothes blossomed out of the bile-yellow houses with pushchairs full of plump infants. A lot of the mums looked young enough to be my daughters, and yet it was I who felt younger than they because they seemed so at ease in marriage and motherhood. I've never felt grown-up enough for either of these commitments; but I suppose it happens the other way around – you never feel grown-up until someone calls you Mummy.

There was no real need to roll your eyes like a stricken cow, P. I meant it when I proposed to you, but I knew really that marriage to you was never on the cards.

Rain again by the time I reached the Vicarage.

Slept all evening in front of the fire. Didn't mean to, but I can't keep my eyes open half the time. The other half, I'm like a mad thing. I'll probably be up all night now. *Quel* bummer.

I can't believe this awful grieving can go on and on and not gnaw itself to death. It even goes on when I'm asleep – I wake up with my heart eaten away to a sliver of ache. I feel more worn out than when I started. My throat is all constricted. I have to cry mechanically, cranking out the tears, to relieve it. I'm not even crying for you any more. It's myself I'm blubbing about – my wasted pointless selfish life.

Well, enough of *that*.

All the same, P., I have to go on a bit more about marriage. I am sorry. But if I can just say it, then we can both forget it. I promise this will be the last mention of it. Don't panic – it's not about marrying *you*. It's about this odd experience I had on the No. 11 bus. You're the only person I can tell because it's just possible you'll understand. Besides, apart from being lovers, we were stupid enough to become friends. It's the friend I miss most right now. (Press on, I hear you say.)

I was on the top deck of the No. 11, on my way to see you that last time. I knew it was more than my life was worth to go on seeing you, but I knew I'd never be able to stop myself. I had to get my fix. As each stop passed and as I failed to get off at any of them, this crisis came over me: I had to make a *choice*. Not a choice between things. More a question of whether or not I'd choose my own life. You know, choose to be *me* instead of just waddling on, passing myself off as a human being. I suppose you helped to bring this crisis on; but you weren't the cause of it.

The bus slowed down in the traffic and I saw this black girl striding along beside it. She was all dressed up, very stylish in her red jacket and tight black skirt. I thought how *brave* she looked, somehow, taking on London like that, at full tilt, head on; yet also *sad* because she looked nervous and a little lost, glancing at her reflection in shop-windows, not out of vanity, but just to check she was there.

The bus picked up speed, leaving the black girl behind; and it seemed that no amount of bravery could prevent her from being left behind all her life. I felt her anxiety as my own. I thought, 'What shall I *do*? I can't go on *like this*.'

The bus stopped at traffic lights. A pale lad of about twenty was leaning defeatedly in a doorway, his hands pushed into the pockets of an old overcoat, staring at nothing. My heart went out to him. He looked as though he needed a good hot meal. I was so absorbed by the scenes outside the window, yet so preoccupied with this sense of crisis like a cleaver over my head, that I felt no particular alarm at the old burning inside as my soul came unfurling in waves of flame. I was too tired to resist.

He stood up like a fountain inside me. There was a jolt in my head; my ears popped. He was *there*, right behind my eyes, looking out; and, at the exact same moment, I saw the pale young man step out on to the pavement, his face suddenly flushed, and into the path of the striding black girl who threw up her hands and with a scream of laughter flung her arms around his neck.

It came to me then that I would be married. Not that I was especially desperate to, or even wanted to. Just that I would. I didn't seriously imagine that I'd marry you, dear P., but one can't leave these things to chance. So, that evening, while I was chopping carrots and you were standing with your back to me at the stove, I said in the course of conversation and in the lightest possible tone:

'Don't be an eejit all your life, P. Marry me. It'll be the making of you.'

You rolled your eyes like Marlon Brando and pretended I was joking. We had a fine evening, perhaps the finest. You were *specially* nice to me, for which I thank you.

People in love are always superstitious, aren't they? Always consulting fortune-tellers and seeing signs everywhere? The collapse of *Weird and Wonderful* was a sign. My last chance, somehow, of making myself worthy – that marriage may be as simple, as inevitable, as surprising, as the way the black girl flung her arms around the pale neck of the red-cheeked boy.

Woke abominably early, thinking, What if the cellar flood is rising unchecked? I sprang up to investigate. I didn't like opening the cellar door one bit – I imagined a tidal wave of scummy black water, full of decomposing things, crashing over me. I couldn't be sure, by torchlight, but I think the water-level's about the same, judging by the rungs of the step-ladder.

The cellar was quiet. Too quiet. Are there such things as water-spiders? Could big ones be breeding down there, lying in wait? The previous faint sickening plop was still vivid in my ears. I listened anxiously. There was no sound.

I was still a bit jittery, when I looked out of the library window and saw the old leech-gatherer woman disappear behind the church again. I couldn't resist sneaking out into the grey early morning light and following her. I don't know what I expected to see. It was truly macabre, P.

On the far side of the church there's a hawthorn hedge growing along a ditch. At a break in the hedge and ditch there's a sizeable depression filled with water, probably by the spring which is converting the whole area into marsh. The woman was kneeling with her back to me at the edge of the pool, stripped to the waist, her faded sandy-grey swatch of hair hanging down her back. She seemed to be washing or, at least, scooping water on to her stomach and chest. Honest to God, P., she was as creepy as the banshee. I wouldn't have been surprised if she'd started combing her hair and keening. Instead, she stopped scooping and began batting the water with her hands. I cleared off. She must be a madwoman.

Electricity reconnected, phone back on. I immediately rang Mr Salmon and asked him to do something about the flooding. In other words, to get the remote hard Zetterberg to do something. He hummed a bit, obviously as disinclined to beard her as I am. I suggested that two men with a pump and a sack of cement would probably do the trick. Mr Salmon laughed nervously, as if I'd made a joke. The real problem, it turns out, is that Mrs Z. – who owns other properties apart from mine – is notoriously tight-fisted. Her buildings are all decrepit and, according to Mr Salmon, 'it's deucedly difficult to persuade her to see to them.'

Well. The Vicarage is still a snip at £70 a month, despite the state of the cellar. *I* don't call Mrs Z. mean.

Dad knows where I am. Of course. I wrote to him almost at once, without disclosing anything about you, dear P. He hates whingers. Besides, I know how he worries about me. Actually he'll probably be delighted that I've put my job out of its misery. I mean, he'd bite his tongue off rather than say so directly, but I suspect it physically pained him to see me hacking out 'books for non-readers', as he called them. His passion for books is, to say the least, unusual in an academic biochemist. Yet, as he says, 'One can't do science without a moral vision, and for *that* one must go to Plato and Dante and Milton' – all of whom he reads in the original. So galling for us monoglots who never mastered Latin's passive subjunctive. I've seen him shake his head in mock despair over some of his colleagues. 'They're scarcely *scientists* at all, but rather some new species of technocrat, forever harping on about gadgetry and applications! Beauty and truth are strangers to them, Lulu.' (Yes. He calls me Lulu. 'Eileen' was Mum's choice.) 'I hope *you'll* never become estranged from beauty and truth,' and he laughs as if he were not deadly serious.

Why *shouldn't* I write a book just as I said to the Zetterberg? What else is there to do while I'm waiting for it to happen? (Or, God, am I unconsciously competing with you, P.?) What would it be about? More to the point, how can I prevent it from being about a girl who leaves her writer-lover (better make him a painter) and flees to Nature in order to Find Herself?

'Lulu stared out over the green corn. A small rain, simple and cool, refreshed the dour earth whose sudden rich exhalation seemed to promise New Life . . . ' Fade out; tumescent violins etc. Back to the drawing-board, I think.

I could write something anthropological (but what?). I've always meant to follow it up. Cambridge really only whetted my appetite for it. On the other hand, (a) would it be dead boring? and (b) why bother?

CALCINATION

*

Drove into town and bought:

Two fan heaters, a blanket, firelighters, a second-hand brass curtain-rail, a non-stick saucepan, Bio-Tex, bleach, bog rolls, Proust, a jumbo economy-size pad of paper, packet of biros, stamps, pair of thick oatmeal socks; and, at the health-food shop, 5 lb muesli, 2 loaves real bread with the density of Jupiter's moons, assorted nuts and dried fruit, multi-vitamin pills, 4 organically grown leeks. There's to be a new ascetic but healthy régime. I shall be svelte in mind and body.

Ran heaters in the back bedroom all day. Set up curtain-rail in library and hung long, red, slightly mouldy curtains from dining-room. Lit fire. Brought 2 bedside lamps from bedrooms to replace naked overhead light. Instant cosiness. Scrambled eggs in non-stick saucepan. Put half Proust on the empty bookshelves – sad sight – and went to bed in new bedroom with other half, plus assorted fruit. Read 2 pages Proust. Put fruit in wastepaper bin. Wrote this. Goodnight, dear P.

Ghastly dream about Mrs Zetterberg. I was trapped in a huge snow-filled valley with sheer cliffs on all sides. She was standing on the top of one. She wore a long black fur coat. She shouted instructions as to how I should get out but her words were garbled by a complicated echo. At last she disappeared from the cliff-top, only to reappear a moment later out of a burrow at my side. She was small and round and her black fur was not a coat but her skin. I realised she wasn't trying to help me at all. In fact, her mouth had opened very side – as wide as I am tall – and it was filled with razor-sharp little teeth, festooned with saliva. Woke, in a state.

P.! I was woken this a.m. – at two o'bleeding clock – by *the* most almighty crash. I lay there, stunned, rigid, every pore tingling. I ran through all the things it could be, eliminating all the unlikely ones, and finally paring the options down to:

(1) A psychopathic axeman had broken in.
(2) A psychopathic rapist etc. etc.

In fact, the sound wasn't – on reflection – very psychopathic, nor even very burglar-like. I strained my ears. Silence, except for a distant owl. Then it happened *again*: a great smash as if a cupboard had been tipped over. No phone by the bed so no choice but to display Bravery.

I armed myself with two spray cans – one of hair-spray which I never use because it makes my hair sticky; and one of deodorant which I never use because of guilt about the thingamabobs buggering up the ozone layer every time you give yourself a pssst under the arms. I reasoned that if I missed whoever it was with a jet of lethal deodorant in the eyes, I could at least ruin his hair and, maybe, box his ears with the two tins. I didn't feel like joking at the time.

I tiptoed about with heart convulsions at every creak. There was no one there. No sign either of a break-in. Not even a piece of furniture out of place. Bad one, eh? The library door *was* open and some of my bits of paper *were* on the floor; but I couldn't swear that I hadn't left them like this, although I don't remember doing so. I don't understand how nothing could have produced those fucking great noises that put the heart across me and have me up now with tequila-laced tea, looking over my shoulder and scribbling away with all the lights on. I mean, let's face it, poltergeists hang around pubescent girls, don't they? Am *I* a pubescent girl? It *has* to be the house itself. Old houses 'settle', don't they?

Anyway, if my corpse is found tomorrow, mysteriously frozen into a posture of horror, I'd like to leave this message for humanity:

[Unfortunately no message seems to have been forthcoming.]

More Shock Horror. A ghastly Face at the window. By the time I'd gone outside and said loudly and icily, 'Can I help you?' – meaning 'What the fuck is the Phantom of the Opera doing at my window?' – the Face's owner was already carrying logs from a trailer attached to a mini-tractor, to the woodshed by my back door. Just the job, of course. But how did *he* know? And how dare he assume that I want his logs?

When I looked more closely at the poor fellow I could see that he really is an Igor-style person. Crippled down his left side, his left leg is thinner than his right, and it drags. His left arm, too, is wasted and ends in a mangled hand, more of a purplish claw really, which he uses to steady the logs while the other arm – massively strong – takes the strain. He was wearing corduroy trousers, a checked shirt and a donkey jacket.

He kept his face averted so that only his raw, wizened ear was visible, like a shrivelled fruit; but the face I'd glimpsed at the window was similarly half-devastated, obviously burned, so that the skin is scrunched and painful-looking. I'm pretty sure there's only the one eye. He lets his long hair, black but tinged with grey, sweep down over the other to hide whatever's left. I'd say he was in his late forties or early fifties. He makes an excellent Igor, bar the hunchback; for in fact he's tall and holds himself upright, only spoiling the effect by sinking his head and holding it away from you.

When I accosted him about the logs he did say something but I couldn't make it out, partly because he limped along all the faster. I gave in and began to help him carry them to the shed. We passed to and fro in silence.

I braced myself to look into his face and asked how much I owed him. He waved his good hand dismissively and then pointed across the green to the manor. It suddenly struck me that, of course, Mrs Zetterberg lived there. Who else?

'The logs are from the Manor?' I said. 'From Mrs Zetterberg?' The poor man was already shambling off, but I thought his head bobbed in assent. 'Will you tell her I'll come and thank her?' The man stopped, and shook his head and gestured. I understood that I was not required to thank her. He climbed on to the little tractor and, with great deftness for a village idiot, puttered off. I felt that my nightmare about Mrs Z., as well as my impression of her as haughty and cold, had been unjust. I took in half a dozen of the new logs, which burned beautifully.

TWO

Solution

SMITH

I spent the bulk of the night on my knees. I let no food pass my lips, allowing myself only a few sips of water drawn from my well. At dawn I placed the two oil lamps on either side of my electric athanor. I took hold of the pelican and boldly (but gently, gently) eased the calcined dragon down its throat. Its body coiled itself at the base of the glass. I set the temperature, as our Philosophy dictates, at a heat just warm enough to hatch an egg.

Next, I carried out the simple instructions which Philalethes gives in his *Marrow of Alchemy*:

> Take then our mercury (which is our Moon)
> And it espouse with the terrestrial Sun.
> Thus man and wife are joined, and to them soon
> Add the reviving spirit; this when done
> A noble game you soon shall espy, because
> You have attended nature's noble laws.

From the pure candour of his noble heart, he repeats the instruction even more explicitly in the next verse:

> Of the Red man one; of the White wife three:
> Take thou and mix (which is a good proportion).
> Then of the water four parts let there be,
> This mixture is our lead, which unto motion
> Will be moved, by a most gentle heat,
> Which must increasèd be until it sweat.

I will speak more plainly yet. To my White wife (our mercury) I joined the Red man (our terrestrial sun) in the proportion, not of 3 : 1, but of 9 : 4. This is *the marriage of Venus and Mars*. As to the 'reviving spirit' or 'water', this refers to our solvent which issues from the marriage and it is *the means by which the dragon dissolves itself*. It does not refer, as so many have ignorantly claimed, to the actual water which needs to be added in order to drown the dragon. For this, it has been the fashion to follow the *Mutus Liber* which depicts in dumb show the gathering of spring dew,[1] which may be supposed to possess magical, if not heavenly, properties. In fact distilled water will do as well. For my part I have used my own well-water whose magical attributes are as efficacious as any.

It is advisable also to add a small amount of some flux. Like the water, this has been subject to all kinds of dark mystification as if it were the secret fire itself. Poppycock! I say openly, and probably for the first time in the history of the Art, that three or four grams of borax or nitre is all that is required. I favour the latter because it is easier to work with.

Once water and nitre had been added to the espoused Venus and Mars, I made haste to seal all four elements hermetically into the Egg. I took an iron nail and scored the top of the stopper with Solomon's sigil,* which, depicting the union of the elements, is the emblem of our quintessence.

I could not help checking and rechecking the seal because of my great fear that it might be faulty – allowing Mercurius to escape and, apart from destroying the Opus, blasting me to Kingdom Come with his venomous breath.

I kept watch for upward of three hours and all seems secure.

But I am staggered at how eagerly, how quickly the dragon has stirred! I didn't expect any movement for at least three days. Instead, by the time I was near fainting with fatigue, I had seen the matter spread its scaly wings over the water, ready for flight; and the waters, viscous and bilious in hue, trembled – as they trembled on the day of Creation when the spirit of God passed across their face.

She 'found the door open'. A lie. She 'only came down to tidy up, like'. She had no intention of disturbing anything. The enormous slack grin was the same as ever but her lips were pale with lies.

---

* i.e. presumably ✡ which represents the combination of water ▽ and fire △, plus ▽ and △, earth and air respectively.

I blame myself. I could have guessed that Mrs Beattie would not be able to contain herself concerning the cellar. But somehow one is, in general, unwilling to confront human frailty until it can no longer be avoided. I am very angry at this betrayal. She must have gone to great lengths to gain admittance, even down to taking the key from my desk.

I caught her standing *within feet* of my Egg, her mouth hanging open in the imbecilic expression her Neanderthal-jawed face assumes in contemplation. The hurt to the Work could be incalculable; its components are so finely balanced that a single ill-willed or impure glance can upset its equilibrium – let alone Mrs B.'s gawping. She had the gall to ask me what it was. I should have invented some disarming story. As it was I had breath enough to speak only with the greatest economy, forbidding her to work out her notice. She was taken aback. Almost, I think, lachrymose. (I should not have revealed the importance of the Opus.) Uniquely, she said nothing before she left.

Despite my reservations about the time and manner of her sacking, I am glad it is done. I had almost forgotten what it is to feel light-hearted, to read a book during a solitary meal – to be free! Because it crept up on me, insidiously permeating the house like the stench of her cooking, I did not realise how enervating and stifling her presence had become. I want to throw open all the windows to expunge her spore. Never again will I have to watch the excruciating movement of her scalp as she works her big jaw through a plate of stewed offal. Bliss.

Of course, much as I relish shifting for myself, I shall have to replace her. Bad enough being a bachelor, positively *eccentric* being without a housekeeper. *Dare* I think that Janet might come occasionally?? But no, Farrar would never allow any wife of his to cook for another. Besides, the village would never recover from the scandal. I remember Mrs B. intimating that it was not 'wise' to associate with Janet who has 'a reputation'. When I was sharp with her, she looked hurt – she did not wish me to make a fool of myself; I have not been in the village long and don't 'know its ways'. Mixing with the likes of Janet, not to mention that 'queer stand-offish gentleman' – she meant Robert – does me No Good. Far be it from her to cast the first stone etc., but I must be protected from myself, I am 'too kind', my virtue blinds me to the truth ...! Well, now I am free to mix with all manner of publicans, sinners (and papists) without having to suffer Mrs B.'s 'you'll learn' look.

I am haunted by my interview with Stebbins. Did my reticence imply any endorsement of Caldwell's action? Did I *fail* the Stebbinses? Better if their licentious little girl had not had relations with young Caldwell, better if he had checked his lust – best if our little village were wholly rid of him.

But surely, *surely* since it *is* done, it's better after all if Jenny has her baby away from scandal and possible vilification? Surely it's best that she learn her lesson while still young and mend her ways hereafter? If she had remained, God alone knows what disruption to the parish would have ensued, with the fruit of her fornication looming larger every day. Imagine the whispers, the side-taking, the apportioning of blame. And how could I remain disinterested? My position demands that I condemn the young couple; but who would bear the brunt of judgement? Not the Caldwells, who couldn't care less what the Church or anyone else says of them; not even Jenny, I suspect. No, her parents would bear the brunt. Their disgrace would be multiplied far beyond what it is now. Mr Stebbins may have imagined for a moment that he might brazen it out, may have thought that I'd support him. But how can I? My hands are tied. Whatever I may think as a man must in *this* case be subordinated to the larger interests of the congregation. I should perhaps have made it clearer to him that I do not condone Caldwell's hushing-up operation. It is always repugnant to see one immorality compounded by another. But without such compromises the Jennys of this world would be ruined by a single venial sin.

Or would they? Might not the village have rallied round as they must have done in the old days when illegitimacy was not uncommon? Was it perhaps waiting for someone in authority to take the lead? To repudiate Caldwell's cash offer and show him that he has not got us all over a barrel? It is easy to pray for the Stebbinses. It's the Caldwells who keep me up at night, beseeching God that he may prevent me from hardening my heart towards them.

Solve et coagula [dissolve and coagulate], the Philosophers never tire of repeating. Again *solve et coagula*, as if they were fearful of forgetting that in this simple process lies the whole of the Magnum Opus.

The goal of solution is only this: to divide that which is Above from that which is Below.

When this, and this alone, is done, then may we begin the process of separation, which is the divorce of mercury and sulphur, soul and body of our matter. We call it *the slaying of the dragon*.

Daily the clouds increase. Wafts of deadly vapour rise up from our sea and grow denser, like a preamble to some mighty deluge.

Thus our Earth was before the beginning of time. In its fiery inchoate state it sent up just such poisonous clouds which cooled, condensed and shed their load of moisture on the Earth. I can hear the global serpent's long-drawn-out hiss as it breathes vast billows of steam up into the Above where again it cools and rains the more on the Below. For a thousand years Heaven wept at its separation from Earth until the oceans were formed. Yet I, with my little world within a glass, can do as much – and in a shorter space of time.

Neglected my duties today. The lifting of the rain and my vague perturbation of soul prompted me to take a walk along the high ridge of Grimm's Down. A heavenly day of clear blue light and steady breeze with no one about but the swallows. The smells of civilisation were soon blown out of my clothes and hair. The cramped, stifling village straggled along the valley below. Its inward-looking inhabitants were too busy keeping an eye on each other to notice me sailing along like a cloud high above them! From my skylark's-eye view nothing moved save the thin scribble of smoke from Robert's kiln and the green barley rippling light and dark like the glossy flanks of a thoroughbred.

I headed for the great stone column, known locally as the Blind Dancer, which provides a natural focus and resting place on the crest of the down. As I drew nearer I saw that someone was occupying its shade already. I couldn't tell who it was at first because their back was turned towards me. Nor was I noticed, with the swish of my footsteps concealed by the wind. Closer still, I saw that it was Janet.

I was about to call out, but something in the strange movement she was executing prevented me. I hoped she would catch sight of me and wave. However, she seemed oblivious of everything except the massive, fifteen-foot-high standing-stone. She was pressing her back against it and, with bent knees, rubbing up and down against it. Then she turned to face it and stretched out her arms as though she would embrace it. Her head was thrown back and her eyes were closed in pain or ecstasy. I quickly changed course and made off down the hill.

Her little, somewhat perverse, ritual stays with me. It's disquieting. I wish I had not seen it. I don't want there to be anything odd about Janet, the bastion of my sanity. Still, I am haunted by the sight of her – lips stretched back in some primitive emotion, body taut and straining as if it could melt into the surface of the megalith.

There is danger in the stale air of the cellar. I sense the spirit gathering itself up for flight – sense that the pelican barely constrains it. Still, so far Robert's work has been proved sound, God be praised. But, strain as I may, I cannot *see* the nature and condition of the body, our matter. It is shrouded in cloud and mist which drift around the Egg, frustrating all my efforts to read its heart.

I am hedged about by fears. For three days I have been cut off from the body of our earth except in brief tantalising glimpses as the atmosphere eddies and swirls. I peer and peer, shining my torch into the dim interior; for my two lamps, standing like sentinels on either side of the Egg, fail to penetrate the fog with their diffuse yellow-flaming light. Increasingly it seems as though the fault lies with me – as though the smokiness were in my eyes. I rub them obsessively but it's like trying to clean a glass from the outside when the dirt is within. I am numb from waiting and watching; I cannot entertain thought or activity; I am swathed in tendrils of fog which magnify my fears and yet, as soon as I distinguish them, disappear in puffs of smoke. Is there too much moistness? Too much heat? Or cold? My hand darts towards the temperature control a hundred times a day but I snatch it back.

I must learn *patience*. My master used to say that patience was the cardinal virtue of the Art. Nevertheless, I am gnawed by the desire, against all reason, to try and accelerate the work, knowing that it is pride on my part to imagine I can do anything by interference except contaminate the natural process of purgation.

But how to look on while Mercurius may be dying before time, suffocated in sulphurous fumes? *Patience.* He will tell me by infallible signs when to alter the vessel and the heat. He will tell me, yes, *providing* my calcination is true, providing my exoteric fire is not too forceful, providing – but it's futile to torment myself when the prima materia has torments enough of its own. I can do nothing of myself but watch, wait, pray.

She shouted above the high-pitched engine and the rushing wind:
'*I'm thinking of leaving Arthur.*'
A coldness passed through me. It seemed to numb my brain so that, although I recognised that a crisis was upon us and the importance of saying exactly the right thing, my mind refused to deliver an appropriate response. Cravenly, I wished I had not accepted once again her offer of a lift.

'*For Heaven's sake*,' I heard her say, '*don't look so shocked. People do leave their husbands, you know.*' She tossed one of her rapid dazzling smiles at me. The hedgerow flashed past at an alarming rate. She changed gear with a deft stab of her left hand; the car whined as it veered around a tight corner.

'Don't even think of it,' I said. She pulled the car over on to the grass verge and switched off the engine. It continued to tick like a bomb in the enormous abrupt silence.

'I can't go on . . .'
I stared straight ahead, swept by cold anger. God knows, Janet is often enough taken for a flighty sort of creature. It is a mask. I flatter myself that I am one of the few people to have seen through it to the serious and deeply perceptive woman beneath. In the same measure I fancy that she sees beyond my clerical crust and knows something of the man it cloaks. We do not speak of this; our mutual understanding – our essential contact – surfaces only in the undercurrent of our speech, either in what we choose not to say or, with others present, in the small, barely audible ironies we utter for each other's ears alone, like private jokes.

Her strident announcement not only shattered, as it were,

our reciprocal vow of silence, but also caused me to wonder if I had not misjudged her altogether. We have never discussed the sanctity of holy matrimony, but I would have sworn that she held it to be as inviolable as I myself hold it. Indeed, if there is one tenet which inclines me favourably towards the Church of Rome, it is the high value and deep gravity it attaches to marriage and the impossibility of subsequent divorce. The fact that my own Church has grown lamentably lax in this matter serves only to lay heavier responsibility on the individual conscience never to wed without being absolutely prepared to remain so until 'death us do part'. Why, as God is my witness, I myself might easily have married – no attachment could have been stronger – had I been able to blind myself – as Annabelle apparently could – to the knowledge that our union would take place in, and remain under, the eyes of God.

I couldn't look at her. She was weeping. I was afraid her tears would lead me astray. I asked her if she hadn't better speak to her priest about this.

'Oh, *priests*,' was all she said. There was hopelessness in her dismissal. I asked her how long she had been married to Farrar.

'Ten years. He was turned down by the army, you know. Dicky heart. He still gets palpitations. The drink doesn't help. You know about that? Of course you do. Everyone knows, no one says. Anyway it's not *that* . . . I felt sorry for him with his dicky heart and his one good suit and his big sad face . . . ' She had stopped crying now. Her voice was flat, with no bitterness. 'Things were different in the war, weren't they? No one thought about the future. Least of all, people of our age.'

'But he's not such a bad chap,' I said lamely.

'No. He's not such a bad chap. It's just that our marriage is a travesty. For a long time I tried to keep it going . . . to keep the life from going out of it, but it's no use. He seems to have given up. He just goes through the motions. It's not the drink, that's just a symptom. It's a full-time job to stop myself being . . . *dragged down* by his dead-weight . . . I can't do anything for him any more . . . ' And so on. It was most distressing. 'Don't tell me to pray,' she finished by saying. 'I pray all the time. If we had children, then perhaps . . . But no such luck.'

'What do you want me to say?'

'I don't know. I want you to understand. But how can you? You'd never get yourself . . . your life in such a bloody muddle. You're too good. I think that what I want is your . . . *permission*.'

'It's not mine to give. What God hath joined together— '

'I know, I *know*. But it's more complicated than that. I might put up with it – I *have* put up with it – if it were just a matter of going on and on, day after day; but it's different now . . . ' My legs stiffened of their own accord, bracing themselves for a further blow. ' . . . Please don't hate me, I couldn't bear it, but . . . what if I were *drawn* . . . to someone else?' The inconceivable possibility began to dawn on me. Please God, I thought, don't let her say any more. I wanted to stop her but my mouth would only work soundlessly. 'Someone I could talk to . . . who was kind and strong and not at all like him. Someone— ' I could not listen to any more. She was looking at me pitifully.

'Stop, Janet,' I almost shouted. 'You *must not* talk like this, it does no good. I can't forbid you to leave your husband, but I beg you not to. It won't always be like this, it *will* pass, God won't desert you . . . Have patience, persist, pray— '

'Don't say any more,' she said softly. The car started. We drove in silence. From time to time a freezing tear flew out of her eyes and hit my burning cheek.

Once again I slept a bare three hours before being jerked awake out of some blood- and cobalt-coloured dream. I hurried down to the cellar. The Egg was warm – too warm? – to the touch. Above and Below were linked by a central column of opaque spiritous vapour which overflowed at its zenith into the twin necks of the pelican. Doesn't a volcano send out such distressed plumes of smoke prior to eruption? The flags felt suddenly very cold under my bare feet. I detected a whiff of something noxious in the air. I examined the vessel anxiously for any indications of crack or leak. It seemed secure. I breathed again, and remembered my dream:

I was in the cellar. I could see nothing except the Hermetic egg which gave off a terrifying light. Silhouetted against the unclouded glass was a tiny black feline animal standing in a human posture. As I looked at it, a kind of horror crept over me. It pressed its paws against the glass and returned my look with a peculiar cold inhuman stare of its own. I heard Mrs B.'s voice say quite distinctly, '*He'll never marry now. Who on earth would live with him down here?*'

Is the dream a sign? Mercurius spoke to my master more than once in dreams. I have to watch everything, all the time, even when I sleep. *Vigila dormiens* – 'watch while sleeping' – as Khunrath advises in the engraving of his laboratorium. Nothing must be overlooked, for what is the secret but some infinitesimal thing which goes unheeded?

My first crime was to dupe myself with the notion that somehow I would *control* the Opus. Foolish pride. The Opus cannot be controlled any more than Nature herself.

My second crime was my overweening *curiosity*. In this, I have been tainted by what so often passes nowadays for science. It is not true science, of course, but a kind of technique which presupposes a right to investigate everything *to its limits*. Its curiosity is unbounded and, for the most part, idle. It probes Nature as if she were a corpse, laying out her innards on the dissecting table, oblivious to her sensitive soul. What wonder then if she drives us mad with her vast soundless scream? What wonder if, at last, she retaliates from the depths of her farthest atoms and, stirring into devastating life, brings down destruction on our heads?

I can't undo what I have begun. I can only kneel at my prie-dieu and do penance before the wonderful Egg for my presumption. It will not be manipulated, only ministered to. I pray that the spirit within will guide me in this task, for I am in a mist and don't know which way to turn.

What does it mean to have a *vocation*? Do I have one?

In one sense I am unsuited to the ministry because it is hard for me to sympathise with those people – they seem to form the majority – who *take no interest* in the things of the Spirit. For me, the Spirit has always been of absolute interest. I can take no credit for this. I do not see that one can somehow *will* to be spiritual. It's more a matter of being born to it. As a small child, for example, I remember kneeling by my bed all night and calling on Jesus until my eyes were swollen and closed with tears and my knees bled; I cannot remember what possessed me to do this. I suppose it is precisely a pastor's task to interest people in the Spirit; but I do not readily see how, unless they have already to some extent known what it is to be stricken, sick at heart, *faint* with yearning for a glimpse of it.

It is a strange passion, this desire for the Spirit, because it is a desire to know what cannot, by definition, be known in itself – yet, without some inkling of it, life is, strictly speaking, insupportable. Any fool can desire the attainable; but to crave the unattainable, to go on hoping when all hope is lost, is to effect a violent uprooting of one's own nature. Then when one is nothing other than a detached boundless passion, all but exhausted in the cold unreciprocating void, it sometimes happens (because with God all things are possible) that one is suddenly wrapped about by the unimaginable paradoxical fire of Grace as the spirit – ah, at last – grasps the patient surrendered empty soul and burns it up with a kiss.

It is as difficult to describe this passion as it is to depict the sensation of homesickness to one who has never suffered from it. Indeed, homesickness is itself a highly instructive state, providing in my case the first intimation of the lengths to which a desire to know the unknowable might go. Homesickness is a long-drawn-out longing, a bottomless pit in the stomach, an ineffable pain in the heart. Longing for what? For home, of course. But what *is* this home? It may appear at first to be a place, a particular house or country; it may appear to be the loved ones associated with the place – mother, father or wife, perhaps. But these only temporarily assuage the craving. Soon enough the restless homesickness returns. No place, no person – perhaps nothing on Earth – can contain the vast amorphous world-pain of the homesick, unless that Garden for which Adam yearned with dreadful nostalgia as he laboured in the wasteland of sin and death.

For the secret of true homesickness is that it's the soul's longing for repose; a longing of which the ache for our actual homes is only a pale reflection. The lesser exile recalls the greater: existence itself. Our heart's desire is to discover the resting-place where all the contradictions of existence are reconciled.

My first experience of homesickness occurred in a curious way shortly before my fifth birthday. I was hiding behind the sofa while my mother entertained a distraught friend (who, as I later found out, was the vicar's wife). The night before, this friend and her husband had been woken up in the early hours by an almighty crash, as if a pile of china had fallen through the ceiling. In fact, something of the sort had happened because their bedroom floor was littered with their best dinner-service. Despite the force of the crash not a single piece was broken. Investigation revealed that the same dishes were absent from the sideboard in the dining-room where they had been put away the previous evening.

Absorbing the implications of this event, my infantile soul was filled to bursting with the mystery of it. *I wanted to know* how it had happened, what it meant, how it tied in with God; I wanted to know with an intensity – an *illness* – of longing I was later to identify with the sensation of homesickness. (For me, perhaps, simply *knowing* is home.)

(Subsequently I learnt that more poltergeist activity plagued the vicar and his wife, in the form of apports: books from one room materialised in another; mud appeared in the meat-safe, coal in the younger daughter's bed and finally – absurdly – a shoulder of pork arrived in the kitchen. One second there was nothing; the next second it was dripping blood on to the scrubbed table. The woman was at her wits' end. There was no possibility of a prankster – even the elder daughter was away at boarding-school. The vicar surreptitiously attempted exorcism, but the phenomena only grew more frequent, messier, and more menacing. My mother recommended that the daughter be removed from her school. I have an idea she was. I have an idea the apports ceased. I cannot say what connection, if any, my mother perceived between these separate events.)

Mrs Crowther's brood have more or less recovered from their whooping cough. I like Mrs Crowther; I even like her reprobate husband. In fact, on the whole, I like nearly all my parishioners very much. They are good people. It's only when I consider them as an entity – 'the village' – that they seem narrow and provincial; and that's my fault. Individually, they often surprise me by being far from narrow and provincial. It grieves me therefore to find that, on the whole, they would rather I did not call on them. I am not the bluff country parson they could take to their hearts; I lack the simplicity and candour that might chivvy them closer to Christ. My speech and manner estrange them but they are too polite to say so.

Perhaps they will get used to me in time. Meanwhile I will continue to call, to do my duty by them, and to drink the cups of tea it causes offence to refuse.

I returned from my rounds this evening, wearier than my exertions warranted. It is the strain of perpetual civility behind which I try, as it were, to learn their language. I am like a foreigner who knows what the words signify but misses the nuances of meaning. They talk about the past a great deal, and of people whom they seem to assume I know, whereas it often turns out that these people are long dead! I am learning to pay attention to this. I am learning that their recital of names is a sort of shorthand way of affirming continuity with the past and of drawing me into that continuity. Naming the dead is their way of invoking a whole range of associations, left unsaid, by which the past is shared. How can they welcome my calls when I have nothing of value to share?

My front door is never locked (it seems unChristian somehow to lock it). I should not have been surprised therefore to find someone lurking in the corner of the darkening hall. Nevertheless, my heart skipped several beats. It was Nora Thomas. She took a step forward and I saw that she was formally dressed in a white cotton blouse, cream twin-set, and, if you please, white gloves. The unwonted make-up on her face had the paradoxical effect of making her appear younger rather than older than her twenty years.

'I thought for a moment you were the White Lady,' I said. She startled me by letting out an incongruous booming laugh. It was so unexpected that I laughed myself; and, hearing the unusual sound, I realised how little laughter there had been under Mrs B.'s régime, and how little there was likely to be now that Janet and I must keep out of each other's way.

Nora stated the purpose of her visit: I was in need of a cook. She was ready to step into the breach, if I liked. In fact, if I liked, she would light a fire in the library (thus does my study, with all its books, appear to her!) and bring me a tray there at once. The thought of this arrangement, so unutterably different from Mrs B.'s demanding meals, rather overwhelmed me. I asked what had given her the idea of coming here.

'It was Grandma's suggestion,' she said. I pointed out that Mrs Beattie was still here when her grandmother lived, but she only shrugged. Mrs Maltravers – wise woman – must have foreseen that I could not put up with Mrs B. any longer than she. I felt a fierce pang of nostalgia for the old woman I had never known.

Nora's tray was excellent: cold gammon with a delicious cauliflower *au gratin*. She refused food for herself, having had her tea earlier; but she agreed to sit with me while I ate. She curled her legs underneath her, adopting the position in which I first saw her. One constantly expects her long limbs to be gawky, her movements clumsy, when in fact they are not. Similarly, I expected her to fidget like an adolescent when she sat; but she was perfectly still. Her tumultuous blonde hair has been bleached by the sun so that it contrasts even more sharply with her brunette's complexion.

She asked me if I believed in the White Lady. I said I did: every ghost-story sanctioned by local lore usually has some genuine apparition behind it. She told me that most people in the village laugh at it, but, if pressed, will offer a theory.

'They say she's the ghost of some old vicar's wife who killed herself for love of the local squire. I've heard one or two say that she's Saint Uncumber and that it's good luck to see her. Others say she appears before a death.' Interestingly, no one thinks that she's the shade of the old dyer woman who saw the Virgin Mary – perhaps because the White Lady is unanimously agreed to be on the youngish side.

Nora herself, uniquely, does not believe that the Lady is a departed saint nor someone whose violent death has stamped their image on the vicarage's stones. Rather, she thinks of her as the 'spirit of the spring' – a kind of Nature spirit connected with the 'holy water' of the spring.

'The only trouble is,' she admitted, 'there's no reason in that case to be hanging around this house.' I mentioned the well. 'A *well*, is there?' – she opened her eyes wide – 'well, that settles it then.' We both laughed; and I, thinking of Mrs B.'s outrage at the notion of this slip of a girl in 'her kitchen', laughed again while Nora watched me with her watchful eyes under straight dark brows.

De fonte et origine

Concerning the fount and origin [of alchemy], my master would speak eloquently about our founder and 'patron saint', Hermes Trismegistus the Egyptian who taught Moses the technique of turning staves into serpents. By the knowing way my master ran his acid-stained fingers through his discoloured beard I judged that he spoke allegorically.

At other times, he discoursed on the historical origins of the Art – or, at least, the earliest records of it in the West. By the time of Bolos of Mendes and Zosimos of Panopolis who wrote in the first centuries AD, our Philosophy had already been known in Hellenistic Alexandria for four hundred years. Zosimos believed that it had indeed started with the Egyptians amongst whom the working of gold was the prerogative of priests, and he even examined a furnace in the temple of Memphis. My master was a great student of chemical apparatus, and I almost think he was half in love with the two women who towered over the practical Art in those days – Maria Prophetissa [the prophetess], also called Mary the Jewess, and Cleopatra the gold-maker.

Prior to these inventors, distillation, he said, was little more than the condensing of liquids on the lids of covered pots or on animal hides. The crucial innovation of the alembic was to heat the matter in one vessel, cool it in another to condense the vapour, and add a third to receive the condensation. Mary the Jewess was also credited with the invention of the water bath – her *bain-marie* – and of the kerotakis, a closed vessel in which leaves of metal were treated with different vapours, especially mercury vapour.

However, I revere her as much for her profound epigram from which the whole of our Philosophy can be inferred: 'One becomes two, two becomes three, and out of the third comes the one as the fourth.' (This riddling formula has special significance for Solution where the dragon begets Sol and Luna who in turn give birth to Mercurius. Thus the One is dissolved into Two who are united in the Third – who is also the Fourth, corresponding to the original One raised, as it were, to the second power.)

On the whole I could wish that many more women had devoted their talents to the Art. All hail to the three wise Marys – Prophetissa, Sidney and South![2]

At the end of the fifth century, the impetus of our Philosophy passed from the Greek to the Arab world. It faltered after AD 622 when the many Arab tribes, united under Islam's banner, were somewhat hostile to infidel arts; but, by the middle of the eighth century, the Arab world was again hungry for Greek works of philosophy, science and mathematics. By AD 760 world-famous Jabir ibn Hayyan, renowned in Europe as Geber, was at the height of his powers. His writings are so profound, yet so careful to guard the secret of the Art, that the ignorant pronounced them 'gibberish'. He was born in the Persian town of Tus,[3] and sent to Arabia for his education, afterwards returning to Kufa, his father's birthplace, where he quickly won fame as a brilliant philosopher and scientist. His great influence on European chemistry was largely owing to his new theory of the elements.

He probably derived it from Aristotle who, as well as his earth-air-fire-water theory of matter, had another one up his sleeve: that minerals are produced in the earth through an 'exhalation' like 'earthy smoke', while metals are produced by a second 'exhalation' likened to a 'watery vapour'. The 'earthy smoke' consisted of earth particles changing into fire, the 'watery vapour' of water changing into air.

Jabir thought that Aristotle's exhalations passed through an intermediate stage – the 'earthy smoke' changed into 'sulphur' and 'watery vapour' into 'mercury'. Sulphur and mercury then combined in varying proportions to form the minerals and metals. The perfect mixture, naturally, produced gold. Jabir knew, of course, that ordinary sulphur and mercury combined to make cinnabar [mercuric sulphide] and could not therefore form the constituents of metals. His mercury and sulphur, from which ours derive, were a kind of ideal variety – a dual principle out of which all matter arises.

Two hundred years after Jabir's death the ruins of his laboratory were unearthed. Nothing of interest was found except, in a corner of the room, a mortar of pure gold.

EILEEN

To Town. Bought hot-water bottle, hair conditioner, and staple foodstuffs from the supermarket which is cheaper than the village shop. Ran into sweet Mr Salmon and tortured him with compliments on his appearance – the brogues, the four-piece tweed suit, the *fob watch* – until he squeaked.

I put it to him point-blank that the Vicarage was haunted and that he had failed in his duty to warn me. I was mostly teasing, of course, but he was so disconcerted that I realised I'd hit on some sore point.

'Come clean, Mr Salmon,' I urged. 'What class of a haunting are we talking about?'

'Oh I'm sure, Miss Er . . . that it's, you might say, non-applicable.'

'Press on, Mr Salmon.'

'Well, there *is* a reputation attached. A former incumbent is said to have been seen.'

'And this old vicar drives tenants away?'

'Oh, I think, Miss Er – Er, that it's more a question of inconvenience than of terror.' He leaned forward and added roguishly, 'I believe it's a local sport to try and frighten tenants with grisly fabrications concerning this vicar. So be warned, Miss Er . . . mmm.'

Fascinating stuff, eh? What a pity that people like me who believe in ghosts never see them. It's the idea that the villagers try to frighten us tenants that's really spooky.

Igor turns up this a.m. with a young lad and a sofa, which they wordlessly carry in and place in front of the library fireplace. I'm in my dressing-gown and only half-awake; but I have enough presence of mind to ask their advice on a pressing problem. I address myself to the lad, who looks intelligent. I lead the way to the cellar, explaining about the flood. Only Igor follows me. To my amazement, as soon as I reach for the cellar door-handle, he turns and shuffles off as fast as he can. I catch him up. I am really quite irritated. Before I can speak, he says clearly and firmly: 'I'm sorry. I'm not going down there.' What is even more surprising is his voice – educated, as middle-class as my own. He fixes me with his good eye, and it's far from being the eye of a village idiot.

Dear P.,

My first cloudless, rainless day. I walked along a track on the far side of the village. It leads to a path up to a lovely hill-top wood where golden liquid sunlight splashed through the trees. They'll be shedding their leaves any minute. I made the most of them, pain helping me to see them more clearly. Their beauty pressed in on me like thorns. I miss you horribly.

On the way back I followed a fork in the path that led down (instead of up towards the wood), and found a greasy-looking, overgrown lake. Big pond, really. I felt like the evil Cardinal in *The Duchess of Malfi* (you never forget a play you do at 'A' level):

> 'When I look into the fish-ponds in my garden,
> Methinks I see a thing arm'd with a rake,
> That seems to strike at me.'

Methinks I know what he means.

Remember that Sunday we spent in bed? Remember how the light faded behind the drawn curtains and I suggested we go out before the sun clouded over for the day and have some lunch at the pub on the river before it closed? You laughed. You said: 'It's seven o'clock.' I couldn't *believe* it. I felt peculiar, as if I'd been enchanted. A whole day had flashed past without my being conscious of it.

There was a kind of enchantment, wasn't there? We talked a lot and had jokes. We lay quietly for a long time reading each other's thoughts, feeling each other's hearts beat in time, not knowing where one body ended and the other began, so warm we seemed mutually melted down like butter into some simpler amorphous shape. Our souls were in our eyes, just as the Elizabethans said, and transparent to each other. I saw little sparks dancing around your pupils, dear P. I swear I did. I didn't mention it because you smiled as if you knew. Seven o'clock. It frightened me.

That day was a model of our entire friendship. It had a darker side. We lived in a self-contained twilight where the enchantment could turn morbid, even claustrophobic. We had no context to put each other in, except each other. So, whereas at times returning from work to you was like entering a more intense level of reality, at other times it was like drawing heavy curtains that shut out a whole world of air and sunshine. Either way, we were, I think, eating each other up.

Seven o'clock. I couldn't get over it.

You 'had to' go to some party to which I had not been invited. I didn't resent this. Except that I know you could have taken me if you'd wanted me there. I watched you shaving and dressing up in the way you used to when we first met. Why were you taking such trouble if not to attract other girls? I had to stay very still for fear of some huge green globule of jealousy rising up through my body and into my mouth where I'd have to spew it all over you. Dear P. God, how I hated you.

After you had gone, it would have been sensible for me to go back to my flat. Instead, I mooned around. I buried my face in your bath towel and your smell filled me with such a profound inexpressible longing that I think I knew even then that it was too huge a thing for you, or perhaps for anyone, to assuage.

I dreamt there was something long and thin and sharp in bed with me. I woke with a start to total darkness. The dream was true. There was pain of exactly that shape in the bed. Other shapes swirled about in the blackness like the huge mutant water-spiders in the cellar.

I must do something about that cellar. How can I work with black water slapping about beneath me? *Work*, I hear you say. All right. So I'm not working. But I've got to pretend, haven't I? I've got to sit at this desk and write something, anything, in the belief – based on no personal experience whatsoever – that writing might help me ravel up the frayed threads of myself into something resembling a person.

*

It's a curious thing, but I can't remember what your face looks like. I can visualise individual features and even expressions perfectly, but the whole face is as vague and elusive as the face of my soul. Perhaps I always looked at you too closely, missing the big picture; perhaps I never looked at you properly at all. Is it possible that I made up your face to suit myself?

I feel I ought to make myself known to my landlady. It seems rude not to. We are practically neighbours, after all. I wouldn't have to mention the logs and the sofa since Igor thinks it inappropriate; but I should make it clear that they are appreciated. The trouble is, I get terrible butterflies in my stomach when I think of meeting Mrs Zetterberg. She sounded so fearsome on the phone and, somehow, her generosity towards me makes it *worse*, because it contradicts the way she seemed and the way Mr Salmon sees her. I keep thinking I'll pop in casually, but I always put it off until tomorrow. I had another dream about her too – she's obviously preying on my mind – and the dream, though imprecise, was full of dread.

Dear P.,

It's a pity you never met Dad. I badly wanted you to when he came down to London with Tanya for that conference – although I probably played it down. Anyway, you couldn't or wouldn't. I was disappointed but secretly glad, too, because Dad can be intimidating.

When I was a teenager, and after, he always enjoyed meeting my boyfriends and was always nice to them. He can't help being a bit frightening – being so *distinguished* etc. – but I reckoned that if the boys couldn't cope with that they probably weren't worth the trouble. Dad and I discussed them after the meeting. It was a little ritual we had. Dad was penetrating in his assessments. I don't know how he did it: after the most casual conversation with the boy in question he seemed able, like an Intelligence expert, to sum up their entire character. Of course, he'd never deliver a verdict unless I badgered him, and he was unfailingly fair and generous. However, he always detected anything phoney or 'second eleven' about them. 'So-and-so's a thoroughly good sort,' he'd say. 'But I wonder how long he'll keep you *interested*.' He was right. Almost at once my interest would flag. Dad could even predict how long a boyfriend would last – two weeks, or a month, say – while I, madly in love, would protest violently. Once again he was invariably right. As the appointed time drew near, I'd find that I was not nearly as keen on the bloke as I'd thought at first. Dad would console me and soon have me laughing over the whole affair.

I thought Philip Allegro was different. I was crazy about him. He was everything a girl of my age dreamed of – dark, handsome, saturnine and terribly kind. He used to hold my face impulsively between his hands and gaze into it as if his eyes were eating me up. Even better, he was brilliant and already writing poetry up at Cambridge where I was desperately hoping to follow him.

I nearly died when Philip misquoted a poem of Andrew Marvell's to Dad. Not that Dad betrayed the slightest sign that he had noticed. In fact he made every effort to take to Philip, but, at our post-mortem, his honesty compelled him to recognise that Philip's mind was not 'of the first rank', perhaps not even of the second. Dad had divined what, in my passion, I had been blind to – that beneath a superficial intelligence and a poetical enthusiasm, Philip was 'thin'. Surprised that he was up at Cambridge, Dad thought that Philip might be happier 'at a place like Sussex'. Sure enough, Philip dropped out of Cambridge and ended up . . . at Sussex.

I saw him all one summer and, after that, never again.

I was getting into such a neurotic state over the Zetterberg that I really had to get it over with. I thought we might've run into each other by now, in the natural course of things; but since I haven't had a peep out of her, I swallowed a large brandy and walked through the Manor's wrought-iron gates.

The gravel on the drive was barely visible through the weeds. The ground-floor windows were curtained like shut eyes. An ancient Wolseley with a 'Disabled Driver' sticker on the window was parked near the front door, but there was no sign of Igor. I pressed the doorbell and nerved myself for the response. I didn't hear it ring inside, but I waited a minute, pressed again, waited and decided the bell was broken. Honour satisfied, I was inclined to chicken out and beat a retreat. Only the thought of how feeble I was being – altogether unlike me – kept me there.

As soon as I lifted the heavy brass door-knocker, the door swung open. In front of me was a vestibule which gave on to a dingy hall – quite different from what the Manor's mellow red-brick exterior had led me to expect. In the distance I could hear raised voices.

I called out rather half-heartedly. No one replied. A door on the right-hand side of the hall was ajar. I took a peek through it. The room was a surprise: large and low and light, thanks to the addition of long windows on the garden side (the original windows, at the front for example, are small for the size of the rooms). The antique furniture was worn, but thin-legged and elegant in the French style; the floor of dark polished wood was strewn with old glowing rugs from Turkey or Persia; a jet-black baby grand gleamed in the corner; porcelain and an ormolu clock stood on the mantelpiece above the fireplace; the wallpaper looked like faded yellow silk; the ceiling was pale blue. The overall impression was of contrasting light and shade, and a musty faded grandeur.

I jumped at the sound of a slammed door and running feet. They came from a dark corridor leading from the hall towards the back of the house. I advanced tentatively along it. There was a crash and a high-pitched cry. Alarming. I called out. Again no reply. Then everything happened at once, and very fast.

A door on the right was thrown open. Igor lurched across my line of sight and disappeared through the doorway opposite. He was pursued by a woman. She was only before me for a split second yet she branded herself in her entirety on my eye as if she'd been moving in slow motion.

She was about fifty, I'd say, tall, bony, dressed in a torn tweed skirt, holey grey cardigan, broken-down slippers. Her hair, somewhere between fair and grey, was unkempt and straggled down her back. Her face was striking in profile: strong nose, thick straight eyebrows, small even teeth displayed in what might've been a snarl. But the most pertinent thing about her was that she was carrying a steel-grey gun. A Second World War Luger, I think. I froze.

Furniture was heard to overturn, Igor to swear, a body to fall. I edged forward and poked my head around the door into a large unmodernised kitchen. Three chairs lay on their backs, as did Igor, with the woman straddling him, pinning his bad arm to the ground with one knee and his strong arm with the other and with one hand. The other hand pressed the gun down on his throat. I wanted to shout for Mrs Z., tell her the staff were killing each other, but I was too mesmerised to make a sound.

'Where are they, Pluto?' the woman said menacingly.

'You'll never know,' he choked.

That my Igor should be named 'Pluto' was strangely apt; he *is* like some god of the Underworld, deformed but powerful, half ugly and dangerous, half handsome and benign. But, unlike the myth, this witch-like Persephone was getting the better of him.

She leaned forward. A blob of spit appeared on her lips. 'No!' cried Igor or Pluto. He thrashed his head from side to side.

'Tell,' said the woman fiercely.

'No!'

The spittle began to elongate. Pluto's thrashing became more desperate as it threatened to drop on his face.

'*All right*,' he shouted at last. '*Stop*. They're in the blue flour-tin.'

The woman sucked up her spit like spaghetti and rose stiffly to her feet. She saw me immediately, and fixed me with her startling deep-set eyes that didn't blink. Even as she raised the gun I couldn't move.

Without taking her eyes, or the gun, off me, she took a blue tin from a shelf, opened it and fished out a packet of cigarettes and a lighter. She was still a little out of breath and her face was flushed. Although it was lined it retained a kind of haggard beauty. She lifted the gun higher and aimed it at my head. My heart stopped.

'Hello,' I said. 'Sorry.' I've no idea what I meant. She lit a cigarette. Pluto was in some sort of convulsion on the floor. He was gasping.

The woman pulled the trigger. A jet of water hit me on the left cheek. 'Hello,' she said, blowing smoke out of her nose. Pluto was in a fit of laughter. I went as red as a beetroot, backed out of the room and ran for it.

I'm actually *shaking*. The Manor episode really frightened me. Not that I really believed the gun was real or anything, or even that they were seriously brawling. I don't know what I believed. I kept telling myself that it was simply two adults behaving childishly – he had obviously hidden her cigarettes and she was threatening him with a water-pistol (and spit!) in order to retrieve them.

Then why am I so shaky? There was something truly bizarre about their carry-on. Something sinister. I had the feeling that, had the gun been real, that woman would've pulled the trigger just as nonchalantly. She seemed completely anarchic, capable of anything, a nutter. The way she straddled that crippled Pluto, watching his raw head thrash like that. Obscene. Perhaps she's his wife? The housekeeper?

Oh no. I know who she is, of course. She's the woman I saw batting the pool on the other side of the church. The half-naked one who sloshed water all over her front. Raving bonkers. Except that her weird slanting behaviour *wasn't* raving. She was in control. In control yet giving off lightning, on the lines of Mrs Rochester! Oh God, she couldn't be Mrs Zettterberg. Could she? Oh *God*.

P.! Brace yourself. This is going to amaze you. First of all let me assure you that I have *not* gone barking mad. OK? It's been the oddest day, but packed with personal triumph. I'll get to that. Meanwhile, I have discovered genuine *treasure* . . .

Why isn't the psychological idea of *projection* taught at school? Wouldn't it save people from a lot of heartbreak and misunderstanding? We do it all the time – or, rather, since it's a function of the unconscious mind, *it* does it all the time without our realising it. We blithely think that we're looking at an absolute, real and objective outside world when actually we're looking at whatever the unconscious has projected on to it.

God knows what a welter of projections I'm swamping you with, P.! I can't face my own jealousy so I call you an unfaithful bastard. And so on. I don't see *you* at all. I'm a typical sad blind misguided woman who can't distinguish a single personal emotion from what is the case; who is so ignorant of her own deepest needs and desires that she seizes upon the nearest man – you! – and uses him as a screen on which to project a succession of images: Swine! Saint! Friend! Idiot! Bastard! Darling! I've made you a set of exclamations when, in fact, you're probably a perfectly ordinary, reasonably affable bloke.

The great task is to become aware of our unconscious projections, to make them *conscious*. This enables them to be withdrawn into the subjective realm where they belong. The more the unconscious projections are made conscious, the less power they covertly exert over us. Consciousness is enlarged and, simultaneously, we begin to perceive the world more as it is and less as we have been colouring it. In other words, the withdrawal of projections promotes both self-knowledge and a knowledge of reality.

It's easy to spot other people's projections, hard to recognise our own. Knowing how much I project on to you, dear P., doesn't magic away the hurt. But it helps – helps me to be a little dispassionate, a little sceptical about my overpowering feelings. It's painful to know that you are different from images of you, but truth has a habit of being painful.

Do you remember how we used to sit up at night arguing about Jung's psychology? You gave me his last great book, remember? *Mysterium Coniunctionis*.[4] I never finished it at the time, but – it must be pretty obvious – I've had my nose stuck in it all day. I'm deeply grateful to you. Without it I might never have recognised my treasure for what it is!

This is what happened:

I woke from another dream about the cellar. There was ghastly anxiety attached to it. It was getting me down. And since there was no way I was going to start hassling the Manor for help, I decided to knock it on the head myself.

It was a bad business going down the ladder, and worse wading through the water, but I did it with hardly a scream. I dragged the ladder across to the middle of the cellar, clambered up it and inserted a new light bulb in the fitting. There's nothing worse than water all around you in the dark, especially if it has Things in it. I moved very slowly in case I panicked myself, and thrust all thought of what might be down there with me out of my mind.

I tried the light switch just inside the doorway. It worked!

The water looked ordinary and dirty in the light. The cellar walls are of ancient stone, badly blackened – as is the vaulted ceiling – as though someone had been lighting bonfires down there. Some attempt has been made to scrub and whitewash one of the walls but the effort peters out, as if some poor old vicar had begun to convert the place into a ping-pong room for his kids but given it up as a bad job. At one end there's a very large crumbling fireplace which shows that the room was not always a cellar; at the other there's a few bits of shoddy modern furniture obviously stored here, forgotten, and now ruined by water.

I sloshed carefully about for a while, scanning the flood for monsters. No sign of anything untoward, just a scum on the surface and some broken glass crunching underfoot. I found a coil of copper tubing curiously distorted as though it had been melted by some terrific heat before hardening again. I used it to poke around near the centre of the cellar where one or two bubbles were rising. I struck iron. Plunging my hands in (a nasty moment since I didn't even have rubber gloves . . .), I discovered a kind of ill-fitting manhole cover which levered up quite easily. Glugging noises! The water definitely went down the hole a bit.

I straightened out the copper tube as best I could and jabbed it down the aperture. It was clogged with mud and stone. I stirred and scraped as hard as I could until, suddenly, there was a gush like a waterfall down the hole and a distant splashing as if the water were pouring into a deep cavernous drain.

It was brilliant. The cellar began to empty! After a few minutes tiny islands of stone floor began to appear. I was thrilled and relieved. It wasn't long before I could see that the 'drain' is really a *well*. Three feet or so down from the opening a fine grating had been fixed across the shaft, presumably to prevent things or people toppling down the shaft when the lid's off. At some point the masonry between grating and lid disintegrated – probably when the water surged up past the lid into the cellar – and bunged up the grating so that the water couldn't drain away again when the flood subsided.

I went down on my knees and scrabbled out some of the muck while the water went on pouring back down the well. About two feet down, just above the grating, there was a breach in the well's wall which I attempted to patch up with some of the larger pieces of masonry. An obstacle prevented me from plugging the hole properly so I reached in and used it out. It was some sort of uneven lump of ore that had been used to wedge in a package, tightly wrapped in oilskin. *Drama*.

I got the package upstairs. Honestly, my hands were trembling! I don't know what I thought it would be. I didn't think anything. In my state of mind, here in this odd place, nothing and everything surprises me. I had to take scissors to the package which was sewn up. Inside was a metal box. Inside the metal box, inside the oilskin covering, were some sheets of paper. Not really treasure, of course (although they may be valuable). Not even a treasure map (although I thought at first they were). They are an alchemical manuscript.

I've had time to think about this. I can't tell you what it was like reading it for the first time – all those strange images and all that odd archaic language. It was like digging up the bones of an exotic prehistoric beast. It's a real gift, isn't it? What's to stop me finding out about it and publishing the results somewhere? I could write a learned paper like a proper scholar. Or maybe the colour supplements in the Sunday papers would publish a feature on it. I feel quite evangelical about it, eager to correct the popular misconceptions about alchemy. Why is it still seen as a futile attempt by superstitious crackpots to turn base metal into gold? It never was that; it was always, surely, a spiritual quest – as even a cursory reading of Jung's work makes clear. 'Our gold is not common gold,' the alchemists never tired of saying. It was a lifelong search for the secret Prime Matter which, once it was made or found, supplied 'our mercury' which transformed the Prime Matter into 'philosophical gold' – the Tincture, Elixir, Stone!

The idea, too, that I am in all likelihood living in an alchemist's house makes me look at the place with new eyes. It doesn't seem quite real. Why did he hide this manuscript in the well? Was someone *supposed* to find it or not? Basically, I'm *thrilled*.

SMITH

The European quest for the Philosophers' Stone began on 11 February 1144. On this day a certain Robert of Chester finished the first translation of an Arabic chemical text into Latin. Called the 'Book of the Composition of Alchemy', it was written by Morienus, a Christian ascetic who taught the Art to Prince Kallid ibn Yazid, one of the first Moslems to study our Philosophy.

The book had fallen into Robert's hands (in Toledo, I believe) because Christians had recently begun to recapture those parts of Europe such as Sicily and southern Spain which had fallen to Islam. They also, of course, captured Arab manuscripts amongst which were chemical treatises and the first copies of Aristotle. (Thus Europe received its classical heritage from Arabic versions of the Greek originals.)

By 1200 the great Smaragdine Tablet had been translated.* Across Europe the cry went up: 'As Above, so Below!' The Philosophers had their Bible, the Hermetic Art its foundation stone.

In the ensuing century the two books of specifically European provenance which in my opinion stand out as superlatively useful to our Philosophy are *Liber Octo Capitulorum de Lapide Philosophorum* ['The book of eight chapters concerning the philosophers' stone'] and *Speculum Secretorum Alchemiae* ['The Mirror (of the Secrets) of Alchemy'].

The author of the former arranged a dinner for William II, Count of Holland. Although it was midwinter he had tables set up in the garden of his monastery in Cologne. Thick snow lay on the ground and a freezing wind was blowing. But as soon as the Count sat down at table, the snow and wind disappeared and were replaced by a balmy spring breeze. Fragrant flowers pushed up

---

* See p. 432.

through the frozen earth, the trees blossomed and songbirds flitted from branch to branch. However, as soon as the meal was over, the garden reverted to its former state.

The author of the book and of this miracle was Albertus Magnus [c. 1200–80] who laboured for thirty years to make a brazen head with oracular powers – only to have it smashed by a pupil called Thomas Aquinas who was sick of the head's constant chatter.

It is a tribute to Albertus' genius that even so early in the western development of the Art he was clearly intimate with Mercurius. My master quoted his description warmly, claiming that, if no other were available, one might still proceed from this alone: 'It is the serpent that rejoices in itself, impregnates itself and gives birth in a single day, and slays all metals with its venom. It flees from the fire but the sages by their art have caused it to withstand the fire, by nourishing it with its own earth until it endured the fire, and then it performs works and transmutations . . . '

Meanwhile, in England, the author of the second book ['The Mirror of Alchemy'] was working wonders in his laboratory. Although only a humble friar, his name lived on down the centuries as belonging to one of the most brilliant scientists of any age. He was the *doctor mirabilis* himself, Roger Bacon [c. 1219–92]. When he was not making the Stone (as well as the usual brazen head), he was making breakthroughs in orthodox chemistry and in optics. Realising the dangers of gunpowder he hid the secret of its composition.*

In 1315 the martyrdom of Ramón Lull signalled the end of the first wave of our Philosophy in Europe.[5]

If I ever had a *specific* vocation, I had it at the age of sixteen. I am still convinced that it was the type of experience which is called 'mystical'. I believe such experiences are more common than is generally acknowledged, especially those which – like mine – may be tentatively termed 'visions of Nature'.

My vision displayed the usual features: it had an absolute

---

* This is a contentious statement, although it is true that Bacon *may* have made gunpowder. The recipe can be obtained from a questionable anagram in his tract *De Mirabile Potestate Artis et Naturae* (c. 1242).

and unshakeable reality; it was unforgettable; it is inexpressible.

I was walking alone across the school playing-fields on a summer evening. I was homesick. I wanted to die. My suffering, as is often the case, made the world seem more cruelly beautiful than ever. I was concentrated on the sound of the wind rustling the millions of leaves on the trees, on the sound of birdsong. I could hear my own quick heartbeat as if in the presence of a lover. The bell in the clock-tower was chiming eight. The sinking sun was a blinding bronze arc between two hills. The last thing I can record with any accuracy was the overpowering, poignant scent of newly mown grass, like a distillation of all the richest and most evocative perfumes in the world. In the ecstatic fraction of a second between two steps, two heart-breaking heartbeats, I smelled, or was suffused by, this essence of a childhood and a home I had never known, but which also hid other tantalising scents – of spicy far-off places I longed to see.

My breath was crushed out of me; my own essence, like gold beaten infinitely into thin air, mingled with the golden aroma of mashed grass. I heard, as before, the singing birds and rustling trees; but now I knew that they were singing the overture to some tremendous announcement which would take place at the stroke of eight. It came to me quite distinctly, as I looked directly into the great brazen sun, that I was about to hear the Word that was in the Beginning, that single intolerable ululating syllable by which the Elohim created Heaven and Earth.

The bell struck eight. The gong of fire sank behind the hills and, like its visible echo, a vast shadow rippled towards me across the face of the earth. I heard it then, but it was not what I expected. It came up through my feet, juddering my bones, shivering my flesh, like a dissonant bass note too deep for hearing; the groan of *anima mundi*, the Soul of the World.

This was the calling which I came – rather comically – to interpret as a vocation in the Church of England, having fled in disgust from chemistry. But it now appears that my master was perhaps wiser than I knew, or could know, at the time.

I met him soon after I arrived in Paris through a painter called Jean-Jacques who, heir to a fortune and title, was the leading light of our circle. Being older, more intelligent and worldly (not to say more arrogant) than the rest of us, it was he who arbitrated in our philosophical disputes and had the last word in our debates. He was a glamorous figure who moved at will in the higher, more illustrious circles to which we aspired.

One evening three companions and I joined him at a corner table in one of the small restaurants we favoured in Montparnasse. My companions took no notice of the elderly man who sat with him because Jean-Jacques, suffering from incurable *nostalgie de la boue*, was in the habit of collecting 'interesting' vagrants who were only too glad of a free drink. I, on the other hand, was struck by the man's appearance. Despite his sunken eyes and cheeks, his long hair and uncombed beard, his archaic dress which suggested he had stepped straight out of the last century, he sat very upright but perfectly relaxed in his chair, drank only water and took no part in the ensuing lively discussion about art. His exclusion made me uncomfortable and so, wishing to be polite and to flatter him a little, I asked him whether he also was an artist.

He appeared to be sunk in reverie. I had given up any hope of an answer when he suddenly fixed me with a cold amused eye and said:

'What if I am? What do you know of art, sir?'

I was abashed. I could only mumble apologies for my impertinence, adding that although I knew next to nothing I was eager to learn. The old fellow, however, seemed to have returned to his reverie.

Shortly afterwards he stood up abruptly to leave. Nodding civilly to the others, he handed me, without explanation, his card. I recognised the address of an unfashionable suburb.

Jean-Jacques was put out – he had been trying for some time, he explained sulkily, to cultivate the eccentric old boy in the hope of just such an invitation (if the card could be thus interpreted); for it was part of Paris lore that this same fellow possessed fabulous old art-treasures which very few had ever seen.

With racing heart I called at the address. Needless to say I was disappointed in my expectations. But not for long. My master's art was of another kind. He conducted me to his laboratory and explained its rudiments. I was seized immediately. All other enterprises seemed trivial in comparison. I begged to be allowed to assist him in his Art. He had already prepared my room.

I was dimly aware that, in this as in all spiritual disciplines, there was a providence at work: when the disciple is ready, the master appears. What I did not then realise was that I was answering the call on the school playing-field – taking up the challenge, laid aside these many long years, to minister to the unfolding of a Creation which (as St Paul says) groaneth and travaileth in its hunger for the perfecting Spirit.

De Lapide Philosophorum

The goal of the Great Work, the Philosophers' Stone, goes by many names, not least 'the Stone that is no Stone'. Little or nothing can be known of it except by manufacturing it. It is both square and round, says our Philosophy, which is to say a *four-fold unity*.

'For there is one stone, one medicine, to which nothing from outside is added, nor is it diminished, save that the superfluities are removed.' If the artifex bears these words of Arnaldus in mind,* he cannot go far wrong.

The Stone is called gold; not common gold, but philosophical gold. As the Red Tincture it occurs as a species of glassy powder which, projected on to base metals, transmutes them to gold. Imbibed as the Elixir of Life, it renders the flesh as incorruptible as gold.

To speak more revealingly – and here I approach the boundary of what it is permitted to disclose – *the Stone is an hermaphrodite* by which we signify the marriage of the White Stone with the Red, Heaven with Earth. Our hermaphrodite is sometimes known as *filius*, the divine son arising from the union of Sol and Luna.

At the point where Heaven meets Earth, in the wonderful instant where Time intersects with Eternity, there and then you will find the Stone.

It is a great sadness that I can no longer see Janet on our old familiar terms. Living alone can breed habits of thought, of manner – even of

---

* i.e. Arnold of Villanova (*c.* 1240–*c.* 1313), the famous wandering Dominican who is credited with the authorship of *Rosarium Philosophorum* (the Rosary, or Rose-garden, of the Philosophers), a perennial favourite with alchemists down the centuries.

morality – which can grow monstrous even before one has the wit to recognise them. Once or twice of late I have caught a glimpse of myself as if in the reflection of a looking-glass for which I was unprepared, and my naked face is not a pretty sight. I scarcely recognise the stiff pedantic vicar with the apologetic, hypocritical half-smile. Janet held up another glass altogether – one in which I appeared as the same young man, full of *joie de vivre*, who threw himself into chemistry at the feet of his master twenty years ago. What happened to him?

Janet used to tease me about sounding like her prim old maiden aunt, tease me out of my cold guarded self. She would wonder aloud why I had never married when I was, after all, 'not unattractive'. I saw myself differently through her eyes. The blood flowed more warmly in my veins, my constricted heart eased. I have been too much alone. I am out of touch with the times and, I dare say, with myself.

Let it be said: I am distinctly unsober. I can't remember why. Yes I can. One always remembers what one drank to forget. I regret it. I daren't go near the Work in this condition – yet it might need me. I resent this. I resent the way it leaves me more worn out and *raw* every day, without reward. The flesh is being stripped away from me, leaving me a mass of exposed nerves vulnerable to the slightest knock or pinch. For instance, I received a letter today from one Councillor Fielding. It is headed *Re* Nightingale Wood. *Re* indeed. It would be hard to contrive a more mealy-mouthed prevaricating document. He speaks of Caldwell's good sense and high reputation in the locality. Ha! Is this some secret Masonic code for the fact that they play golf together, or worse? Fielding will obviously not help; he has clearly never walked in a wood. He stands four-square with all the dead jargon of bureaucracy behind him. I shall be forced to go directly to the villagers in order to save the wood. But why are they strangely apathetic whenever I broach the subject? It's as though Caldwell and his *Weltanschauung* have a paralysing power on others and a momentum all of their own which no justice can stem. Over my dead body.

Feeling curiously depleted by the letter, as if the battle were already lost, I stopped by the Green Man for a pint of stub-toe [i.e. strong local beer]. I wore mufti, which I regret, because it must seem that I am appearing deliberately off-duty, like a policeman. I heard Joan Thorpe giggle. God knows what she's doing in a pub at her age. Her laughter was echoed by her companions: Bradley and two motor-bike cronies whom I do not recognise. They are not from the village. One of them had his feet up on the bench.

My entrance is like a chill draught which causes the candle of conversation to gutter. I assume the benign, cretinous expression of a vicar willing to be talked to yet unwilling to obtrude; a vicar who will not frighten anyone by mentioning Jesus Christ. The ruddy faces of the men are wreathed in tobacco smoke as they bend over their dominoes; three wives – a sherry, a port and a stout – sit silently in the corner. I stand between them, an intrusion of Sunday morning into Saturday night that they cannot help but deplore.

There is a forlorn hope that Robert will be there; or even the good Doctor Sparrow. They are not. Instead, to my horror, I find that Farrar, the last person in the world I wish to meet, is already buying me a drink in a way that suggests that I, as a clergyman, can't be expected to know how to get one for myself. I have an urge to cry out to all of them that I have not always been a priest, that I have committed sins to make their hair stand on end. I say nothing as Farrar, exercising the right that a bought drink gives, closes in. I register the glances full of relief which are thrown at me from all sides. As long as Farrar has collared me everyone else is safe from the numbing tedium of his monotonous conversation. It reminds me uncomfortably of what I have condemned Janet to. After he has gone, it requires a further two pints of stub-toe to pull me round before I, too, leave, smiling and nodding, hearing as I close the door unrestrained conversations rise up like trout through the swirling blue smoke in the low-ceilinged room.

De alcohol

The philosophical process of fermentation has produced strong drink for aeons; but it was small beer compared to distillation. The unknown philosopher who first took wine and raised it to new spiritual heights by distillation was a brilliant scientist. Having placed the wine in his still and heated it, he observed that it was giving off a faint mist. This was called 'al-kohl', an Arabic word which referred to the fine mist-like black powder which, derived from antimony trisulphide, was used since early times as a hair dye and mascara.

The mist rose as a vaporous spirit, cooled, and condensed into liquid. He tasted it. It burned! It was a clear *fiery water* – in fact, *aqua vitae*, the mercurial 'water of life'. (Isn't it still called 'aquavit'?) The spirit of wine, trapped in his still, was powerful; it revivified and rejuvenated, driving away the cold and moist melancholy humours. Other spirits, with similar medicinal strength, were captured from almost anything that would ferment – potatoes, barley, even juniper berries (though gin came *much* later) – spirits which now stand sadly on the shelves of pubs.

No one knows for sure when this first magical preparation occurred. The twelfth century perhaps; or even earlier. (Probably much earlier in China.) Certainly, by the mid-thirteenth century, the burning 'water' was in general use as a medicine – distilled liquors were not drunk for fun until the late sixteenth century. Further experiments showed that alcohol was ideal for dissolving many of the organic compounds (fats, resins, etc.) that were insoluble in water. Applied to plants, the *quintessence* of wine could extract the quintessence, or celestial part, of a plant to make herbal medicines. In 1510, for example, a chemist called Dom Bernardo Vincelli extracted and distilled the quintessence of many herbs with alcohol and, adding a spot of honey perhaps, came up with the efficacious medicine we call Benedictine.

Being in low spirits I decided to visit Robert. Half-way up the hill I turned back. His company is a temptation; it's too congenial. I was using him as an excuse to shirk my duties.

The clouds abate! Clearly visible, just above the horizon of our wonderful matter, *Sol begins to rise*. His triumphal car climbs the arched vault of our miniature empyrean. This is what I have been waiting for – the sign that my calcination was true and my solution sound. The Spirit ascends into the Above and soon, as dawn matures to noon, he will shoot his bright glancing spears down into the dragon who holds his dear sister Luna enthralled beneath our sea. Then I can begin the grand reunion of Above and Below, the marriage of Sol and Luna, on which the whole of Hermetic philosophy rests.[6]

Tonight I walked out by the light of a huge yellow moon to Nightingale Wood, seeking some balm for the soul. I cannot bring myself to call it the *psyche*. I do not see that it is any part of mine to trick out the soul in Greek simply in order to sound more scientific – as if 'psyche' can dispel any residual suspicion of churchy hocus-pocus and reassure us that henceforward we are dealing with a proper *mechanism* we can poke around in. (It's more complicated than we thought at first, but only slightly more than the average sewage plant.) The appearance of this 'psyche' seems merely to be part of our modern attempt to remake ourselves in the image of our own machines, and so, by demystifying human nature, make it easier to bear. The soul is retained only as a sentimental metaphor – the ladies, bless 'em, like it – or as the property of pale overwrought poets in Slavic novels.

Nor, I believe, do we profit by returning 'psyche' to English as 'mind'. This only serves to suggest falsely that we are identical to our conscious lives, which are in turn functions of the brain. (We haven't made *all* the connections yet, but it's only a matter of time.) And whatever actions cannot be 'explained' by reference to the brain, can be explained by social conditioning. Personal freedom, we are told, is an illusion; all action is a mere behaviour-pattern, not very different from that of the average fruit-fly. All behaviour and thus all theories of behaviour are socially conditioned (except, it seems, the theory that all behaviour is socially conditioned).

So, all in all it won't be long before the soul is done away with for good.[7] It's not necessary to root it out; it's atrophying naturally like the fuddy-duddy theologians who cling to it. We, meanwhile, are encouraged to press on with the great twentieth-century labour of enlightenment.

Why then, on nights such as this, when the body is lulled by the rhythm of its own movement and the mind is at peace, why is the soul palpably present? Drawn out by the moon's beauty, expansive under the stars, it slips from its fleshly envelope and luxuriates in the warm night air.

I am afraid of this fashionable dilution of soul. We can lose it but, no matter how devoutly we wish to, we cannot destroy it. The soul always returns to us, call it what we will, in whatever image we choose to remake it. Our sin is to think that we can remake the soul in our own image because, make no mistake, it will return to us in the nightmare scarecrow shape of that sin. Stifle the soul and it returns as madness; cast it out and it comes back as terror.

What we must do, if it is not already too late, is watch out for those images *by which the soul chooses to represent herself*; and, once observed, we must hold the image of our own souls like a lantern before our inner eye and let her guide us as we stumble through the shadow of the valley.

I have it on good authority that the soul is *imago Dei*, the image of God. What can this mean?

I have never *taken* to God as *Father*. It always made him sound too far away, too transcendental: 'Our Father which art in Heaven'. It is time to replace God the Father as He replaced the wrathful tyrant Jehovah. I find God *the Spirit* more congenial. This has the disadvantage of being rather too abstract compared to our picture of God as a white-bearded patriarch, but He has in any case lost the power to seize our imaginations. The advantage of Spirit is that it does justice to the paradox of God. It is transcendental like God in Heaven – but, as the power which sustains all Creation, it is also immanent. Thus it is both Above and Below, the goal as well as the ground of existence. (As the third person of the Trinity, the Holy Ghost, it can also be seen as both *within* us and all around, or *outside*, us.)

The relationship of soul to Spirit is absolute; for they share the same nature. The soul is simply the particular embodiment of the universal Spirit. Again, every individual soul, as a microcosm of the collective Spirit, is capable of realising the Spirit in all its fullness – and that is what *imago Dei* means.

Sadly, we deny the presence of Spirit in the world – but that is not the same as abolishing it. Spirit always returns to haunt us with the same degree of force we use to drive it out. It is Spirit which holds up the mirror of Nature so that, the more we coerce a world we suppose spiritless and dead, the more monstrous and frightening our own image will be. When we exploit matter, as if it had no spirit, the latter will reflect this and, obligingly, manifest itself as a material power. For example, the atom bomb.

Meanwhile the Church, which is supposed to be the Spirit's guardian, flaps its hands and squabbles over liturgical reform. It bows and scrapes before Science like a poor curate before a belted earl. Its God has receded into the far reaches of astronomical space. Like the hexed African its soul is lost, and it sinks to its knees, shortly to lie down and die.[8]

All this was in my mind as I walked in the moonlit wood, and I was afraid. Never has our Philosophy been more needed. Never has Spirit been such a scarce commodity. It must be sought out in that quarter where it is least expected – in matter. Only our Philosophy can retrieve it from the shadowy subterranean kingdom; only our Art ceases to look vainly to the vast Above and begins ... with the Below.

The moon rose in quiet glory high over Grimm's Down, tugging the tide of sap in the feverish trees. More than my personal salvation depends on the Great Work. For Nature's sake and the world's health I have to summon the earth-spirit back, like the lost nightingales, from his dark exile. I called out to him from the depths of my soul and, for a long moment, feeling the turning earth beneath my feet, I seemed to hear his distant crystalline singing echo in the silence of my skull.

De difficultate operis

Current wisdom has it that there are ninety-two elements in Nature,* and not one can be turned into another. Current wisdom, then, provides the Magnum Opus with its great incentive: it is impossible.

Only the impossible is worthy of the supreme effort; only the impossible is, finally, *serious*.

---

* My dictionary says there are 105 elements, *ninety-three* of which occur naturally.

Christ told us to take up our crosses and follow him. This is, strictly speaking, impossible. Also, 'Be ye perfect even as your Father in Heaven is perfect' is (strictly speaking) an impossible command to fulfil. In short, it is *impossible* to be a Christian – and yet that is exactly and absolutely what we are commanded to become.

'With God all things are possible' – the conversion of metals no less than the conversion of sinners.

A curious unsettling event took place last night.

I was watching the pelican as usual and, with my card-table and chair drawn up to the athanor, was attempting to write some reasonably coherent notes on the condition of the matter. I was very tired. My eyes hurt and the effort of writing made my hand tremble. I must have fallen into a kind of reverie.

Then, all at once I rose from my chair. I was wide awake. I felt irritated at the amount of light in the room. It did not illuminate as much as emphasise the shadows – a sickly dark yellow light. I saw that it came from the pelican where it was so penetrating that I had to look away. Whereupon a woman's voice called me. I glanced back and recognised Annabelle.

She had her hands on her hips as if she were parodying the shape of the vessel. She had changed her hair which, no longer short, hung in curls over her bosom. Her skin glowed. Her face was in shadow. I was wrenched by the old, old longing. I also began to experience such considerable excitation that I couldn't speak to her at all. It was pleasurable at first but became more and more disturbing as it seemed to me that her posture was a mocking one, even lewd. I was alarmed and excited at the same time. I was certainly confused. I was sweating from the heat she gave off, and I couldn't catch my breath. She moved her legs and I saw that they were covered in what looked like tiny iridescent green and blue fish scales which crepitated as they rubbed against each other. The sound had an exquisite effect on me. She bent towards me and, stretching down her hand, did something so utterly uncharacteristic that I can scarcely believe it. The sensation sent spasms of mingled alarm, pain and intense pleasure through my entire body.

I reawoke in my chair to a bewildered shame and a curious

empty sticky exhaustion. Her image had been so *real* that for an hour I could only sit watching the shadows from my oil lamps make macabre shapes on the cellar walls, and wonder if I had been the victim of some weird succubus, who had said softly, 'I'm still waiting.' What does it *mean*?

I woke this morning at dawn with a sense of great – what shall I say? – great *ease* of mind. The anxiety which was in danger of becoming habitual has suddenly flown away.

For the first time in weeks I had no qualms about descending to the cellar. Sure enough, the glass was clear, the clouds had lifted! Joy cometh in the morning.

Noon: *Sol rising in bright splendour to his zenith.* Said a prayer of thanksgiving; ate a great deal; scythed the orchard, singing at top of lungs.

EILEEN

I can easily imagine some old sixteenth- or seventeenth-century cleric pottering about my cellar among the retorts, alembics and cucurbits which together formed the single mystical vessel the alchemists called Our Glass or the Philosophers' Egg. At the centre of his laboratory was his athanor or furnace – from the Arabic *al-tannur* – in which he had to maintain for weeks, months, years without cease the precious fire which transformed his mysterious Prime Matter. Day in and day out he ground the matter and purified it, dissolved and coagulated it, sublimed and distilled it.

It's no wonder, in a way, that his unconscious projections on to the blank screen of his matter should have been so vivid, so visionary. In a way I envy him. For, instead of seeing a boring gas or vapour rising from a solid, he saw the mercurial soul of the matter – perhaps in the form of the moon or a bird – leaving its sulphurous body. When the matter blackened, he saw a crow's or a raven's head; when it began to whiten, forming an iridescent skin, he saw a peacock spreading its tail. When he fused two noble metals in the vessel filled with 'our mercury', it was a sacred moment: a king and queen were married and drowned. Blackness, whiteness, redness – these were not merely attributes of his matter but spiritual states through which the matter, together with the unconscious psyche of the alchemist himself, had to pass in order to attain the Red Tincture or Philosophers' Stone.

Pluto arrived with some elderflower 'champagne' he had made himself. I understood that it was by way of a peace offering or an apology for the unfortunate episode at the Manor. I invited him in and fetched some glasses. When I returned he had only advanced a few feet into the hall. He seemed nervously disinclined to enter farther in, completely ignoring my bright suggestion that we adjourn to the library. He said quickly: 'I can't do anything about that cellar.'

I told him that he needn't worry about it, and he seemed relieved.

We stood absurdly in the hall, sipping the champagne which sent delicious scented bubbles up into the nose. Small talk is not Pluto's strong suit, so I put it to him point-blank that the lunatic woman was Mrs Zetterberg. For some reason I was terribly frightened that he'd say it was.

He nodded, surprised that I had to ask. I felt myself going cold. Why do I feel I'm in the grip of a psychotic? She's only my landlady, for God's sake. She doesn't have actual power over me, does she? Pluto volunteered the information that she was 'not well'. I took this to be as near an explanation of their joint behaviour as I would get. I pushed him a bit, trying to find out if 'not well' was a euphemism for barking, but he wouldn't be pressed. All he would say about Mrs Z.'s circumstances was that Mr Zetterberg was 'no longer with us'. Does he mean he's brown bread [i.e. dead] or what? The trouble is, Pluto isn't exactly with us either. He's not completely out to lunch, but he's not all there either.

What gets me so *steamed up* about alchemy is that as soon as I establish some nice crisp meaning for one of its maddeningly obscure terms, another meaning crops up. I've no sooner learnt to live with the fact that the prima materia, whatever else it is, is a paradoxical bloody article – it's *matter* except when it's *spirit*, *fire* except when it's *water* etc., etc. – than I find that things are even worse: the prima materia is the same bloody thing as the Philosophers' Stone which is 'the stone that is no stone' in the first place!

It's no use losing my rag over this. *Think*, Eileen.

OK. Isn't it true to say that prima materia and Stone are not the *same* exactly? The latter already potentially exists in the former. The purpose of the opus is to *realise* that potential. This is another way of saying that 'our mercury' (either extracted from the prima materia or identical with it) is the raw material of the Stone. So in one way prima materia and Stone are 'one thing', yet composed of four elements (or two lots of two elements!). It depends on one's point of view.

It gets me down to think of all those undoubtedly brilliant minds labouring for centuries over every conceivable substance, organic and inorganic, in search of a 'spirit' *which isn't there*.

Jung is quick to point out that, in a way, they did everything right. They noticed for instance that of the seven 'metals' the six solid ones (gold, silver, copper, lead, iron, tin) were, when melted, very like the one liquid metal (mercury). Naturally they assumed that all metals were formed from a spiritual principle which was most obvious in mercury – what could be more like a spirit than quicksilver, flowing in a silvery stream out of a metal and easily sublimated by heat into an airy vapour or 'spirit'? Next, to account for the differences between metals, they had only to propose another principle, sulphur, which mixed in varying proportions with mercury to create the specific properties of each metal. After all, it's true that metals rarely appear in a pure state. More often than not they do occur mixed with sulphur, e.g. pyrites (iron sulphide), galena (lead sulphide), cinnabar (mercuric sulphide). So, nice try, lads – but *wrong*.

But *were* the alchemists simply wrong? I feel uneasy saying that. They weren't stupid. Quite the reverse. Some of them must have got something out of it, labouring so long and hard. Besides, *I* don't know the secret, so who am I to say they were wrong?

If Jung is to be believed, their endeavour was more psychological than material – they might not have made an Elixir, but at least they achieved something like wisdom or peace of mind. He says that the prima materia was the substance which carried the alchemists' unconscious psychic projection. It wasn't possible therefore to specify the actual substance because the projection from which it was indistinguishable was entirely personal and consequently different in every case. All the odd contradictory statements about the prima materia can then be seen as intuitions about the paradoxical nature of the unconscious itself, which was identified with the unknown qualities of matter. And because matter is impersonal, the projections on to it were impersonal – that is, archetypes of the collective unconscious rather than images from the personal unconscious. Above all, as a reaction to the prevailing world-view, an unChristian (Gnostic) image was projected on to their matter: the image of a Spirit imprisoned within the darkness of the earth. They couldn't look at their prima materia, presumably, without seeing it charged with meaning and life – without seeing the Spirit, 'our mercury', rising like the moon over the earth's dark horizon.

*

Through the dark glass of their vessels, then, the alchemists watched the unfolding drama of their own unconscious psychic lives mirrored in the chemical reactions. Their matter was, like the night sky, a dark unknown abyss fit to receive the projections, not of the personal unconscious, but of the collective unconscious – the archetypal images such as Sun and Moon, King and Queen, dragon and raven, which paraded before their dazzled eyes like the bright signs of the Zodiac, projected by the old astrologers on to the stars.

As I understand it, the collective unconscious is the most profound level of the psyche, shared by everyone, just as we share a common anatomy over and above all individual or racial differences. It surrounds our puny ego-consciousness on all sides as the sea surrounds an island. It doesn't so much belong to us as we belong to it. The archetypes – those monsters of the deep – are unknown and unknowable in themselves; but as they rise to the surface of consciousness and become perceptible, they take on the shape and colouring of the cultural and individual consciousness in which they appear.

I've always found it hard to grasp the archetypes.[9] They're as slippery to imagine as Plato's forms (whose descendants they are). To make things worse, Jung also seems to use the word 'archetype' confusingly. For instance, he insists that an archetype is an empty *form*, an unconscious disposition to form universal symbols. On the other hand, he sometimes uses the word to refer to its *content*, that is to the symbols themselves. If he were to say that the ancient Egyptian Osiris or the ancient Greek Prometheus were archetypes, I sort of know what he means. But in fact they are archetypal *images* or symbols, comparable in their own cultures to other culture-heroes such as Dionysus, Siegfried, various Amerindian heroes, and even Jesus. The archetype which underlies all these, and is distinct from the particular cultural image, is something like the idea of the sacrificed hero. However this has no existence apart from the real or mythical heroes by which it manifests itself.

The sacrificed hero occurs in alchemy as well, but not as any consistent image – he can be Mercury, the King, Sol, even the dragon. He can even, paradoxically, be the sacrificer.

In fact Jung saw alchemy as an archetypal process which enacted and expressed in symbols the development of the personality. He called this process *individuation*. It is the development that every individual has to undergo in order to attain that state of 'wholeness' where all aspects of the personality, conscious and unconscious, are integrated into what he called the self.

The self is Jung's great unifying image. It is the totality of the psyche – not only the centre of this totality, as the ego is the centre of consciousness, but also the circumference that embraces both consciousness and the unconscious. He thought that the Philosophers' Stone was the alchemical equivalent of the self.

There's a funny old codger who pokes around the graveyard. He's got a little fork with which he does a bit of feeble weeding among the graves for about ten minutes; then he stops and wanders about, vaguely gesticulating at the overgrown parts. I brought him out a mug of tea today because the sky's clear blue but there's a real autumn nip in the air.

He was excessively grateful in a whining sort of way. He's called Mr Simmons, and he lives in Upper D— but used to live here (his wife is buried in the graveyard). He's very keen to talk about the old days 'when the Vicarage *was* the Vicarage'. It hasn't been a vicarage for twenty-five years, he reckons, and for most of that time it has been shut up. He used to be the church's verger – he's very proud of this – until they closed it down in the fifties. The congregation wasn't large enough to justify it. If you want to pray now, you have to go to Upper D— . Mr Simmons hasn't missed a Sunday morning service for twenty years, despite chronic ill-health.

In fact he's remarkably well preserved for his age and neat in appearance, with thin white hair parted down the middle. His expression is permanently lugubrious; his hand movements are fussy and his speech ever so genteel. He tends to rest his eyes on the church while he's talking and to shake his head with resigned melancholy. There was a move, he says, to convert it into a Craft Centre, but nothing came of it – apparently 'She' (he indicated the Manor) was against the idea.

This was more like it. I urged Mr Simmons to tell me more about Her.

'She owns a lot of property in the vicinity. She doesn't like changes in the village. She tends to get her own way. Mind you, she's not as wealthy as she was. According to Mike Bruford. He lives up the valley but he farms her land. EEC regulations have begun to bite. She's had to borrow from the bank to buy new machinery. Nearly killed her, Mike Bruford says. She's close with her money. Hates spending a farthing.'

It's difficult to keep him to the point. I asked when Mr Zetterberg had died.

'Died? He might have died, I suppose. He left her ten years ago or more. An American, you know. That's where she lived. America. Came back here when he left her . . . ' A sly look came into his watery eyes. He lowered his voice confidingly. 'I wouldn't normally tell this to a soul, but, do you know, I saw her the other week round the back of the church there, by the old spring . . . ' He began to jiggle about with excitement. His voice dropped to a stage-whisper. 'Early in the morning it was. I don't know if she saw me or not. Anyway, she wouldn't care who saw her, that one. She was splashing about in the spring *stark naked*. In broad daylight.'

I tried to look suitably aghast. I remarked that Mrs Z. was perhaps 'not well'. The old man didn't take my meaning.

'She's not ill. I've never heard of her being ill . . . ' He was still picturing the sight of Mrs Z. bathing herself. Then he turned to me abruptly. 'You know what she's up to?' I shook my head. He glanced over his shoulder. '*Pagan worship*,' he said fiercely. I nearly burst out laughing.

I have scarcely thought about you, dear P., for forty-eight hours. Is this a record? It means I'll recover – am already recovering – as people do. But I don't want you to think that I don't still hump your dead-weight around with me, like lead sewn into my clothes.

Dear P.,

I confess I did a stupid thing last night: I phoned you. The bloody apparatus was just sitting there, waiting for me to use it, like a powerful drug. I thought, Hey, why don't I give the bugger a bell? I'd like to hear what he thinks of this alchemy thing, it'd be strictly a business call – besides, I ought to let him know I'm OK, ought to see how he's keeping, I'll make it light and breezy – I'm over the worst, after all – no reason we can't be pals, etc. In other words, the eternal self-deception of the junkie. I knew that, even as I lifted the receiver; I despised myself for dialling. The ringing tone sounded. A bell was *actually ringing in your flat*. In a few seconds you'd pick up the receiver your end and I'd *hear your voice*.

Well, I had to drop everything, go and throw up. This is one letter I won't be sending. A girl's got to leave herself with *some* dignity.

According to Jung, the Great Work of alchemy is a way of individuation, a way of realising the Self. Individuation, like alchemy, is dangerous because it requires an encounter with the unconscious. Not many people can sustain the integrity of the ego, as they must, against the violent influx of unconscious contents.

Individuation follows a course which shows a certain formal regularity: a number of archetypes act as signposts, although the actual images by which they manifest themselves vary according to the person concerned. Once the ego enters into direct relationship with the unconscious, its first encounter is with the *shadow*, which broadly corresponds in alchemy to the Nigredo or Blackness.

The shadow is our dark *alter ego*.[10] It is constituted from whatever is undifferentiated or undeveloped in ourselves, from whatever we have rejected or repressed because it contradicts our image of ourselves or of our conscious principles and morality, from whatever we can't face. However, the shadow continually thrusts itself upon us, either directly (in dreams, for instance) or indirectly, through projection, which casts this dark side of ourselves on to an object or person so that it's always the other who is guilty and never ourselves.

The shadow has either a personal or a collective form of appearance depending on whether it belongs to the realm of the ego or to the realm of the collective unconscious. Accordingly, it can either appear as someone we know or have seen etc., or as a dark mythological figure such as a sorcerer, satyr, devil, etc.

The shadow stands on the threshold of the collective unconscious. Only when we have come to terms with it can we proceed to the second stage of individuation: the encounter with the *anima* which, meaning 'soul' in Latin, can be thought of as the 'soul-image'. Unlike the shadow which is usually of the same gender as ourselves, the female anima occurs in the *male* psyche; its equivalent in the female psyche is the male *animus*. It's as though we carry around with us a 'soul-image' of the opposite sex, just as (biologically) we carry around a number of genes of the opposite sex to those which determine whether we are male or female.

Naturally the anima/animus tend to be projected on to actual members of the opposite sex. Thus I experience my own animus, the male elements in my psyche, in whatever man is unlucky enough to receive the projection. (Say no more, eh P.?) If I go farther and unconsciously *identify* with the animus, then it's like being possessed by a strange person. I've seen this a lot in people whose conscious control has been temporarily weakened, by anger for instance, or drink – or 'love' . . . I suspect that I didn't fall in love with *you*, but was seized by my animus – all my repressed masculine traits – which was projected on to you. No wonder I'm obsessed.

The unconscious as a whole acts in a *compensatory* way towards consciousness; and nowhere is this more true than in the anima/animus figures who, more than any other archetype, personify the unconscious itself. To know my own animus is to know the mystery of the opposite sex in the depths of my own psyche. In alchemy, this is the Albedo or Whiteness.

Beyond the anima/animus there are further archetypes that I don't really understand. For men, there seems to be an encounter with the masculine principle itself. Typically it appears as a wise old man or a young boy who, Jung says, represents the principle of spirit or *meaning*. For women, the equivalent archetype is the principle of matter or Nature, typically appearing as the Great Mother.

The unconscious archetypes are integrated with consciousness through that common mid-point Jung called the self (or, as I prefer, the Self) whose birth is a complete transformation of the personality. Narrow ego-consciousness is subsumed by a broader, deeper consciousness which can't be described, only experienced. The Self is the whole of which the ego is only a part – we mistake it for the whole because it's the only part we know. In relation to the Self, the ego is no longer a subject but an object; for the Self is a 'supraordinate personality', the goal of individuation – and indeed of life.

*

SOLUTION

I saw Mr Simmons drifting around the graveyard and nipped out to accost him. By the time I arrived he was standing in front of his wife's grave. He seemed to accept my presence as natural, if indeed he really registered it, and without preamble began to speak as if he were already in the middle of a train of thought:

'She was sweetness and light, was Lydia. Used to play the instrument in church, you know. Meek as you please.' He sighed heavily. 'She was got at, of course. She grew very hard. Gave me a rough time of it . . . treated her own sister shamefully. I don't blame her. It was the vicar's doing . . . ' He poked the ground with his stick and raised his vague eyes to look at the church.

'What about the vicar, Mr Simmons?' I prompted.

'Eh? Oh, he was a fly-by-night . . . wasn't with us for much more than a year before he disappeared. The fellow who came after him tried to pick things up. So did his wife. But the damage was done, you see . . . people had lost heart. Once you lose the habit of church-going, well . . . ' His voice trailed away. He screwed up his eyes as if trying to bring the church into better focus. He pointed at it with his stick. 'It closed down after that . . . left to sink into the earth.'

'What was he like, the first vicar? The one who was only here for a year?'

'They say he killed a man.'

'Killed a man? What man?' Mr Simmons wandered off, craning his head forward occasionally like a tortoise in order to read the headstones. 'Winter's coming on,' he said. 'I shan't be coming here again till spring. If I live that long . . . '

'About the vicar, Mr Simmons . . . ?'

'Eh? Ah yes. He was always most appreciative of my work. I was the verger, you know. Most appreciative . . . He went over to the Devil, of course. I remember him preaching about it. He wanted us to follow the Devil. The Devil doesn't need a second invitation. I had nothing more to do with him after that. The Lord knows what he got up to in that vicarage . . . Devil worship, fornication, all sorts . . . shocking business . . . '

I couldn't get much more out of him. As you can imagine, I was all a-flutter at this news – it's pure Sunday newspaper fodder!

*

I am a dozy cow: my manuscript is not that old. How can it be? It's not even written in Latin or on parchment. The fact is, it must have belonged to the Devil-worshipping vicar whom Simmons was rabbiting on about! He was an *alchemist*, of course, not a diabolist. Wasn't alchemy sometimes called the Black Art through a mistaken identification with the Nigredo? Simmons has got it all muddled up.

On the other hand, alchemy is supposed to be an extraordinarily powerful Art. If it *were* used for evil ends . . . ?

THREE

Separation

SMITH

After some eight or nine circulations,[1] all the signs are that the brightness of Sol is opening up the matter. As fast as the dragon reconstitutes itself below, so Sol's shining rays thrust down between its grey-green scales, causing it to writhe and seethe. The death is liable to be a slow and painful one – but how could the separation of mercury and sulphur be otherwise?

The thought of the Nigredo already forms a shadow at the back of my mind. I must try to concentrate on the Albedo beyond.

Another day of tiresome and tiring duties. They compel me to pursue my Art at night. However they must *not* be neglected – and, besides, they are only tiresome in retrospect when, weary, I review the day. It's to my advantage that, feeling so useless – so superfluous – any little instance where I can be of help becomes a triumph and a joy. For example, I overheard a conversation at the bus-stop to the effect that a fellow called Fresnell (I've heard of him but do not know him. He's not a churchgoer) has not been seen about. I forgot this snippet of information until I happened to pass his cottage later on. On an impulse I dropped in, to find him laid up with a badly swollen foot and ankle. Somehow he set me at my ease and our conversation was lengthy and animated – about the farm (he works Caldwell's land), education, the Church, General Eisenhower, hares (why they 'box') and Nightingale Wood which, he agreed, it would be a shame to cut down. He astonished me at the end of it by asking if I would give him communion, then and there, but without letting on to his wife! I obliged him of course, and we held between us a most heart-warming service, using only the Body which I fetched from the church. I shall have to start carrying wine about with me as well for just such contingencies.

Yet it is always a relief to return to my laboratory. Perhaps relief is no longer the right word. I certainly feel more and more that it is where I *belong*; and when I am down there the world above seems unreal – grey, thin, watery compared to the contents of my Egg. At the same time, even as I am utterly *fascinated* by the Work and hurry towards it every morning and evening with fluttering heart, increasingly I find myself pausing at the top of the steps, overcome by a nameless dread of descending. It's not just a fear of some disaster having befallen – a failure of heat or a crack in the Egg – but a sweet anxious fear (such as I felt as a child in the dark) at confronting again the slow, scaly, uncoiling of the matter as it dissolves and coagulates painfully in its own poison.

De tempore

On the time required to complete the Great Work there are many opinions. It is not uncommon to spend a decade in wasted labour. Abbot Cremer avers in his *Testamentum* that he strove in vain for thirty years.[2] The great Flamel himself spent twenty-one frustrating years in study and experiment before his fateful trip to Spain. Bernard of Treves,* poor fellow, used two thousand hens' eggs in one of his attempts during ten years' worth of fruitless experiments!

It is impossible to succeed in the Art without its secret. Once this grand arcanum has been obtained, whether by vision or by some acknowledged master or by Providence, estimates of the Work's duration range from the four days claimed by Helvetius' mysterious visitor, to a year, the period of time favoured by the noble Canon of Bridlington [i.e. Sir George Ripley].

Three, seven or twelve months are popular estimates; but these numbers, being magical, are not to be taken literally but rather as an indication of the numerological importance of the operation, with its tendency to reflect fundamental arrangements in Nature. In his *Ordinall* Thomas Norton, emphasising the Stone's susceptibility to

---

* Concerning the alchemists mentioned in this passage, I know nothing about Bernard of Treves, or Bernardus Trevisanus, except his alleged dates (1406–90), nor about Petrus Bonus (*c*. 1330). Details of Helvetius and his 'mysterious visitor', of Norton and Charnock, can be found in later notes.

astrological influences, says that the first purification should take place with the sun in the Archer [Sagittarius] and the moon in the Ram [Aries] and that the Work should be 'consummated during the conjunction of sun and moon in the Lion [Leo]'. This is a period of nine months.

Philalethes, whose name never fails to set the pulse beating a little faster, tells us that our silver might be found in five months, our gold in a further two, three or four months; but he warns that these are not identical with the Stone: '*that* glorious sight will not gladden your eyes until you have been at work for a year-and-a-half'.

How long then does it take to acquire the secret? 'The whole Magistery of our Art', says Petrus Bonus [in *The New Pearl of Great Price*], 'can be learned in a single hour of one who knows.' Elias Ashmole had it even more quickly from William Backhouse as he lay on his deathbed [see Introduction]. As soon as Ripley sent for Norton, the latter rode over a hundred miles post-haste to Ripley's abode where he was initiated into the secret in a single philosopher's month [i.e. forty days]. The extraordinary Thomas Charnock had the secret *twice* – once from a priest in Salisbury (who, we are told, had no master himself, but received the secret from God) and again from a former Prior of Bath who was able to reveal all in a few words, perhaps because Charnock was already far advanced in the Work.

I know the Secret as surely as I know that I have found the prima materia. I will reveal more than has ever been revealed before, more than I should (as much as I dare).

A man does not seek what he knows but only what he does not know. I know the secret. What I do not know, what I must know, what cannot be known from books, is *the secret of the secret*;[3] and this can only be revealed by the Great Work itself.

The secret is a secret for a very good reason: in the hands of the uninitiated it can do untold harm, not only to the uninitiated themselves but also to others. For the secret gives access to powers which it can take years to learn how to control. Neutral in themselves, these powers do nothing but evil if they are unleashed by the foolish and weak. The extent of that evil can be incalculable.

The wise Mary Anne South always opposed her friends' demands to reissue her profound *Suggestive Inquiry* by quoting Norton's *Ordinall*:*

> So this science must ever secret be,
> The cause whereof is this, as ye may see,
> If one evil man had hereof all his will
> All Christian peace he might easily spill,
> And with his hands he might pull down
> Rightful Kings and Princes of renown,
> Whereof the sentence of peril and jeopardy
> Upon the teacher resteth dreadfully.

(Although Miss South interpreted our Philosophy according to her time, hinting at the importance of manual manipulations, as in mesmerism, and at astral projection, she did not make the mistake of turning the Art into a purely speculative venture or a simple spiritual discipline – she knew that it is an affair of power, both of spirit and matter, and that through the secret the dark forces at the root of metals may be released and, in the hands of wicked men, abused to bring the world to ruin.)

So far, Nora is a success. The antithesis of Mrs B., she is quiet, intelligent, efficient, undemanding. And, I suspect, more thoughtful than she pretends. I have caught her watching me in quite a . . . *fierce* way, before looking away with pink cheeks. Above all, she makes no fuss. She accepts without question my work in the cellar, with its irregular, unpredictable and often long hours, and either leaves food out for me or prepares it when I have surfaced. On the whole I prefer the latter because then we can eat together, mostly in silence, but in an easy way. We use the kitchen, for convenience, where it is cosier besides; but if I am very tired or engrossed in study she will still bring a tray to the 'library'. She is able to stay later now because, her father having returned to his ship, her brother Tim is boarding with Mrs Crowther and her brood. In fact, she tells me, he comes and goes as he pleases between the Crowthers and his own house. She is worried by this because she cannot guarantee to be at home to keep

---

* See p. 449.

an eye on him when he is there. I myself have yet to be convinced of his existence; besides which, Nora spoke as though she had no very lively hope of keeping an eye on him under any circumstances. He seems to be a free spirit who is as likely to be found at Robert's or even wandering the Down as at the places he is supposed to be. However, she is pleased with the Crowther arrangement because it means that Tim goes to school more regularly than in the past: he catches the early bus every morning with Michael and Gabriel Crowther whom he likes.

I suggested that instead of trying to keep up two establishments, mine and her father's, she should close up his for the time being, move in here, and encourage Tim to drop by whenever he feels the need to see her or to get away from the rather overcrowded Crowthers. This struck her as a good plan, and more economical. She is going to consult her brother before deciding.

As Sol moves past his zenith and begins his descent, so his rays grow dimmer, changing from their pure translucent golden hue to the colour of our sulphur. Thus separation begins in earnest.

The goal of separation is to make the volatile fixed and the fixed volatile. This occurs when the dragon, goaded beyond endurance by Sol's spears, flies up into the height of our Hermetic heaven and drips its venom on to our matter, *which is nothing other than the dragon itself*. This is the meaning of the Ouroboros,* perhaps the oldest depiction of our Art, who by devouring itself releases the divine Luna from her imprisonment and allows her to rise.

I can't rid myself of Annabelle. It's no use pretending. It's driving me mad. I'm terrified that she will appear to me again as that infernal succubus with her hands on her mocking hips. Worse still, I keep remembering little gestures of hers, little idiosyncrasies that I didn't even realise I had noticed at the time. They bring her back

---

* i.e. 'tail-eating'; and, more specifically, the serpent or dragon who forms a circle by eating its own tail. It is found very early on, for example in the *Gold-making of Cleopatra*, a page of symbolical drawings from about the second century AD, in which the Ouroboros encircles the words, in Greek, 'One is all'.

so vividly it's as though time had not passed – what's been the point of all these *years* of work and prayer, all those long days of duty which send me to bed dog-tired, if they have done nothing to obliterate or even *palliate* the awful sick pain which her image summons up?

If I am to remember, then I will remember accurately. (Even now my pen, wishing to spare me pain, resists the writing of her name. How tender we are with ourselves! All knowledge of the past, and therefore all self-knowledge, is false because willy-nilly we would rather spare ourselves the slightest suffering than face the unadorned truth. Nevertheless, I will try to distinguish between my own scars, prejudices, delusions, emotions and what was the case.)

I remember I was quite unprepared for the sight that greeted me when I walked into the drawing-room. The maid was arranging the tea things, my mother was chattering to her mother, a cart was rattling outside in the street. Making sense of all the clatter and bustle, encased in a self-contained silence as perfect as her white skin inside her shimmering dove-grey dress, her bobbed hair like a halo against the tall window, she sat on the sofa. All the cockiness and quasi-sophistication which a university education and nine months in the glittering subculture of Paris can bring, deserted me. I who disliked English girls, despising their tightness compared to the generous French women – *I* bristled and shivered like a furry animal. When she smiled, her top lip stretched tight across her teeth in a way that made my body capable of atrocities. I wanted to lunge across the table and crush her and, in crushing her, crush some strength back into my weak bloodless body just as I now want with equal impotence to crush her out of my memory. My violence dissolved in a desire to weep. I frog-marched my legs out of the room and stood trembling in the hall like a whipped dog. I was done for. I had no experience to compare with this white-hot melting-down of my whole personality which streamed out of me like hot ectoplasm and burned to extinguish itself in that cool pristine shimmering dove-grey pool of beauty. I had only agreed to turn up for tea to please my mother. I had been within an ace of missing her.

I was due to return to Paris in three days' time. I had only returned to England at all to appease my parents and especially my dear open-handed father who was beginning to wonder how wisely I was spending his liberal allowance. He rather hoped that I was squandering it on wine and predatory *demi-mondes*, as he had once done in the nineties. I did not disillusion him. He could see that I was in love and longing to get back to Paris; he could not guess, of course, that my love was the chaste passion for Lady Alchymia! Now, however, my deep preoccupation with the Sacred Art, my intense excitement over the Work's progress, my sense of pride and privilege at having been chosen to participate in it – all this was expunged by the top lip of a girl I neither knew nor particularly liked. Annabelle became an obsession with me *instantly*.

It was not difficult to find out about her. She was the daughter of the senior partner in my father's firm. She was (my heart lurched) unattached. She had refused higher education or the opportunity of being 'finished' abroad in favour of becoming a nurse. She had refused her father's offer of a flat and chosen to slum it in a rented room near the hospital. I found out the times of her shifts.

For two and a half days I rehearsed the scene of our next meeting. At the end of this time, knowing that every second that passed was making it more difficult ever to face her again, I drank a lot of brandy and went to her address.

She was in. She wore no make-up, no shimmering dove-grey dress. Her complexion was not as white nor as flawless as I had supposed. She was as I'd hoped and feared she would be – ordinary. Eager to pass beyond small-talk I disclosed myself freely to her. She listened politely. I told her how impressed I was that she should have refused the more frivolous options open to her and have chosen a serious calling in medicine. She was puzzled. She was without wit or ambition; she was uninteresting. When she conscientiously enquired about France, I obliged her with the most extravagant, exotic and humorous descriptions I could contrive. They failed to hold her full attention. What's more, she was inclined to interrupt with irrelevant observations which plainly showed her lack of intelligence and imagination.

Within minutes of arriving I could not believe that I had been in the thrall of someone so unexceptional. Mentally I began to calculate whether I could catch an earlier boat-train from Victoria. I even began to shape my brief infatuation into a comic tale to entertain my master. As soon as I decently could I made my excuses and left with a sigh of relief.

After two months, almost to the day, we exchanged our first kiss.

*

> One thing was first employed,
> Which shall not be destroyed:
> It compasseth the world so round,
> A matter easy to be found:
> And yet most hard to come by.
> A secret of secrets, pardye,
> That is most vile and least set by,
> But it is my Love and Darling,
> Conceived with all living thing,
> And travels to the world's ending.

I woke this morning with these lines from Ashmole's *Theatrum* running through my head.* Like so much that is written about the prima materia or the secret fire, it is in the form of a riddle. However, it is not an ordinary riddle, to be solved by a quick intelligence. It is a *philosophical riddle* to which there is no single answer. As I lay in bed, racking my brain over the lines, I realised that although I was no nearer the solution I was nevertheless, in some sense, *moving nearer to Mercurius*. He, of course, is the answer to the riddle but it does not help us because *he is himself a riddle*.

The secret of solving philosophical riddles is to submit to them, I decided. In racking our brains to the utmost we find ourselves teased into a different realm of thought where the answer is not some piece of information we can grasp, but a mighty insight *which grasps us*. All the endless mind-paralysing paradoxes and contradictions of the Art are riddles which goad us on to think what cannot be thought and so drive us either into madness or into that passionate intellectual ecstasy in which the world's multiplicity and complexity is *comprehended* as concretely as we embrace a lover.

I had no sooner understood this about riddles, and ceased to torture my brain, than the answer came to me as if in mockery.

The answer is *time*.

I should add that time is not the whole answer, which, if it

---

* i.e. *Theatrum Chemicum Britannicum*, a collection of alchemical treatises made in 1652 by the famous antiquarian, alchemical enthusiast and founder member of the Royal Society, Elias Ashmole (1617–92). The quotation is from the tract on Experience and Philosophy.

exists, consists of the thousand names of Mercurius. But it seemed to me then, as I lay staring back in defiance at the grotesque mocking face formed by the damp patch on my white ceiling, that time is an essential part of the secret fire. For instance, it flows swiftly and passes slowly. It is both abstract and concrete. Since it is measured by space – the movements of planets or of hands on the face of a clock – it is also a property of space. It is locked up in matter on which the cycles of Nature – the seasons – depend. Time heals and destroys, restoring what once was lost, taking away what once we had. It dissolves all things and reconstitutes them, as spring follows winter.

The Philosophers' Stone is *that moment in time when time's serpent turns back on itself, destroys itself,* to form the strait circular gateway to eternity.

I sprang up and consulted Ashmole. The poetic riddle continues:

>A child begetting his own Father,
>   and bearing his Mother,
>Killing himself to give life and light to all other,
>Is that I meane,
>Most mild and most extreme.
>Did not the world that dwelt in me
>Take form and walk forth visibly;
>And did not I then dwell in It,
>That dwelt in me for to unite,
>Three powers in one seat to sit.

At that miraculous Moment, as on the Last Day, when time and eternity enfold each other, the mortal body and immortal soul will *mutually indwell* within the Spirit, all three becoming that One who was before time began.

I have just finished an excellent supper which has done much to raise my spirits. Cooking comes easily to Nora, and with a lightness of touch which puts Mrs B.'s ponderous concoctions to shame. Nor does she expect or exact tribute for her expertise as Mrs B. did. (If I pay her a voluntary compliment, she expresses pleasure by blinking her eyelids very quickly while otherwise remaining impassive.)

There's less meat of the stewed gnu variety and more imaginative flourishes. Today I asked her about a particular flavour and she replied: 'That's basil, sir. I'm surprised you don't know, being so keen on Nature and that.' I asked her where she had found it. 'It grows all over your garden, sir!' I was shamefaced at having overlooked this profusion of basil. She promised – if I liked – to bring some herbs she and her grandma grew at Goose Farm and to plant them in my beds. Rosemary, parsley, mint, sage, chives and so on. It was a crying shame, she said, to see a big garden going to waste when I could be growing all sorts of vegetables and saving money. For a second she sounded so much like Annabelle that I suffered a stab of pain. I pointed out that the garden, though untended, was not a complete wasteland – witness the roses. 'Oh, *roses*,' she said scornfully.

She has decided to move into the vicarage, with Tim's blessing. He himself will not have a great deal of time to visit because much of it has, apparently, to be spent 'helping Robert'. Must ask Robert what *he* thinks of this . . .

Nora chose the east-facing bedroom across the landing from mine. She was a trifle overwhelmed at the idea of such a large room all to herself. Conditions at home are not, I gather, as sumptuous. The room looked a little bare and unwelcoming to me – she made me aware of how my house lacks a woman's touch – but by the rapid fluttering of her lashes I guessed she was satisfied.

De operis gradibus

Any description of the stages of the Work must begin with the stern reminder: 'One is the Stone, one the medicine, and therein lies the whole magistery.' The Work is a single operation.

But, as my own manuscript makes clear, it is also a two-fold work, divided into two Regimens (or Regimina) which produce first the White Stone and secondly the Red.

However, the chief means of ascertaining the health and progress of the Work is by the appearance of the three colours – black, white and red, in that order. No *Rubedo* [redness] without *Albedo* [whiteness] and no *Albedo* without *Nigredo* [blackness]. As that old wind-bag, von Hohenheim, insists,[4] the matter must grow 'blacker than the crow... whiter than the swan; and at last passing through a yellow colour, it turns out more red than any blood'. Here, he includes a fourth colour, *citrinitas* [yellowness], between the white and the red, which was more characteristic of early chemistry than later – although it must be said that the wise Philalethes also espoused this scheme: 'See to it that you prepare the couch of Venus carefully, then lay her on the marriage bed, and in the fire you will see an emblem of the great work: black, the peacock's tail, white, yellow and red.' (The peacock's tail is no more a *stage* than the raven's head but rather a brief heralding of the albedo as the latter presages the nigredo.) Nigredo is the matter's mortification, purgation and contrition; Albedo is its purification and dealbation [whitening]; Rubedo, its exaltation and consummation.

The number of steps required to achieve the three colours varies a good deal. Geber's *Summa* [*Perfectionis*] cites eight lab operations from sublimation to ceration [making the matter malleable like wax?]. The *Rosarium Philosophorum* claims ten stages, a perfect number composed of $4+3+2+1$, which cannot but recall to the Christian the ten stages of St John of the Cross in his Ascent of the Soul. In *Splendor Solis* the charming Salomon Trismosin (who describes his rejuvenation by means of 1/2 grain of the Stone!) advances a predictable seven stages for the Work. In his *Compound of Alchemy* Ripley envisages the Opus memorably as a round castle with twelve gates, each representing a stage and ending, naturally, with *projection* – the testing of the completed Stone by casting it on to molten base metal, which (if the Stone be true) turns it into gold.

After two months Annabelle and I exchanged our first kiss. It was a delicate matter. Even in my frenzied condition I was dimly aware of the inherent contradiction: I could not fulfil my desire to kiss her without tainting the purity which was the very object of the desire.

I took her to a show – some nonsense I hoped would please her. She did not remove her arm when I squeezed it while we stood in her doorway. She did not prevent me from entering her room. I kept up a stream of teasing banter, both to hide my excitement, and to make my attempt at a kiss appear as a nonchalant afterthought, a natural extension of my teasing. Without this pretence the attempt was out of the question because it served to shield me from the unbearable possibility of her refusal as well as the unbearable bliss of her acceptance. In either event I could try and pass it off as a light-hearted impulse – a simple kiss.

I kept putting the moment off, babbling desperately, searching her composed face for a glimmer of willingness. When, in mid-sentence, she stepped forward and put her arms around my neck, her expression did not change.

Her kiss was hard and long. I had to pull away. Her lack of reserve took my breath away. I could not meet her eyes which were searching out mine with a gaze both frank and equivocal. I saw her top lip, though, and it stretched across her teeth in that maddening feral smile. She could have no idea what it did to me, of course, just as she had no idea what a torment her guileless trusting kiss inflicted on me. I realised with awful satanic clarity that I could do with her whatever I wished while she in all innocence would acquiesce.

Almost weeping for shame and revulsion against myself, I fled her room and sat up all night writing letter after letter to my master which I did not send. I had already posted a whole series of lying, self-pitying tirades to which he hadn't replied. His silence was a reproach. It spoke eloquently of my weakness and unworthiness to pursue the Great Work. It banished me more cruelly than any *anathema sit* to the realm of common men who will throw over their very salvation for a bit of skirt. I hated myself, but no more than I hated him. And no less than I hated her.

I went to Cornwall and stayed by the sea.

I have increased the heat by a cautious 8° [Fahrenheit]. Each stage in the Opus must be subject to greater heat than the one before. The rise in temperature, though slight, seems to have rendered the cellar airless. At any rate my head aches and my body is beset by lassitude. It may be that I have a slight fever, a touch of influenza perhaps; or perhaps I am simply tired and overwrought.

The Opus has reached some kind of impasse. I have lost track of the number of circulations it has undergone. The dragon writhes and heaves but will not give birth to the fire which will perform the separation of our mercury and our sulphur. In addition there is a worrying *unwholesomeness* about the body: it seems putrescent long before it should. Decay must not precede death. There is blackness, but not the blackness of Nigredo; there is whiteness too, but not that of Albedo. Rather, it is *leprous*, as of flesh decaying in spots on the living body, with bone showing through. It is hard to bear.

I have searched within myself for some ineptitude on my part, something mishandled or overlooked and, beyond that, some thought or deed which may have tainted the Work. I have done much repentance. Sol continues to decline like the sickly king he has become, swathed in greenish fog; but his queen, Luna, remains below, in danger of asphyxiation beneath the dragon's stinking belly.

I want to intervene – but I'm terribly afraid that I am too gross and clumsy and, like a ham-fisted midwife, will bring the Work to ruin. And yet, when the patient atrophies, the surgeon doesn't hesitate to use the knife. I have prepared green vitriol and Sal ammoniack,* in spite of the fact that no scientist worth his salt would coerce the soul from the body. One does not burn down the house to roast pork.

Dear Lord, guide me, I beg you, for without your help the Work I do in your name will come to nothing. Amen.

A hot sultry June day. It's an effort to lug one's carcase about. The roses on the churchyard wall loom large and luminous in the haze, their petals puffed outwards to embrace more air. The grass is a feverish jazzy green. My head seems to be holding too much pounding blood. Perspiration drops on to the page as I write. I must be sickening for something: the feeling of oppression is not only one of anxious tiredness but also one of having my organs turn against me. It is cooler in the cellar. I burnt my hand on the athanor, fancying in a jolt of panic that it had stopped working.

The matter lies there in its morbid condition, steeped in its own prison. It's four days now. I fingered my fiery solvents longingly, but still I do not act. The matter is after all (I tell myself) no worse.

I must remain calm and follow the advice of Dionysius Zacharias'

---

* Smith pretentiously prefers to use the old alchemical names for sulphuric acid (not ferrous sulphate, the greenish crystals more usually called green vitriol) and ammonium chloride. Even so, it's not certain that he is referring to these – although there's no doubt judging by the context that he has some drastic solvents in mind.

'most excellent religious doctor' not to waste money on 'diabolical sophistications' but to study the works of the old masters wherein lies the 'true matter'.* Despite an attack of deep despair (from which he emerged only with the help of the Holy Spirit), Dionysius studied, meditated and worked in his laboratory night and day until at last he saw the three colours appear. Thus, only a year later, on Easter Day, 1550, he says, 'vidi perfectionem' – 'I saw the perfection of the Work: my "quicksilver" was changed into pure gold before my very eyes'.

Woke abruptly in the small hours. A white figure stood by the bed. Suddenly it emitted a flash of energy so intense as to be almost tangible. The whole room was jarred by its electrifying presence. My body jerked into a sitting position. A shattering report rattled the window-panes. I was so bewildered that it took me a moment to make out that the figure was Nora in her long night-dress. She was apologising for disturbing me, gabbling on about how thunderstorms excited her as a child but now frightened her.

The storm was overhead. Nora stood very close to me by the window where we felt, rather than watched, the almost continuous snaky flickering of the lightning. The faint fragrant smell of her soap was soon obliterated by a disturbing burnt metallic odour. The thunder was terrible: bang after bang had a peculiar deafening texture as if the sky were a skin stretched tightly over a vacuum which, tearing and cracking, let out a flat shockwave that popped the ears and battered directly against the brain. I could not make myself heard to reassure the girl. Not that I myself felt reassuring – the storm *was* frightening, like a cosmic war above our defenceless heads. There was no refuge from the din, nor from the ghastly lightning that seared our eyes even behind closed lids. So we simply stood in silence, every sinew tensed against the hammer blows of the storm as it rocked the house around us.

At last the worst of it receded. I raised my hand to point out the sensational display of lightning over the hills, lit in staccato bursts like a battlefield. It passed close to her hair which crackled and stood out from her head. I saw that she was looking at me almost wildly

---

* Dionysius Zacharias, also known as Denis Zachaire (?1510–56), recounts his success in *Opusculum philosophiae naturalis metallorum*.

and shivering as if her whole body had been charged by lightning. I was frightened for a moment. Then she gave a nervous laugh and, opening the window, thrust her head out into the rain which had begun to fall in a deluge of biblical proportions, an iron-grey sheet that shook the roof and hit the windows like bullets. She pulled in her drenched head and, her eyes averted, slipped back to her room.

I lay awake until dawn, hearing the drumming rain long after it had ceased, troubled by the frailty of mere houses and humans in the face of Nature.

EILEEN

[The following is Eileen's psychological interpretation of the second part of Smith's key alchemical text, the Regimen of Luna, which can be found on p. 55]

I have been rereading Jung long enough. Time to put my money where my mouth is. Leaving aside the rather daunting opening speech by 'Mercurius', I have to ask myself what Jung would say about the Regimen of Luna were he to stumble across it.

First of all, the text stresses that the Above must be joined with the Below, and vice-versa. This signifies the need to unite consciousness (Above) with the unconscious (Below). However, before this can happen, they have to be separated out of the Prime Matter, which is more or less synonymous with the 'sea', 'chaos' and 'dragon' — all symbols of the dark, dangerous, undifferentiated unconscious. The division takes place through a preliminary grinding, or calcination, of the matter, followed by a dissolution of it.

At this stage, the text makes it clear that 'beautiful Luna' is associated (if not once again synonymous) with the 'dragon' unconscious. She is freed from its 'fiery embrace' when her 'brother' – Sol – slays the dragon. Sol symbolises consciousness. Paradoxically, the dragon gave birth to him 'before time began'. Thus the unconscious gives birth to consciousness which turns on its source, its mother, and slays her. This signifies the dissolution of the unconscious by self-reflection – it is brought to light, or pierced by Sol's 'bright spears'. The same idea is expressed a little earlier by the winged dragon that flies up into the Above and drips its venom on to 'our body'. The winged dragon is a version of Sol or consciousness which ascends (as an actual vapour), condenses, and drips back (as a liquid) on to itself. The foundation of consciousness is seen as the process of reflux distillation.

In the margin of my manuscript there's a small diagram labelled

Solutio (Solution). It therefore represents this first stage of the Great Work:

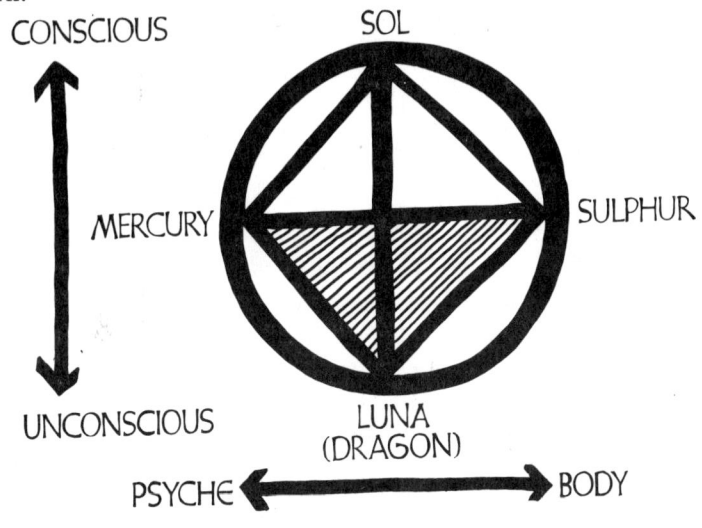

The circle is a schematic representation of the Hermetic vessel or Philosophical Egg. The square inside is the Prime Matter which is a four-fold unity. I have added the labelled arrows to show how Jung would interpret the diagram. He was unconcerned with the chemical side of alchemy. For him, the Hermetic vessel was a mirror in which the alchemist witnessed the psychological transformation taking place within himself.

In the text I notice that the dissolution of the 'dragon' by Sol is also seen to bring about the division of 'mercury' and 'sulphur', the 'volatile' and the 'fixed'. This represents the beginning of the separation between the inner mental life (psyche) and the outer physical life (body).

According to the margin note of the alchemist whose text I have, the second stage of the Regimen of Luna is called *Coniunctio* (Conjunction). The text itself also calls it 'mortification'.

Sol, we are told, sinks into the sea and is devoured by the dragon. This is the descent of ego-consciousness into the unconscious – a familiar mythical motif whether the hero is swallowed by a sea-monster like Jonah, or whether he descends into the infernal regions like Orpheus. In all cases it's an extremely hazardous undertaking because consciousness is always in danger of being irrevocably swamped by unconscious contents. The ego or

'I' can be shattered and overwhelmed, the individual plunged into psychosis.

In effect, this stage of the Work represents part, or all, of the Nigredo when the 'I' encounters its shadow, the personal unconscious containing the personality's negative aspects. Only when this has been faced and assimilated can the collective unconscious (and its representative, the anima) be broached. However, Jung reminds us that the shadow, too, extends its roots deep into the collective unconscious so that it can appear not only as a complex of relative evils but also as absolute evil, the dark side of the Godhead. This is not something one would wish to confront . . .

As Sol sinks, so Luna rises 'not in refulgence but in darkness'. The rising of the dark moon is the ascent of the unconscious – the counterbalance to Sol's descent – which overshadows the 'I' like the raven's wings. At the same time, Sol's descent and Luna's ascent are presented as the deathlike conjunction of King and Queen (Rex and Regina), who are synonymous with Sol and Luna. Since we already know from Solution that Sol and Luna are brother and sister, the conjunction is incestuous – an illicit 'marriage' from which Luna has to 'veil her mourning face'. This expresses the dark, uncanny, forbidden, sexual atmosphere which surrounds the perilous descent into the unconscious realm where, at this stage, a number of alchemists perished.

Following the precedent of Solution, then, Conjunction can be represented like this:

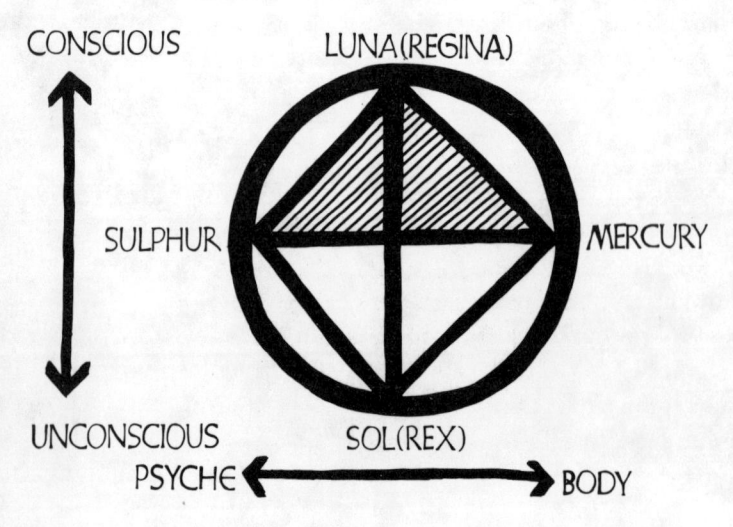

SEPARATION

The entire picture has been inverted through 180 degrees to create a reversal of the 'natural' order which prevailed at Solution: darkness reigns above, where the light of consciousness should be, while, below, the light of the 'I' – Sol – is drowned in the dark tide of the unconscious.

The text further complicates matters by interpreting Rex and Regina as 'the body and soul of our matter'. The latter are explicitly related to sulphur and mercury since they are joined in 'the mercurial fountain' and 'burned by the sulphurous fires of Gehenna'. In alchemical terms, the usually 'fixed' sulphur has become 'volatile' and the usually volatile mercury, fixed. Psychologically, this seems to express a variation on the main theme: the bodily unconscious aspects of the psyche – perhaps sexual desires – become activated or 'volatile', while the more conscious aspects, such as intellectual control or moral attitudes, become passive and 'fixed'.

The important thing to remember here is that Jung tended to see the whole alchemical process as being 'infra-psychic' – as taking place, that is, entirely within the psyche or mind. Alchemy, however, always included the relationship between 'mind' – or, as it prefers, soul – and body. 'Body' signifies the 'extra-psychic', including matter and Nature. Thus the conjunction of Rex and Regina has another aspect: it not only represents the joining of consciousness with the unconscious (Above with Below, Sol with Luna), but it also represents the interpenetration of psyche and matter, soul and body (volatile and fixed, mercury and sulphur).

The situation can be summed up by this modified diagram for Conjunction:

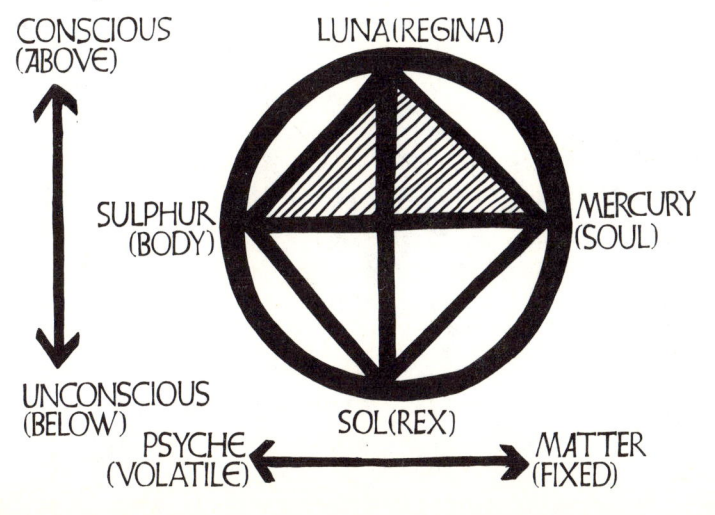

The third stage is the *Albedo*, or Whiteness, which produces the White Stone. We are told that the wheel of alchemy has turned full circle, and so the diagram will look the same as at the first stage, Solution, but will obviously be very different.

Luna has paradoxically descended 'to her zenith' and, in so doing, has raised up Sol. Thus Sol and Luna have been joined together again but not, as before, in darkness below but in the light above. This can also be seen as Sol's successful completion of his passage through the unconscious depths. In returning to consciousness, he has brought up with him Luna who, as representative of the unconscious, is the anima or soul-image. As the moon, she is no longer dark and new, but full – fully lit, fully realised, fully conscious. Her complete circle symbolises the wholeness consequent upon the marriage of consciousness with the unconscious, Above with Below, which the author describes as 'Heaven'. Psychologically, some revelation or illumination is indicated – perhaps a vision of light or of the anima as moon goddess. It is presaged by that curious phenomenon called by alchemists 'the peacock's tail', when their matter is arrayed in the 'thousand colours', suggesting a rainbow-like iridescence in the Hermetic vessel.

The author clearly felt that the full moon alone was not powerful enough a symbol to express this new, higher, expanded state of consciousness. Besides, he needs to suggest the union of the moon herself with the sun. And so he compares their marriage with a 'star set in Heaven'.

It's tempting to say that the White Stone symbolises the Self – but that honour, I suppose, must be reserved for the Red Tincture or Philosophers' Stone whose manufacture is described in the Regimen of Sol. Jung might say that, after the 'death' during the Nigredo, the Albedo or White Stone represents a rebirth which contains the *potential* for Selfhood: that is, the 'I' is no longer the personality's centre, but has been superseded by a larger, more comprehensive and objective sense of Self. It's this potential Self which becomes actual in the course of the Rubedo, the reddening of the White Stone.

I must have dozed off on the sofa because all of a sudden it was twilight. Big patches of pink sky were framed in the windows, but the room was growing darker every second. I don't know why I crash out like this. The country air, perhaps, or am I relaxing at last, catching up on all the hours of sleep I've lost over you, dear P.?

I didn't feel relaxed. My heart was going like an alarm clock, as if I'd been roused by hearing my name suddenly shouted, as one does sometimes think one hears it, in the middle of the night. Perhaps some noise had woken me. More to the point, I had the impression that someone had been watching me as I slept, someone who moved away from the window just as I opened my eyes.

I walked around the outside of the house. When I reached the back door I heard a sound in the woodshed. I waited, expecting Pluto to come out. He didn't. Mrs Zetterberg did.

I must've been still half-asleep, my imagination still loose, or something, because I had a moment of pure unreasoning fear. When she stepped out of the shadows she could, as far as I was concerned, have been holding anything – a gun, an axe, or worse.

In fact she was holding nothing. She looked pale and harmless. Perhaps a little too pale. A touch of the vampire, I like to think, compounded by the unblinking eyes set rather deep in their Gothic sockets. But really, P., that's about as Hammer Film-like as I can make her. Having not studied her too closely before, I was struck by her sort of emaciated beauty which overruled the rather hawkish impression she gives in profile. She was more shrunken and stooped than I remembered. She must once have been pretty much as tall as I am.

She waved a vague, imperious hand at the shed and spoke half to herself:

'That miserable Pluto stole them from me. You can't trust anyone.'

I took her to mean the logs. I was intensely nervous, and breathing much too fast. 'You can have them back,' I said. This amused her. 'You'd better keep them now. Don't set the chimney on fire. Have you got a cigarette?' I hadn't. She shrugged. 'That sod hides them from me. But you already know that.' This was her only reference to our first meeting.

'A drink?' she said. It wasn't really a question.

'I think I've got some tequila left. Is that any good?' My fear – and my fear of showing it – made me sound narky and aggressive. I regretted it instantly. Mrs Z. opened her eyes very wide like an owl and then, smiling in the most disarming way, said:

'*Tequila* would be *awfully* nice.' Her drawled emphasis made me think she was taking the mickey. I can't be sure. You don't know where you are with her. Her accent wasn't the one I'd imagined her to have on the phone. It wasn't Scandinavian at all, but there was something funny about it – sort of 'refined' but with a trace of American perhaps. I wondered if she was schizophrenic, speaking in two voices. I wanted to run into the house and shut the door on her, but I didn't dare.

She held the glass of tequila in both hands and sucked at it like a child, walking slowly around the room, taking everything in. There's little enough to look at. My alchemical manuscript, plus my library books, lay on the desk. Guiltily it occurred to me that I should tell her about my discovery – strictly speaking, the manuscript was hers, being found on her property – but the moment passed.

'And how's the book coming along?' she asked, reading my thoughts. My mouth was dry; I didn't know what to say. 'You told me on the telephone you were writing a book,' she accused mildly. I sort of shrugged. 'I have a great many books.' She sounded like a child boasting of her toys. Maybe she realised it because she added sadly: 'Not that I'll read them now.' Then she turned on me irritably, making my heart jump: 'You're entitled to arrange things as you like of course. But I'd prefer as little change as possible.' I nodded. I hadn't thought of changing anything.

'I recognise that sofa,' she muttered, 'the sod.' I suppose Pluto had also 'stolen' it from her. She seemed resigned to this. 'I can look around.' I took this as a question, though it wasn't quite.

'Feel free.'

I could hear her climbing the stairs and then changing her mind, come down again and go into the kitchen. After a while I heard her in the hall once more. I waited for her to return. In the end I followed her – only to find her empty glass on the hall table and the front door open. She'd legged it! I was both relieved and angry. I told myself she was not rude, just batty; not dangerous or threatening, just eccentric. All the same, my heartbeat hasn't recovered yet and my hand still shakes.

Energetic today. Felt impelled to give the cellar a good seeing to. Did hosing down, slopping out, mopping up. Piled junk in one corner and rubble in another. Cut finger on broken glass. A lot of crap has gone down the well, but I expect its water will be potable again once it has settled. It's good clean crap anyway. Scrubbed walls, really dished out some stick. Calculated where the old aborted chimney comes out at the side of the house. It's covered with a ventilator grille now at ground level, or just below, and choked with earth and weeds. Dug down and cleared it. With the door open I can actually feel a suspicion of through-breeze.

Funnily enough, you'd like my Ma, P. Pity you won't meet her now. I was remembering the way she gives snorts of laughter out of the blue at some odd thing she's seen. I never grasp what she's laughing at. I suspect you have the same sense of humour.

She's a dark horse. In retrospect I see that she was only waiting for me to grow up a bit before she left us. I turned nineteen before she felt she could decently push off. That's been a lot for me to swallow. But I don't really take it personally. It's not as though she didn't love me. She's just a bit weird, that's all.

I've been up North to see her, naturally, but only twice since she moved in with Larry. I don't know how she could, after Dad. Larry calls a spade a shovel, never opens a book, keeps pigeons – they're divine – listens to Gilbert and Sullivan, never tells a joke without messing it up. The complete opposite to Dad. He's deeply nice, though.

Mum won't marry Larry because she's a Catholic and won't divorce Dad. She can't be all that happy because she has taken to going to church again. She never went when she was with us. I used to tease her about mortal sin! When I asked her why she didn't go, she said: 'Your father isn't keen. He's rather jealous of God.' See how weird she can be?

Another example: she said it didn't matter if I didn't go to Cambridge. She meant well, but it goes to show how little she understood me – going to Cambridge was, for ages, the only thing that mattered to me. 'If you don't get in, lovey,' she said, 'Dad will get over it, you know.' I see now how out of touch with him she already was. It would've killed Dad if I hadn't gone to his alma mater. He'd set his heart on it. It was bad enough when I changed to Arch. and Anth. [Archaeology and Anthropology]. 'Ah, the soft sciences,' he said, smiling bravely. 'Aren't they done rather better at Oxford?'

I slogged my guts out, as you know, to get my first and make up for it. I wasn't shocked when I didn't: in my heart of hearts I think I've always known that my mind is not of the first rank. Dad never shows his disappointment.

[This is Eileen's transcription of the third part of Smith's manuscript:]

I [Mercurius] say that the whole of the Great Work is but one thing, to which nothing is added and from which nothing is taken away. I am the one by whom and through whom everything is achieved (*omnia perfecta sunt*); for I am the *penetrative water* and the *transforming fire*, the spirit of light and dark, the *mother* of our mercury and our sulphur, and the stone that is no stone.

Here begins the Regimen of Sol.

It is necessary to make the volatile fixed and the fixed volatile, the fruit of which operation the philosophers call *Earth*. This is a species of spiritual body which must be wedded to the corporeal spirit we call Heaven. Then will you see the *Lapis Philosophorum* [Philosophers' Stone] or Red Tincture, the greatest sight that ever befell human eyes.

To which end, dissolve and coagulate the matter, turning the wheel of our philosophy, as it is written, until the *separation of mercury* and *sulphur* begins to take place. This you will know when you see the noble king weaken and fall, fainting, to earth. Let him lie there *ten days and nights* until the earth becomes as a scorched desert, whose sign is the gradual *reddening* of the king (which betokens the sinking sun). On the tenth night his sister, our divine *queen*, will begin to rise. Then loose the *green lion* upon the king and let him tear the royal limbs, scattering the king to the four corners of the earth. And let the royal blood sink down into the parched earth and gather below. Again, I say, as often as the green lion, which is *fiery, combustible* and *sulphurous* in nature, overpowers the sick king, so allow his *moist, penetrating, mercurial* blood to bring forth Luna's dark bloom from the earth and fix her upon the horizon. Coagulate and dissolve until such time as you see the blackness of the *raven's head* begin its carrion-feast upon the sinking king.

Now, with God's help, make our queen volatile and our king fixed by immersing them in the *mercurial fountain*, which must be sealed tight as a tomb wherein our sulphur begins to blacken, as the body rots and the soul prepares for flight. Maintain a *steady heat*, twice as hot as the heat of digestion and half as hot as that of roasting. As soon as our sulphur stinks of the grave, suffer our mercury to *fly into the Above* and in no wise suffer her to descend again until all dross has *sunk Below*. Neither weep nor despair at the melancholy body's decay, for know this: that there is no *regeneration* without *corruption*. Have patience, for only when the body is black, blacker than black, can the soul begin its long descent to revive the body.

Now all is in readiness for the *Tremendum*.

Of Sol take three parts, and of Luna, nine; and with her marvellous moist fire sublime *Sol* five, seven or *nine* days and nights until the red sulphur is separated from the white. For our most excellent celestial fixed water will open up the fiery volatile body and draw out a secret running white sulphur which the philosophers call *chrysosperm* ['gold seed'], that is, the soul of the metals. To complete the Regimen of Sol it remains only to apply the utmost degree of heat, which will fix the white sulphur, *our mercurial soul*, and render volatile the red, *our fixed body*, which together constitute Earth. And in the same moment when our *Earth* is thus constituted, so the heavenly Queen shall descend in stately splendour, amidst great rejoicing, to Earth and lead Sol to the fiery marriage-bed of immortality where *I, newborn, will step forth and speak in my own voice*.

Before I attempt a psychological reading of the first part of this Regimen of Sol, I think it'll be helpful to construct a diagram of it as I did for the first three stages.

Its main purpose is the separation of mercury and sulphur. The main events are, firstly: the King (or Sol) falls fainting to earth and reddens like the setting sun. Secondly, the Queen (or Luna) rises to become fixed on the horizon. Sol and Luna therefore comprise the horizontal axis.

The Green Lion is a problem because I assumed that he invariably appeared *before* the Albedo, but here he is in the run-up to the Rubedo. He may signify a powerful solvent such as green vitriol (sulphuric acid) which, like a lion, is 'fierce' or caustic. At any rate I can assimilate him to sulphur (because he's described as 'fiery, combustible and sulphurous') while mercury is the 'moist' and 'penetrating' blood of the king which 'gathers below' and brings forth 'Luna's dark bloom from the earth'.

Sulphur and mercury thus form the vertical axis:

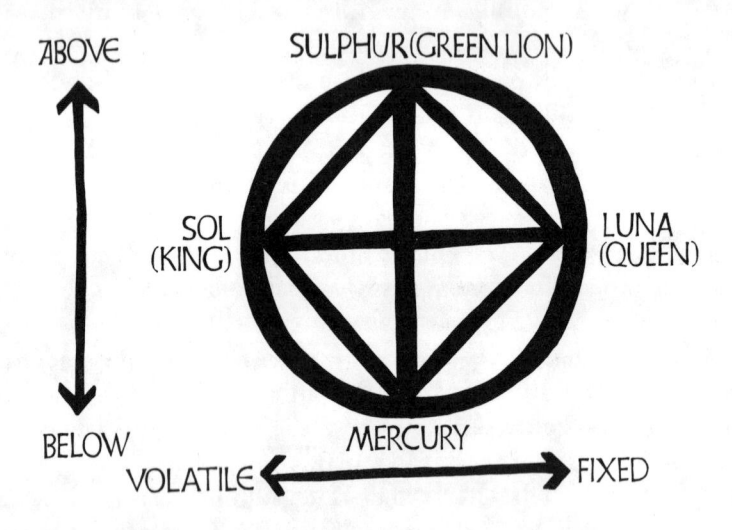

Diagram: A circle containing a square and triangle. Labels: ABOVE (↑) / BELOW (↓) on the left vertical axis; SULPHUR (GREEN LION) at top; SOL (KING) at left; LUNA (QUEEN) at right; MERCURY at bottom; VOLATILE ← → FIXED horizontal axis.

But wait a minute. This stage ends with the blackening of the king and the raven's head appearing. These events, surely, point to the advent of the Nigredo! So this stage *must* come before the Albedo. And if it does, so must the next two stages. Obviously the whole Regimen of Sol comes *before* the Regimen of Luna. There's been a mix-up – or, more likely, a deliberate attempt to confuse the would-be alchemists. (Is this what I am?! In a way I am trying to 'dissolve and coagulate' my manuscript as if it were the Prime Matter!)

My theory is confirmed by the second stage: the King and Queen are joined into a single body which rots until it is 'black, blacker than black'. This must be the Nigredo. In so far as the King (Sol) and Queen (Luna) are separate, they are fixed and volatile respectively – that is, the reverse of the previous stage. In so far as they are one body, they are identified with sulphur which remains, blackening, below while the soul, or mercury, flies into the Above. Hence:

SEPARATION

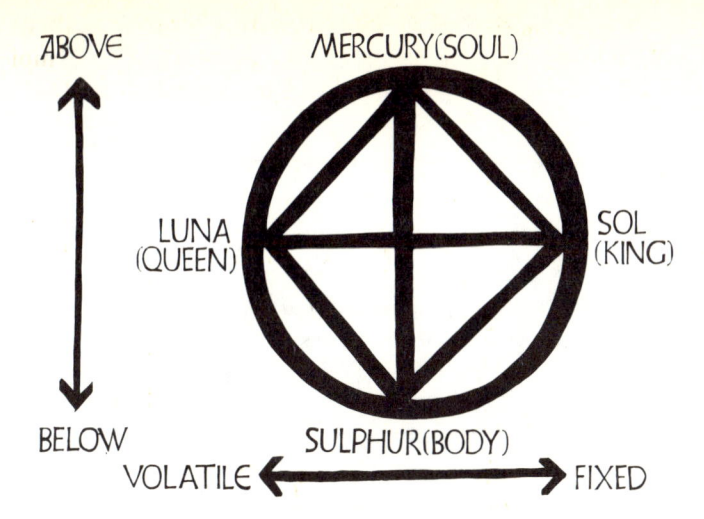

```
ABOVE ↑↓ BELOW
MERCURY (SOUL)
LUNA (QUEEN)        SOL (KING)
SULPHUR (BODY)
VOLATILE ← → FIXED
```

But *wait a minute*. The third stage is *definitely* the Rubedo. It must *come after* the Regimen of Luna – after the Albedo! And yet the Albedo must come after the Nigredo. This is bloody confusing. I'll have to think again.

Through the letter-box today a card headed with the Manor's address:

'Come to tea the day after tomorrow. If you can't, never mind. No reply required. Please bring drink.'

Palpitations. Do I dare go? Do I dare *not* to go? What *time* shall I go?

Come to think of it, that day you didn't come to dinner with Dad and Tanya – it wasn't that you *couldn't*. So what was it?

It was a Saturday and you were in a bolshy mood, watching some bloody sport or other on the box while I got ready. With only half an hour to go, whereas I was all kitted out – hair washed, legs shaved, full warpaint, new dress – you hadn't moved. I stood in front of the telly. Did you remark on how lovely I looked? You looked at me and said: 'I thought he was your *father*, not your . . . tutor.'

I nearly tore your head off. You didn't mean 'tutor', did you? You almost said something else, didn't you? Some obscenity, like 'lover'? Your pause was fatal. I dragged you around that flat, remember?, forcing you to shave, practically stuffing your arms into a clean shirt. I was seething. You were quiet, amused or, more likely, pretending to be. In either case it was intensely infuriating. 'Why all the fuss?' you said. 'I've only been invited to make up numbers. Your Dad's got his bit of fluff and you've got yours.'

I stormed out of the house. It wasn't just the idea of Dad having a 'bit of fluff' – a ludicrous idea as you'd know if you met the formidable Tanya who is severe and beautiful like a ballerina and doing a Ph.D. in medieval French literature – but more the fact that you'd missed the *whole point* of the occasion. What you didn't know was that I had so far deliberately kept you and Dad apart, because, I suppose, he's so daunting if you don't know him. And, of course, he'd ask you about your writing and it would sound so *thin* because, I suppose, it is rather thin, as you yourself admit.

But the point, dear P., is that *you* aren't thin. You are just yourself in the way that Dad is. In the way I'm not. You're your own man (at least, that's the impression you give). And it came to me, with sudden joy, that Dad wouldn't be able to sum you up; nor could he possibly predict how long we'd go on seeing each other! You'd be safe. You'd simply enjoy Dad's brilliance and appreciate him as my other boyfriends couldn't, because they felt threatened. But he couldn't overpower you because the things you know about – the Manichaean heresy, the European Cup-winners' Cup, bloody Kierkegaard – don't interest Dad. Do you see? *That's* why it was important to me that you should have dinner with him and Tanya.

Anyway, I made your excuses. The actual meal was grim. The restaurant in Victoria was new and empty; our voices sounded loud and stilted; the Spanish waiters outnumbered us four to one. Dad was a bit on edge to begin with, a bit snappy with Tanya. She was anxious, of course, but composed. She knows him by now, having been with him much longer than any of the others – about five years, I guess. They're almost like a married couple.

Dad loosened up after a while. He was killingly funny about the political jockeying and backbiting of his fellow dons. He seems quite detached from them. I don't think he's able – even after all this time – to take provincial university life seriously, compared to his old life in Cambridge. We had a good laugh together while Tanya, who isn't on our beam somehow, did the ordering and so on, making sure that Dad had everything.

When he went to the loo, she apologised, as if an apology were needed:

'He doesn't usually go on about his department. It's just that it could be hit by government cuts unless it gets hold of some geneticists. They're flavour of the month. That's why he's a bit hard to please at the moment. But don't worry – I'm sure his job's safe.'

I saw Tanya in a new light. We got talking about her Ph.D. I don't know how Nicholas Flamel came up – I knew nothing about him then – but I remember being curiously stirred by her brief description of his search for the Philosophers' Stone. Not that alchemy has anything directly to do with her studies. She simply came across his story in the course of them and told it to me as part of ordinary conversation. It seems, with hindsight, a significant moment. She told me, in passing, that Flamel's pilgrimage to St James's shrine at Compostela in northern Spain – next to Jerusalem, the most popular pilgrimage of medieval times – could be a kind of allegory or visionary journey because other alchemists (Ramón Lull, for instance) refer to it in a way that suggests it was a code for some magical or spiritual operation rather than a literal journey. I was actually disappointed when Dad returned and we had to turn to less whimsical subjects.

While Dad was hailing a taxi I asked Tanya if I might read her thesis. She laughed. 'It's not finished,' she said, 'and I doubt it will be now – I've hardly touched it for the last two years.' Why not? She laughed again, and shrugged. 'I don't know. Your father's very time-consuming. I sometimes think he can't do up his own shoe-laces without help! It's a wonderful thing to find someone so remarkable, yet so childlike. Besides, my thesis is no great loss to literature.'

They beetled off in a black cab down Ebury Street. I remember thinking how Ma and I had always looked after Dad – I, with devotion; she, with ... something less than that. With resignation perhaps. We were 'his girls'. Now Tanya is his girl. I haven't really thought about our conversation until now. I'd like to talk to her again. I know how she feels about Dad. I know what she means about him not knowing how to tie his own shoe-laces. It seems disloyal to think of it, but isn't it a bit childish of him not to do such things for himself?

*

If only I knew what sulphur and mercury *are*. (But if I knew, would it help?) Jung found himself in deep water when he tried to sort them out. Not only do they differ in meaning from one alchemical text to another, but they also seem to mean different things in different places within a single text!

Sulphur is sometimes gold, sometimes the prima materia of gold; it can be red or white and, as such, the active 'power' of sun and moon respectively. It exudes a corrosive, consuming, diabolical fire and also a gentle, light-bringing warmth. Jung suggests, rather weakly, that sulphur represents the 'motive factor in consciousness', either as the conscious will or as compulsions emanating willy-nilly from the unconscious.

Mercury is worse. But since it is by all accounts *the* key concept in alchemy, it's worth struggling with. It is a 'water' – or, at least, a liquid variously called dew, milk of the virgin, balm, our honey, water of Azoth, etc. It's also *aqua ardens*, a burning water, a corrosive, 'philosophical vinegar', a 'water that does not wet the hands'.

Mercury is also a fire; just as much a fire as sulphur, in fact. It is an invisible fire. It is, in fact, the Secret Fire. If I knew what mercury was I could do the Work in a jiffy.

It's also the *anima* or soul of the matter which, when it flies into the upper part of 'our glass', becomes an airy volatile *spiritus* or spirit, symbolised by the eagle, dove or swan.

I'm convinced that the important Green Lion is not an adjunct to the Work, like an acid, but an integral part of it. It is Mercurius in one of his many guises. Psychologically it represents the overpowering effects which immediately precede or accompany the upsurging of unconscious contents. It's the King's 'animal nature' – the lion is the royal beast – which turns on him and causes uncontrollable emotions. Its greenness does not so much refer to some literally green substance, but to the fact that it's still contaminated with the *viriditas* which characterises the raw state of the prima materia or dragon.

The dragon (serpent, toad, etc.) is a cold-blooded, primitive and reptilian creature which is replaced by the warm-blooded, but still dangerous and predatory, lion as the Opus progresses. They represent stages in the transformation of Mercurius or, as Jung might say, stages in the 'evolution' of unconscious contents as they rise towards the surface of consciousness.

After the Green Lion, bird imagery appears: eagles, crows and, in my case, a raven. The *caput corvi,* or crow's head, signals the onset of Nigredo—

Hold everything. I see where I've been going wrong. I see how the text works. It's so *obvious*. How could I be such an imbecile?

SMITH

Arriving home from a round of those on my Old and Ill list, I was startled to hear laughter in the kitchen. Reflecting that there has been too little laughter in this gloomy pile (it reminded me uncomfortably of Janet) I went to investigate.

A small woman was standing on the kitchen table with her back to me. On top of the flowery dress that came down to her ankles she was wearing, if you please, a surplice whose baggy incongruity betrayed it as one of mine. The woman was intoning in a high nasal voice and making the sign of the cross. Nora was in fits of laughter. Only when she caught sight of me and instantly tried to strangle her giggles did I realise that it was I who was being parodied.

As soon as 'she' turned round I saw that it was a boy. Nora introduced us between gasps of laughter. The little blighter had the nerve to 'bless' me with a condescending wave of his hand. His appearance made me laugh as well, largely out of surprise, for he was wearing cosmetics – not smeared on anyhow as one would expect of a boy who had painted his face as a joke, but meticulously and professionally applied. The effect of this make-up under his cropped schoolboy's hair was of a bizarre gamine, like a rather macabre fairy-tale angel.

My laughter was an obvious relief to Nora; Tim, on the other hand, was completely unabashed. He climbed down from the table and gravely shook my hand while his sister tried to explain that he is fond of dressing-up, that the surplice was her idea (which I doubt) etc. I asked him his age. He is nine and three-quarters. I put it to him that he wanders around the graveyard in a crimson evening-gown and gold earrings. He conceded that the description might fit him. He has his dead mother's wardrobe; he likes to wear it, especially when he is 'paying her a visit'. She is buried in the south-east corner of the graveyard. He speaks in a comical pedantic way: 'I'd be obliged, sir, if you did not tell Gilbert about this episode.' I understood him to mean his father. I agreed not to tell Thomas. Tim seemed gratified; he extended a gracious hand and we shook on it. Why does he dress up as a girl? 'Oh, I think girls are much nicer than boys on the whole.' As if that explained everything . . . !

Last night I thought I saw the Raven's Head. I said to myself, 'At last it is coming – the Nigredo.' I addressed the Spirit aloud: 'Be patient. One long dark night and then you'll rise into the daylight.' My voice sounded oddly. The cellar walls echoed with a dull boom of foreboding. I laughed at my own fancy, and the walls returned my laughter with a hollow ring. For a moment I thought something was loose in the room. I pulled myself together.

God forgive me, but I half-repented of having begun the Opus. I dwelt too long on its thrilling devotional aspects, eager to suffer for the Spirit's sake, as the neophyte dwells on the Passion of Christ, thinking it can be imitated. He overlooks the brute pain of it, the humiliation, the *obscenity* – as I overlooked the imminent necessary obscenity of the Opus, grinding monotonously on, day after day, dragging Sol inexorably down towards that which he cannot bear.

It was not the Raven's Head. Yet I was not altogether mistaken in my detection of change: Separation is beginning. Or rather, I should say, Separation is manifesting itself – because of course it has been going on invisibly all this time. It's a reflection on me rather than on the Opus that I'm not more, shall we say, enthusiastic. I am not myself. My long vigils are taking their toll, or *something* is – I cannot fix my mind on the matter, I cannot, as it were, feel my head from the inside, it's as though it had come loose. The concentration on which I pride myself has deserted me; dark thoughts spurt up into my mind. Hot dark oily thoughts which nauseate. And memories. Dear God, I can't be doing with them. I can't rake over the past again; and yet, it seems, if I do not, the past will submerge and sicken me. I dread the violence of Separation and long for the calm darkness and inertia of Nigredo where all the elements sink down into that blank zero of equilibrium, the empty centre towards which the world falls.

I pray that my soul be fed, as starving Elijah was, in the desert, by an unkindness of ravens.

*

I don't know what I thought. Did I think that Mercurius was some quaint impish little spirit to be kept like a specimen in a glass pot? Small my Egg may be, but it constrains Heaven and Earth. Like Blake's grain of sand it holds the universe;* like the mustard seed it is a potential Kingdom of Heaven. For the truth is, *the part* – no matter how small – contains *the whole*. If the Spirit is present, it is present in its entirety. And God help me, it is present.

I can't prevent myself from obsessively checking and rechecking the seal, the temperature, the glass. I feel so helpless. When I first shut up the dragon in its glass prison, I thought only of how the blessed Stone would form itself out of our Chaos. I did not think of its *power*. One does not play with fire; one cannot even countenance the Secret Fire of the Philosophers. If it is imprisoned, it is no more imprisoned than a wild ravening beast before whose bars one stands aghast in dreadful fascination, wanting to run yet rooted to the ground, unable to meet the sulphurous green fire of its eyes below the burning halo of mane. As it moves around its cell it is I who feels the coldness of iron closing me in.

At noon I returned to my study. I sat at my desk, wishing for sleep. My eyes itched from sleepless staring but had somehow jammed open. Nora brought food I couldn't stomach. I saw my face reflected in her appalled expression. It was a dash of cold water. She is a dear girl; a daughter could not be more solicitous. I agreed to drink some tea and change my clothes which were damp with perspiration. At last I slept where I sat, plunging immediately into profound dreams – of palpable darkness and its fire-breathing denizens. I jerked awake and hurried down to my laboratory. I could not look into the pelican where Sol is being drawn and quartered. I simply satisfied myself that the seal was intact.

When the sun shines after a small rain, and God smiles on the world, it's easy to vow that you will pursue the Devil to the ends of the earth and depths of the sea. But when he is finally cornered and the lance is raised to pierce his plated hide, and his great leathery

---

* Not quite. 'To be a World in a grain of Sand/And a Heaven in a Wild Flower' were William Blake's actual words (see 'Auguries of Innocence', *c.* 1803).

wings are folded over his face, what if he suddenly draws them back and slides towards you with a cold mocking smile?

I went to Cornwall and stayed by the sea. I barely left the rooms I had rented except to stalk the cliffs and howl into the squalls of wind and rain. I wrote long letters.

I had come to see that of course Annabelle was not *ordinary*. She was merely unawakened. The girl I had seen that first time, in the drawing-room behind the teacups, was the true, the extraordinary Being whose very virtue lay in being unaware of her innocence and loveliness. How I despised my own superficial talents, my lack of virtue, my *unworthiness*. At what length I detailed this to Annabelle.

And yet I told her, too, of the high hopes I had always nurtured for myself – how, despite my unworthiness, or even because of it, I felt called to some higher Destiny. I did not mention the Great Work, preferring only to compare myself favourably with the reprobate Francis of Assisi.

She wrote back in her slow rounded childish hand. She 'understood'. She thought I could not be 'as bad as all that'. She had always liked St Francis for his kindness to animals. She recounted some little event or other at the hospital which had made her think of me.

I wrote longer letters, reviling myself. I explained how our love was doomed, how my congenital melancholy, my dissatisfaction with myself and the world, could bring her nothing but unhappiness. I slashed at the writing-paper, pouring out turgid analyses of love. I wrote of Proust, and the frailty and self-deception of love which, after its first brief fever, turns into the long disease for which there is no remedy in this world. She thanked me for my 'amusing' letter. I explained how the first moment of love is the greatest and, in a brilliant analogy, compared it to death in the Tibetan *Book of the Dead* where the initial illumination of White Light is succeeded by a deadening progression through remorse and judgement and tribunals of bird-headed gods, all the way back down to another murky incarnation on the lowest plane of existence – Earth. I blamed my own imperfection, my immaturity, my need to become more worthy of her, my uncertainty about the truth of my feelings, the impurity of my love.

I received no letter from her for three days. I broke on the rock of her silence. In a flat panic I raced back and proposed marriage to her. She took a little step forward and said with the utmost simplicity: 'Yes. I will marry you.'

De Elixir Vitae

As soon as I heard the legend of Wei Po-yang,[5] I knew that Chinese Philosophy had a special grasp of the Philosophers' Stone as panacea, universal medicine, Elixir of Life. In fact I know nothing of the Chinese Art except a few anecdotes my master sometimes recounted during some tedious period of digestion [i.e. of the alchemical matter]. He reckoned the Chinese a highly spiritual race who were never much interested in gold-making as so many debased occidental chemists were. (Was it because gold was not a currency in China?)

In the course of his travels my master learnt a great deal, he told me, from a Chinese adept he came across in Smyrna. He grew a second set of adult teeth as a result of taking the 'lesser Divine Elixir' compounded by this sage. They briefly studied together the composition of the Cinnabar Pill which confers immortality. He told me how, ironically, the search for this Pill, their Elixir, was responsible for the deaths of a great many Chinese Philosophers and their disciples – for ingestion of actual cinnabar [mercuric sulphide] causes painful poisoning. In the ninth century six emperors were killed by so-called elixirs which they took to attain immortality. This unfortunate sequence of events probably contributed to the decline of true Philosophy in China at that time, and to its transmutation into a decadent 'physiological chemistry' of the Yoga variety.

However, without doubt our Stone can bring the body of man or woman to incorruptible perfection as easily as it can change base metals to that pure Gold which cannot be found in Nature.

A sad bitter day. Being unfit for active service because my head was full of fire and solvents and serpents I allowed myself the luxury of a visit to Robert. As I walked up his rutted lane I could see a small person standing by one of the chapel windows. Although I could only see him from behind, the grey flannel shorts, blazer, beige socks and brown shoes were unmistakably those of Tim's school uniform. There was something about the boy's frozen stance that made me think he was eavesdropping; and I was furious that Robert's kindness and patience should be thus rewarded.

Hearing me approach he broke his statuesque pose and looked around. I expected his face to bear traces of guilt but there was only the usual powder and lipstick and, beneath these, an expression so stricken that I was immediately shorn of anger. Above the pink chiffon scarf which he wore in place of a tie, the little made-up face was clenched around staring eyes. His ears were bright red above the diamanté earrings.

Before I could speak he seized my hand and began to pull me away from the chapel. I asked him what the matter was. He shook his head violently and pressed his finger to his lips. I gently disentangled his hand and tiptoed guiltily to the window.

Janet sat on a straight-backed chair. Tears were drying on her cheeks. She looked tired out by a kind of total exhaustion: her body was drained of life; her face, empty of any animation, looked old. Robert was kneeling at her feet. His hands gripped her hands where they lay indifferently in her lap. He was still crying, soundlessly, without facial contortions – huge teardrops simply flowing from his intensely dark eyes. He spoke too low for me to make out what he was saying but the tone was imploring, pitiful. There was terrible devotion in his abject prayer-like position. His voice rose suddenly, repeating the same hypnotic monosyllable:

'*Please . . . Please . . .*' Janet shivered from head to toe. She shook her head wearily, turning it in my direction. I had no time to duck away; I was rooted to the spot in front of this small, almost silent cameo which seemed timeless, more vivid than life, as if impressed on the canvas of the world in the brilliant raw pigments of a medieval painting. My heart seized up as her eyes came level with mine; but she no more saw me than if the window had been a wall. She was oblivious, sealed off within a trembling film of pain and hopelessness.

Tim and I walked in silence down the lane. Surprisingly, he took my hand. Hard to say who was the more comforted. After a while he said: 'Best not to mention this on the whole.' He was crestfallen at his hero's obvious ignominy. Not trusting myself to speak I nodded agreement, hoping he had not noticed my burning face. Of *course* it was Robert. All along it had been *Robert*. Who else would it be?

'Why were they crying?'

I wasn't certain how to answer the boy. I remembered with angry shame how I had wanted to introduce them to each other, like a foolish old pander, when all along... Why had neither of them trusted me enough to tell me? Perhaps Janet had tried. But Robert – Robert had stood mutely by while I described his lover to him. I could not suppress an obscene little pang of pleasure that Janet was now spurning him. It quickly passed; more than anything I was sad that I had been instrumental, however correctly, in dampening Janet's ardour at least.

'I think they are in love,' I said.

'Oh, *love*,' said Tim airily and with some embarrassment. Then, after a pensive pause, 'So it's not all kissing and that.'

'No,' I agreed. 'It's not.' He removed his hand and walked nearer the hedgerow, scrutinising it.

'Robert was my best friend.'

'Well, I should think he's going to need his friends more than ever,' I replied. Yet the past tense was appropriate. Tim realised before I had that our relations with Robert would undergo – had already undergone – a radical change. We might still be friends, but not with the same Robert. *Why* had he interfered in Janet's marriage? Why could he not leave well alone?

'Was *she* your friend?' he asked.

'Yes. She was.' I knew I would never have the old Janet back. How could she forgive me for refusing my assent to her affair? For being a party to that ghastly scene? It was difficult for me too at that moment to forgive *her* for laying herself open to Mrs B.'s insinuations. How sordid her liaison would have become in Mrs B.'s version of it – but how *base* of me to see the matter in this light. I disgust myself. Neither Janet nor Robert would *ever* cheapen themselves. If anything their mutual love *proves* it. What would they have cared if scandalmongers had made a meal of them?

'I'll be your friend,' said Tim casually. 'If you like.'

'And I'll be yours. If *you* like.'

'Do you have any medals?'

'Not proper ones, for bravery, like Robert's.'

'And you don't make glass or anything, I suppose?'

'I'm afraid not.'

He sighed. 'Nora says you just read books. And write things.'
'Yes.'
'Nora says you're nice though.'
'I'm glad.'
'I'll just have to make do with you, then. What things do you write?'
'Oh, just what happens to me. That sort of thing.'
'Will you write about what happened today?'
'Do you think I should?'
He thought for a while. 'Yes, you should. As long as you keep it private. Will you write about me as well?'
'Yes, I probably will.'
'*What* will you write about me?'
'How you look. What you say. That's all.'

He seemed to brighten up a bit. He ran to a nearby gate, clambered over and, dipping his handkerchief in a horse trough, began scrubbing at his face. 'Gilbert doesn't like all this,' he said cheerfully, pointing to the discoloured cloth. 'He whacks me if he catches me at it. Thinks I'm a cissy. *I* don't care.' He returned to my side, neatly unclipping his earrings. 'See? I can be a boy if I want to.' He laughed. '"Uneasy lies the head that wears a throne."'

'Shouldn't it be "crown"?' I suggested.

'That's the joke. "Throne" is funny. It's from *1066 and All That*.' I was puzzled. 'Haven't you read it? It makes history funny. I should have thought you'd have read it,' he reproached me.

'Sorry. But why did you quote from it just then?' He looked at me as if I were retarded.

'I wanted to say something memorable, of course. For you to write down.'

'I say the Green Lion who in truth is the Babylonian Dragon, killing all things with his poison.'[6]

Philalethes is right, as usual. However, although he here tells us that the lion and the dragon are the same *in kind*, he omits to say that they are not the same *in degree*. No one who has witnessed the slow poisonous dissolution of the dragon's creeping self-slaughter can think that any death is worse – until he sees the green lion clawing the soul from the body of the King [i.e. Sol].

*

She took a little step forward and said: 'Yes. I will marry you.' I was so resigned to a rebuff that I was devastated, even a little nettled, that she had accepted my proposal as natural, as inevitable – as if my agony had been simply the thrashing of a man hopelessly enmired in her quicksand. Above all, I was filled with an enormous sense of relief that it was all over.

The following day the feeling I have always identified with homesickness, and which her acceptance had instantly assuaged, returned. I knew at once that I must go back to Paris and devote my days and nights to the service of my master and his Work in order to purge myself in that ordeal by fire and so become worthy of her love. Annabelle was crestfallen. Her lovely eyes were blind to my faults and inadequacies. However, I hinted at the vow I'd taken – a private one, but as binding as any other – and I asked her to put her faith in me and our love. The Work – I could not specify it, of course – would not perhaps take too long, and then we could be married. She agreed at once, or as soon as she saw the seriousness of my intent. She told me that she had loved me from the first because she saw that I was marked out for some spiritual purpose. She had never wanted to obstruct this, only to share it.

My master was much changed. He seemed older and slower. He took such a long time to get anything done. He did not once show any interest in my absence or question me about the shattering developments in my life. He barely paid me the slightest attention for days at a time. He did not answer my reproaches for not replying to my letters. He took no notice of my suggestions for the advancement of our Opus. All the things which had formerly intrigued me about him were now simply irritating. He seemed to make no progress with the Work – the operations which had thrilled me with their mystery and promise of occult knowledge were really only the confused and futile potterings of a misguided old man.

It was like waking from a deep chemically induced sleep. I saw with sudden clarity where my true path lay – not in obscure esoteric ramblings but in the fresh air of hard work and clearly defined duty. I thought of my vision on the school playing-fields and saw that the way to realise it was not in some self-indulgent heterodoxy but in good clean Christianity. For me the hard thing was to knuckle down to discipline, to give up fancy notions of spectacular transmutations, to lead an outwardly dull and unrecognised life attempting to be *good* and, failing that, at least exercising virtues in the hope that, over the years, they would become instinctive. This was the strait gate through which I'd enter the Kingdom.

I relayed this to Annabelle and enrolled in a theological college in the north of England. It was the only one which would take me at short notice, but I was secretly pleased that it placed me far away from my fiancée. I did not love her less. Quite the reverse. But her presence never failed to arouse me to such a pitch of desire that I shook for a day after seeing her. I wrote to her of her distracting influence at a time when all my energies had to be placed at the disposal of God and my studies. The darling understood, as always. I saw her in vacations, of course, when I was not on retreat or cramming for exams. The time before ordination would pass so quickly and then my new life with her could begin. Or so I thought.

Today I noticed how no one, with a single exception, shook my hand after matins. This is partly because, in spite of my efforts to be friendly and useful, I have so far failed to establish myself with my congregation. Partly, too, though it pains me to say it, they take their lead from Caldwell. None of them would admit that he has any special standing in the village. But he has. Not so much because he has money or owns the Manor but because he is a forceful character. Above all, perhaps, he has cast himself in the role of Squire and the people are glad to acknowledge him as such.

He resents my middle-class upbringing and my education. He suspects that I'm going to try and put one over on him from the pulpit. I know this by the way he tried at first to enlist me on his side. We did a lot of handshaking then. He even made jokes about my sermons to show he had been listening. But there was a veiled threat in the jokes, too. He wants a nice quiet compliant vicar – which, to my shame, I have been. My opposition to him over Nightingale Wood has merely unearthed a more fundamental opposition. Certainly we fear each other. I fear him for obvious reasons; he fears me – I've seen it in his eyes – for reasons which neither of us, I suspect, can articulate. He has a natural contempt for the clergy, a distaste for anything that smacks of the intellectual; but neither are cause for fear. I think it's to do with the materialist's latent fear of the supernatural. For the brief period that I'm in the pulpit, he is powerless. At any second I could be seized by the Holy Ghost and, instead of mouthing banalities and platitudes, I might be suddenly tongued with fire fit to drive the crying congregation to their knees. As it is, he gives me a curt nod as I stand outside the church with all the dignity and presence of the doorpost.

Out-of-sorts Simmons has got the idea. He ferrets past me, his shifty eyes avoiding mine. Mrs B. simply sails past like the carved figurehead of a galleon. They both hurry to catch Caldwell and engage him in what they are pleased to call conversation.

It is Lydia Simmons who offers me a birdlike claw and thanks me for the service. I thank her for her organ-playing. (Actually it is a harmonium, electrically bellowed, which she plays in an untutored but occasionally very moving way.) Her pale eyelashes give her a myopic look; but her eyes, as I realise for the first time, are sharp. We watch her husband and sister perform their mincing curtseying little mating-dance around Caldwell who expands fatly, his self-congratulatory gestures fanning outwards like a peacock's tail. She sees me thinking that the two of them are more like a married couple than she and Simmons; she sees that I am sorry for her just as I see that she is sorry for me, having to put a good face on the snubs I receive. I touch her shoulder lightly to distract her from a sight that is painful to both of us, and I feel bone not flesh. She also understands from my touch that she has no need to feel sorry for me; that I have other resources (as perhaps she has) which disqualify me as an object of pity. We humans are so wonderful – so complex and quick that all this, and more, can pass between two of them in a flash, so subtle that it passes undetected by anyone else.

I went in for my lunch with a lighter heart, blessing Mrs Simmons whom, as far as I can see, no one loves except at this moment myself – and she the easiest person in the world to love because of her soul's magnitude.

Beard's Pool is a rum place. Once upon a time some minor glacial action must have gouged a sheer-sided hole, corrie-like, out of the landscape which filled with water. It is larger than a pond but smaller than a lake, and reputed to be extraordinarily deep. Trees and scrub grow right up to the edge where there is a straight drop of about four feet to the still, dark water. This vertical slippery perimeter is supposed to have prevented Sir Gregory Beard from scrambling out when he changed his mind about drowning himself. He was Lord of the Manor some 250 years ago and he threw himself into the pool in a fit of despair after heavy gaming losses, so they say.

The path which leads down to Beard's Pool forks to the left off the track which leads up to Nightingale Wood. I had never taken it before, probably because it leads on to Caldwell's land. Today, however, Robert was standing at the fork with his angling gear. He had seen me toiling up the hill from the village and had waited for me. He was smiling what seemed to me a false smile, perhaps because his smile is so rare. I shocked myself with the sudden rush of aversion I felt towards the man. I did not want any company, let alone his.

'I take it you're not too busy, padre? Care to take a stroll down to the pool?' I did not care to; but strangely I felt deprived of all volition and found myself being shepherded down the path to Beard's Pool. Whereas for so long I had done the talking while Robert remained largely silent, our roles were now reversed:

'I haven't seen you for a long time, padre. Have you been under the weather? You look a bit peaky. Nora looking after you all right? My place hasn't been the same since she stopped coming to clean up. I miss that little devil Tim as well. I suppose he's caught up in life at school and so on. That'll put a stop to his antics – a chap can't go on wearing women's dresses all his life; although, come to think of it, there *was* a fellow in my regiment . . . but never mind that. Anyway, I thought that since it's a fine day my work could go to the Devil. Not that I've been up to much recently. I've had one or two ideas on the glass front but I can't seem to drum up the enthusiasm these days . . . trouble concentrating or something. Glad I ran into you actually. Been a long time since we had a chat . . . '

I did not want a chat. The one subject lay between us like a barbed fence. I have thought more about Robert in the last week or two than I care to admit. Perhaps I should say that he has cropped up in my thoughts. I see those awful tears plopping out of his eyes, and the twin scars very white on his clenched jaw. Every time I try to feel sorry for him or wonder whether I should visit him, I make excuses, telling myself that it would be an intrusion on his grief or that it would look as though I were exerting spiritual pressure on him – taking advantage of his sorrow to make a convert, like some brutal evangelist.

The pool is an enclosed, oppressive spot. The silence is not a tranquil one. It is somehow ominous as if at any moment it could be broken by the sound of old Sir Gregory's fingers scrabbling impotently at the smooth bank. Robert settled himself in a break in the surrounding undergrowth and prepared his rod. He had stopped his chatter and was sunk in a despondent silence. With an effort I asked him what he hoped to catch.

'Pike,' he said at last. 'There's a great bastard of a pike in this pool that's eaten practically everything else in the water. It's been here just about for ever, and I'm going to . . . get it.' His voice rose in pitch alarmingly on the last words and he turned his head away. The idea that he might be blubbering again was deeply perturbing. I wondered if I could decently slip away. However, when he spoke again his voice was once more under control:

'Sorry, padre. I don't know what's come over me lately. I'm all in . . . *pieces*. It's just that . . . I was wondering if you might have a word with Janet. I know you've spoken before . . . I know she *listens* to you. You see, we are each other's last chance for any sort of, well, happiness. You must know her marriage is over . . . effectively. I wouldn't normally ask. It's just that, well, I love her so bloody much.'

Poor old Robert. It was obvious that Janet had not told him *what* exactly I'd said to her. If it had not been so distressing, it would have been almost laughable that he should try to enlist me to intercede for him.

I didn't know what to say. My head was aching so hard that I was dizzy. His *atheism* angered me. He just does not see the importance of certain things because he is completely without the category 'in the eyes of God'. Maybe he has some intuition that this is what sets Janet and me apart from him. Maybe that's why he instinctively seeks my help. But the idea, deeply distasteful to me, that I should act the pimp and persuade Janet to do something with which I strongly disagree – the idea's preposterous. He should *never have allowed* Janet to become so attached to him. He knows, for God's sake – he must know – that he is attractive to women. The trick is to avoid pitfalls and temptations. My own clerical garb incites certain sorts of women – yes, even married ones – to protestations and endearments which it has not always been easy to nip in the bud. But it *must* be done, and with the ruthless speed of a surgeon's scalpel. It makes me ill to hear him indulge in talk of 'love'. I had always thought of him as so splendidly aloof and self-sufficient, so far above the grubbiness of an illicit affair. I've *tried* to see his *amour* in a good light, to find some compassion for him, but when I think of those demeaning tears, the sheer selfishness of his affection which doesn't care what it destroys as long as he is gratified, I feel only disgust.

Since I couldn't marshal my thoughts sufficiently to say anything rational or useful to him without revealing the contempt which, God knows, I don't *wish* to feel but rises up unbidden in me like bile, I simply mumbled and shook my head vehemently and (because I knew it was wrong to leave him in this way) patted his shoulder – and sloped cravenly off.

I stood up a moment ago to fetch the *Tractatus Aureus* from my shelves,* when I chanced to see Nora loitering at the gate with Bradley Caldwell.

The sight of that youth puts all thought of work out of my head. It's hard enough to concentrate as it is with my mouth all dry and my skin all scratchy and my thoughts all scattered around my mind like broken glass – it's well-nigh impossible with him hanging around my front gate.

They've been talking now for more than five minutes. What can they possibly find to say to each other? Nora leans on the gate. She looks composed enough. The top half of her body is bent slightly back, the bottom half thrust slightly forward. Caldwell jun. has his hands in his pockets and slouches to and fro in front of her, scuffing the ground with his shoe, shooting glances in her direction as he talks but never looking at her steadily.

She says little. Her eyes comb the sky, the hills, the church

---

* *The Golden Tract of Hermes, concerning the Physical Secret of the Philosophers' Stone* is another alchemical classic of great antiquity. Its anonymous author ascribed it to Hermes Trismegistus. Often praised for expounding (like Smith's manuscript) the whole Art, it can be found in *Ars Chemica* (Strasbourg, 1566). An excellent, if idiosyncratic translation of it exists in Mary Anne Atwood's *Suggestive Inquiry* (op. cit., p. 435).

tower. She doesn't seem interested in what he's saying yet she makes no move to come in – she has even put her shopping basket down at her feet. She swivels her head and looks at me directly. Can she see me through the glass, watching her? I feel like a peeping Tom, which is *ridiculous*. She takes off her headscarf, shakes out that damned hair of hers which shines in the sunlight. Bradley looks at it. There's something about that boy I can't abide, something about his movements that grates on my nerves, something about the very smoothness of his olivey complexion and his red lips. I can't have him hanging around here, looking at Nora like a wolf. He's young, I know – only nineteen – but he already has considerable experience of callousness. Nora would be appalled if she knew about Jenny Stebbins. She sees no harm in anyone; she thinks Caldwell is the same little boy who, she told me, followed her around at primary school. Well, he has no doubt been brutalised by public school since then, and by worse.

He puts an almost proprietorial hand on the gate. He leans towards her. He is fashionably dressed as always, his glossy dark hair comes down to his ears giving him a rakish Bohemian look. She throws her head back and laughs – and again glances in my direction. I raise a hand in greeting. I will not be thought of as spying on her. Either she does not see it or she chooses to ignore it. I refuse to feel slighted. I turn my attention to the neutral view of the graveyard in front of me. His languid *predatory* gestures do more than disturb me. They frighten me. I'm frightened for Nora. She doesn't know what she's doing adopting those womanly poses. Caldwell isn't the childish acquaintance he was; he is not innocent. How can I warn her that her goodwill, her very *purity*, could be her undoing – without destroying those very virtues? How can I keep that insolent youth away from here?

Separation is almost complete, I'm sure of it. It is profoundly disturbing to see with what ferocity the green lion dismembers the dying King. To watch the inexorable agonising division of his sulphurous body from his mercurial soul is to experience a kind of dumbstruck paralysis of the will, while thought and feeling – they grow harder to distinguish – run amok.

*

SEPARATION

As the King sinks down, Queen Luna rises out of our sea like his reflection. Our sulphur, like the King of the beasts, holds sway above. Our mercury, dark as the blood of Sol, rules below.

9 a.m.: the Raven's Head appears! Nourished by the King's carrion, black as the new moon, it broods over our matter. *Success.* Yet here begins the black tunnel of Nigredo in which many lose their way and not a few perish. Lord of Heaven and Earth, guide me, protect me, have mercy on my soul.

EILEEN

The Regimen of Luna and the Regimen of Sol *are not consecutive, but alternating*. The first stage of Luna is followed by the first stage of Sol, followed by the second stage of Luna, and so on. That must be right. Just as every 'solve' implies a 'coagula', every separation a conjunction, so the two Regimens go on simultaneously.

Here is the diagram of the Magnum Opus. There are six stages, three from each Regimen, but seven if you count the preparatory Calcination and eight if you count the last irrepresentable stage – the production of the Philosophers' Stone.

Since the Opus is in reality a continuous, dynamic process, the diagrams can only roughly represent the state of affairs at the *completion* of each stage. Lastly, it also occurs to me that the first five stages at least correspond to those in Sir George Ripley's *Twelve Gates*,[7] so I've labelled them accordingly:

SEPARATION 171

(CALCINATION)
↓
SOLUTION

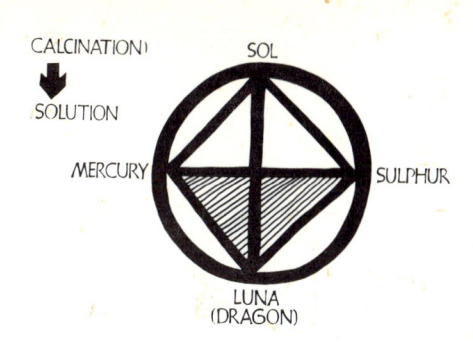

SOL
MERCURY — SULPHUR
LUNA
(DRAGON)

6. (SUBLIMATION)
(PHILOSOPHERS' STONE)
↑
SULPHUR
SOL — LUNA
MERCURY

← WHITE STONE

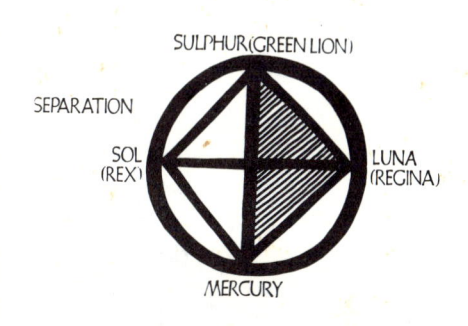

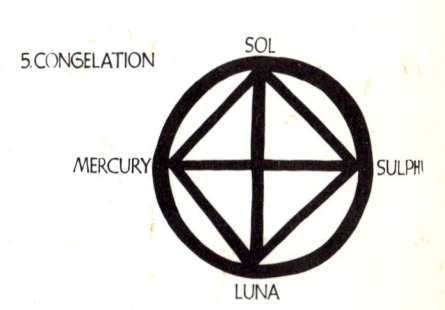

SEPARATION

SULPHUR (GREEN LION)
SOL (REX) — LUNA (REGINA)
MERCURY

5. CONGELATION
SOL
MERCURY — SULPH(UR)
LUNA

← PEACOCK'S T.

(RA)VEN'S HEAD →

(CO)NJUNCTION
LUNA
SULPHUR — MERCURY
SOL

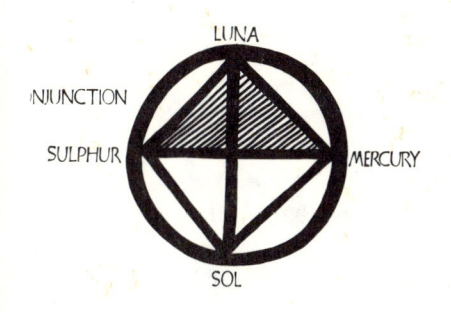

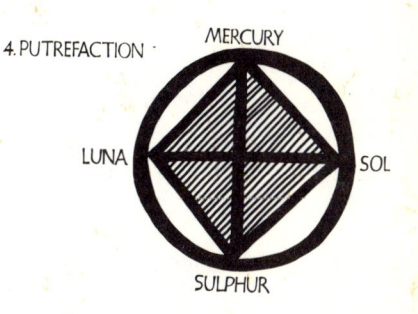

4. PUTREFACTION
MERCURY
LUNA — SOL
SULPHUR

Suddenly it's possible to see the wider meaning of the alchemist's 'circulations'. Each stage comprises many solutions and coagulations by the circular process of reflux distillation; but each stage also represents an anticlockwise turn through 90 degrees in the larger 'wheel of Alchemy'.

At every turn, the two pairs of opposite elements – both chemical and psychological – change in relation to each other, being either separated or joined. The odd stages, 1, 3 and 5, are primarily concerned with the separation and conjunction of Sol and Luna, Above and Below; the even stages, 2, 4 and 6, are mainly to do with mercury and sulphur – making the volatile fixed and the fixed volatile. However, both processes are carried out simultaneously and continuously with each other.

In Solution, the division between Sol and Luna out of their undifferentiated unity in the Prime Matter, or dragon, enacts the separation of consciousness from the unconscious. Sol's return to the Below, through the process of reflux distillation, initiates the further division of the Prime Matter into mercury and sulphur – the volatile and fixed, spiritual and physical, aspects of the psyche. At the same time Luna moves up to the threshold of consciousness while Sol sinks towards the unconscious, displaced from his ruling position in consciousness by the fiery bodily effects of the sulphurous Green Lion. (Sol and Rex are more or less synonymous; Jung suggests that whereas Sol represents consciousness, Rex stands for its 'dominant', e.g. a set of traditional moral principles.) As the four elements of the personality are thrust apart, it experiences a conflict of opposites which, at their extremity, begin to move towards reunion. This moment is marked by a blackening of the matter, called the raven's head. It is the beginning of the Nigredo.

It's not possible, I now realise, to correlate the Nigredo with any one stage of the Opus. It begins at the end of Separation and ends with the completion of Putrefaction – that 'darkness of purgatorie withouten lights', as Ripley describes it. Its central point is the Conjunction, that strange illicit funereal coupling of King and Queen. Perhaps, paradoxically, the Albedo begins at that same moment, as the seed of the White Stone is sown and left to germinate in the dark. In that case, the Nigredo overlaps with the Albedo which comes manifestly into its own at the beginning of Congelation when by the curious phenomenon Jung called enantiodromia – the changing of one thing at its farthest extreme into its opposite – the profoundest blackness blooms with the first pale flecks that herald the whiteness.

This process has an interesting parallel in the author's use of bird imagery: the raven's head is transformed into the peacock's tail – the sign that the adept's mystical totality is approaching, as the multiple colours are unified in the purity of white light. Between these two events, during Conjunction, Luna is pictured as rising up into the Above where she 'spreads her wings as black as the raven's' and eclipses Sol. The image is one of increasing volatilising of the matter, which is at the same time becoming blacker, as the raven emerges head first, struggles free, spreads its wings and finally shows its tail which, surprisingly, is that of a peacock.

The incestuous copulation of Rex and Regina at Conjunction is either accompanied, or immediately followed, by their death. This is the near-extinction of consciousness in the unconscious, the overwhelming of the 'I' by the dark negative aspects of the anima, symbolised by Luna, the 'baleful new moon' who is still hedged about by her dangerous dragon attributes.

In Putrefaction, the single 'body' of Rex and Regina is left to rot. It is represented by sulphur which sinks into decay Below, as mercury, its soul, is separated out and rises into the Above. (Jung says: 'it is not the adept who suffers all this, rather *it* suffers in him' – 'it' being 'our matter', the mysterious Secret Fire – ' . . . *it* is tortured, *it* passes through death and rises again. All this happens not to the alchemist himself but to the "true man", i.e. the "true inner self", who he feels is near him and in him and at the same time in the retort . . . ')

This state seems to correspond to what tribal societies call 'loss of soul' – a profound dislocation of psychic and physical life, which may also be a period of gestation as the impact of overpowering unconscious contents is absorbed. At any rate, at its lowest point, when the matter achieves a 'black, blacker than black', the work begins to turn: the body's putrefying becomes the purifying process of Congelation, the fifth stage of the Opus.

Here the body is washed of its dross and impurity by the distillatory action of that very mercury (now identified with 'Luna's tears') whose loss initiated the decay in the first place. As the body is thus prepared for the soul's return, the first signs of whiteness appear, often as bright flecks. Jung identifies these with 'soul-sparks' or 'multiple luminosities of the unconscious' which express the paradoxical fact of the unconscious having consciousness, like secondary or multiple personalities. These merge and expand to form the peacock's tail, which presages the emergence of the unconscious anima, symbolised by the full moon or star, into the light of consciousness. The adept's dark feminine side, glimmering in unconscious night, has been raised up from Below like the soul of the metals and unified with the Above to form 'Heaven'.

According to Jung, many alchemists accounted this stage the end of the Work – he himself finds such strong images of union indistinguishable from images of the Self. However, my text, like many others, goes on to another sixth stage which I've called Sublimation. It corresponds on its own to the Rubedo, which culminates in the marriage of Congelation's 'Heaven' to 'Earth' – a union of which I can't imagine a psychological equivalent.

'Well,' says Brendan, 'beam me up, Scotty, if it isn't little Eileen.' I pointed out that I was at least three inches taller than he. 'I may be small,' he said with dignity. 'But I'm beautifully marked. Plus, I have many of my own teeth.' He smiled hideously to demonstrate the fact. There was a large gap where his upper right molars should be. I suggested sternly that he might have more customers – the bar was empty – if he were less familiar with them. He loves to be teased.

'You're gorgeous when you're cross, did you know that? I knew an Eileen once, all legs and red hair, the toast of Ballinskelligs. She was so lovely, poets killed themselves for love of her. I even gave myself a Chinese burn. Let's get down to serious business now.' He stood back and, striking an attitude, gestured negligently towards his attire. 'What do you think? Marks out of ten, please.'

I awarded him a harsh six for Colour Co-ordination. He was so indignant that I had to give him a generous nine for Style. He gave himself a punitive ten for General Gorgeousness. 'Shall I tell you the secret of my personal confidence?' he asked rhetorically. 'It comes from the knowledge that *there's not a stitch of unnatural fibre on my body*.' He stared meaningly at the 20% Terylene in my shirt.

He poured me another drink. I tried to pay for the first two I'd had, but he waved my money away – 'Ah God, we'll not kill ourselves for a bob or two' – and leant towards me confidentially.

'Have you come across yer Man?' he whispered.

'Who?'

'Yer Man up there at the Vicarage?'

'Who?'

'*Who*? Only the Black Vicar, that's who.' He was rather put out when I told him it was too late to scare me, and impressed when I told him his Black Vicar had worshipped the Devil.

'Is that a fact? Well, pluck me eyebrows, I hear a lot of things behind this bar, but I never heard that one. I only heard he was up to no good and the top man for haunting little girls like yourself.' I begged him, of course, to keep his ears open for any more titbits concerning the 'Black Vicar'. He tapped his nose.

The Secret... If the secret were the actual substance, or substances, used, it would have leaked out by now, wouldn't it? Couldn't it be like the secret of the ancient Greek Eleusinian Mysteries whose participants swore not to betray the 'secret'? The oath was a sort of formality, surely, because all the aristocrats of the time underwent initiation so the secret must have been an 'open' secret. (On the other hand, no account of the secret has come down to us.)

In the same way the alchemical secret, like the secrets of all magical or 'Secret' Societies, was designed to produce that effect which every child who has a secret knows – the effect of *inner pressure*. Because it is forbidden to tell, it works on the mind, exciting it and stimulating it to creative effort. The discipline of secrecy speeds up the pulse-rate and concentrates the mind, enhancing learning, and, above all, attention. This is why the tribal lore taught to circumcision candidates at their puberty rites is secret. In fact, certain of the so-called secrets they're taught are perfectly well known, for example, to the women of the tribe, who nevertheless pretend not to know them. Often a secret may not be worth keeping but just because it *is* secret it has its effect – specifically it activates the deeper layers of the psyche where 'secret' contents – secret because they are as yet unknown – seize upon the opportunity offered by a receptive, attentive consciousness to manifest themselves.

*

I was far from sober by the time I left Brendan. A drink at lunchtime is worth two in the evening, as the old Irish saying goes. I felt better than I have for a long time, and more importantly, I felt calm – calm enough to take tea with Mrs Z. Back at the house I topped myself up a bit with a can of lager or so, just to maintain the right level of calmness, and at 4.15 p.m. – the time I'd decided was about right – I set off for the Manor with a litre of plonk. In a fit of honesty, I also brought the manuscript. Best to come clean. (But I have copied it out in case Mrs Z. should want to keep it.)

The front door was open. As usual it seems. I felt calm. I went in and called out. Mrs Z. replied faintly from the drawing-room.

Although it was not yet dark, the curtains were drawn. The only light came from the fire and from two dim table-lamps, an arrangement which struck me as deliberate. It left Mrs Zetterberg, who was reclining on the sofa, in shadow. A note of trepidation sounded in me as I approached her, but I quickly calmed myself.

She had assumed an air of faded elegance for the occasion. Her long legs were outlined, as if joined, beneath an old-fashioned dress of silk-satin. It was of an indeterminate dark colour and gleamed in the firelight like the pelt of some aquatic creature. For a moment, as I moved nearer, her disturbing eyes had the watchful, glossy, near-human sheen of a seal's eyes. Then, for the first time, I noticed how tired she looked, now scraggy her neck was, as though she had abruptly lost the flesh from under the skin.

She pushed out her bottom lip in what might have been a greeting, and graciously indicated the armchair, close to the sofa, where I was to sit. On a small table between us there were two tumblers, two expensive-looking pastries on a plate, and no sign of any tea. Her right hand was hidden behind a cushion. As she drew it out my heart gave a frightful lurch. She seemed capable of producing any of a number of terrible objects.

She pulled out a corkscrew and tossed it over to me. It's impossible to describe the freaky aura of danger which surrounds her or which she barely contains, like a wild animal coiled to spring at you out of her skin. You tend to forget it or think you've imagined it when she's no longer present. I even forgot it from moment to moment as I was talking to her: she seems to withdraw, to lull you into a sense of security and, in doing so, to draw you out. Before I'd finished opening the bottle I found myself talking freely about myself, telling her much more than I intended, as if I were desperate to interest and please her and keep her contained. She seemed completely absorbed in, and sympathetic to, what I was telling her about my family, education, jobs and, yes, even you, dear P. I poured it out higgledy-piggledy, amazed to find that I had drunk most of the wine, not she – I'd vaguely assumed she was an alcoholic – until it seemed to me that my whole life has been so meagre, so *thin*, that I came over all weepy and made a complete arse of myself.

And then, without moving a muscle, she can change; or, at least, change your whole attitude simply by pulling out some small remark like a switchblade, a comment so oblique and wacky that you remember with a jolt that you're alone with a lunatic who splashes in springs at dawn and spits on cripples; and you start to think *you* are the mad one . . . She can make a harmless interjection such as 'Pluto's in town for provisions, so we won't be disturbed,' sound very disturbing indeed. I was intensely curious to know more about her, of course – if only to put her in some more normal context – but she slides out of enquiry; and, then again, there's always the fear that the slightest unwitting impertinence might break her awful fragile surface tension and send her flying towards me with flailing nails.

'I've never been keen on having tenants at the Vicarage,' she said. 'They won't let things *be*.'

'Surely they were driven away by the ghost of the Vicar,' I said defiantly, put out at her scornful dismissal of us tenants.

'Oh, he's not a ghost,' she said. 'It's the White Lady who's the ghost. Haven't you seen her? I have. She's been there as long as anyone can remember.'

'What does she look like?' (You see? Before you know it you're sucked into her barmy world. I wouldn't put it past her to claim to see almost anything. I felt drunk and unhappy at the turn the conversation was taking.) She paused for a moment. Then she said, drily:

'White.' We both laughed. It was so ludicrous. 'Dressed in white, with hair the colour of yours,' she elaborated. 'She was bending over a desk. I didn't see her face.' I asked if this was a recent sighting but she didn't answer. She seemed bored by the subject.

'What have you brought me?' She pointed at the folder I'd put the manuscript in. I showed it to her, explaining how I'd come across it. She wasn't particularly surprised or curious; she was more interested in the extent of the flooding in the cellar. I mentioned pointedly how *I* had cleaned it up. She was oblivious – or pretended to be – of her landlady's obligations.

'I have a lot of papers like that.' She tilted her head on one side and made her eyes big and round like a bird's. My sudden excitement at her words changed just as abruptly to dread. 'Do you think they're worth anything?' she asked slyly. I couldn't speak; I didn't know. 'I wouldn't sell them anyway. I suppose you want to see them.'

She led me to the stairs. Half-way up she stopped and clutched the banisters. For a second there was a twisted, sort of hopeless expression on her face.

'Oh, fuck this,' she said, and began to descend. 'You go on. It's the third door on the left. Shut the front door behind you when you're finished.' I was dismissed. She disappeared into the recesses of the house, slightly bent and scuffing her feet, before I could thank her for the 'tea'.

I've an idea that Jung got started on alchemy after his pal Richard Wilhelm showed him an old Chinese alchemical text called the *Secret of the Golden Flower*. The 'Golden Flower' was the equivalent of the Philosophers' Stone – which, for the Chinese, was the attainment of immortality through the transformation of the body into a '*diamond body*'.

In his commentary on the 'Golden Flower' Jung says that the diamond body is 'a symbol for a remarkable psychological fact which ... could be best expressed by the words "It is not I who live, it lives me"'. He concluded that the aim of alchemy, in both the East and the West, was to produce a *corpus subtile* [a subtle body] – that is, a body which is at the same time spirit, a transfigured 'diamond' body.

I don't think Jung could really bring himself to believe in such a body. He didn't rule out its possibility, but he preferred as usual to see it as a symbol of the Self. And this, too, is how he saw the Philosophers' Stone.

Aren't there really *three* secrets of alchemy? The prima materia, the secret fire and the Philosophers' Stone?

The last can't be made without the first two – but in some sense the first two are the same (the prima materia, extracted from the Raw Stuff, seems to transform itself through the secret fire ...) Another three-in-one and one-in-three mystery.

The manuscripts were in dusty brown cardboard folders, stacked in boxes. Books were piled up everywhere. Some piles had toppled over, scattering books over the bare boards. The room was otherwise unfurnished. There was a single overhead light.

The books were mostly 'classics'. I recognised many of the authors who were of the kind I've often *meant* to read: Plato, Plotinus, St Augustine, Cornelius Agrippa, Bonaventura, Dionysius the Areopagite, Marcion, Pico della Mirandola, etc. There were fewer works of fiction, but most of the Big Boys were there – Chaucer, Dante, Milton, Shakespeare, Cervantes, Goethe, Racine, etc.

I knew at once, and not only because of the predominance of theological and ecclesiastical stuff, that the books belonged on the empty shelves in my library.

As for the manuscripts ... P., I can't tell you what it was like taking the first folder from its box, opening it, drawing out the handwritten pages, each punched with twin holes so that they can be bound together by string. Their musty smell was incredibly rich. It was like breathing in wisdom. I began to read. Such a strange feeling. Everything was suspended. There was like a clunk or crunch in my head as if my brain had settled like an old house on its foundations; yet it was an oceanic sensation, a feeling of vastness as though the halves of the brain, like continental plates, had shifted and interlocked. I can't describe it.

There's nothing too surprising about the papers themselves – they're alchemical tracts all right, copied out in the same hand as my cellar manuscript. I recognised some of the titles from Jung: *Turba Philosophorum, Tractatus Aureus,* Ripley's *Duodecim Clavibus,* Norton's *Ordinall,* Dee's *Monas Hieroglyphica,* and so on. Seven boxes, about ten to a box. All meticulously translated, often in parallel texts with the original Latin on the left-hand side, and the English on the right. Nothing remarkable really, *except* this sense of immensity – of being the first person to step on to a vast Dark Continent and finding these small, precisely formed, black ink inscriptions which seem as familiar and intimate as a love-letter. And dotted about the margins, like the PS disguised as an afterthought that every lover longs for, are little notes and exclamations – *cris de coeur* added by the translator.

I read for a long time. At one point I became aware of Pluto standing in the doorway. We said Hello. He left me in peace. Later on I suffered an aching neck and leg cramp from my contorted reading position. Later still I was distracted by the weight of silence in the house.

When I arrived home, covered in dust, the clock – I could hardly believe it – said 1.30 a.m. I went to bed, but couldn't sleep. I made tea and sat at my desk – *his* desk – with the lights out, looking at the yellow Chinese moon through the mist over the graveyard, and thinking about everything – Mrs Z., Ma, Dad, you, me – until there was no one left in my thoughts except him whose name was inscribed in the books. John Smith.*

---

* Smith has been a bit naughty. His name seems to have been his real name and not, as he claims earlier, an alchemical pseudonym.

FOUR

Conjunction

SMITH

The Raven's Head marks the completion of Separation and the beginning of Conjunction. I'm afraid. Sol follows the left-hand path into our sea where in blackness he will commingle with the horned Luna.* Can one behold this act and not go *mad*?

I ran into Janet while crossing the Green. I did not know quite what her reaction to me would be. Actually it is the same as before in theory, but in fact everything is missing: try as she may to put on a brave front I can see that all her old spontaneous gaiety is gone and she is only going through the motions. Our conversation quickly became stilted; she was anxious to leave me – I guess because I am a reminder both of former happier days and of her decision to part from Robert. (I could detect no *personal* aversion to me.) She wears the same bright, light-hearted outfits, the same make-up and perfume, but now they seem rather to be concealing her true feelings than expressing them. The change is subtle, and might go unnoticed by a less affectionate eye. Her underlying sadness gives her the seriousness which some might have thought lacking before, and the result is a loss of what one might call voluptuousness – but a gain in beauty.

She has had to sell her car. I gather that Farrar is in some financial difficulty – temporary, I hope – and not unconnected with his rather-too-habitual drinking which, Janet implies, has shaken public confidence in his legal abilities.

I wanted to mention that I'd seen Robert but she, guessing what my next words would be (as she so often has in the past), shut

---

* 'horned' presumably because Luna is appearing as the ill-omened new moon. Also, Smith would not be the first Philosopher to see in the conjunction of moon (☽) and sun (☉) part of the symbol for mercury (☿).

her eyes very tight and raised her hand with fingers stiffly splayed: 'Don't. Don't talk about it.'

We said goodbye; I added, fatuously, 'Keep in touch,' as if she were moving far away instead of crossing the Green to her house.

During our fateful interview in the car, when she first intimated that there was 'someone else', she claimed that I couldn't understand her predicament – I was, ha!, too 'good' – ha! again. Oh, she was wrong. I wanted just now to tell her how wrong. I wasn't constrained as she is by the ties of matrimony, granted; but my ties were no less binding, surely. Bound over to obey a higher Will than my own, I gave up my greatest happiness. The Lord only knows what I endured as a result.

However. I survived it. I went on – as Janet will, *must*, survive and go on through the Grace of, and so on – and she'll be the *better* for it, she'll be *purified* (what other word is there?) as I'm pleased to believe that the Spirit has been gracious enough to purify *me* so that I can truthfully say I'm in the world – God knows how far in – but not *of* it. Oh Janet, I'm so sorry, sorry. If only I could say he's not worth it but I'm terribly afraid he is, damn him, afraid that perhaps it *won't* pass as in some ways it hasn't passed for me – although it has, hasn't it, in all essentials – I *am* free of all that, free of *her*.

The Green Lion has spent his force. His work is done: soul and body, being separated, begin to *turn against* themselves like a retort. Not for nothing is our Philosophy called 'the Work against Nature'. Thus sulphur descends into the realm of the volatile, and mercury ascends to the realm of the fixed. When the first is a clear volatile water eclipsed by the fixed black earth of the second, then Nature is *involuted* into the base image of our Stone. This is Conjunction, which we also call mortification, because it is a deed of darkness.

Heraclitus says: 'God is day night, winter summer;'– that is, all the opposites – 'he undergoes alteration in the way that fire, when it is mixed with spices, is named according to the scent of each of them.' Just so is our fire named differently according to its manifestations. And just so is the soul (which Heraclitus deems composed of fire) variously named according to the image by which it represents itself to itself (to us).

*

The last time I saw Annabelle was on a day of snow in January. We met, for some reason, in the park in the early morning. The memory of it is blurred as the snow blurred the hard outlines of our surroundings. It is somehow muffled as the untrodden snow muffled our voices, bestowing on them the intimacy of a conversation in a soundproof box. But it *will* keep coming up. I can't recall it clearly but I can't keep it out of my mind. I remember the black trees, frozen stiff and miraculously outlined in white by some giant unseen hand during the hours of darkness. As a child who could never colour a picture without going over the black lines I marvelled at the precision with which every twig had been delineated with a white powdery shadow.

Why is it always incidental details like this that one can clearly remember in moments of tremendous decision, while the main event, so to speak, can be recalled only as a faint splash in the distance, a twinkle of unheeded feet disappearing into the sea, like the fall of Icarus in Breughel's painting? Humans have a low pain-threshold beyond which merciful oblivion veils our experience and makes it inaccessible to memory. I am fairly certain that this oblivion is summoned up by shock, which is not a way of waking ourselves up but a way of consigning horrors to our own dark depths. They will only resurface – in idle moments, in dreams – if they have not been shocking enough. Beyond a certain level of horror, shock jolts the experience directly down into a permanent black forgetfulness where the light of awareness, even if we will it to shine, won't penetrate.

There were tears, certainly. I remember those, and the pain. But tears and pain seem now to have belonged not to us but to two strangers. I remember sitting on a bench and, watching Annabelle's tense little profile against that enormous wilderness of whiteness, realising I had to make some simple yet irrevocable choice between them. I cannot forget her words, spat out like a gob of blood on snow, 'If you don't marry me now, you never will . . . ' I remember thinking that if she smiled, if she stretched her top lip across her teeth, I was lost. If she did not smile, I was . . . what? Saved? I don't know. I can't be expected to remember all those years ago. She didn't smile. Instead she grabbed my hand and pulled it towards her. The air was too icy to breathe properly. I had to get away to think. I could never *think* properly with her near me. She muddied every issue with her irrelevant asides, her illogical convictions, her endless bloody smiling and her little round breasts always rising and falling in front of me – I tore myself away. It was intolerable the way she was always trying to sidetrack me from my purpose. Christ knows it's hard enough being anything remotely like a Christian let alone a vicar without having to contend with her constant harping on about marriage and didn't I love her and couldn't we just kiss and 'be kind' to each other when she knew *perfectly well* that our future happiness depended on *unbending* dedication or else we may as well give the whole bloody thing up and just wallow around in some sensual sty while the world goes to hell, damn, *damn* her.

Anyway, whatever the point of that God-awful last scene in the park was, the next day Nora* wrote to me and broke off our engagement.

Mercurius is dark and dangerous but he is not evil. He is good *and* evil like the refulgent Lucifer who mysteriously displays attributes of both Christ and the Devil.

I regard him as beyond good and evil. Or, one might say, *below*. Or, perhaps, *before* good and evil became distinguishable. Those who follow him are led neither up nor down but *back*, into that frightening Chaos which men have never set eyes on before – a spirit realm, far underground and yet near at hand, of which we are completely unaware.

As the poison-dripping dragon and the marvellous Hermaphrodite Stone, Mercurius begins with evil and ends with good.

The excrescence that is Nigredo spreads. Luna rises, hiding her beauty. She is the dark *dragon-moon*,** who will devour her brother

---

* *Sic*. Smith, of course, means 'Annabelle'.
** All the passages concerning what Smith sees in his vessel are obscure. Luna was formerly the spirit imprisoned by the dragon in the depths of the sea. As she rises up (from the depths of the matter) it is apparent that she and the dragon are, if not identical, part of each other's nature or (so to speak) different aspects of the Spirit. At this stage she is still dark and possibly dangerous because her draconian attributes still cling to her.

Sol and hold him in her womb for two days and three nights, purging him with terrible heat before he can be reborn.

Blackness spreads over the Above; Below Sol shines ever more weakly. Mercurius with brooding black wings oversees the conjunction of Below and Above.[1]

I'm actually *trembling*. Partly with anger, partly with – what? Outrage? Mostly *anger*.

He was actually *sitting in the kitchen*, on our big scrubbed table, swinging his feet. No question of standing when I came in. Just an 'Evening, Vicar . . . '! Nora washing potatoes at the sink, calm as you please, barely turning round, merely saying over her shoulder, 'Bradley's dropped by for a minute. He helped me carry these' – indicates a sack of spuds on the floor – 'May I offer him a cup of tea, sir?' A *cup of tea*. Why not ask him to supper? I didn't realise what an expression I had on my face until she turned around and visibly flinched. As for *him*, if he had betrayed the smallest diffidence or awkwardness I'd have shown him the door without a second thought; but his damnable self-assurance left me speechless. When he pulled out his packet of cigarettes I simply had to leave the room. Next thing, Nora will be smoking *his* cigarettes. Has the dear girl *any idea* of what she's playing at? I can't put off facing up to the gravity of the situation any longer.

She has just popped her head around the door to ask if I'll be eating here or in the kitchen. 'Bradley's gone,' she adds. Her tone, I think, may have been apologetic. I didn't trust myself to speak – but I will speak, oh yes, and very soon.

Later. Nora appeared with a tray. I'd been unable to work, what with the image of that man kicking his impudent heels against my table leg. I hadn't noticed how hungry I'd become. Fresh-baked bread, sardines, cheese, chutney, apple, tea – all helped to settle my spirits.

Nora asked timidly if she might sit with me while I ate. I said she might – it was the ideal moment to broach the subject of Caldwell jun. I decided to wait until I'd finished. Nora took a book from the shelf and, tilting it towards the window, began to read. The last of the light (I'd no idea it was so late) was filtering, almost spent, through the windows. The silence grew to enormous proportions and then, as softly as a bubble-burst, seemed to dissipate all tension. As the darkness deepened, an enchanted stillness filled the room which neither of us with speech or lamp wanted to break.

At last I asked her quietly what book she had chosen. By way of reply she began to read aloud from *Samson Agonistes*. The Latinate cadences rolled through the air, sounding oddly in her sweet voice, grave and moving as only a young girl's voice can be. As the heavy furniture lost weight and substance, letting go of its stored light and drifting away into the dark like small ships slipping their anchors, I thought of the old blind tyrant-poet himself,* softening into reverie, all passion expiring in the limpid peace of his daughter's voice.

I gradually became aware that Nora had stopped reading. Out of the darkness I heard her voice:

'He's only a boy.'

I imagined her pushing out her slightly bee-stung bottom lip as she said it, and then smiling. It seemed there was no need to speak to her after all. Irrelevantly I remembered an odd remark of Mrs Beattie's: 'That Nora Thomas says she's going back to live in the Manor one day,' and she lifted up her nose as if to add 'Hoity-toity'. Then she laughed incredulously.

Strange summer weather. The light is diffracted through the thick mote-laden air, foreshortening the fields I can see from my window, giving odd perspectives. Almost-ripe wheat gives off a disturbing musk. The sun is hazed, the sky blanched. It's very dry – the water in my well is too far down to see; it gives off a sour shallow splash when I drop a pebble into the shaft. The days are long and enervating; the nights bring no freshness, no relief. Birds suddenly beat off into the darkness. Cottages shift uneasily in their heavily scented little gardens. Trees rustle their millions of tinny leaves, but there's no discernible wind. I prefer to stay below with the Work, but there is a certain . . . menace there as well. I can't keep my mind on it – can hardly think at all now when I most need to. If only one could *breathe*,

---

* i.e. John Milton.

if only I were in some cold northern pine-forest where the clean tang would clear my head.

It is right that Janet and Robert should cease to see each other. I'm certain their liaison hadn't yet reached the carnal stage. One sees it in their faces, senses it, on reflection, in their mutual attitude on the hateful day Janet and I took tea with Robert. They have been subject to temptation, then – but they haven't fallen too far into sin.

Temptation, sin. Unfashionable words. But, surely, apt. Any other vocabulary demeans the gravity that they themselves would accord their situation. The language of the Church Fathers is not for children, not for this increasingly childish age, but it still applies to adults – and those two are nothing if not adult. I pray that as time bears them away from the occasions of sin (as a Catholic might say) their suffering will diminish and they'll be *glad* they did not fall as I'm glad that my own imperilled soul [next words crossed out]. They will see that I [crossed out] it is right. In the meantime it's no use seeking to *cure* their suffering – by distractions or idolatries or false hopes – they must *use* the huge energy that suffering releases, put it to the wheel that they may grind their souls into pure lenses for the magnification of the Lord. *The soul must be scoured until it is fit to receive the spirit.* What does it matter if it hurts when, the little pain past, a soul is ravished by its own whiteness? If they will but climb the mountain of themselves they'll look down with pity on their muddy pasts, wondering what all the fuss was about – and yet I pray that somehow they will be spared – if only because they'll then be spared the doubts and memories driven in like nails . . .

I dreamt there was a great fancy-dress party on the Green. The whole village turned out in elaborate colourful costumes, some wearing masks, others wearing the heads of animals. It was about two in the afternoon. The sun was high, a sickly yellow disc which cast a dull light over the bacchanalia. There was wild dancing to the sound of drums and dissonant guitars. A little piglike creature was turning on a spit, mewing piteously. I tried to prevent it being roasted but I was distracted by an uproar for more drink. An odd fellow, not unlike Out-of-Sorts Simmons, entirely clad in what looked like moleskin, thrust two short rods into the ground. A geyser of dark oil fountained out of the ground and people began filling mugs and pitchers from it, and drinking.

The party went on and on, getting wilder and wilder. I couldn't stop it though I knew I had to. Bradley was there on his motor-bike – except that it was an animal of some sort with its front legs bent painfully back to form the handlebars. He was drunk, dribbling, and wearing clerical clothes stolen from me. Nora was spreadeagled across his saddle and every now and then he pushed a distracted hand up her skirt. It was indescribably horrible. I shouted myself hoarse but no one would listen. I knew something awful was about to happen. A clock struck. I went very cold. It struck twelve times. *I knew it was midnight* but the sun was still high in the sky. A hush fell over the company. The sun began to jig up and down as if pulled by invisible strings. Then it began to move backwards, from west to east. I knew it was the end of the world.

The Nigredo is *alive* and instinct with power. I can't watch its inexorable growth without the vertiginous sense of falling – falling into an infinite abyss. May the Spirit have mercy on me.

The blackness fills the Above as only metal-sickening, moon-induced Cancer can;* but it also grows *inward*, increasing its *intensity* to a darkness that no longer merely baulks the sight but *opens up* under the eyes and leads their gaze into such astronomical blackness that one becomes one's own precarious ledge on the sheer dizzying cliff of endless Night.

When Annabelle broke off our engagement, my despair was mingled with an extraordinary exhilaration which she herself had inspired; for paradoxically, even as she scotched our marriage for ever, she also asserted that she would always love me. I suddenly realised how wise she was, how sublime her intuition that we must part. She had realised, as I had not, that in renouncing me she was in fact

---

* This obscure image seems to include (a) the idea of Nigredo as a cancerous growth; (b) a reference to the constellation of Cancer which is (c) astrologically ruled by the moon and (d) doubly appropriate because Cancer is in fact overhead, in the macrocosm (as well as in Smith's glass), during this stage which is taking place in July when the Sun is in Cancer.

joining me on my spiritual pilgrimage. In renouncing each other, we were in reality renouncing the world and serving a higher destiny. From now on neither of our lives would be 'normal' but a process of threshing and grinding by which earthly desire would be milled into divine love. *Our* love was not lost but found. Henceforth we would run in parallel, drawing strength from the knowledge that somewhere the other was struggling equally with chaste solitude and selflessness until at last, perhaps, like Dante and Beatrice we would stand side by side with our eyes directed towards the blinding illuminating Love of the Creator.

In the years to come I thought of her often. It was a comfort in times of stress to imagine her perhaps travailing in some wretched diseased country. It gave me strength, when I was let down and angry, to remember her fidelity. At times she leapt so vividly to mind that I believed she was thinking of me; and I'd dwell lovingly on her image, in silent communion with her. Whenever I had difficulty in fixing my gaze upon the Eternal, praying for the importunate body to fall away from the long-suffering soul, I had only to summon up the image of her determined guileless face to renew my resolve.

One day, at the beginning of the war, I received a letter from my mother. Tactfully she had never before mentioned Annabelle, although she knew little enough about our romance except that we had been engaged. I suppose she thought that enough time had elapsed to heal whatever lacerations I had sustained. I suppose she thought I'd be glad of news concerning my former fiancée. She mentioned, quite casually, that Annabelle had given birth to her second child. When I remonstrated with her for this tasteless mistake, she sent me a faded newspaper cutting stating that Annabelle was married to a general practitioner from Leigh-on-Solent. The wedding had taken place *less than a year* after our final parting in that snowy unbesmirched park.

And that's the end of the story.

Two days' almost continual attention to the Opus have taken their toll. My intermittent bouts of feverishness come more frequently. With each remission I feel weaker and more drained. I have begun to welcome the illusion of strength which fever brings; but I am also afraid of it because, while I have the temporary energy to perform my duties, I feel also that I'm eating into some essential reserve which won't be recovered in a hurry.

The Work moves towards its excruciating nadir, its dark heart, which is the base reflection of the ultimate marriage between the White and the Red. Obediently *solvo atque coagulo* [I dissolve and I coagulate]. Luna continues to heave herself up as Sol declines; our dissolute sulphur contends with clotted mercury.

Prayer seems almost pointless. I can't hoist the words more than a foot above my head, it seems, where they are dissipated in the unnatural opaque aura which presses around my aching head. I dread being led back by Mercurius, through Nature and down to that inarticulate realm where our divine gifts of reason and speech revert to simian gibbering; and, beyond that, to the cold silence of stone.

EILEEN

There have been no repetitions of things that go bump in the night, thank God. On the contrary, I've been sleeping like the dead. (Even last night, when I woke, or dreamed that I woke, in the middle of a highly erotic dream, I went straight back to sleep again. It seemed that P. was in the room and I was on fire to receive him; but when I turned over, it wasn't P.) On the other hand, I wouldn't say that the house is entirely noiseless, nor entirely – how shall I say? – unatmospheric. It's not that I expect to *see* anything, even if I were psychic which mercifully I'm not, it's more a feeling that comes out of the blue, perhaps when I've come in from a walk and I'm a bit dreamy – it comes to me that someone was in the hall or library a moment before. It's not at all alarming. I somehow don't think it's Mrs Z.'s White Lady! It's as though the house itself is glad to be lived in and is welcoming my return. The 'presence', if that's the right word, is really an absence, as if whoever was in the room has tactfully, discreetly, withdrawn on my arrival.

What on earth *are* Sol and Luna, sulphur and mercury? I keep thinking that they're code words, as if Sol (for example) stood for a simple substance, like gold. It does look as though the two pairs are related in some way. The alchemists sometimes spoke as if sulphur and mercury were a kind of dual prima materia from which all metals were generated; that they were not separate from Sol and Luna but were 'secret essences' hidden inside whatever substances Sol and Luna represented. It may be that, in asking what the latter are, I'm asking the wrong question or not asking it in the right way.

Anthropology taught me something which might have great explanatory power for alchemy – the *universal* proclivity of humans, from ancient Greece to Africa, from China to South America, to classify the world according to a system of oppositions. Moreover, out of the countless number of oppositions to choose from the same ones in fact crop up over and over again. A typical example of this dual symbolic classification goes like this:

Right	Left
North	South
East	West
Sun	Moon
Light	Dark
Even	Odd
Male	Female
Day	Night
Senior	Junior
Bones	Blood
Political power	Religious authority.

Not all cultures use all of these by any means; but most, if not all, use some of them. According to the rules which govern this system of classifying the world, the terms in each column needn't hold any property in common. They are not synonymous but *homologous*. Secondly, the relationship between each pair of opposites is *analogous*. You never say 'right' equals 'sun', or 'moon' is synonymous with 'dark' – you have to say right : left :: sun : moon [right is to left as sun is to moon].

Alchemy has a well developed system of opposites by which it classifies the world. Some of them are unique, e.g. sulphur/mercury, volatile/fixed, while others overlap with the typical oppositions of other cultures. The principal ones are:

Sol	Luna
Sun	Moon
Gold	Silver
Rex (King)	Regina (Queen)
Light	Dark
Above	Below
Sulphur	Mercury

Male	Female
Fixed	Volatile
Fire	Water
Body	Soul
Matter	Spirit.

On the same principle as before, one must resist the temptation to say that Sol 'stands for' gold or that Luna is the equivalent of dark – one can only say that Sol : Luna :: gold : silver :: light : dark [Sol is to Luna as gold is to silver as light is to dark].

It's this principle of analogy which Jung never consistently got to grips with. He tends to think in terms of 'symbolism' – as if Sol *symbolised* consciousness and Luna *stood for* the unconscious. The correct formulation, however, is Sol : Luna :: Above : Below :: consciousness : the unconscious.

It can be misleading to talk about 'dual classification' because it's not a conscious thing. Everyone uses it but no one thinks about it. They certainly don't draw up lists of opposites in columns. On the contrary, like all cultural ideas or beliefs – all collective representations – dual classification is by definition taken for granted in the same way that we take for granted the grammar of our language. It's something we absorb, like air, as we grow up.

At first sight the dual classification of other cultures (and I include alchemy) can be baffling. An African tribesman's assertion that, say, blacksmiths and circumcised males are 'right' while potters and uncircumcised males are 'left' is incomprehensible. It begins to make some sense when we understand the implicit analogy behind his statements – right : left :: blacksmiths : potters :: circumcised : uncircumcised. It makes more sense when we realise that our own classifications can be not very different. For example, right : left :: blue : red :: Tory : Socialist; or, east : west :: bear : eagle :: Russian : American.

On the whole, the difference between our system of dual classification and those of more 'primitive' cultures is that our opposites are often abstract – good/bad, subject/object, emotional/intellectual, democratic/totalitarian, etc. Such opposites are comparatively late accretions, subsequent to our division of the world into distinct spheres – the moral, the psychological, the political and so on. However, the fundamental building-blocks of dual classification remain those of the kind I've listed. They are not abstract but *concrete*, deriving from perceived contrasts in the physical world. They operate simultaneously at levels which we have come to regard as separate. The alchemical opposition volatile/fixed, for example, implies the analogy volatile : fixed :: gas : solid :: spiritual : material. The opposition Above/Below implies that the top (of the vessel) : the bottom :: Heaven : Earth :: consciousness : the unconscious.

Similarly, it might surprise us to find that the contrasts, hot/cold, moist/dry, point to moral or psychological, as well as physical, opposites. But it isn't so surprising when we consider that a similar wealth of such primary oppositions is embedded in our own language. We speak of temperaments as being fiery or watery; of warm- and cold-hearted people; of hot- and cool-headed people; of politicians who are 'wet' and of a sense of humour that is 'dry'. Often we don't spot the analogies which underlie such expressions, e.g. warm : cool :: heart : head :: emotional : intellectual; or, hot : cold :: fire : ice :: sexually ardent : sexually frigid.

I have the feeling that Dad never quite got over leaving Cambridge. Anywhere else was a kind of exile, the provinces even more so than America, perhaps.

I'm not sure why he *did* leave. There was some sort of row, not of the explosive kind but of the silent electrical kind which children (I was tiny at the time) can sense without understanding. Dad doesn't discuss it, nor would I dream of mentioning it. It just isn't done. But I have the vague impression from Mum, who was distinctly bitter about it (though not, I think, because Dad was sacked), that he was too hard on one of his students. It must have been difficult for them to understand, as I do, his exacting nature. He's nothing if not a perfectionist.

The thing I remember most clearly about our Cambridge house is Dad's study. It was set apart from the other rooms by its own narrow passage, doubtless a short one, but immensely long and dark to a three- or four-year-old. It was an almost holy place where Dad hid himself away to write or to supervise the students whom Mum ushered quickly through the house and left at the beginning of the passage to proceed alone.

I did venture into the study myself once, although I knew it was forbidden territory. I may have been looking for something. I don't know. I only recall poking timidly about while my whole being filled up with this sick feeling of dread. I did find something behind Dad's green cupboard. It was a cane. A thin, whippy one. For some childish reason I was certain that if I mentioned this cane *it would be used on me*. By Dad, of all people. I still tremble and feel queasy to think of it.

It seems absolutely absurd to me now – I think it did even then – that I should have believed Dad capable of thrashing anyone, let alone a little girl, his daughter. And yet the fear persisted. Later, I came to associate the cane with homework. I was always in a state over homework. I applied myself to it feverishly, working myself up, terrified of failing at it. I see now that it was this fear of failure that caused me to fail, in the end, when the work became more demanding and required real thought. I was always too nervy to think properly. Still, as long as I could get by on a certain native quickness and capacity for slogging, I succeeded. I never needed the cane. Dad was never upset – I made bloody sure of that. Fortunately we were always so close that there was never any question of conflict between us arising.

Mrs Zetterberg knocked at my window this morning, putting the heart across me. We're not exactly on an easy footing, but she seems marginally less formidable – if no less unpredictable. At least she appears to have given up her early morning 'bathing', if my attempts at vigilance are anything to go by.

She was in a hurry, somewhat distracted and high-handed:

'I've just called to say that you may come when you choose, to look at those papers, if you find them at all interesting.' Once again even her accent can throw me into confusion. It seemed 'put on', deliberately 'refined', and yet with an edge to it which was not perhaps American after all, but simply a good old West Country burr. 'The door's always open, as you know. Just give me a shout to let me know you're in the house.' I thanked her, adding, 'They came from here, didn't they, the papers?'

'Yes.'

'They were the vicar's. John Smith's.'

'Yes.' She was not in a communicative mood.

'Have you read them?'

'I've glanced at them.' She glanced at her watch, keen to get away.

'You know they're about alchemy?'

'Alchemy . . . yes.' She didn't sound sure; she seemed uneasy. I wanted to press my advantage, so I said:

'It's the art of turning base metal into gold. Did you know that?' She stared at me stonily.

'Everyone knows that.' She turned abruptly and walked off, leaving me flustered and feeling foolish. Her look was suddenly so hard and bitter.

I stayed in the front garden, enjoying what may be the last warm sunshine for a long time. Frost the night before last and wind last night have conspired to strip the trees of their leaves. I thought about what I should do for Christmas. Last year, Dad went abroad with Tanya and so I spent it with Ma and Larry. I don't see myself going again this year.

I was still wondering what it would be like to stay here, alone, over Christmas, when Pluto rolls up. He's breathing hard and, while he speaks as usual with his face averted, there's no mistaking the anger in his voice.

'What did you say to her?'

'I didn't say anything' – I found myself stuttering guiltily – 'I mean, we were talking about those papers. She said I could look at them when I wanted.' He jerked his head up; his shiny eye was startled:

'She never has visitors.' It was my turn to feel cross.

'Well, she's had me to tea and she wants me to come again.'

He limped a few steps down the path and back again. He was agitated now, his commanding air quite disappeared. I felt sorry for him. His concern for the old bat is transparent – though God knows why, since she does nothing but wage war on him.

'Look,' I said. 'I'm sorry if I upset her in any way.'

'No,' muttered Pluto. 'I'm sorry.' He lifted his good hand

hopelessly. 'The slightest thing sets her off. It's not your fault . . . ' He had lowered his head once more but he shot little darting glances at me as if in a quandary. 'In fact, I'd be glad if you did come to see her. She has rather . . . cut herself off recently. Only, please, don't make it obvious. She can't stand to seem dependent on anybody. Just act as if you're popping in as you pass through – and please don't brink drink or cigarettes. She really isn't well.'

'What's the matter with her?' I asked boldly.

'Her stomach. And listen, please, if you must root about in those old papers, don't pester her with them. It unsettles her to rake over the past. She has to rest.'

'You know whose — ?'

'Yes, I know whose papers they are.'

'Did you know him? Smith?'

'Yes. I knew him. Don't believe what you hear about him. He wasn't understood. I don't know anything about his experiments. It's up to you if you want to go digging around. They didn't do him any bloody good.' The oath sounded oddly on Pluto's lips. He has never given such a series of long speeches. He really is entirely *normal* – except for his over-protective obsession with his employer. I had no wish to collaborate with this, but I wanted to reassure him. I wanted us to be friends. So I told him I'd do my best not to upset Mrs Z. in any way and promised not to supply her, if I could help it, with booze and fags. He nodded, taking all this in, and then awkwardly stuck out his hand, which surprised me so much that I shook it.

One of the great stumbling-blocks to an understanding of alchemy is the way that it combines, recombines and jumbles up different pairs of opposites so that you never know where you are. The principle of analogy provides a key to the apparent confusion – each pair of opposites implies other pairs in an analogical sequence, enabling the alchemist to operate on several levels at once.

It's possible to arrange the specifically alchemical opposites (as against the more general ones, such as light/dark) in a sequence of diagrams which suggest both this simultaneity of levels and the progression of the opus. The first diagram shows the four basic attributes (hot/cold, moist/dry) which combine to form the four elements (earth, air, fire, water), which in turn give rise to the four alchemical 'elements' (Sol/Luna, sulphur/mercury):

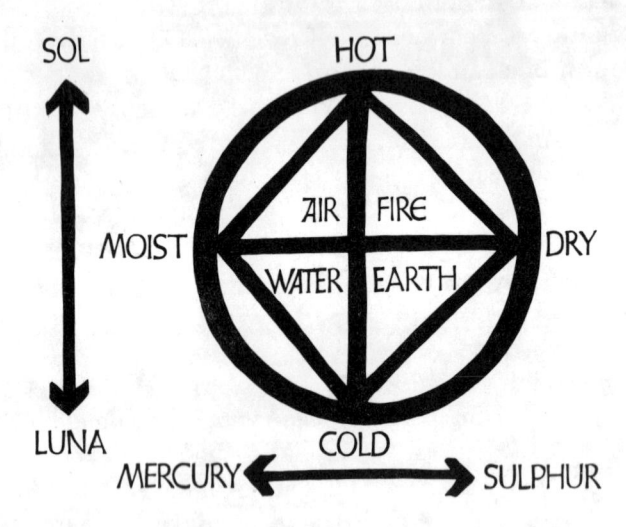

![Diagram: circle with AIR, FIRE, WATER, EARTH inside; SOL↕LUNA vertical axis; MOIST-DRY horizontal; HOT at top, COLD at bottom; MERCURY↔SULPHUR]

This scheme can be overlaid, at a higher level, by another – like a grid:

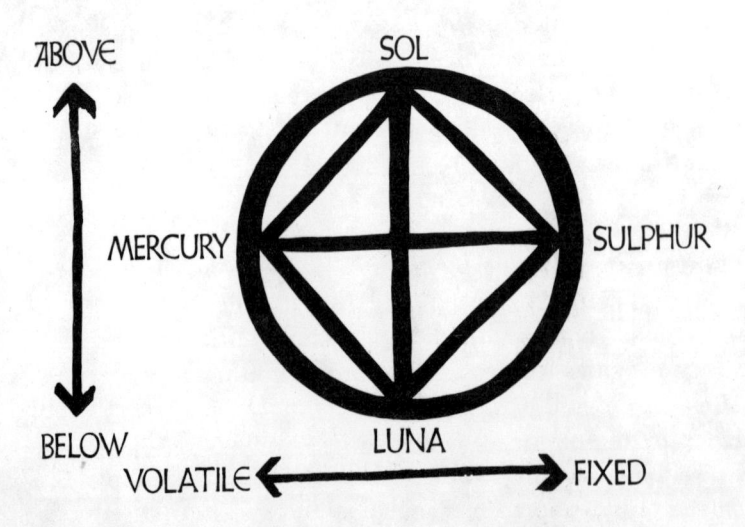

![Diagram: circle with ABOVE↕BELOW vertical axis labeled SOL at top, LUNA at bottom; MERCURY-SULPHUR horizontal; VOLATILE↔FIXED]

Finally, when Above and Below have been joined at the Albedo and the volatile has been made fixed (and the fixed, volatile) at the Rubedo, the final union of Heaven and Earth takes place:

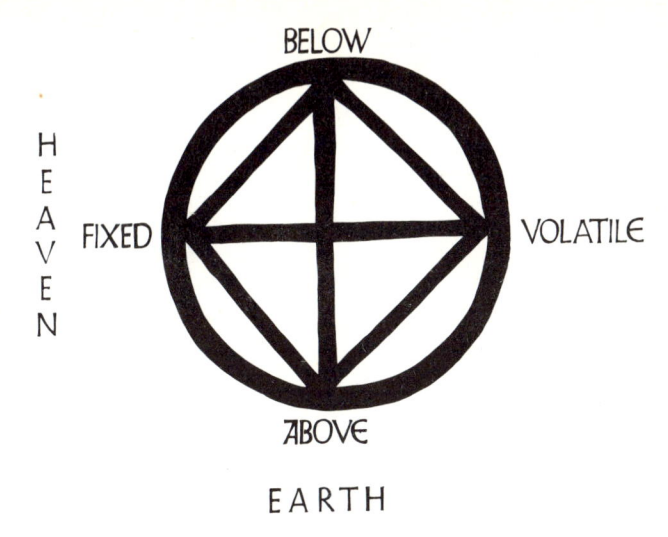

```
                    BELOW
   H
   E
   A      FIXED          VOLATILE
   V
   E
   N
                    ABOVE
                   EARTH
```

In theory one pair of opposites is no more important than any other pair. They are all equally related through the system of analogy. In practice it does sometimes look as if one pair acts as a kind of rubric for the others – in some tribal systems of dual classification, right/left might fulfil such a role. (Alchemy, incidentally, does not employ this opposition, perhaps because it is itself a 'left-hand path' – in which case we can say, alchemy : Christianity :: left : right :: dark : light.) The best example is probably the Chinese yin/yang. Yin does almost seem to embrace its homologous set of terms – e.g. moon, dark, female, passive, etc. – while yang covers sun, light, male, active, etc.

I spent some time trying to make a similar case for sulphur/mercury as the sort of Western equivalent of yang/yin, but I was forced to admit that there are certain oppositions, such as Above/Below, which can't be subsumed under their general category.

Now it strikes me that, *if* there is a key pair of opposites which underpins the others and serves as a rubric, it has to be MALE/FEMALE (masculine/feminine). This pair above all lies at the heart of the Great Work.

*

For people in Elizabethan England (as for tribal people perhaps), the world was not – as it is for us – '*out there*'. They were intimately related to everything in the universe, either as the critical links in the great Chain of Being which stretched from the throne of God down to the meanest stone, or through separate but closely corresponding planes, such as the angelic realm, the universe (macrocosm), the social realm (body politic) and man himself (microcosm). This complex web of interrelationship did not so much *occur* in some space 'out there'; it *was* space. The universe was not an infinite void in which galaxies hang at intervals; it was more like a cathedral, vast but finite, the harmony and order of whose architecture inspired awe and a sense of man's littleness – but never the indifference, uneasiness or fear that our universe so easily evokes. The planets and fixed stars were at an immense dizzying height and yet each person – even each part of a person – maintained a spiritual affinity with them which it was the astrologers' job to chart.

Such a unified world-view was not without its conflicts and discontinuities. Chief amongst these was the felt discrepancy between matter and spirit which had existed from the earliest days of the Church. Yet, except perhaps for a few acutely sensitive – and pessimistic – contemplatives, the conflict between matter and spirit did not, it seems to me, lead to a dualistic way of thinking. For the natural world, like man, was conceived as being compounded of matter *and* spirit, and so man experienced its tensions as his own, as the contrary soul and body. More than this, unlike dualism, the opposition was not simply a barrier to integration but could be used to serve it; for, by virtue of his double nature, man could uniquely bind together the whole of Creation from the angelic realm above to the inanimate material realm below (although the alchemists believed otherwise, it was generally held that spirit ceased to operate below the level of vegetative life).

Something like this, I guess, was the world-view of the educated man-in-the-street during the English Renaissance. But during this critical period, which some say originated as early as the fourteenth century in Italy (and which saw the most sophisticated developments in alchemy), another world-view, qualitatively different, was emerging. It was in fact our modern world-view.

The question as to how it began is the question as to how the Renaissance took place at all. I don't know the answer. I only know the usual stuff about the sudden spread of classical learning, the advent of scientific and geographical discovery, the new spirit of secularism, the new sense of man's individual potential, etc. All these seem to beg the question. The notion that the Renaissance was the effect of some cause seems contentious, since the notion of cause and effect is in itself a product of a way of thinking which began with the Renaissance. I've even heard that it began with the invention of perspective in art, before which the medieval painter simply depicted most clearly and largest what interested him most, regardless of its position in what we call actuality.

At any rate, whether we regard the Renaissance artist as having discovered space or as having invented it, it's evident that the way we regard space is a crucial characteristic of the modern world-view. Descartes,* of course, provided its most famous formulation in the 1630s, when he divided the world into mind on the one hand and, on the other, matter – which was identified with geometrical extension. From now on there was to be an inner, subjective, mental realm as opposed to an objective, material realm 'out there' – a space in which objects existed and events occurred wholly separately from us.

We are now as far from the medieval world-view as the first man to stand on two feet was distant from the primates who moved on all fours; (but what the new *homo erectus* gained in improved eyesight and longer views he also lost in a reduced sense of smell and sensitivity to the earth . . .)

Alchemy would also succumb to Cartesian dualism, dividing into a kind of speculative mysticism on the one hand and into modern chemistry on the other. But meanwhile, in an individual isolation that to some extent adumbrated the Cartesian separation of man and the world, the alchemists strove to reunite matter and spirit. In a way they refused to subscribe to the new spatial model which gained nothing by moving from a vertical scale (Above/Below) to a horizontal plane (inner/outer). The new model was even deleterious, because it destroyed the correspondence between microcosm and macrocosm – the alchemist knew that his soul and body, mind and spirit, were analogous to Heaven and Earth through the common terms Above and Below. Dualism denied the analogy by denying

---

* René Descartes (1596–1650), French mathematician and philosopher.

man's double nature, reducing him to a single term in the opposition, mind/matter or subject/object.

Heaven and Earth meanwhile lost the concrete connotations which Above and Below supplied, and, relegated to the sphere of religion alone, became a metaphor whose vitality diminished over the centuries as it was steadily removed from the model that originally gave rise to it. We retain only an inkling of this model, as when we refer to Heaven above or when we say that a thought came into our heads from above (like a bolt from the blue), or that emotions and desires 'rise up' from below.

The secret of alchemy can only be imparted verbally to a chosen disciple by a divinely appointed master; and 'of a *million*, hardly *three* were ere Ordained for Alchemy'. So says Thomas Norton whose *Ordinall of Alchemy*, copied by Smith from Ashmole, I've been reading this afternoon.[2] Nor are these lucky three-in-a-million likely to be eminent academics, for 'Almighty God/From great Doctours hath this *science* forbod,/And graunted it to few Men of his mercy,/Such as be faithfull Trew and Lowly'.

When I went on to Charnock's *Breviary of Alchemy* I was amazed to read that he was given a second chance to learn the Great Secret,[3] having *forgotten* it the first time!

When Captain Cook anchored in Botany Bay, the Aussie aboriginals on the shore took no notice of his ship. Only when he took to the rowing boats did they go wild with excitement. The ship was too big, too far outside their experience to spot.

I think alchemy is like that. It's hard to keep away from the Manor these days. I can't remember when I was last so intellectually wired up. It's like being set in front of an immense crossword puzzle on whose solution your whole life depends. Dammit – those alchemists weren't fooling around. They're on to something BIG – possibly *too* big for our blinkered primitive vision.

Pluto has reluctantly set up a card-table and chair in the manuscript room. I read more or less at random, taking notes. The *mss*. [manuscripts] are murder. I understand, or think I do, about one sentence in every five. I tend to impose a psychological interpretation on the texts, but this is possible less often than I thought, going by Jung's works. I sometimes have the uneasy feeling that I'm missing the whole point. My only hope is to try and absorb as much as possible – to stuff my head with pieces of the jigsaw – and have faith that they'll arrange themselves into a pattern.

The texts are definitely recipes for the most part. They are there to be tested in the laboratory. They can't be written off by psychology; but, then again, nor are they simply a primitive chemistry. I still long to know what *actual* substances you're supposed to start with! Just as I'm about to give up in frustration I see some small reminder of my own cellar text and I take heart.

After all, it's still my aim to elucidate '*my*' text. It was obviously precious to John Smith: why else would he hide it in the well? Pluto doesn't seem to think that he had much luck with it.

Who wrote it, apart from 'Mercurius'? Not Smith. He only translated it from the Latin. How old is it? I don't yet know enough about different styles to date it.

Anyway, on, on.

SMITH

I wouldn't say that Nora is *sulky* exactly. Rather there's an edge to her reticence. Nor is she exactly disrespectful. However there is a coolness towards me coupled with a certain carelessness, a lack of *decorum*. She takes baths at odd times. She doesn't lock the door, as I know to my cost – I inadvertently burst in on her yesterday afternoon and caught a glimpse of her long supple body in the tub before I could avert my eyes. It's really *very* trying. She didn't seem in the least put out, so unconscious is she of the effect she might have. When she serves my food there's a distinct tendency to *flounce*. It really won't do. She's becoming harder to ignore. I heard footsteps on the ceiling above me last night. It must have been Nora of course; but for a second I imagined it was the restless White Lady and, to my surprise, I was terror-struck. I can't understand it. Why should I think all of a sudden that the sound of footsteps was made by a ghost? Why should I be frightened? I'm not afraid of ghosts. I'd be less resentful of a ghost disturbing the contemplative state of mind that I now have to struggle so hard to reach. If Nora continues to act so irrationally, to disturb me so often with her silences and baths and thumping across the ceiling at all times of day and night, I'll have to let her go. *She* must understand that *I* must have complete peace and quiet in which to work, with no distractions. If people knew that she was having baths with the door unlocked there'd be hell to pay. It makes me shiver to think of it.

I thought the dragon's venom and the lacerating Green Lion were the worst of Mercurius. They were nothing. Nothing compared to this slow heat, this storm-laden stillness, numbing my wits with a kind of creeping black foreboding. Darkness is the heart of the work, the black *liebestod* [love-death] of the Spirit.

Twilight gathers; God hides his golden face from the world; Nature convulses with a single long-drawn-out shriek that no one hears but I. Blood-stained banners stream across the western sky. I can do nothing but wait for the night that brings that other Night, like night's eclipse.

I spoke sharply to Nora about the baths. I told her not to wear so much make-up, during working hours at least. It's not appropriate, nor is it particularly hygienic. I went down to the cellar for a couple of hours but couldn't settle. There's something unbearable about the Nigredo, something . . . *sly* in the way the blackness seems to advance only in my absence.

I have increased the heat – but minimally. Things can't be rushed. The cellar is stifling. My skin prickles and itches but scratching does no good except to produce a kind of irritating heat-rash. I immersed myself in cold water which brought some relief. I wanted to go for a walk to work off my restlessness but it's too muggy outside, making me sweat and scratch. Actually I'm not at all well. It's not like me to start weeping for no reason. It's just the fever, I suppose, and the frustration – patience is so hard and the Work so long.

I wandered about the house. No sign of Nora. It struck me that I'd been too harsh with her, even unjust. I searched everywhere for her, amazed at my own panic. I wondered if she had gone for a walk, if she had met Bradley and gone with him up to Nightingale Wood, curse him.

Her bedroom smelt sweetly of sandalwood. A petticoat lay in dishevelled abandon on the floor. I could see Nora from the window. She was sunbathing in the orchard, lying in the long grass with a book. Is there anything lovelier than the intent expression on the face of a young girl absorbed in a book? I forgot my own discomforts. I wondered which of my books she was reading. She has borrowed a number recently, mostly poetry. I make no attempt to conceal my pleasure. It's a wonderful thing to share books, and to think that – useless as I am – I may be indirectly contributing to the enrichment of her young life. The skirts of her faded blue dress were artlessly tucked up to show her long golden legs to the sun; the bodice was twisted tightly across her chest. And she, all unaware of the idyll she created, deaf to the skylarks pouring down their liquid song, read on.

I'm genuinely *shaken*. Am I such a coward? There were times in Italy when I cheerfully trotted out in full view of enemy snipers, without the cover of the Red Cross, if a wounded soldier needed me. Even discounting the element of bravado, I *did* overcome a real fear. Why then should an inconsequential encounter with a sullen teenager leave me in such a *state*?

I hadn't planned to accost Bradley – but isn't that often the best way? We can do what we dread simply by plunging thoughtlessly in. It was the roar of his wretched motorcycle, disrupting my attempt to work, that gave me the first furious impetus. I was already crossing the Green to the Manor's outbuildings before I decided to beard him over his scandalous conduct towards my Nora.

He didn't even bother to look up as I approached the garage he was working in front of – he went on removing the oily chain from his machine. The sinews in his unexpectedly wide forearms flexed and unflexed. I disliked him at that moment as much as I've ever done. My charitable thoughts towards him are at an end. It was typical of him not to look up: it sums up his whole attitude – the arrogance, the want of ordinary decency and civility, the ignorant contempt for religion, the belief that people exist as his playthings. It made my blood boil. I managed to say:

'I want a word with you, Bradley.'

He stood up slowly, the chain dangling from his grease-stained hand.

'All right.' His voice has that irritating flatness, part insolence, part affectation – his father sent him for years to a public school to rid him of that very accent the family brought with them from the North. He doesn't quite close his mouth, which, with its red lips, gives him a permanently libidinous expression. I can picture only too easily the effect of that confident sensual mouth on the Jenny Stebbinses of this world. She must've been child's play. My fury made me cold and hard. I wanted to slap him down once and for all. All I could manage was:

'I don't want to see you hanging around Nora again. I don't want to see you anywhere near the vicarage, d'you hear?'

I could feel my rash flaming up and irritating my skin unbearably. I wondered briefly if I'd overdone it – been too crushing.

Quite the contrary. Bradley wasn't crushed. He took one step towards me and my rage drained away into the ground. The chain swung in his hand. I was suddenly afraid. All he said was: 'Oh yes?' He didn't need to say more. He has something of his father's innate power to intimidate. At this point two of his cronies came out of the garage's dark interior. It's another of his affectations to mix with the rougher good-for-nothing elements in town. All three were taller than I. They couldn't do anything to me – not to a vicar, not in broad daylight – but simply having to tell myself that compounded my fear and I felt a weak half-smile taking possession of my lips and I hated myself as much as them.

'Look here, Bradley. Be reasonable. You know as well as I do that you shouldn't be pestering Nora . . . ' I was going to mention Jenny but felt it might be fatal. Instead I tried to give him a meaning look but it broke harmlessly on his blank wall of a face, impervious to shame.

'I should think I can see Nora when I like,' he said. 'Unless,' he added, 'you want her all to yourself.'

I felt ill, inclined to shake. One of the cronies gave a short laugh.

'You go too far . . . ' but I couldn't finish the sentence. I turned and walked away, my neck pricking, half-expecting to hear the swish of Bradley's oiled chain.

Another thing: when I went down to the orchard Nora had already gone indoors, leaving her book behind. The buzzing of insects was very insistent, the odour of grass acidically sweet. I felt weak and dizzy. I lowered myself, slowly and precisely, prone on to the long imprint her form had made in the grass, and for a minute or so I knew some respite from illness and anguish. My large volume of Keats was open near my head; but when I picked it up to see what poem she had been reading, I saw that it concealed another book, a cheap paperbacked piece of trash full of autoerotic fantasy masquerading as romance. An annihilating sadness I've no way of explaining swept over me.

*

Almost as if he were expecting me, Robert was standing at his door as I climbed the muddy lane. My heavy heart lifted. No one has seen him for days. I'd begun to fear he'd returned to his old reclusive ways – in which case I was deprived of perhaps my last bastion of sanity. I was seriously tempted to tell him about the Work and seek his help.

However, before I came within hailing distance, I saw him raise his arm and then wave it in a single irritable dismissive gesture. I turned around and trudged back down the lane.

Tim knew he'd revert. As soon as he witnessed that terrible scene with Janet, he knew Robert would no longer welcome him. I would like to help Robert, but the blind can't lead etc. How flimsy friendship proves itself in the face of unrequited love. Our friends teach us true estrangement, as marriage (according to Chekhov) shows us what true loneliness is. The closer we are to each other, the more conscious of our inviolable otherness.

It's possible (I believe) for advanced souls to imagine others so truthfully that they can take on those others' suffering and alleviate it. I do not see who can do this for Robert.

There has been lamentable unforgivable behaviour. I don't know why I did it. Yet I feel no remorse, only renewed anger. That bugger Bradley again.

As I emerge from my laboratory I see him, through the open back door, accosting Nora. She is picking early beans in the vegetable patch and talking to him earnestly. I am calm. He is staring moodily at the ground, taking short puffs on his cigarette. Then he throws the butt down and seizes Nora's hand. It's as much the wanton littering of my spinach with his filthy cigarette as anything else that propels me forward. It's the last straw. However, I keep control of myself. I am not going to allow that youth to aggravate me as he has in the past.

I hear myself telling him to accompany me to my study. He nods. This is a relief. My fingernails cease to dig painfully into my palms. Nora gives me a look. I can't describe it, I don't know what it signifies. A burning look full of – anger? No. Surrender? (What do I mean?) Some anger, certainly, and a silent enquiry; a hint of impatience, too, and a plea for lenience.

In my study I close the door on him. He seems subdued, but I'm ready for any monkey business. I remain calm. I state my position succinctly: I cannot tolerate him in my house again, I will not have him pestering Nora like a meat-fly. He takes a comb from his back pocket and passes it superfluously through his long, possibly brilliantined hair. I brace myself; but it's not an act of defiance, only the automatic movement of a man ill-at-ease.

He speaks in a low voice, to begin with. His face is white and his jaw wobbles like a child suppressing sobs. I don't want to listen but there is a terrible fascination about his words:

'At school, when we were young, she had all the good ideas. Nora was never like the others, she was . . . she is out on her own. If I ever saw *anyone* . . . if I caught them, you know, mucking around with her, they were . . . *for* it. You know? She's always been like . . . like a sister. Kind of like a sister . . . And when I went away, to school, I used to write and sometimes she'd write back.'

I don't see what he's driving at. I am calm, though. Then he goes on, saying such extraordinary things that I can only conclude he has lost his reason as well as his self-possession:

'She was fine till you came along, *fine*. Now she's not the same person – she's moody, odd, you don't know which way she's going to jump . . . whether she's going to laugh at you, or be angry at you for no reason, or flirt. All she can ever talk about is you, it's not right, you've . . . *you've bewitched her*. Oh yes, *Vicar*. Everybody knows you're up to no good in that cellar of yours . . . ' The man's fancies begin to disturb me. There's as much fear in his eyes as anger. 'You're worse than Nora's old witch of a grandmother. She eats out of your hand. It's sickening. You're old enough to be her father — '

But I'd heard enough from him. I took three strides across the room and hit him. Not a real punch. More of a smack in the mouth with the intention of shutting it. Immediately I think of the time it will take to neutralise the crude energies, inimical to the Opus, which my violence has called up. The thought is sobering. I tell Bradley how sorry I am. He has sat down abruptly in a chair, holding his mouth. There is blood on his lip. We are both strangely polite. He tells me the wound is nothing.

I open the door for him. As he leaves he says matter-of-factly: 'You've done it now, Vicar.' I smile vaguely as if he were complimenting me on a sermon. Of course his damaged pride requires a threat. Nora is in the hall. He leaves without looking at her. I return to my study. I write this in the hope that it will ease my misery and confusion. I don't know what's come over me. I can't remember the last time I lost control like that. All those insinuations – all those lies. What put them into his deranged head?

Nora rebuked me, rightly, for striking Bradley. She admitted to listening at the door during our abominable interview. I was, she said, *quite wrong about him.* Bless her. Blithely she sees no harm in anyone.

She embarked on a breathless rambling tale about her childhood and her school where she was persecuted for putting on airs and graces and for repeating what her grandmother had led her to believe – that one day she would live in the manor formerly owned by the Maltraverses. At the same time the poor darling was afflicted with shyness, and with shame at her comparative penury. 'He was the only one who was kind. Pluto was the only one who stood up for me.' *Pluto?* 'The others called him that because they said he followed me around like a dog. *You* know, like Pluto follows Mickey Mouse.' Mickey Mouse. It's hard to follow her drift sometimes. I didn't want to disillusion her too violently; but I couldn't altogether let the opportunity for truth pass. I tried to point out gently that whatever canine devotion he was capable of in the past, his present character shared more similarity with a rabid wolf – that his behaviour towards the fairer sex had been less than impeccable. Nora shook her head impatiently, making her thick blonde hair swing to and fro.

'Oh, you mean Jenny,' she said. 'Everyone knows about that. She's been asking for it for years. I doubt if Pluto was the first. He probably isn't even the father!' I all but blocked my ears so as not to hear her speak in this shameless vein. For a minute Nora – who has been almost like a daughter to me these last trying weeks – *Nora* was like a stranger.

Noon. Heat and glare. The sun's black after-image blinds my eyes. Stench of stale flowers in the graveyard. The ears are assailed by stupid bestial sounds: plangent sheep, blatant cows. The stifling air is unbreathable sawdust, the litter of treetops sawed by the rooks' caw. I stare at my arm's alien jut, wondering that it's mine.

*

Night. Sky's black carpet has shaken out its stars. To look up is to look down into the black unfathomable earth.

The light fades in my poor distorted flask, like a blindness not of the eyes, but of the soul.
 Breathless I wait for our earth to crack, and topple me from my fragile ledge. God have mercy upon – but God, God is absent: *He can't reach this far down.* His Son, too, is too high on His Cross.
 I light another lamp and watch its light thrown back, thwarted by the blackness. Sol emits his last expiring glint, like the last thing in Pandora's horrible black box. The earth is given over to Mercurius. This is the last dispensation as Joachim of Fiore foretold.[4]
 May it not go too hard with me, Lord, spirit of the abyss. May I see another sunrise . . .

Someone's down here with me. It's, damn him, *Bradley*. No, impossible, of *course*. Could've *sworn* someone . . .
 There's something, *something in the corner*. Slipping away – no *control* over the body – some idiot thing oh god it [*sic*] drooling and makes me [illegible].

Write write must keep writing. If I stop, if I move, some mad black dog horror may leap on the body.

It wants me *to think about Nora*. She lies in bed upstairs wrapped in crisp white dreams – it *reads thoughts*, she must *not* be thought.

Writing. Cellar filling with . . . *fumes*. Gas, poison. Can't find a leak in the Egg. It's cloudy, shifting.
 Can't move my legs. Neck. Head.

Dark. Smoke congealing. Spirit is loose – *fumes*. No. Comes from the walls. They go at odd neck-break angles. They *crawl* – soft, disgusting turd walls crawling with evil . . . It's in the well not the walls *the well*. It comes up horrible boneless clicking [illegible] the

WORM. Head waving blindly looking for pure white *Nora*. It wants her WRITE write don't think write our father which art in heaven hallowed be

WORM. It's burning burning to possess oh god the body. Clot of dark. Bat wings closing in can't move. It's soft insinuating *pushing* in behind, brushing over brain nerves its mad lust *lust* wriggling in the groin looking for Nora NORA LOOK OUT FOR its long its stiff lust sticking out [illegible] it opens its red eye, it *sees* you, it's seen you there's no escape it moves my legs my body must go up to you push it up fuck   FUCK

EILEEN

The villagers are not unfriendly. They say 'Good morning' and remark on the weather, as I pass them on one of my walks. I find that I don't at the moment want any more contact than this. I'm happy to wander about Timothy's Wood where it's so peaceful, or to march against the wind along the high crest of Grimm's Down where the sky brushes the top of your head, pausing at the standing stone to rest my tired eyes on the horizon, before descending again into the shelter of the valley.

I don't want to talk to people because my thoughts must be allowed to run their course in silence. The exceptions are Brendan, whom I can rely on to provide amusement without interrupting the flow, and Mrs Zetterberg. I often long to talk to her – more than that, to interrogate her, despite my residual foreboding. I sometimes run into her on arrival at the Manor (I always call out but don't always receive a reply). Questions form themselves. I need to link up John Smith's archive with the man himself, to connect up his Art with his life, and I'm certain Mrs Z. can help me do this. But she's not someone to be interrogated or even questioned. If she shows any inclination to talk it's usually just as I'm leaving for the night – but, by then, my brain is bubbling like an alembic and I can hardly wait to be back at my desk, condensing ideas and dripping them painfully out of my pen.

Brendan brightens up when I walk into the bar. Today he immediately began to wind up the poor farm workers who had stopped by for a quiet drink on their way home – 'Pint of Babycham lemon top coming up, sir', 'cherry with your bitter, sir?' etc. They accept his antics placidly, deserving better. They don't know what an awful snob he is behind their backs. 'The clientele here is *agricultural* altogether, wouldn't you say? Not at all what I'm used to.'

He used to serve cocktails in London where he came to escape the stigma, real or imagined, which attached to him in Ireland. For, as he confided to me in the lull between the early and late evening custom, 'I'm what you'd call a *homo*.' As his confession suggests, he's nothing of the kind. He doesn't really fancy other men. What he likes is a good giggle with the girls and dressing up in his 'outfits'. Today it was matching lavender socks and tie (9 out of 10); light grey 'slacks' *with* turn-ups (7); light blue pullover (6 upgraded to 8: 'Look! There's no disgusting little *logo* on it!'), etc. Brendan hated London, found it a 'filthy place', was glad to come down here. 'I may be a homo but I still have the solace of my religion. Oh yes. You can riddle me with bullets where I stand. You can beat me over the kidneys with telephone directories. You can circumcise me, feather and tar me – but I've lived a Catholic and I'll die a Catholic, with the name of the Blessed Oliver Plunket on me lips . . . '* All good stuff.

Brendan also passed on a fascinating and terrible piece of information overheard in the bar: my Reverend Smith died, quite young, in a fire.

Was it the fire in the cellar??

The days fly past. I want them to. I want them to go as fast as my thoughts. I want my thoughts to go faster, to whirl like falling leaves inside me, weaving a golden pearl around my poor scratched heart.

Thanks to dear old Claude,** I've been able, I think, to begin to discern some sort of order in the chaos of the Great Work. It shares common features with the tribal way of thinking and of ordering the world. It not only uses the same system of dual classification, it also uses many of the oppositions – light/dark, sun/moon, etc. – which are found in all cultures. These can truly be called archetypal elements –

---

* Brendan is out of date. St Oliver Plunket (1629–81), the Archbishop of Armagh martyred by the British, was canonised in 1976.
** i.e. Claude Lévi-Strauss (b. 1908), the eminent French anthropologist who was a pioneer and leading exponent of the structural approach to anthropology.

but they are by no means the only ones which alchemy shares with practically all other cultures. The colour sequence black-white-red seems to be universal. So does the incidence of certain numbers, such as two, three, four, seven, twelve, and of certain elementary designs, such as the square and the circle.

The great lesson of structural anthropology is that these archetypal elements have *no consistent value*, no absolute meaning. Their value changes according to context, according to the relationships between them.

I remember being very struck by this insight while reading an account of the colour symbolism of some African tribe whose classification system uses, among other things, bodily fluids. I had just grasped that blood symbolised both 'darkness' and 'redness' when to my irritation, I was asked to swallow the fact that it also symbolised 'light' and 'whiteness', that is, the exact opposite. (Jung had the same problem when he found that his archetypal symbols equally contained their own opposites.) The trick, of course, is not to think in terms of 'symbolism' but, as usual, in terms of analogy. Thus I was able to put together a sequence which ran something like this:

mother's milk : blood shed by a warrior :: light : dark :: white : red. But, in another context,

blood shed by a warrior : menstrual blood :: light : dark :: red : black.

In this way 'blood' does not *in itself* take on an opposite signification; it is simply 'dark' *in relation to* one thing and 'light' in relation to another. Reciprocally, light and dark or red, white and black don't mean anything in themselves; they take on meaning only as members of pairs of significant oppositions.

A Roman Catholic friend once told me that a novice nun wears white to symbolise her purity. This may well be the case. But since a fully fledged nun wears black the novice's white is just as likely to be a term in the relationship:

novice : nun :: white : black.

And this relationship may in turn be a special application of:

white : black :: wedding dress : mourning clothes :: bride : widow :: marriage : death. In which case:

novice : nun :: 'Bride of Christ' : 'woman who has died to the world'.

A priest's clothes are coded differently; he wears black while going about his everyday business, but a white surplice when saying mass – black : white :: profane : sacred. I have a strong suspicion that the wedding party at a traditional Chinese marriage wears red; but mourners in China wear white. So, in China, red : white :: marriage : death.

This idea, that the same elements have different significations, has profound implications for the Opus – its apparent contradictions are due to the fact that is elements assume *opposite qualities in relation to each other* during the transformations they undergo in the Hermetic egg. This is something my tentative diagrams [see p. 171] have actually made clear already. In Solution, Sol : Luna :: Above : Below :: light : dark and mercury : sulphur :: volatile : fixed. In Conjunction, the terms are reversed:

Sol : Luna :: Below : Above :: dark : light, and mercury : sulphur :: fixed : volatile. This perfectly fulfils the alchemists' prescription to 'make that which is Above like that which is Below' and 'to make the volatile fixed and the fixed, volatile'. (As Jung might say: 'make everything conscious that is unconscious and make everything "inner", "outer" and everything "outer", "inner"'!)

The second and fourth stages of my text represent an exchange of terms with stages one and three. In Separation, we see that mercury : sulphur :: Below : Above, and Sol : Luna :: volatile : fixed, while Putrefaction again reverses this scheme. (Dark/light are not opposite here because Putrefaction : Congelation :: dark : light.)

From Solution to Congelation, then, the 'wheel of alchemy' turns full circle (anticlockwise, to the left). The two pairs of elements, Sol and Luna, mercury and sulphur, pass through all positions, all possible transformations in relation to each other, in order to be synthesised into a new unity, analogous to the prima materia, but at a 'higher' level.

Lévi-Strauss noticed that the number of contrasts used by mythological thought varies from one set of myths to another.* Some sets merely contrast sky/earth, high/low. Others subdivide these categories into subsets in order to convey equally fundamental contrasts, e.g. male/female can be placed entirely in the 'high' category, as sun and moon perhaps, where they either coexist or clash. Equally, male/female can be transferred to the 'low' category,

---

* *The Raw and the Cooked* (London, 1970), pp. 332–3.

as earth/water, vegetable/mineral. Exactly this sort of shift of levels takes place in my text: Solution sees the *separation* of light/dark, male/female, sol/luna, mind/spirit (consciousness/the unconscious) under the general category Above/Below; Conjunction sees the 'dark' *reunion* of these opposites under the same category. But at Congelation, which looks the same as the diagram for Solution, there is in fact a substantial difference – Above and Below have themselves been reunited under the category 'light' or 'whiteness' as opposed to the blackness of Conjunction. Now, Sol and Luna are united 'Above'; but since they represent Above and Below, a new opposition has to be introduced, namely Heaven/Earth, of which they comprise 'Heaven'. This will be joined with Earth (formed by the volatilised sulphur and fixed mercury in the 'Below') at the Rubedo.

Jung described the male psyche as complementary to the female psyche, and said that, since the Opus was invariably performed by a male alchemist, its structure doesn't apply to a female. Whereas in the male psyche, sol : luna :: consciousness : the unconscious, the reverse is true of the female:

Sol : Luna :: the unconscious : consciousness.

All I can say is, either I've misunderstood him (which is not unlikely) or he's not entirely clear about the Work. The *whole point* of it, as far as my text is concerned at least, is that it recognises the astonishing fact that each gender contains the other; and the Work's aim is to transform male into female and vice-versa. Sure enough, the second analogical set, which he says characterises the female psyche, would of course be exactly the one represented in my text by Conjunction. The difference is, that the female alchemist would begin with it – it would be her equivalent of Solution.

The problem about Jung's opposition, conscious/unconscious, is that the unconscious has a disconcerting tendency to *know more* than consciousness. It often anticipates, and provides incentives for, our psychic development as if it were a 'higher' consciousness than mere ego-consciousness. Somewhat desperately (it seems to me), Jung attributed this tautological tendency of an unconscious consciousness to certain 'psychoid factors', whatever they are.

Actually it's not too difficult to see how, as the Albedo approaches, consciousness is widened or deepened to include material from the unconscious – material which is collective rather than personal in nature – so that consciousness is no longer 'mine' but something in which 'I', as an individual, participate. This anticipates the Self, concerning which consciousness can't be defined as being personal or even 'inside' – it is both inside and outside us, just as the Self is both Above and Below us, both immanent and transcendent, both 'I' and 'not-I'. At the microcosmic level it is as if the body were to develop a consciousness which embraced that of the mind; on the macrocosmic level it is perceived as that awful experience of Nature as a living, thinking, purposeful Creation.

The cellar has dried out nicely. Today I played truant from reading and writing to drive into town first thing for a visit to the DIY emporium. By the time it was dark, I had finished the whitewashing – on three walls at least – which someone had begun. I couldn't bear the thought of those scorched walls. I imagined I would have to shut out any idea of the gruesome event that took place in the cellar; yet, funnily enough, there's nothing morbid about the room. I was cheerful, and worked easily and hard. Perhaps it's only my fantasy that John Smith should have perished there.

I removed the grating from the well and lowered in a bucket. The water is icy cold and clear. I tentatively tasted it. Delicious. I took refreshing swigs throughout the day. I could bottle it and sell it – a bona fide cottage industry – except that Mrs Z. would no doubt want ninety per cent of the profit.

It's difficult not to feel *near* to someone whose writing you study so closely. Their idiosyncrasies are like familiar and well loved tricks of speech. How well I know his stutter on the letter 'g', his hesitations on the 'sh's. How easily I sense his tiredness in the repetition of a word or phrase, or his frustration in a sudden crossing out, his irritation or exultation spilling over into the margins.

I used to be a day person – up at the crack, early to bed – but no longer. My routine – rise, read, walk, eat, write, read, eat, write, sleep – gets later and later. I've discovered the joys of working at night. No distracting view from the window, no people, no sound. You tick on while the world sleeps, tapping into its dreams.

It's 2.30 a.m. The magic hour when the metabolism suddenly dips, when people who are going to die, die, and mystics in their lonely cells see angels. The hour when the mind is loose, when dream comes down on furious thought like ice-cream clouds over a volcano; the hour when God knows what ideas come wailing like klaxons into consciousness and huge intuitions beach themselves on the shores of the brain.

I have only to sit very still to sense the sudden stirring, the vertiginous unravelling – my golden soul's molten surge as he makes to *stand up* in me and stare with brazen eyes through my eyes – I feel the mould cracking and cling to the desk and say aloud, 'Not yet, *not yet*.'

I keep coming across bits and bobs of information about Alexander Seton. He seems to have been a mysterious character, a Scot who appeared out of nowhere in around 1602 and caused a furore across Europe with a series of projections [i.e. transmutations] in Holland, Switzerland and Germany. For instance, Smith mentions how two sceptical university professors, Jacob Zwinger and Wolfgang Dienheim, were allowed by Seton to collect the materials for a projection – a crucible, plus lead and sulphur – from different places to prevent trickery. They themselves dropped a small packet of Seton's yellowish powder into the molten mixture of lead and sulphur. In fifteen minutes the molten matter turned to gold, which, assayed by a local jeweller, was pronounced purer than 'Arabian gold'.

Seton apparently continued his operations in Strasburg, Frankfurt and Cologne. In the summer of 1603, for example, several witnesses in Frankfurt saw him transmute six ounces of mercury into gold, which was described by an assayer as 23-carat. Inevitably he attracted the attention of Christian II, Elector of Saxony, who threw him into jail when he performed a projection in front of the entire Court, but refused to reveal how his 'powder' was made. The unfortunate Seton – he's described as short, stout, highly coloured, with a beard in the French style – was pierced with iron spikes, scorched with molten lead, burnt by firebrands, beaten with rods and racked until his limbs were disjointed. He still refused to say a word.[5]

It almost looks as though, with the sudden rash of public transmutations in the seventeenth century by the likes of Seton and (possibly) Philalethes, the alchemists were deliberately drawing attention to themselves.[6] It was as if they scented the cold wind of the new approaching world-order that would blow them into historical oblivion; as if they were staging a last-ditch attempt to impress the world with the reality and pre-eminence of their Art.

There was something *hysterical* in my passion for P. Nothing to do with him, of course; more to do with some deep sense of release on my part – relief that I'm capable of normal feelings and desires towards a bloke. I had begun to lose my nerve, to lose heart, even to panic ever so slightly – and to panic more at the panic itself. It had been so long since I'd even remotely felt as I felt for him, feel for him. I had begun to despair of ever falling in love.

Looking back, it's ironic that I should have 'saved myself' for Mr Right all those years – only to give up my virginity to David. It was tough being a teenager in the abysmal swinging sixties, tougher to know that you were probably the only virgin left. Still, I might've hung on if the sixties hadn't gone on well into the seventies. As it was, I became a victim of peace and love. My nerve failed. What if Mr Right didn't come along? Dad's romantic stricture that I should save myself at all costs for Love seemed less and less binding. The treasure I guarded became more and more like a jailer. I tried to summon my soul for guidance but Dad's face always got in the way, fastidious and dismissive of the lads I fancied. In the end I had a few drinks and in a spasm of fear, excitement and shame, hurled myself into David's arms.

On the whole I've never regretted it. By a pure stroke of luck David was just the ticket: handsome, wholesome, sexy, good fun, but, above all, kind and thoughtful. His pleasure was as much in my pleasure as his own. My load was shed without fuss and with only a little blood. It might have been better to have remained intact if I could have done so for the right reasons. As it was, best to get shot of it. OK.

I told P. about David. He listened patiently. He was non-committal but not unsympathetic. I remember he expressed surprise that David was American. I didn't really say what I wanted to say. I didn't *know* what I wanted to say. I instinctively omitted two facts. First of all, I didn't mention that David was married. I didn't know it myself at the time. Not that he hid it from me. He assumed I knew. Indeed, it was blindingly obvious. I would have laughed at anyone who, in my shoes, didn't realise it at once. But I suppose a kind of vanity intervened to throw up a smokescreen. I wanted my first lover to be all mine. I didn't want to marry him. Far from it. But I suppose, like a trembling virgin, I wanted him to want to marry me.

Anyway, the second fact, which I'd like to believe was casually omitted, was probably suppressed: David was a professor. Only an American one, as Dad might say laughingly, but nevertheless I can see P.'s Amateur Shrink expression coming over his face: 'A professor? You mean, like your father . . . ?'

The only thing that caused me any real pangs of distress over this episode was how *little* I did in fact feel for sweet ingenuous Californian David, with his lovely straight American teeth and his sensitive close-together Jewish violinist's eyes. And I went on feeling so little for subsequent chaps, as much as I liked them, that I can't be blamed for thinking that perhaps I was a trifle neurotic, a teensy bit blocked in the old Deep Feelings department, just a touch father-ridden, etc.

But I couldn't give a monkey's about this now. The chaps I've been out with were all fine and good; but they never seemed to have what I longed for (thought I glimpsed it in Philip Allegro) – what I didn't *know* I longed for until I began to study Smith's texts. I mean: spirituality.

I don't care how embarrassing this is. It's what attracts me, what I can love in a man. It doesn't mean I'll become a priest groupie; I don't mistake the uniform for the fact (although being a priest doesn't necessarily rule out the spiritual). Nor do I want to play Héloïse or Clare, hankering after some Abelard or St Francis. I just long for the divine folly, the mad otherworldliness of people like the alchemists. It's what P. wants too, if he only knew it. That's what I saw in him: a kind of weariness with the streetwise shrewdness of what people have the gall to call the 'real world', and a desire for some Archimedean point of truth outside it. In a way he's smarter than I am because he doesn't hope to find it in a woman. But he pointed me in the right direction, unlocked the door, let out my cramped feelings. Through him I have been freed to love. My error was to identify the freedom to love, with love itself. I'll always be grateful to P.; but I have to press on now, to make myself worthy of love, should it happen along.

Everything is utterly changed. I was beginning to feel happier about the Zetterberg. I was beginning to believe that she was human. *God*. My gorge rises to think of it. She really is the foulest, most loathsome – she's a *savage*, for God's sake, a wild animal.

SMITH

It's here. Darkness. The Horned One. One eye one leg. *Monstrum*.

EILEEN

The Magnum Opus is patently related to what Lévi-Strauss thought of as the central problem of anthropology, viz: *the transition of Nature to Culture*. His contention is that man is preoccupied with his own paradoxical existence: we are *part* of Nature and yet we can't help seeing ourselves as *other* than Nature. At the same time, in order to survive, we have to keep up our relationship with Nature. The way we meet this contradiction, Claude reckons, is by cooking. We don't *have* to cook but we do so for symbolic, as much as for gastronomic, reasons.

Just as there's no human society which doesn't have a spoken language, there's no human society either which doesn't cook in some way. Like language, cooking is a prerequisite of Culture as against Nature; and the key feature of cooking is *its transformation of raw materials by fire*. (Hence, presumably, the widespread motif of the culture-hero who procures or steals fire from the gods; and whoever, Prometheus-like, procures fire, also teaches man the rudiments of culture, e.g. arts and crafts.) Fire is the agent by which Nature (raw food) is transformed into Culture (cooked food).

Significantly, the alchemists also describe their Art as one of 'cooking'. Their aim is simply to transform the right 'raw stuff' into the Stone by means of different degrees of 'natural' fire, plus the one 'secret fire'.

However, the outstanding differences between alchemy and culinary operations are firstly, of course, that the former is a purely *individual* activity while the latter are *collective* (social). Secondly, the alchemist is not dealing with organic material – food – but with inorganic material, 'metals'.

Our relations with food are the opposite of those with 'metals'. That is, we're in the *most* direct relation possible to food because we eat it; the inorganic 'metals' are what we're in *least* relation to. My guess is, therefore, that the inorganic signifies that to which we are *absolutely* related – ourselves (or, to put it another way, God). Thus alchemy becomes a kind of internal cuisine or a 'meta-cooking' which doesn't so much transform Nature into Culture as transform Culture back into a transformed Nature. It's a reversal of social 'cooking myths' because it starts with the individual who is, by definition, acculturated and whose task therefore is to reunite himself with Nature in some wholly new way. To achieve this he can't use the ordinary fire which transforms Nature into edible Culture, but must resort to a 'secret fire' which will, paradoxically, transform the inedible inorganic realm into an edible 'meta-Nature' – the Elixir, which in turn transforms the adept into supernature (an immortal).

Alchemy strove to overcome the contradictions of existence – the fact that we are self-transcending beings who are both continuous and discontinuous with Nature. The task therefore was to separate Above from Below, Culture from Nature, soul from body, and then to reconvene them in that mysterious Stone which can withstand any fire because it is itself composed of fire – the self-transforming 'secret fire' which is both the means of the Opus and its end.

In tribal societies, people who are most deeply embedded in Nature commonly have to be 'cooked' in order to return them to the fold of Culture. By 'embedded in Nature' I'm referring to those periods of life, such as puberty or pregnancy, when people are profoundly subject to physiological processes. In other words, symbolic cooking is a *rite of passage* which serves to socialise those who are under the sway of biology. For example, boys are typically classified as 'raw' until they are 'cooked' during puberty rites to become men – cooking is symbolised by circumcision, say, or by tattooing. Some Amerindian tribes place pubescent girls and women who have just given birth into 'ovens' hollowed out of the ground; among the Pueblo Indians women give birth over hot sand to 'cook' the newborn baby.

Isn't the Opus like a rite of passage in which raw matter is 'initiated' by the alchemist, who thereby initiates *himself*?

The Hermetic vessel is certainly analogous to the ritual womb or tomb or oven in which rites of passage take place. It is like the liminal, or threshold, zone between 'village' and 'bush', 'habitat' and 'wilderness', Culture and Nature, in which the initiate's transitional physiological state is symbolically correlated with a transitional social status. One could say that, by analogy, the physical changes of the matter in the philosophical egg are symbolically correlated with the spiritual changes of the alchemist.

Which of the rites of passage is the Opus like? They are associated with the major changes in natural life – birth, puberty, marriage (and childbirth), death. I suppose puberty rites fit the bill. They're often the most important (contrary to one's own experience of them: confirmation in the Church). They commonly involve elaborate preparation, fasting, hardship, tests of manhood (e.g. slaying a lion), ritual circumcision, tattooing or scarification, the learning of sacred lore, symbolic death and burial before a rebirth into society with a new status and even a new name. But hang about – am I being thick? I am, I *am*. The Opus incorporates *all* the rites of passage: the first five stages correspond to the crucial stages in life. Solution = the *birth* of Sol; Seperation = his initiation at the hands of hitherto unconscious desires and affects such as occur at *puberty*; Conjunction = *marriage* (and *death* in the forbidden union between Sol and his mother/sister/daughter Luna); Putrefaction = *burial* (a mixture of cremation and burial, perhaps – cooked: rotting :: cremation : burial); Congelation = *rebirth* (the same configuration as solution/birth but transformed to a new spiritual status); Sublimation (Rubedo) = ? Some state for which Nature supplies no equivalent. The Opus re-enacts one's whole natural life in a short (or shorter) space of time in order to raise it up into consciousness and recreate it.

I ought to set down Mrs Z.'s atrocity. OK. I was in the manuscript room as usual. I had taken a break from reading and was standing at the window which overlooks the weed-infested courtyard at the back of the Manor. It's surrounded by old stables and outhouses where farm machinery is kept and, in winter, cattle. Mrs Z.'s hens were pecking about in it. On the left there's an open-fronted outbuilding where the wood is stored. There's a chopping-block in front of the wood stack and an axe. A movement caught my eye and I – I feel sick.

*

This morning, a note from Dad:

> Darling! Must get away from the maelstrom of university life over Christmas. Have booked in at Green's [a London hotel] to escape the usual tinsel, turkey and general sentimentality. Will you join me for lunch *à deux* on Xmas Eve and stay for some, if not all, of the *soi-disant* festive period?
>   Your loving father.
>
> PS Please may we dispense with presents this year? I have enough unreadable books and unwearable ties to see me out!

He *is* funny. He writes as though he spends every year deafened by the Christmas hoo-ha when in fact he invariably spends it abroad! No mention of Tanya. Has he given her the elbow after all this time? I thought she'd last. I doubt if he'll do better.

Still, Dad and I haven't been properly '*à deux*' for years. There's *so much* I have to tell him. I can't think of a nicer – or a more exciting – way of spending Christmas (there's something a bit *naughty* about hotels!).

There's one anomaly that bothers me about sleeping with David. On the fourth (and, as it turned out, the last) occasion, I was lying in his bed, giving myself up to that delightful dreamy relaxed state, idly glancing around his room, when I was seized by a deep irrational fear at the sight of something poking out from behind his chest of drawers.

My body began to shake alarmingly. David attempted to put his arms around me; but, while *I* remained perfectly rational and almost amused, my body was terrified of him. It was all I could do to prevent it from leaping out of bed and fleeing in horror. The immediate occasion of this fit was an innocuous ivory walking-stick which David's uncle had picked up in India. It awoke my childish memory of the cane in Dad's study.

For a moment I relived all the dread of that walk down the dark narrow passage, the sensation of entering that forbidden room (but Dad hadn't forbidden it, had he?), the excitement and terror of finding the cane behind the green cupboard (I *knew* I'd find it. But how? Had I been beaten by it already and forgotten? It's unthinkable). I think

I recall the tentative way I made the cane swish and then, with all the anguish of a self-inflicted wound, the way I tested its power by feebly swiping the leather settee. For a moment, too, I feared that David would use his stick on me, just as I had secretly feared my father wanted to use the cane if I didn't excel at my homework.

I was more upset by this episode than I cared to admit at the time. I tremble still to remember it. Ought I to allow the cause of it all to surface? *Is* it always best to wake sleeping dogs? Are there some you should let lie, lest they spring up and savage you?

Myths. For example: people at all times everywhere have believed that they have devolved from some pristine culture – a Golden Age – when gods walked among the ancestors who were better, wiser, stronger and happier than we are now. Some natural or moral evil – a catastrophe or sin – caused a Fall from this state of harmony; and, ever since, we have been trying to recover it. The only way to advance is to rediscover the past, to recreate the conditions of Arcadia, Eden or Atlantis. The alchemists, for instance, sought to reproduce the operations originally taught to man by Hermes Trismegistus. Their aim was to restore man's unity with Nature and to heal the rift between Heaven and Earth.

The complementary myth – evolution – is much rarer. I can't think of one outside Christian-influenced cultures, for it is millennial ideas, I suppose, which foster belief in some *future* condition of peace and happiness. The Marxist Utopia is a popular evolutionary myth of the sociological kind, but our favourite is probably the biological one credited to Darwin but foreshadowed, so C. S. Lewis tells me,* in Leibniz, Kant and Diderot, and more or less articulated by Schelling, Goethe and Herder. In other words, there was a demand for it which Darwin supplied.

As the wise Philosopher-Scientist, the alchemist was, as it were, the culture-hero of the devolutionary myth just as the modern scientist is the hero of the evolutionary – a Romantic hero, in fact, who has been known to dramatise himself as a lonely, alienated, struggling seeker after pure truth and facer of unpalatable facts. Not content with a simple *forward* evolution (as the alchemist wishes only to go back) his

---

* In *The Discarded Image* (Cambridge, 1964).

movement is also represented as *upward*, towards some biological peak of which he is himself the forerunner. We are confronted with the myth of 'the Ascent of Man' which not only makes use of the old opposition, Above/Below, but also that other, more emotive opposition, Light/Dark. 'Benighted' alchemy is cast out into some Dark Age of superstition while our progressive 'enlightenment' (inviting favourable comparison with the 'illumination' of the saints) moves smoothly onward and upward.

There was a time when the white coat of the scientist, contrasting so starkly with the dirty, black-clad magician of old, was viewed with the same reverence accorded to a priest during his holy offices. Is there anyone now who doesn't regard it with the darkest suspicion?

Creation myths. Alchemists were divided over the question of Creation. Earlier adepts took their lead from the Bible and adopted the *Creatio ex nihilo* theory [Creation out of nothing]; later Paracelsists held that the prima materia was *increatum* – an eternal uncreated substance. In other words, they subscribed to either a Big Bang or a Steady State theory.

The Big Bang theory begins with a marvellous mythical *thing*. Once this thing big-banged it rapidly generated neutrons, protons, etc., all the raw stuff of the universe. Before that moment it was simply itself; it had being but it didn't *exist* because existence implies becoming and changing in space and time – and space-time didn't yet exist. It was still potential, coiled up like a spring or a snake in the original mythic 'fireball' where all the opposites were as yet undifferentiated. The alchemists' idea of the prima materia may well have been something very like this.

That day when P. didn't come with me to have dinner with Dad and Tanya ... He hung back; he ignored my carefully prepared appearance; he deliberately provoked me by referring to Tanya as Dad's 'bit of fluff' and referring to himself as mine. In all this he had divined, rightly, that I was setting him up in competition with Dad. He refused to collude with me. I was furious because I thought for once that a boyfriend of mine stood a good chance of 'winning'. I didn't want Dad to approve of him. I didn't want him to pass my

Father Test. I wanted him to fail – *without me giving a stuff*. I wanted it to make no difference to me, to my feelings for him. Really I was testing myself: did I care enough for P. to go on loving him regardless of whether my dear Dad approves or not, regardless of whether he writes P. off or not? But, oh God, when has he *not* written my boyfriends off one way or another – with faint praise or mild disparagement or the ironic remark which I appeared to force out of his unwilling lips, hanging on every word, struck to the heart by his slightest bias? I wanted, of course, *of course*, to please Dad in my choice of boyfriends as *I want to please him in everything*.

The wretched Pluto has been around to enquire if I'm all right. Needless to say I haven't been to the Manor since the Incident. I spoke to him coldly, snootily. I didn't mean to. I just wanted him to go away quickly. I believe he is – he must be – innocent of any involvement in Mrs Z.'s obscenity; but I can't help lumping him in with her. He's so like a ghastly *familiar* or something.

On the doorstep, a parcel. In the parcel, a letter:

> You were interested in my boxes of papers. You may be interested in these. I have often regretted that I myself did not make an effort of understanding. It is too late to begin now. My excuse must be that I never had your education. I suppose I might have tried – but that's of no interest to you.
>   These papers concern our vicar's experiments. I give them to you because you can understand and share his work in a way that I am not able, not being much of a one for ideas, science and the like. I believe he is still waiting to be understood and is pleased to think that you, who have so much in common with him, are willing to pursue the truth. He set much store by the latter. I had my chance perhaps but was not up to it. You don't see the importance of a thing when it is under your nose.
>   Yours sincerely,
>   Eleanora Zetterberg.

PS If you are not too busy I would be pleased to see you. Any day will do. I do not get about much now. Better not bring a bottle.

Extraordinary. The papers seem to be *John Smith's laboratory notes.**

At every twist or turn of the Great Work I am confronted by Mercurius. But just as I think I have him pinned down he slips through my fingers.

What is Mercurius? *Who* is he?

'This invisible spirit', says Basil Valentine, 'is like the reflection in a mirror, intangible, yet it is at the same time the root of all the substances [*radix nostrorum corporum*] necessary to the alchemical process or arising therefrom.'

If I were a Taoist or maybe even just Chinese I'd probably have no problem grasping Mercurius. He is as tricky as a Japanese Zen master. In fact it would be easy to make a case for alchemy as (amongst other things) the Western equivalent of Zen.

In seventeenth-century alchemical engravings, the stages of the work are often pictured as being directed or presided over by Hermes Trismegistus. The ancient sage is thus a personification of Mercurius who *mediates* between Sol and Luna as he does between mercury and sulphur. (Is it merely fortuitous that Mercury is the only planet to bear the same name as the 'metal' to which it corresponds?)

That old codger Simmons called Mrs Z.'s behaviour 'pagan worship'. I laughed. But could it be worse? Could my landlady be a species of satanist?

In the glimpse I caught, I saw no magical accoutrements. Nor was there any sign of a rite. All there was, in the courtyard below the window of the manuscript room, in broad daylight, was the sudden movement of a woman coming out from behind the wood stack. She was dressed in a brown coat and wellington boots, and she was cradling a hen against her chest.

---

* Or, as it turns out, probably only a part of them and not including his 'journal'.

In a single movement, horrifying in its precision, she seized the axe, thrust the hen on to the chopping-block and decapitated it. It was all over in a flash: the headless bird flapped like a nightmare in her hand and I could see the blood pumping in little spurts out of its stump of a neck.

Mrs Zetterberg, God help me, pressed the stump to her mouth. The bird's wings beat feebly around her face. When she detached it, her mouth and chin were red.

I went on quietly working for a while, unable to credit what I'd seen. At last my stomach began to heave. I dashed home, threw up. I'm careful to lock my doors at night.

We don't inhabit the world – we inhabit our models of the world. I take 'model' to mean not a small-scale replica, but an illustration by analogy. The implicit model for electricity is water, for instance. This is evident from the metaphors, drawn from the model, which describe electricity's behaviour – it 'flows' in 'waves' or 'currents'.

Models aren't conscious inventions; they are collective representations of the unconscious. However, they may crystallise in an individual mind as did, for instance, the Newtonian model of the universe. We talk about the world in terms of metaphors which derive from our models. Our use of the words space, time, matter, etc. is metaphorical. We don't usually realise this; we mistake our metaphors for the thing itself, the map for the landscape.

Our consensus of belief in the space-time continuum and the solidity of matter prevents the earth opening up under our feet. Our metaphors prohibit equally our disintegration in chaos and our union with the Source of all being: only madmen and mystics live without metaphors.

Our models can be modified – up to a point. They possess a kind of critical threshold beyond which no one transgresses with impunity. In the old days, anyone who crossed this threshold by expounding ideas too different from those which the official, orthodox model allowed, was condemned as a heretic, e.g. Galileo. More recently, such people were simply ridiculed. How Science laughed at the idea of stones falling from the sky! How it slapped its thighs at reports of a furry, web-footed, amphibious, egg-laying mammal with a beak! Its scheme of things didn't yet allow for meteorites and duck-billed platypuses.

How are 'heretics' treated nowadays? How, for instance, does the average enlightened progressive scientific wholesome individual regard alchemy? He confidently asserts – purely on the basis of ignorance, prejudice and intellectual idleness – that alchemy was merely a superstitious myopic groping towards modern chemistry. An alchemist would not now be treated seriously enough to be persecuted, or even ridiculed. He'd be ignored. The Philosophers' Stone – that winged platypus of the Art! – is dismissed as a *myth*, by which is meant the fantastic invention of childish minds. Well, bugger that.

What's good enough for Smith is good enough for me. Just because alchemy's not possible in *our* model of the world, that doesn't mean it's not possible. Since our models create the world, why shouldn't there be a world in which one element, like lead, can be converted to another, like gold? It's no good telling me that elements can't change – that the hydrogen atom always has one electron. (No one's seen a hydrogen atom; and, if they had, what would it prove?) The alchemist might say – as the Buddhist certainly would say – 'Of course the hydrogen atom has one electron. Of course there are scientific laws. But these laws are neither eternal nor immutable, and neither is the hydrogen atom. It has been created as it appears to be by our perception of it. To change our perception of matter is to change matter.'

Appearance and reality. Appearance is real *as appearance*, but unreal if it is identified with reality.

In a sense the secret of alchemy is to imagine a world in which it is possible to transmute base metal to gold.

FIVE

Putrefaction

SMITH

[This stage of the Great Work, part of the Nigredo, seems to have been the longest, lasting from the end of Cancer to the beginning of Libra, i.e. just over two months. However, it is also the stage in which Smith makes the fewest entries.]

Been down there almost three days, it seems. Light hurts my eyes. Hungry and very weak. The vicarage is empty and unlived-in. I called for Nora – I must *say* something, explain. How can I explain? More appropriate to ask her forgiveness.

When I went to her room I knocked but could not bring myself to go in. It reminds me – I remember both too much and too little of Conjunction's madness. Anyway she is not there.

My desk was tidied. On it a note from her: she has left me. She hopes it will not cause me too much 'inconvenience'. Her father has returned on leave and she must return to look after him, she says. There is hope that this is not merely an excuse, although I would not be surprised if she were simply exercising tact. I know now that it was (at the very least) irresponsible of me to expose her to the danger of that stage of the Work. More than that, it was diabolical pride – to think that 'I' could control it. Where was I when the dark Spirit appeared? I can't think of it. My world is unsteady, as light as thistledown which one blow will annihilate. I must keep writing – to make an inventory, anchor myself, keep what is left of things intact. They won't be the same again. What underlies phenomena is now known; and I am the forlorn explorer who writes on the blank edge of the world 'There be dragons'.

Was it me? And whose hand writes 'was it me'?

*

Fitful sleep. Weakness persists. Feel as if I've come in from a fearful battering by high winds. My body is loose at the joints, loose inside. I walk gingerly lest I fall apart. I am *scorched*: my skin is dry, my bones brittle, tongue swollen.

Went out on my rounds but had to turn back. Spent two hours sitting in the window, watching the beautiful speckled birds going about their mysterious business. I thank the Spirit who has let me live.

I have been to her room. Her scent fills it like a vast ache, evoking memories, yes, but too turbulent to set down.

I must remember what happened. We only truly experience what we recollect. If I cannot recall it, who knows what will spring on me unawares as my unquiet mind already springs on itself in those drugged vulnerable moments between sleeping and waking?

I found Tim red-faced and bothered among the kitchen utensils. He was, for some reason, trying to concoct a meal for me in Nora's absence. He told me I 'looked awful' and apologised for neglecting me. When I remonstrated with him, saying that it was not his duty to worry about me, he gave me a long-suffering look as if to say 'It's a dirty job but *somebody*'s got to do it'. He shooed me out of the kitchen; he wanted to surprise me with something nice. I hadn't the strength to tell him that what little food I force down generally disgusts me.

I took a turn about the orchard, dutifully moving my cramped legs, but without pleasure. When I returned, Tim was not much farther on. The labels of certain tins had come adrift and he'd ended up with corned beef, peas and peaches. Not what he'd had in mind. He was even slightly tearful. This took me aback – Tim's mandarin composure seems unshakeable. One forgets he is a young boy. I pulled myself together. I mopped his face with a clean tea-towel and straightened his blouse and skirt. He was soon his old self.

We decided that neither of us liked tinned peas. So, with great daring and a mutual pact not to let on to Nora who would deplore the waste, we ditched the peas in the dustbin. Tim made toast while I fried up the corned beef. Then he arranged the peaches artistically on the beef which I'd put on the bread. The combination of savoury and sweet was strangely successful. We had a big pot of tea and, for dessert, the remains of an apple flan Nora had left in the larder. We both hummed 'Frère Jacques' as we ate. It was the first food I've enjoyed since I last saw Nora.

Of course I *was* terribly tired and anxious. And the descent into darkness took its toll. I tell myself that this is sufficient to explain the aberration of events. But is it?

At the nadir, the total eclipse, there was some ghastly inversion of reality, like a nightmare and yet like a nightmare in which one goes to sleep and wakes on the wrong side of sleep, wakes into some other order of reality at once dreamlike and more real than reality where one is both more and less oneself – no, I can't say what happened.

All violence has ceased. The elements, all passion spent, no longer contend with each other. The conjunction of Sol and Luna, Above and Below has been consummated in the darkness. They are one body, which has yet to rot. There's no triumph, only lethargy. I am exhausted; and yet I must proceed to make the volatile soul fixed and the fixed body volatile. As the body is corrupted and sinks down into the deathlike equilibrium of putrefaction, so must the soul be separated from it and made to rise. Easily said.

I increase the heat but with no very lively hope that it will lift the weight of blackness which spreads like a stain through the soul.

Dryness. Neither thought nor feeling obtain. I work at my circulations, kneel at my prie-dieu. What else can I do? It's not that I've ceased to believe in God. It's just that God has withdrawn. Or perhaps the God I believed in did not exist in the first place.

The Opus has lost all savour. I go through the motions. Putrefaction succeeds mortification. Where once the blackness was alive and volatile, now it is fixed and dead. Our sulphur, that is, the body, must sink down into decay; the worm burns itself out, turns to mere maggots battening on the stinking matter. The soul meanwhile, that is our mercury, will soon (*Deo volente*) be free.

Heraclitus says: 'The path up and the path down are one and the same.'

Accidie. Whenever we say the worst is over, that is the signal for worse to come. I cannot even drum up remorse over Nora. The house is empty without her.

A truth which all the orthodoxies, East and West, have overlooked is that the body also has a life after death. It lies in the earth and decomposes, one larger life breaking down into many smaller lives. When the mystics attain the liberation of their souls in the great oceanic Spirit they may well die to themselves – but they rarely heed their bodies or, indeed, Nature, which is to their bodies as the Spirit is to their individual souls. Only our Philosophy takes *seriously* the imbalance in Nature that a soul without a body creates. (Along with the Holy Ghost, the Resurrection of the Body is the most mumbled, least understood article of belief in the Apostles' Creed.) For this reason the Art is to draw down the soul and raise up the body, making the spiritual corporeal and the corporeal spiritual in the microcosm, so that (in the microcosm) Spirit and Matter may once more be married as they were in the Beginning.

The days pass and still the soul does not separate from the body. Our airy mercury remains trapped in its mortal coil of earthy sulphur. If it does not rise soon it will sink back into its original chaotic condition.

It occurs to me that *the body's impurities are too many and too great to allow the tainted soul to escape.* If this is so, I have to intervene – but at what cost? One does not disturb the dead. But if our mercury is not freed the body cannot properly decay: without *niger nigrius negro* [the black blacker than black] the whiteness will not appear.

Were the Work going well, Nora's absence would be less felt. Tim, the dear soul, strives to distract me. We play the odd companionable game of chess but it's difficult for me to pull my mind into the necessary shape to formulate the exacting patterns the game demands.

The weather continues humid; the sun, heavy-lidded with heat haze, hangs over the dozing fields. Forgotten mutton in the meat-safe went bad and had to be buried. Milk turns sour on the doorstep unless Tim remembers to bring it in. He covers the butter and stands it in water, but still it goes rancid. I wonder, as the days drag by, if the weather is affecting the Opus – whether it, too, is contaminated so that Sol and Luna, mutually entwined, will rot together before they are raised up.

My duties have never been more wearisome. It is surprising how many I can get away with neglecting. No one misses my visits or, if they do, I do not hear of it. I do not actively discourage callers but my feigned interest is so patent that it puts them off. Janet has been but I don't answer the door to her if I know it's she. I could not pretend with her. I have cut out parish councils. I have nothing to say to Caldwell. However, I hear that his plans for abolishing Nightingale Wood have been put back. Not for long, I trust. It's all I can do to conduct a service without apathy. I crib my sermons from old ones I've already delivered, or from books. I no longer linger by the door to greet my parishioners; I hurry back to my cellar and the Work for which I reserve my remaining strength and prayers. My congregation is much fallen off. Soon the harvest will be in.

My mind is numbed. Words come to me from a great distance as if I were in a trance. It is in many ways a relief not to think. I must not try to restore my thoughts as they were. These old charred brains must be swept away and the head emptied to a clean white receptacle. At present there is *vacuity*, yes, but not yet the *emptiness* which will inevitably attract the influx of spirit. There is awareness, but it's not easy to locate. It is diffused inside me as if my skeleton were aware of itself. It seems to impale me. Every movement bruises me. Its vacant eyes look out of my eyes; behind my sad mouth it is grinning.

*

I had to *act*. If I had been more in my right mind I would probably not have dared. But I could no longer endure this twilight life-in-death. I broke the seal and transferred the commingled bodies of our King and Queen into my largest cucurbit. I raised the heat to the fourth degree. Then, quickly, lest the cadaver spoil, I bathed it twelve times in the mercurial fountain. Next, I entombed it in my alembic and attached the coil and receiver. In this way I hope the soul will be able to free itself from the body – which can then proceed to putrefy as it should.

EILEEN

Christmas Eve

I didn't know what to do with myself. The drive back from London was so weird and violent. I bombed mindlessly down the dark M4 with the Chieftains* turned up full blast on the stereo and me wailing along with those piercing tin whistles and nasal heartbreaking pipes, both sad and gay.

I went straight to the pub because I needed a friendly face. Brendan's was far from friendly. He wouldn't even talk to me at first. I had to worm the reason out of him: his feelings are hurt because I've neglected him.

'You only come here when you want a *drink*,' he complained. There was a good deal of flouncing and several pointed remarks to other puzzled customers about me and my painful hair-do. The pub was pretty much packed. I bellowed extravagantly high marks for his Christmas outfit – grey suit, emerald green silk tie, matching handkerchief – above the hubbub. He only tossed his head, refusing to fall for such obvious blandishments.

'She's so self-centred,' he confided to a woman with prematurely blue hair. 'So vain. She thinks of nothing but drawing attention to her own great flapping ears, with lobes on them'd be the envy of Dumbo himself.'

'Your *earring*,' I shrieked. 'It's gone!' Brendan permitted a rare smile to cross his deadpan face.

'Earrings. They're so seventies, don't you think? So . . . ' he groped for the word ' . . . so *niff*.'

'Naff?' I suggested.

'Also naff,' he conceded sternly. Thank God, we were friends again.

---

* A well-known band of traditional Irish musicians.

[245]

By the time I had driven through Oxfordshire my wailing had changed from anger to tears. It's not every day one loses a father. My crying was not without histrionic elements. The father I've lost was never wholly real. He was partly invented so that part of me could remain a little girl. The Chieftains broke into a fast reel. Behind the wild joy there is all the sorrow of Ireland. The rain on the dry-stone walls, the white foam on black pints of porter in bars filled with the ancient smell of turf smoke. I am sad that some weight – the gravity of adulthood perhaps – has been added to me; happy that another weight, like a satchel full of books, has been lifted. Freedom is never unalloyed. It's the exchange of involuntary constraints for voluntary obligations.

Two lads who work for Mike Bruford on the Manor's land bought me a drink. I bought one for the blue-haired woman. More people came into the pub, recognised me, wished me 'Happy Christmas'. I am not a stranger.

'Yer Man over there,' said Brendan, through the gap in his teeth at the corner of his mouth, 'has been putting them away with fierce determination.' He indicated Pluto, alone at a corner table, drinking steadily. I watched him for a while, watched how the other customers acknowledged him respectfully as they passed. He's no employee. I've assumed that, being disabled, he was taken on by Mrs Z., perhaps out of charity; but, of course, he is less dependent on her than she is on him.

I brought him over a large whisky, a peace-offering perhaps, or a simple gesture of goodwill. I sat on his good side. His dark eye regarded me.

'You haven't been to see her recently.' His voice was slightly slurred, but unreproachful. 'She talks about you. She doesn't often talk about people who aren't in the past. It's good . . . a good sign. I think you remind her of how she used to be . . . before she became the lady of the Manor.' He took a large swallow of whisky. 'Maybe I only think that because you remind *me* of how she was.' Drink had made him loquacious, but (mercifully) not maudlin.

'I'm sorry I haven't visited her.' What else could I say? He looked at me like a hawk.

'You know why I'm drinking too much?' I shook my head. 'Because I always drink too much at Christmas. There are things about Christmas I want to forget, but I always end up remembering.'

Some response seemed to be expected, so I said:

'Things to do with your ... injuries?'

'Worse than that.' He was abrupt, as if realising that he'd gone too far. He changed the subject. 'I have another reason for drinking today. The reason is, I found three dead hens behind the wood stack.' I went very red in the face; my only thought was to get away from him. 'I thought at first it was the work of a fox,' he went on. 'We've had a lot of aggravation from foxes. But, d'you know? It wasn't a fox at all, was it?' I couldn't listen to any more of this. I felt sorry for him, but what could I do? I quickly excused myself and pushed through the crowd. Outside a light frost had turned the Green to sparkling silver. A single light shone from the Manor.

If 'culture' is to be differentiated from 'nature' – that is, if human society is to exist at all – men have to learn to distinguish themselves from each other. They have to establish a social status. In tribal societies they do this by distinguishing themselves in the same way as they distinguish species of plants and animals in Nature. In other words they 'use the diversity of species as conceptual support for social differentiation'.* Lévi-Strauss dissolved the problem of totemism by showing that the social importance of totemic plants and animals is not, as some people thought, to do with their economic value, but simply with the categories they provide as species: plants and animals may well be *'bonnes à manger'*, 'good to eat', but as plant and animal *species* they are *'bonnes à penser'*, 'good to think' (or 'goods to think with').

I remember that Edmund Leach points out, in his paperback on Lévi-Strauss,** that far from being exempt from this practice the English have an elaborate system of classification for animals. For example:

1. wild animals 2. foxes 3. game 4. farm animals 5. pets 6. vermin

Entirely separate rules govern our behaviour towards these creatures. If we juxtapose these categories of animal with the

---

* See Claude Lévi-Strauss, *Le Totemisme Aujourd'hui* (Paris, 1962); English version *Totemism* (London, 1964).
** *Lévi-Strauss* (London, 1970).

following categories of human – A. strangers B. enemies C. friends D. neighbours E. companions F. criminals – it's easy to spot an approximate homology between the two sets of terms. The animal categories can be, and are, used metaphorically as equivalents for the categories of human beings.

The alchemist also finds animals 'good to think'; he uses dragons and serpents, ravens and eagles, crows and doves, lions and peacocks to categorise both states of matter and mind. He does not use plant species (unless he's a plant alchemist) but he does use 'metals': gold, silver, copper, iron, mercury, sulphur are all 'good to think'. However, he is, of course, not seeking to use these categories as a way of distinguishing himself from others; he's trying to distinguish parts of himself from other parts, whether it be the mental part from the deeper spiritual part, or the spiritual part from the physical. Alchemical texts are psychological, not social, 'myths'; they do not concern man's relations with other men but man's relation to himself, to Nature and ultimately to that transcendental Self in which all his relations are brought into harmony.

I was struck by a passage in Nicholas Flamel's *Thresor de Philosophie* in which he says that alchemy is simply the 'knowledge of the four elements, and of their sensuous qualities, mutually and reciprocally changed one into the other: on that the philosophers are all in agreement. And know that beneath the sky, there are Four Elements, not visible to sight, but by effect, by the means of which the philosophers, under the cover of the elementary doctrine, have given and shown this science'.

By distinguishing between the four concrete elements and their four abstract – 'not visible to sight' – counterparts, Flamel shows great insight into the alchemical process. His remarks are modern in tone, reminiscent of Lévi-Strauss's definition of *signs* which 'resemble images in being concrete entities but . . . resemble concepts in their powers of reference'.*

Sol and Luna, for example, are the concrete 'entities', sun and moon; but in relation to the category metals ('below') as opposed

---

* *Totemism* (op. cit.).

to heavenly bodies ('above') they are gold and silver. They are also, of course, a pair of the actual substances the alchemist is using. As 'concepts', Sol and Luna can refer to a whole range, from Above and Below to masculine and feminine to Smith's 'mind' (spirit of the Above) and 'Spirit' (as spirit of the Below) respectively. Psychologically they can refer generally to consciousness and the unconscious or, specifically, to ego-consciousness as opposed to, say, the archetype which personifies the unconscious. Sol and Luna are very 'good to think'. They mediate between all manner of different realms, providing a locus of exchange. The alchemist would call them 'subtle bodies', drawing attention to their capacity to signify both the spiritual and the physical, the abstract and the concrete, the mental and the material. It's hard for us to extract all Sol and Luna's powers of reference because to some extent the metaphors of the alchemical era still obtain – sun and moon are symbols which still have wider resonances for us than as simple heavenly bodies. They belong to that metaphorical system which opposes (in a general sense) light and dark, and (specifically) day and night. The moon is particularly 'good to think' because, whereas in relation to the sun she may be thought of as feminine, dark, sinister, etc., in relation to night (which is when, as it were, she plays the part of the sun) she can signify the light of day or the 'light' of dawning consciousness etc.

When the alchemist set to work on his elements (or signs), there is no sense in which he somehow *interpreted* the concrete substances in terms of abstract concepts any more than, during a conversation, we interpret the expressions and gestures of the person to whom we are talking – the expressions *are* the meaning. The Opus was not a cerebral experiment, nor even that kind of religious discipline in which, for instance, the alchemist manipulated the chemical formulae like a mantra in his mind while carrying out the operations in his retorts. No, it was more like a *drama* of which the alchemist is first the producer and then the audience, wrenched by pity and terror as Mercurius directs his tragi-comedy full of kings and queens and exotic beasts in a tale, both violent and lovely, of death and loss, rebirth and reunion. (But isn't a drama of this kind precisely what we should understand by *ritual*?)

*

The first task of the alchemist is to dissolve the undifferentiated unity of his prima materia and to separate out its elements into their pairs of opposites. At each stage of the work the elements change their signification. The effect is exactly that of a *kaleidoscope*: each turn of the alchemical 'wheel' alters the meaning of the elements by changing their relation to each other and forming a new pattern.

The archetypal elements – perhaps I should call them *primary* to avoid confusion with Jungian terminology – are properties of the unconscious psyche. They enable a social order to be superimposed on Nature. As far as I can see, alchemy is unique in proposing that the primary elements are also properties of inorganic matter.

When an alchemist said that the world consisted of four elements, he used the word much as I'm trying to use it – to indicate both a set of primary psychic factors and a set of primary constituents of matter. He would not have been perturbed by modern chemistry's discovery of ninety-three elements because he was not, as is often supposed, using the word in that way. In a sense he was looking beyond the chemical elements to the structure beneath; he was operating in the profound abyss where the psychic and the physical meet. (In this sense his activity has more in common with nuclear physics.)

The data in his Hermetic vessel told him that the world, of which he is a part, is structured in a four-fold way. This could be seen as a structure of opposition or, in another way, as an eight-fold structure which distinguished between *elements* (e.g. water and fire or mercury and sulphur) and *qualities* (e.g. cold and moist or fixed and volatile).

European alchemists after Paracelsus favoured a three-fold structure – presumably under the influence of Christian dogma which asserted the threeness of the Godhead. This trinity 'above' had to be balanced by a trinity 'below', and so salt was added to mercury and sulphur while Mercurius (as planet/quicksilver) was added to Sol and Luna. The three-fold scheme has the significance of an opposition plus a mediator.

The pressing question is: why do we use a certain limited set of elements and not others? Why, for instance, the principle of opposition in the first place? One answer may be that opposition is a cultural reflection of a natural fact, namely that we have a so-called left-brain and right-brain, each controlling opposite sides of the body (i.e. the left-brain controls the right-hand side of the body). The left-brain is supposed to be characterised by logical, rational, verbal thinking, and the right-brain by intuitive, emotional, visual 'thinking'. (They look suspiciously like Jung's consciousness and unconscious . . .)

I instinctively revolt against the idea of connecting the primary elements to predispositions inherent in the brain because it perpetuates a causal mechanistic way of thinking. It's not that I pooh-pooh *any* connection between psyche and brain; it's more that the psyche may not be exclusively located there. The brain has only recently come into such prominence – it's a purely modern Western collective representation to locate the centre of the personality there. Other cultures (and our own in earlier times) locate it elsewhere – in the heart or blood or liver or solar plexus, for instance.

It seems reasonable to me that our 'split' brain is as much an effect of the principle of opposition as a cause, particularly since the cerebrum (if that's the right word) is a comparatively late accretion. At the same time, it's undeniable that the world really *is* organised according to oppositions, prior to any further cultural organising on our part: our bodies *are* symmetrical on a vertical axis, thus opposing left and right, and days *are* divided into light and dark, and so on.

Our five senses seriously limit our perception of the world, but we tend to think that thereafter we are free to construct all manner of representations. We aren't. The shockingly few primary elements impose definite limits on our power to represent the world. We are less free in our inner creative life than we think; and, since the primary elements are by definition common to everyone, we are also less individual, less 'original', than we think we are.

This doesn't trouble artists of the first order, for whom true self-expression is also an expression of the universal. There is always something anonymous about great Art, as myths are anonymous. The alchemist worked directly with the primary elements – a few pairs of opposites, a few numbers and colours, a few symbols, a few rules of transformation such as inversion, reversal, alternation. He worked *at the limits of the imagination,* as if the imagination, through him, were working on itself to create out of its own paradoxical nature some wholly new resolution.

Boxing Day
I woke yesterday with a hangover. It was a sunny morning, clear and cold. I decided to go to church – a rare thing for me – and felt an odd little pang at abandoning my own sadly shuttered, lop-sided church for the one at Upper D—. I drove slowly through the crisp countryside enjoying the peculiar hush you get on Christmas Day.

The service was traditional, comforting, with its nativity stories and the old carols. Light at heart, strangely relishing the prospect of my first Christmas alone, I managed a reasonably sincere prayer for Mum and Larry and P., whom I pictured in the bosom of his family, at his mother's house in Wiltshire. In a fit of supererogatory virtue I also prayed for Dad and Tanya, for poor Pluto and, yes, Mrs Z.

There was a man with a little girl outside my front door. He introduced himself as Michael Hawkes and his daughter Sophie. His parents are old friends of Mrs Zetterberg's and they have always brought him to spend Christmas with her. Now, he brings his wife, Miriam, and Sophie. He was sent across to invite me to Christmas dinner and, later, tea.

I declined the invitation, of course. Michael spread his arms wide in a gesture both accepting and welcoming. He's a little younger than I, nice-looking, laid-back, intelligent. He talks very quickly and is madly enthusiastic about everything. I didn't want to appear stand-offish so I persuaded him to come in for a drink.

'I shouldn't really, no, I won't, thank you, we'll be late for dinner, it'd be *unforgivable*... Oh well, why not, to hell with it, dinner can wait, the turkey can *burn* for all I care, no, Sophie, I was only joking, the turkey won't burn, in fact it's so big, isn't it, it'll still be raw if we cook it till tomorrow... Good Lord, look at this *hall*, it's pure, pure something or other, wonderful, how'd you like to live here, Sophie, it's brilliant isn't it, I'd love to get my hands on it, it hardly needs anything doing to it, I could just fix up those mouldings on the ceiling a bit...' etc. Michael restores old houses for a living and is happy. Sophie and he obviously interest and amuse each other. She is six, darker than her father, very pretty and natural, with her hair done up in a topknot. Her large serious eyes often rest tolerantly and quietly on her gesticulating father.

We drank more whisky than we meant to. ('I'm doing the *wrong thing*, Sophie – look, did you see that? I took *another* sip, Mummy's going to be cross, you'll have to protect me, what a terrible thing to say, of course you won't have to protect me, oh, you *will*? Well, that's kind of you but I couldn't exploit your filial duty in this way, no, I'll have to face the music alone, serve me right, no, I won't explain what "exploit" means, it's too tricky right now, but I promise you *will* know what it means one day, soon probably, so don't *worry*, now I want to talk to Eileen so nip off and scribble on her walls while I distract her attention.' That's the sort of thing. It's infectious. I was gabbling as fast as he by the time they left.)

Michael and his family live in Derbyshire, about thirty miles away from his retired parents. He travels around a lot, to his decaying houses; Miriam teaches French. They are the only 'family' Mrs Z. has, apart from a relative in Canada, Timothy by name, who used to be – perhaps still is – a lawyer of the radical kind, fighting noble causes such as Indian land rights, illicit whaling, etc. He disappeared three years ago into the North-West Territories, or whatever that huge chunk of tundra is called, where he is rumoured to be living off the land and sea with some tribe or other and studying their religion.

I've been immersed this evening in van Helmont's fascinating *Oriatrike or physick refined* [London, 1662].* He actually describes the Philosophers' Stone:

'For truly, I have divers times seen it and handled it with my hands, but it was of colour, such as is saffron in its powder, yet weighty and shining like unto powdered glass. There was

---

* Jean Baptiste van Helmont (1577–1644), an outstanding chemist and physician, was the first man to realise that there were gases other than air (in fact he coined the word 'gas'). As one of the earliest empirical scientists he had little time, prior to his experience of transmutation, for alchemists whom he referred to as 'a diabolical crew of gold and silver sucking flies and leeches'.

once given unto me one fourth part of one grain (but I call a grain the six hundredth part of one ounce): this quarter of one grain therefore, being rolled up in paper, I projected upon eight ounces of quicksilver made hot in a crucible; and straightway all the quicksilver, with a certain degree of noise, stood still from flowing, and being congealed, settled like unto a yellow lump: but after pouring it out, the bellows blowing, there were found eight ounces and a little less than eleven grains of the purest gold.

Therefore only one gram of that powder had transchanged 19186 parts of quicksilver, equal to itself, into the best gold.'

The man who gave him the powder, he says, had enough to transmute two hundred thousand pounds' worth of gold. But what is interesting about him is that he used his 'stone' exclusively for healing. The man was an Irishman called Butler who was imprisoned in Vilvord Castle where he healed the diseased arm of a Franciscan monk (a fellow prisoner) by dipping 'a certain little stone in a spoonful of almond milk' and giving it to the monk to drink. Van Helmont went down to Vilvord the next morning to investigate the healing, and he made friends with Butler. He soon had the chance to witness another cure: Butler healed an old laundress 'who from sixteen years or thereabouts laboured with an intolerable megrim' by dipping the same little stone in olive oil, one drop of which on the woman's head was enough to cure her immediately; and she 'remained whole for some years, the which I attest. I was amazed, as if he were another Midas, but he smiling on me said:

"My most dear Friend, unless thou come thitherto, so as to be able by one only remedy, to cure every disease, thou shalt remain in thy young beginnings, however old thou shalt become." '

Van Helmont told Butler of the distress of a young prince of his Court, the Viscount of Gaunt, who was so prostrated by gout that he 'lay only on one side, being wretched, and deformed with many knots'. However, the young man was apparently so obstinate that 'he had rather die than to drink even but one only medicinal potion'. Butler was undaunted by this – he said that the prince need only touch the little stone every morning with the tip of his tongue and, after three weeks, wash the knots daily with his own urine, and he would be cured.

Van Helmont immediately set off for Brussels and reported what Butler had said. The prince replied: 'Go to tell Butler, that if he restore me, as thou hast said, I will give him as much as he shall require: demand the price and I will willingly sequester that which is deposited, for his security.' But when van Helmont duly related this to his friend, Butler was angry: 'That prince is mad, or witless, and miserable, and therefore neither will I ever help him for neither do I stand in need of his money, neither do I yield or am I inferior unto him.' Van Helmont was dismayed at the man's proud independence of mind and began 'to doubt lest the foregoing things I had seen were as it were dreams'.

But they weren't dreams. He saw a friend of his, master of a glass furnace at Antwerp, who was afflicted with great fatness, apply the same remedy as had been recommended to the prince. Butler provided a small piece of the stone to lick every morning. Within three weeks the fatness had significantly receded.

Curiously, the stone did not work on van Helmont himself. He refers to his having been poisoned 'by a secret enemy' which gave him painful joints, a vehement pulse and fainting of mind. Butler (who was still in prison) sent him some olive oil 'tinged' with the stone, telling him to anoint the painful places with it. Which he did – but 'felt no help thereby'. On the other hand, his wife, who had been 'for some months oppressed with a pain of the muscle of her right arm' and who now developed 'a cruel oedema' from foot to groin, restored herself to full health with a few drops of the oil.

The Great Work asserted that Nature is *not*, as classical physics later claimed, an assembly of elementary parts, but a complex network of relations between parts of the 'one thing', the whole. Moreover, the alchemist who examined these relations, whether he knew it or not, was (as Jung makes clear) always and essentially *included* in them. Quantum theory agrees with these views.

Well, that's torn it. If there's one thing gets up my nose it's superannuated acid-heads who bang on about subatomic physics to bale out their own half-baked scrambled-brain brand of mysticism. 'Wow, man, *amazing*. I've just seen a neutrino...' On the other hand, half the world's leading astrophysicists seem to be old Californian hippies. You see them on telly in beards and open-necked shirts, obviously posing as artists, never mentioning their mind-numbing maths, just smiling benignly and telling us that time goes backwards in a Black Hole or that (my favourite, this) there are two universes, mirror-images of each other, but going in opposite directions in time. The last time I looked in on them it was all 'string theory', with only one paltry universe but ten dimensions to make up for it. 'It must be true, man, because it's so *beautiful*.' These guys would really like alchemy.

Of course, they're searching for a Philosophers' Stone of their own, namely the unified field theory – Einstein's holy grail. The four forces concerned – electromagnetism, the weak and the strong nuclear forces and gravity – are to be reconciled in a single yet quintessential force. They have to be married to each other in a series of lesser conjunctions (as electricity has already been married to magnetism) before the grand union can be effected. It seems that the union of the first three is in sight, but gravity remains recalcitrant. No one has yet measured gravity 'waves' with any real certainty. It was supposed to have been 'discovered' by Newton when the apple fell on his head. I think it far more likely that he hit upon it during his alchemical experiments – gravity is, after all, not unlike a mechanistic version of the *Anima Mundi* [Soul of the World]. I therefore think it likely that gravity will not prove separate from the other three forces but will be found to underlie them in some essential way. If it *is* separate, then the mathematical formula for the unified field will also be the formula for the *Anima Mundi* or Earth-spirit. However I doubt that even maths is a suitable tool for the task: the unified field may have to be formulated – if that's the word – on an entirely new level. The structure of matter is not in the end separable from the structure of the mind (or, as Smith less misleadingly puts it, the soul). There's only one symbol that's appropriate for the unified field: the ouroboros.

C. S. Lewis [op. cit.] argues that new models of the world – anthropology's collective representations – don't simply replace old ones as a result of newly discovered phenomena. He cites as an example the nova [i.e. an exploding star] of 1572 which contradicted, but did not immediately alter, the prevailing doctrine of fixed and immutable stars. Instead, the human mind seems to grow tired of the old model and hanker after a new one – whereupon phenomena to support the new model promptly turn up. For example, the demand for an evolutionary scheme in biology, as opposed to the old devolutionary scheme, was already theoretically quite far advanced by the time Alfred Wallace and Charles Darwin came along; it remained only to find the evidence. A new model won't be constructed without evidence, but the evidence only turns up when the *inner need* for it becomes sufficiently great. 'It will be true evidence', says Lewis. 'But Nature gives most of her evidence in answer to the questions we ask her.'

This says a lot of important things about our relations with Nature. We have to be careful about the questions we ask her. Science, bless its little cotton socks, tends to ask her single questions under laboratory conditions which, by definition, exclude a great many different questions. This is fine – as long as it doesn't pretend that its observations are answers to the question of Nature's reality. As Mr Uncertainty himself said,* 'what we observe is not nature itself, but nature exposed to our method of questioning.' Thus the *way* we question Nature determines what we see.

Alchemy knew that Nature has every sort of phenomena in store and that to demand unequivocal answers to loaded questions was unrealistic. To know Nature herself, we must question her unconditionally, in her fullness, as the alchemist did who watched and waited for as long as it took before she provided her own answer in her own terms. He never bullied her if he could help it, but simply gave her his absolute attention, letting the secret fire gradually reveal her reality.

It seems to me that we can go on stripping Nature of more and more veils, but we'll never see her naked until we marry her and carry her to the marriage bed.

I had delicious boiled gammon for my Christmas dinner, slightly tainted because the parsley in the sauce was dried, not fresh.

---

* I thank my friend Kenneth Crampton for telling me that this refers to Werner Heisenberg (1901–76), the German physicist who formulated the famous Uncertainty Principle. The quotation is from his *Physics and Philosophy* (London, 1963).

Afterwards I drank whisky and reread John Smith's 'notes'. He describes his progress in more or less conventional terms – yet how alive these now seem to me! At first I was a shade disappointed: I thought Smith would demystify the Opus and make it instantly digestible. *Of course* he doesn't. This is alchemy, not television. Its exotic terminology isn't there to obfuscate – it arises spontaneously from the Opus whose own proper language it is. Alchemical symbols are the syntax of the collective unconscious! How can dear Smith reduce it to bare chemical formulae? He knows that the conventional terms are the true matrix of the Art in which his own personal quest can find expression.

The Work is irreducible. It can't be 'decoded', as I'd hoped, because that supposes it's a simple two-dimensional puzzle whose solution is hidden behind a set of clues. It's nothing like that. Rather, it's a complex multi-levelled Art which must be grasped whole and in the language appropriate to it – which simple formulae, however useful in other ways, can never be.

I climbed down the ladder into the cellar and lit a candle there. Isn't there always the feeling that, at Christmas, the spirits of the dead are near us, especially in places they've loved; that they gather around the tremulous flame of that one day's goodwill and, perhaps, breathe a ghostly blessing on the living? I grieved for the Reverend Smith whose life, if Brendan's information is right, was so agonisingly burnt up in my cellar. I have considered the spiritual danger of handling the Secret Fire on a daily basis, but I've overlooked the sheer obvious physical peril of a laboratory explosion.

I closed my eyes and imagined the sudden roar, the awful sheet of flame in that confined space. I held my breath and invoked the shade of John Smith, and, in the pressure of silence around my head, I seemed to sense a faint ripple of air as if he were nodding his own head in guarded approval.

Dear Mr Smith, I don't mean to intrude on you, or your Magnum Opus. But I can't help it. It has seized me and shaken me awake. My past is a dream. Bear with me, please. Help me to understand.

At half-past five I went out on to the dark deserted Green and looked at the little lights twinkling in the parlours of the cottages. An icy wind hoovered down the valley, making my ears ache. Shredded clouds raced across the sky. I was tempted for a second to visit the Manor – what could she do with all those people about? – but my nerve failed. All the same, the idea put it into my head to creep around the house and peek in at the drawing-room window.

It took my eyes a moment to adjust to the blaze of light from the dozens of candles on the tall Christmas tree. The first person I made out was Michael who stood, relaxed, glass in hand, on one side of the fire. On the other, Pluto leaned casually against the mantelpiece, his purple claw-hand dangling openly from the elbow. His head was thrown back, unselfconsciously revealing the full extent of his damaged face, and he was laughing.

Eleanora Zetterberg lay full length on the sofa, with a rug over her legs. She looked thin and drawn, but she was smiling faintly and leaning forward to give a small elegantly wrapped present to Sophie, who sat on the floor, her back against the sofa, her serious eyes wide with pleasure. Her mother, Miriam, was seated near her on a low stool, stacking the remains of the tea things. She spoke quietly to Sophie who ceased unwrapping the present and, glancing at her father, turned her glowing face back towards her mother. She made a quick funny little movement with her fingers which, instantly understood, made Miriam laugh.

Two older people – obviously Mr and Mrs Hawkes, Michael's parents – sat at right angles to one another in front of the fire. She was plump and grey-haired, with long laughter-lines around her eyes; he was leaner and darker than his son, but very like him. He was watching his wife watching their granddaughter. They both smiled at the same moment; and she, turning her head a fraction, caught his eye. For the space of a candle-flicker a bright palace of affection hung between them in that reciprocal look, and then it was gone, diffused like incense through the warm room. I wanted to push through the window's soft membrane and grasp a handful of it.

I was suddenly conscious of my frozen fingers and nose, my feet like ice in their boots. As I turned to leave, I saw something flash in Sophie's hand. Mrs Z. had slumped back on her cushions, seemingly unregarded. But it was clear by the way the others inclined unconsciously towards her that she was the centre of the gathering. She rested her fingertips on the hair of the little girl, who lifted up her present to the light. It was a piece of glass that glowed like blue fire. And, as everyone looked, the expression on the faces of the girl and of the frail woman on the sofa were identical.

I don't know any nuclear physicists, so where do I get the impression from that they are on the one hand brilliant and boyishly charming, dealing daily with the unimaginable realm of subatomic particles; and, on the other hand, sort of sad and trapped in tired, worn-out *mechanistic* ways of thinking? Isn't it significant that when they coin a new word, as they have to, to signify their findings, they lift 'quark' out of James Joyce's *Finnegans Wake*? It's a bit naughty, jokey, impishly 'unscientific' – like the physicists themselves. They don't seem grown up. They seem to live in the closed world of a mathematical game, curiously removed from real life. And yet they spend their days probing into the very stuff of reality. Why is it unreasonable of me to expect them to relate the restless, vibrant, living realm of subatomic particles to the rest of existence? How can a profoundly *spiritual* view of the world *not* force itself upon them? Are they afraid of being thought unscientific? Surely not, when their field of study makes it plain that it is no longer possible to be scientific – that is, scientistic – in the old sense.

So where are the wild visions that will tear apart our narrow, comfy Newtonian existence and give us a wholly new model of the world? We don't get them. We get plenty of weird cosmologies but they're not connected to our lives. They never leave the nursery. What does a nuclear physicist do if he sees a ghost? It is, after all, only another anomaly, another discontinuity with everyday life, such as he meets with all the time. Does he struggle to create a picture of things which can include ghosts? Not likely. He either tells himself that ghosts don't exist therefore he didn't see one, or he sticks it in the drawer marked Things I Won't Go Into Because They Get In The Way Of My Important Research Into Reality. But what *about* ghosts, angels, fairies, poltergeists, apports, levitations, spontaneous human combustions, UFOs, etc. – aren't they the equivalent of quantum events within our 'reality'? You can't tell me they don't exist – or, worse, that they *only exist in my mind*. A lot of funny things happen. Everyone knows and has always known that. Everyone, that is, except scientists and people who *believe* that scientists are *right*.

To study alchemy is to travel in time. I feel increasingly – almost palpably – connected up to a hidden stream of history which, still flowing through all of us, can with only a small alteration of perspective sweep us back through the years.

I have never considered time. It's curious how we measure it in terms of space, picturing it stretching away into infinity or, perhaps, seeing it as the circular procession of seasons and months or hands on a clock face. The idea of linear history is certainly a recent accretion which traditional societies find it difficult to understand. I remember P. telling me about his pal Charlie who was a district officer in the Solomon Islands. Whenever he was presiding like a judge over land disputes, he found that the natives could only indicate to him *when* an event had occurred by referring it to the particular D.O. of the time – 'such and such happened in D. O. Bloggs's time or in D. O. Jones's time.' European time had to be attached to a European.

To quantify time in terms of space is useful but, surely, misleading. Time isn't a different degree of space as the expression 'fourth dimension' implies, but different in kind. It is only *like* a fourth dimension. The past doesn't stretch away 'behind' us any more than the future extends 'in front of' us. The past – and, for all we know, the future – is present, but hidden. It can be recollected in all its vivid complexity, as Freud and Proust demonstrate. The taste of a madeleine can recreate a world we had thought lost. The totality of time – eternity – is all around us, its hand poised to tap us on the shoulder.

People can't be objects of scientific enquiry because they are its subjects. It's a delusion on the part of psychologists and anthropologists to imagine that their disciplines can be scientific in the way that the natural sciences are. Yet it's a delusion in which for the most part they persist. They seem to suffer from a massive inferiority complex *vis-à-vis* the natural sciences, always protesting how scientific they are even when (*especially* when) the scientific method leads them into areas with which it was not designed to cope.

I remember, for example, my deep shock on reading a collection of essays by eminent anthropologists on the subject of witchcraft and sorcery. They came up with some brilliant analyses of the phenomenon, some excellent theories (mostly sociological) about what was 'really' going on. They sought to explain why tribal peoples worldwide believe that witches are visible at night in the form of glowing lights; why the same people believe that witches can harm or ill-wish others at a distance; and so on. Not one of them gave a moment's consideration to the possibility that anomalous lights do actually appear in the night sky; that it may well be possible, for all we know, to harm people at a distance. They did not stop for a moment to examine their own cultural presuppositions and prejudices. If anthropology seeks to shed light on other cultures without allowing them to shed light on its own, then it is simply another name for bigotry.

True science constructs provisional open-ended models which take account of the incommensurable; scientism ignores the evidence that doesn't suit it and invents a model to which its limited methods can apply. It is quite capable of reducing the soul to 'mind' to 'brain' to computational device. God knows I don't mind attempts to map mental functioning on to the brain; I applaud them. I don't even mind having my brain compared to a computer. What I *do* mind is listening to some jumped up johnny in a white coat tell me in all sincerity that *this is the case*.

Jung was a true scientist; he followed his empirical evidence into a realm to which scientific objectivity cannot apply – the collective unconscious. He struggled hard to map this conventional science on to his conception of the psyche and its historical counterpart, the alchemical Opus, knowing that he was dealing with immutable facts of existence. He never quite got the two to fit. His 'scientific' colleagues ridiculed him as a mystic, which he did not take (as perhaps he should have) as the highest compliment. He pointed out that physics, the doyen of the natural sciences, was beginning to suffer, at its limits in the subatomic realm, the same problems of distinguishing subject and object, observer and observed, as his psychology. I rather think that he was branded as a heretic.

It's sometimes hard to believe that the scientism that outlawed

Jung is still rife in the 1980s. It seems so old-fashioned somehow. When I think of the clumsy paraphernalia of nuclear physics, with its miles of particle accelerator, its bubble chambers and computers, the effect is one of cumbersome, almost Victorian machinery. An alchemist would laugh incredulously at this way of investigating matter. The physicists are not disconcerted – not even by the way the matter under investigation laughs at them. Mercurius the eternal trickster is only too happy to come up with an infinite number of subatomic events – whatever event, in fact, the physicists predict; I suppose he's hoping that at some point those good-natured brilliant little boys will get the joke.

SMITH

One can't meddle with metals and their spirits with impunity. I have only myself to blame. It's in the nature of the Work to call up the lunatic Mercurius, at first in his dark phase and then, *Deo volente*, in his light. What wonder then if some misshapen dwarfish drooling thing should rise from the underworld and look at you with your own distorted face? And if I successfully embraced him, as I did, it's no surprise that I should then fall prey to his familiar and master – the inhuman Worm that burns like ice at the bottom of things. Who can withstand the lure of the Worm whom at root we all long for as much as we dread it? What is it but the brute lust, as impersonal as matter, that underlies all our desiring? There is that in me which, for a long moment, *wanted* to be consumed by the Worm – longed to burn in flames of evil ecstasy. I tried not to think of her, I remember. Tried to put her out of my head but I kept seeing her soft outline under the white sheet in the bed upstairs. I cried out in terror and anguish. I clawed at the creature who wanted to possess me with his black fiery thirst, I tore at him as Heracles tore at the poison shirt which ate into him more deeply the more he tried to rip it off, its awful single eye saw everything, saw where she lay, saw into my thoughts, it rose in front of me leading me on by its sick yellow sulphurous light like the flashes of light I saw as a boy when I had pneumonia and I struck out violently at some thing in the bed sticking its boniness into me – only to find, when the fever broke, that I'd been striking myself.

Memory fails us when we fail to attach ourselves to an event. By 'ourselves' I mean, I suppose, the *sense* of ourselves – Herr Doktor Freud's *ego*. I prefer the pronoun 'I'. It is the same with dreams as it is with early childhood: we can't remember them because we have no 'I' by which we are detached from events in the first instance, and by which we reattach those events to ourselves as data of experience. Whenever the 'I' is diminished or entirely passive we can only remember events (I'm thinking of dreams in particular) in a vague fragmentary way. In the wakeful state, on the other hand, the 'I' is too strong, too sure of itself – or, at least, too active and overbearing, which is not the same thing. In this case the 'I' puts on airs, deluding itself that it is identical with the whole self when it is in fact only a tiny part.

We should be trained to bring the waking and sleeping portions of our life into harmony. This would entail increasing the sense of necessity which is lacking in the possibilities of our dream world; and vice versa for our waking state. We should learn to diminish the self-importance of the 'I' while awake (for example by prayer) and to strengthen the 'I' during sleep (for example by simply willing to do so). This would enhance our grasp of reality and hence our ability to recollect (and profit from) those experiences which, incidentally or by choice, we have forgotten.

When I came up for air today, I found Tim reading in my study. He was wearing silk stockings, torn. I drew the line. In future, if he wishes to continue coming here, he is to wear boy's clothes. I don't mind the odd earring, but silk stockings are the limit. (Where does he get these things? Does he rummage through dustbins, rifle ladies' boudoirs?) Meekly he began to remove the offending articles on the spot, showing parts of a suspender belt beneath his shorts. He told me it was Nora's. It struck me that Tim is here too often, and I do not exercise enough – if any – guidance. He's getting too old for this dressing-up. Thomas is right to forbid it. I ordered him home to his father. Solemnly he announced that his father is no longer at home – he returned to his ship *more than two weeks ago*.

Why hasn't Nora come back? I know very well why. How could I think she could forgive my obscene visitation? And if she could forgive, how could she forget – as I have cravenly persuaded myself almost to forget?

So. I remember, yes, at the nadir, the Worm. How its eye opened, how it lunged blindly forward, carrying me to the stairs, how my feet dragged, how his hot breath came out of my nostrils. I remember standing before Nora's door, hearing the blood throb, feeling the Worm's itch to expunge the body's heat, to plunge it hissing into the cold moist effeminate soul. It pushed the door open I remember. I struggled against the invading dark, moving in spite of myself with the slow wading motion of a nightmare towards her white outline under the cool sheet, yes, I can see how her room was rent by the chiaroscuro of contradiction: exquisite pain, fearful desire, horrified exultation – all the oxymorons of ecstasy. And, Christ, the head I remember turning slowly on the pillow and – and I forget. I can't remember. *What have I done?*

There's hope. Mercury rises and forms a clear lunar water; sulphur sinks down into an earth as dark as the grave.

The darkness is not the *active* dark of Conjunction but the *passive* blackness of Putrefaction. The seed of whiteness matures in darkness (no generation without corruption).

Tim, very serious, asked me: is it true I burn black candles and raise the spirits of the dead to do my bidding? You have to laugh. He picked up this image of my work at a conclave of female pundits which is held with depressing regularity either at the bus-stop or on the Green. I need hardly add that chief among them is Mrs B., whose overwrought fantasising I detect in the lad's question.

On an impulse I determined to disabuse him of these unsavoury ideas, born no doubt of boredom and idle gossip. Dramatically I swore him to secrecy. His eyes grew big as saucers. Then I led him down to the cellar. It was strange to see him there, strange to see the Opus through his eyes.

I explained as simply as I could how I was (in a manner of speaking) cooking metals in order to transform them from their raw state to a higher, more durable condition. He immediately grasped – intelligent boy – the principle of the Spirit that animates all things, down to the basest metal, in the way that (analogously) carbon 'underlies' apparently very different things. We do not see carbon itself – we only see its manifestations – for example it can be hard and black (coal, graphite) or a very hard, clear crystal (diamond).

The colour and texture of carbon changes as it is fired in the great pressure-cooker of the Earth. The Spirit is like the sun whose light and warmth we can see and feel but which we can never know in itself; a dark sun which lies at the centre of the Earth, irradiating it from within, while the Earth itself, like a body to the sun's soul, acts as a stained-glass window to tinge this sun's rays into the many forms of Nature.

I described to him what stage the Great Work was going through and, much moved I think, he stretched out a hand and gently stroked the cucurbit in which the decaying body of Sol and Luna, the royal pair, lay entombed in blackness. He asked me when I would return the soul to its body and I explained that the body had first to be cleansed of all dross after which, if all went well, the Albedo would appear. As to how long – that is up to Mercurius.

Very little to write. The Work's Wheel of Fortune has ceased spinning. And I'm left hanging on to the bottom by my fingertips. But there was *one* thing: Tim brought Michael Crowther round to see me because the lad had been 'a bit upset' – frightened, I guess – by something that happened two nights ago. Tim showed a touching confidence in my ability to assist in explaining it to his friend.

Michael's a likeable fellow, fifteen and large for his age, slow in movement and speech – but not in any other way as I soon found out. In fact I'd say he is mature beyond his years, with all his mother's common sense and all his father's intelligence (which I trust he will not dissipate in the same way).

The story goes thus: at about 10.20 p.m. he had been sent by Mrs Crowther to fetch her husband from the Green Man. Tim, who should have been in bed, went with him. Returning across the village green, Crowther – he was a little the worse for wear – remarked on the size of the full moon hanging low over the vicarage roof. The three of them realised a second later that the moon was not full that night, nor was it in that quarter of the sky. They stopped and looked at it more closely. It was a 'sphere of light about twenty-four feet in diameter'; it began to 'pulse'. Mr Crowther did not like the look of it. The moment he became afraid, Michael did too.

Suddenly the sphere of light shot sideways, or 'jumped', at an enormous speed, stopping once more only to hover about fifteen feet above the graveyard. The Crowthers promptly took to their heels. Tim was amused by this; the whole event 'interested' him more than it frightened him.

Subsequently, Crowther wouldn't discuss the matter at all. Michael was ridiculed by the people he told. It was suggested more than once that he had lingered in the Green Man along with his father. His mother put it down to 'imagination'. He himself wanted to believe that 'gases' were responsible. Somehow they emanated from the graveyard and spontaneously ignited, in the way that will-o'-the-wisps are said to be the spontaneous combustion of 'marsh gas'. None of us, we discovered, really believed this. We didn't even believe the 'explanation' of will-o'-the-wisps – Tim pointed out that, even with his limited school chemistry, he knew that a 'marsh gas' such as methane would not ignite on its own and, if it did, it wouldn't burn in a coherent ball of light for as long as will-o'-the-wisps shone in the course of leading unwary travellers astray. We discussed other possible causes: a mistaken perception of the moon or another bright planet like Venus; aeroplanes; balloons; tricks of the light; ball lightning (whatever that is), etc. The boys ruled them all out in turn.

Then Michael confessed his real fear: that the light was a 'flying saucer'. He had been reading that there is an apparent abundance of these in America. They are disc- or sphere-shaped aircraft, often travelling brightly lit at night; they are manned by people from other planets. In fact, he thought on reflection that he could make out circular patches in the sphere which might have been 'portholes', through which he could see grey skinny shapes moving about.

Tim was quite enthusiastic about this, speculating that the aliens would almost certainly be more advanced than we and, knowing more, could quite well have an important message for mankind; but, seeing Michael's knitted brow, he kindly added that on the other hand his grandma had spoken of seeing a similar light in the vicinity many years ago. She had attributed this (not, he thought, altogether seriously) to witches who fly about at night emitting an intense glow. I hastened to suggest that the whole thing could probably be put down to some freak atmospheric phenomenon. Poor Michael was not so much reassured by this, as simply by having the chance to talk freely about the experience. He left in better spirits, more or less reconciled to the fact that he would never know for certain what he had seen.

All through that terrible Night I longed for daylight; but now that it has come I can't seem to avail myself of it. It's an effort for me to leave this cellar although I hate it here and come very near to wishing that I could break the glass and expose the body like a malformed child to die at the hands of the elements. I'm trapped down here where, if it is not safe, it is at least the devil I know. Above, the world is too bright and shrill and demanding. Besides, the stench of decay clings to me. I can't rid myself of its disgusting taste and smell. If I were to venture abroad I'd be smelt out immediately; so I play possum by day and emerge briefly by night like a stinking fox. If I run into Tim he does not appear to notice the odour of corruption or does not mind, or, most likely, is too polite to mention it.

I don't know why, but I think Tim feels he must come here more often to compensate me for the loss of his sister, to 'look after' me. I taxed him with this – tactfully, of course – telling him that I had looked after myself for many years. He was quite upset. He *wants* to come but won't if I don't want him to. I quickly reassured him that he was always welcome; and, in saying that, I realised how true it was.

Bradley has proposed marriage to her. Tim tosses off this piece of information as if it were a weather bulletin. I've not laid eyes on Nora for weeks. Tim brings the odd piece of news, enough for me to ascertain that she is all right. He does not specify her emotional condition, however, and I have not pressed him – partly I now realise because my own state is far from stable. Now he springs *this* on me.

Young Caldwell has gall, I'll give him that. But Nora will show him the door. I know her. She'll never marry except for love. I wish she were safely back in the vicarage – but why should she trust *me*? Can I be trusted any more than Bradley? She has every reason to think not. All my instincts tell me to rush to her at once – and yet I do nothing, knowing that the sight of me cannot but be repulsive to her. This whole business is a *torment*.

*

Later: it's worse than I thought. Tim showed signs of distress at my reaction to his news. He confessed that he knew more than he was saying, but that Nora had instructed him not to tell me. I coaxed his secret from him. It was becoming a burden for one of his tender years – and, besides, it is already known to Bradley and, of course, to Dr Sparrow. Tim is bewildered but cheered by the thought that he will be an uncle. It's the thought of who the father is that covers me in a cold sweat.

And so, all of a sudden, it suits Bradley to play the loving husband and father. I'd be more certain that Nora will reject him if I could get out of my mind her haunting remark: 'I'll live in the Manor one day.' Would she marry Bradley to recover what her family once owned? It does not seem conceivable; yet who knows how a young woman's impressionable mind can become distorted? And what changes might not her pregnancy have brought about? Perhaps she is already thinking of her child's future welfare?

I must remember, too, that she does not even dislike Bradley as he deserves. A kind of panic seizes me when I think of her alone in her father's house, besieged by Bradley, with no one to turn to and least of all me whom she can only despise or even hate. She *must* be made to understand that she need *not* marry for the sake of her baby – *I'*ll provide for any eventuality, provide for her and protect her. I must go to her.

It's the queerest thing, but I distinctly recall (at the nadir, amidst the obscenity) the thought of love. It was the merest faintest glimmer; and yet it seemed to my feverish imagination as if – I don't know how to put it – as if love were operating more strongly at the very time when it was by definition entirely absent. I can't say what I mean.

All I know is, that it was not love as I have ever known it. I think I've defined love all my life by its opposites. There is a love which is the opposite of hate, a love that is the opposite of desire, another the opposite of power and of fear and so on. As long as love is defined by its opposite it is always *equivalent* to that opposite. In this way our mercury is always defined by its opposite, our sulphur, yet both are correlated in the transcendent singularity, Mercurius. The Love I glimpsed had no opposite. It was certainly not an *emotion*. It is a simple unequivocal thing, like the air we breathe. Like the One Mercurius.

I have not yet reached the point where I am capable of love. Therefore I pray that the Spirit may let love possess me. Let me look at its face and, if it seems good, let me die in the light of its countenance.

At long long last – the end of putrefaction. Our sulphur has sunk down into its final decay. The eye alone tells me this from its quite extraordinary blackness, blacker than pitch, blacker than black. Now begins the process – I pray God it is not as protracted – of washing it free of impurity that it may rise in whiteness!

I decided to leave the matter in the alembic for the moment. However I will return it to the pelican as soon as I can. Robert did a wonderful job with it. Robert! I was possessed of a great urge to see him and tell him of my trouble and dilemma. I immersed the matter in our mercury whose fire, God willing, will purge the dross from the body and allow Sol to rise up and be joined with his queen. I sealed the cucurbit and, leaving Mercurius to do the Work, hurried off to Robert's chapel.

He was not at home. The place was locked, the windows curtained, the chimney smokeless. He was not on the Down, not on one of his favourite walks, all of which I traced as fast as I could. I was on my way back down the track from Nightingale Wood when I remembered Beard's Pond. I veered sharp right at the fork and followed the path until it petered out at the edge of the pond. I looked to left and right but could see very little through the undergrowth. My fast breathing was very loud in the silence which that odd hollow holds in its cupped palm.

The water-level seemed to have dropped a foot or so since I was last there; but the water seemed no less dark or deep. Although it was only late afternoon the twilight had already gathered around the banks. I started to beat my way around the perimeter, looking for Robert. The silence was oppressive. A sudden, seemingly enormous turbulence in the water startled me. I could just make out through the gloom something large and sickly-white turning beneath the surface. Robert's giant pike perhaps. I waited to hear the swish of his cast, but there was nothing. I turned back. I hate to think of that monster down there all those years, watching, growing, with nothing human in its round fishy eye.

I couldn't face going back to that empty house. I can't get over Nora being pregnant. It seems to be part of the awful endless muddle and weakness and lust that swamps everything, part of the inexorable running down of things. It should be joyous but is hedged about with sins. A baby is quite enough to carry without any extra burdens.

I trudged back up to the wood. It was a bad moment – which the dawning autumnal beauty of the turning leaves only made worse. The trees are preparing for their winter sleep; unaware that Caldwell's axemen will see to it that they never wake. Why can't I *rouse* myself to prevent it? I pressed my head against the bark of a great ivied oak. My head felt exhausted, light, spongy, able to pass through the bark and merge with the xylem and corky phloem through which the mineral-tasting sap surged giddily to all parts of the tree. I could feel the oak shutting down like a power station: its roots clench the warm earth more tightly against winter winds, its branches stiffen in anticipation of snow, its twigged fingers growing numb and letting fall its leaves. It had already ceased the heady transpiration of summer and was bedding down with shallow breaths to dream of greenness and the vulgar hallelujah of spring.

I walked on. I could hardly feel my legs, I was so light I barely touched the springy ground; with every draught of air my body expanded, grew lighter, while my heart was so full of nameless ache, of inchoate longing that it almost lifted me up in a great balloon of world-pain. I had to stop and lie down. The ground was soft and porous and perfumed with humus and fungi. I let myself go.

It was a wild exhilarating sensation, like dying. For a moment I clung to myself by a thin silver cord, flying myself like a straining kite until the leash broke and I sailed vertically into the air, dazed by my own daring, my stomach turning over, afraid of never returning to earth – but above all thrilled to bits by the freedom of it! The wind blew through me, whirling me like a sycamore seed over the valley. The world is so simple from high up. I watched the lights coming on in the cottages, wanting to forgive and to be forgiven, feeling the reality of atonement, wanting my flight to last forever.*

I came to earth on the edge of the wood. It was like sinking into a heavy bog. I dragged my mired feet down the hill to the unlit vicarage.

The renewed movement of matter and spirit is an enormous weight off my mind. For the first time in ages my thoughts can flow freely, even if it does mean that they drag up in their wake the more sluggish, massive memories. The timeless interior of the alembic, like a crystal ball, flings my past and future in my face. It is a long time now since Annabelle appeared so mockingly and lewdly in the place of the pelican during that curious waking dream. She is vivid still. And, I fear – as she said at the time – 'still waiting'.

Struggle as I may against it, the barbed wire of truth has been borne in upon me:

I was afraid of Annabelle.

(Good. It's written.)

---

* As so often it's hard to know exactly how to take Smith's descriptions. This passage would seem to be about an 'out-of-the-body experience', most commonly reported by people who are close to death. There is an extensive literature on the subject which unfortunately I haven't read.

EILEEN

Armand Barbault's *Gold of a Thousand Mornings* is a bit of a disappointment.* I collected it from the library this morning and read it at one sitting. He turns out to be a plant alchemist, not a metals man, and he is irritatingly vague about crucial parts of his process. I've got higher hopes for the Fulcanelli book,** which is due to arrive in a fortnight or so. (Why am I bothering with these so-called twentieth-century alchemists? Is it because I want to believe that alchemy is still possible? Am I trying to drum up support for Smith? Do I doubt him? No. I don't doubt him.)

Anyway, Barbault claims to have made his 'first order preparation' in 1960, having begun his Opus in 1948. This medicine, 'drawn from the blood of the green lion', he calls 'vegetable gold'. The 'second order' medicine, 'drawn from the blood of the red lion', is the Great Elixir, 'potable gold', in which metallic elements come more to the fore. He has got as far as producing the 'mercury' which appears as crystalline star-like points in his black mass of 'earth'. There's also, he thinks, the possibility of a third-order medicine 'with its source in the alchemist's powder of projection', about which it is (needless to say) inadmissible to speak.

The two 'anthroposophical' laboratories which tested his medicine achieved some excellent results, particularly in accelerating the general recovery of patients.

Barbault's prima materia is common earth or, rather, it looks like common earth but, to the initiate, it is *living* earth. It must be looked for in Capricorn and acquired in Aquarius. It can't be found without a revelation or a guide – in his case, his mediumistic wife. She perceived the primary colours in a globe shape under her feet at the First Matter's location. It must be 'seized from the ground

---

* First published in France, 1969; English translation, 1975.
** See p. 316.

by a ... process belonging to the sphere of High Magic'. That is, there's a struggle between the seeker and the 'forces of the earth which watch over this spark of life'. The struggle takes place in a dreamlike or meditative state in which the seeker symbolically engages the Dragon in combat and, piercing it with his lance, transforms it into a majestic lion.

The treatment of the First Matter is extremely complex. It took twelve years to accomplish the state of 'Absolute Black'. It has to be 'nourished' by sap gathered under exact conditions, for example just before sunrise when it's most 'concentrated'. Dew is used to 'burn' the First Matter. It has to be gathered by dragging canvases over a dewy field and wringing them out, as depicted in the *Mutus Liber* ['Silent Book'. See p. 434] which, together with the Emerald Tablet, was Barbault's 'bible'.

The power of living things, concentrated in sap and dew, has to be fixed and accumulated in the First Matter as 'salts'. The living particles must cease to fear the fire but settle willingly into the salts and 'thereby acquire the power to separate the soul of the metal from its physical matrix'. This soul can then be 'fixed in itself' to form the medicine.

And so on. All good clean wacky fun. I liked this remark of Barbault's though: 'Nuclear science liberates energy whilst destroying the atomic structure. Alchemy ... utilises this energy to make the matter evolve ... '

Looking back on Christmas Eve, there were omens I should have recognised. When I woke up that day my heart was fluttering as if I were scheduled to meet someone infinitely more exciting than a mere father. I prepared myself with more than usual care. It wouldn't do to look less than impeccably groomed in a hotel of Green's starred, but discreet, splendour.

Then, there was a moment during the application of mascara, regarding my face in the mirror, with its pleased expression because it had inadvertently lost weight, when I brought to mind two wistful remarks of Dad's. First, when I was a student, he once sighed and said of my appearance:

'A pity cosmetics are *de trop* these days. I've always thought that most skin needs all the artifice at its disposal. I suppose this scruffiness *is* only a phase, my darling? It's almost painful to look at you.'

I'm fairly certain that for the next three years I never appeared in front of him without full warpaint. However, at the end of this period, Dad made the second remark. Again, there was a sigh:

'Of course you have your own inimitable style, my darling, but don't you tire of such extravagant make-up? I've always thought the "natural look" most appropriate and most lovely in a young woman.'

From then on I could never decide whether, and to what extent, I should wear make-up or not; and whichever choice I made, I was always convinced that it was the wrong one as Dad, in the first moment of meeting, gazed into my face and, smiling his charming wistful smile, seemed to suppress a sigh.

On Christmas Eve morning I had the usual desire to scrub my face clean as soon as it was perfect. As I stood appraising the reflection of my face, feeling the twin prongs of Dad's contradictory remarks, I struggled to beat down the disloyal thoughts which rose up in front of my eyes. My face betrayed me. Its mask began to crack up with laughter at the comical idea that I was caught in the act of tangibly aping my father's two-facedness. And the idea, the laugh, made me feel extraordinarily carefree.

At the same time, I was filled with foreboding. The laugh was dangerous, an unthinkable flippancy. In retrospect, I think I already knew that my feelings for my father were quite other than those I represented to myself. I could already sense them like a dark torrent, swirling beneath the powdery crust of self-deception. Quickly I averted my eyes and applied more blusher to a cheek from which the blood had drained.

When I studied anthropology I didn't study very thoroughly or very hard. I was too young and stupid. One has to be much farther along than I was at university even to begin to know how to study. But I do remember that wonderful moment, which anthropology is uniquely placed to confer, when for a brief second I stood outside my own culture and saw it as exactly that, a *culture*, with all its culturally relative prejudices and misconceptions that I had all my life assumed to be absolute reality. It's an experience that anyone more sensitive than I can have every time they read a poem or look at a painting – the experience of looking on a familiar world in a wholly new way, through someone else's eyes. Even so, perhaps because the poems and paintings I looked at belonged to the same culture as myself, they never gave me that culture shock – that imaginative leap into another frame of mind – which anthropology gave me. (I might've expected travelling to give it to me but it never did – not even travelling outside Europe. I lugged my culture around with me like a suit of armour; I used travel as *ersatz* imagination, an excuse *not* to make the imaginative effort because the effort of physically visiting another culture was less strenuous.)

It wasn't long before I twigged to the fact that you didn't have to look that far afield to find a different culture – you only had to look a little way back within your own, to travel in time rather than space. I wrote an essay comparing witchcraft in Africa to witchcraft in early seventeenth-century England.

I got another shock when one day I started chatting to a woman at a bus-stop. She seemed to share exactly the same way of thinking as the tribe I'd just been reading about. I couldn't help feeling a sense of superiority in both cases, as if both the woman and the tribe were somehow not as smart or as rational as I. This is a vice which, in the first case, my education had given me, and in the second, my education in a particular system. A moment's troubled reflection told me that most of my thinking, most of the time, was in fact of the same kind as the woman at the bus-stop, of the same kind as the tribe I had presumed to study, and (if anything) inferior in degree to both. I discovered that anthropology can, and should, begin at home, in the jungle of my own soul. Social anthropology is only possible at all because, as alchemy makes so clear, we already contain what is utterly *other* than us.

The more I put my mind to the Opus, the more elegant I find it. Not elegant exactly – more *true to life*. When I think about how my so-called inner life develops, I see it as an uneven process, a series of pendulum swings, an enthusiastic pursuit of ideas and activities (and, yes, people) in one direction followed by a reaction against them in another. I'm always going back to square one.

But square one has changed in the meantime – changed maybe to a circle. There never can be a return to square one. There's always a driving forwards towards some horizon, which recedes or alters in contour as one approaches; sometimes the way forward looks like the way back – to square one.

Jung's individuation process is just such a complex dynamic. It's not a linear development but a circular one – or, better still, a spiral in which – as in a labyrinth – we circle our own centres, drawing near at one moment, only to be drawn out to the perimeter at the next, in order to encompass some apparently peripheral but vital fragment of ourselves. When we seem farthest away we are sometimes nearest, as the Albedo is near to absolute blackness.

The Magnum Opus expresses this movement in its 'circulations' – both on the grand scale, as its end bites the tail of its beginning, and on the smaller scale as each stage contains many circles of dissolution and coagulation, like a fast-turning cog in a larger, slow-turning wheel. There is a constant shuttling between opposites, fixing and volatilising mercury and sulphur, soul and body on the horizontal axis, and ascending and descending between Sol and Luna, consciousness (mind) and the unconscious (spirit), on the vertical axis, always referring back to the beginning, never advancing until the appropriate separation or union has taken place at all levels – which sympathetically reflect and interpenetrate each other.

I didn't play any Chieftains on the Xmas Eve drive to London. I listened to a Radio Doctor instead, dispensing sound advice on his phone-in to the sexually perplexed. I parked around the corner from Green's at 12.20 p.m.

Dad looked greyer, more stooped, almost *old* – but still tall and elegant in a perfectly cut grey suit which reminded me of French aristocracy. (10 out of 10.) At lunch, things did not go swimmingly. He was a little *distrait*; I was a little nervous. Conversation was somewhat forced. We both drank more than we wanted. The hotel's brown ambience and wooden staff exercised their restraint. We rehearsed our old intimacy without achieving the usual ease and naturalness. My mind began to wander in a maudlin sort of way. I was sensible of being an inadequate companion. Thus, seeking to play upon the sentimentality which is never far from Father's polished surface, I reminisced about the past, when our relationship was mutual bliss. In particular, having recently brooded on my early irrational fear of that hidden whippy little cane, I spoke of it to Dad.

'I don't know *why* I was so afraid' – I was laughing – 'you couldn't possibly hit . . . ' I was going to say 'a girl'; but for some reason, perhaps the expressionless fishy look in his eye, the way he lifted his Burgundy stiffly to his pursed mouth, I paused and said, ' . . . me. You couldn't hit me . . . '

We read each other's faces in silence. An awful knowledge began to dawn on me; and he, seeing it, frowned; and, in frowning, allowed me to read the beginnings of what I had so long forgotten.

Dad mistook my knowledge for a realisation of another kind. He started to speak moistly, between melodramatically clenched teeth:

'She ruined my career, you know . . . a hysterical wench who made trouble . . . a lot of accusations . . . claimed I'd hit her . . . ' His voice went loud and soft like an aural lens zooming in and out. I was miles away. ' . . . All I hurt was her vanity . . . self-righteous little bitch had me hauled over the coals . . . college took "a dim view" . . . it was either my job or the Courts. . . . ' Somewhere or other I registered all this. Suddenly it fitted into place. I said nothing. I was too preoccupied with a monstrous blob of memory rising up into my throat. I pushed back my chair and half-ran to the Ladies.

Safely locked inside a cubicle I gave myself up to the squat black images which jerked up inside me like toads: the narrow dingy funny-smelling passage that led to Dad's sanctum. The funny sounds from behind the door. The height of the door-handle as I stretched up my hand to turn it. The door opening a crack.

I was gasping for breath. My stomach was heaving. I knelt down on the cubicle floor and leaned over the dazzling white porcelain, on which I clearly saw the scene behind the study door.

The girl lay face down on the leather settee. Her bare buttocks were flushed. Dad stood over her with the whippy cane raised. Neither of them saw me. I pulled the door to, and scarpered.

I retched once or twice into the lavatory. How absurd Dad looked, standing there in his shoes and socks but without trousers! They were neatly folded on the back of a chair. He was always fastidious about his clothes. Humorous, too, was the way his shirt stuck out in front as if he had a stick underneath. His legs were white and his face was red. What frightened me most, I think, was the incongruity between his jokey attire and his frown of concentration as, with moist lips, he brought the cane down on the girl's bottom.

I didn't bother to combat the vomit any more. I surrendered to it, letting it flow easily out of me, a gorgeous warm wine-tinged ruby stream splashing on the white bowl. I drank some water and splashed my face. I felt weak and sad but, on the whole, better. I didn't bother to reapply my make-up.

'Are you all right, my darling?' Dad was anxious. I told him I was. Perfectly. I drank some coffee. He leant towards me and spoke confidingly, sorrowfully. Tanya had, of all things, *left* him. *Him.* His charming grey eyes were melancholy. The hand that held the brandy glass trembled. On the back of it were three sad liver spots. I felt sorry for the old boy. I wondered what on earth I was doing there, and immediately the answer came to me. I remembered how I had set my heart on his coming to my graduation ceremony. He cried off at the last minute. He had to attend a conference. He had to attend it, it turned out, because his current love was attending it. I began to laugh. It was really too funny. When Dad's in the midst of an affair I sit on the bench, ever ready to take the field if he wants to make a late substitution. No matter what we've arranged, if Miss Current Lover whistles – why, then it's a red card and an early bath for me. I laughed all the harder. The reason I was there, in Green's, was that Tanya had gone and I was the only female replacement he could get at short notice. It was killing.

'You find it amusing that Tanya has seen fit to leave me?' said Dad coldly. A fresh wave of laughter engulfed me.

'Don't worry,' I managed to say, the tears pouring down my cheeks, 'she probably just got tired of being birched.'

When Jung identifies the *Anima Mundi* [Soul of the World] with the collective unconscious he gains nothing in clarity but loses a great deal in beauty.

In fact I'm not sure I can be doing with psychological jargon. I wouldn't mind if it were truly illuminating, but it looks to me more and more like an attempt to be modern and scientific for its own sake without any increase in explanatory power. I don't care that the old theological language is dead – Smith has brought it back to life for me. I long for the old Hermetic days when 'spirit' and 'soul' were scientific as well as supernatural facts. These are the words which do justice to human complexity. It's no good simply abolishing them in the hope that they'll go away.

Lévy-Bruhl's* idea of *participation mystique* provided Jung with powerful support for his conception of 'primitive' psychology. He can't help seeing the tribal person as somehow less differentiated, less conscious than we are. He seems to suggest that because the primitive's unconscious is always projected upon the world, his existence is a more or less dreamlike, 'mystical' participation in Nature. And this goes for alchemists, too.

Jung's view can't be right. The so-called primitive is clearly no less conscious than we; he is just as able, if not more so, to distinguish between his dreams and events in the outside world. All the same there *is* a difference between a member of an African tribe and a member of Western society – a difference Jung recognised but failed to explain satisfactorily.

I doubt if I can do any better; but the first thing I'd want to say is that, while there is no less consciousness among tribal societies than among us, there does seem to be a lack of importance attached to one of our most precious categories: the individual. The tribal member doesn't seem to have our notion of a self. Perhaps I should say that he is conscious but not self-conscious. That is, his notion of a self is not as something separate from contingent circumstances; it's a self defined by a number of external reference points such as his position in the family, clan and tribe, as well as his sex, relative seniority and general social status. There is no part of him which does not find a place in society. His psychic structure is congruent with his social organisation. His relationship with the world might be compared with a craftsman's relationship with the object of his craft – one of complete absorption and continuity.

Actually we find this easy to understand since we also define ourselves in relation to whatever role we are playing – we are

---

* The anthropologist Lucien Lévy-Bruhl (1857–1938).

children in relation to our parents, but parents in relation to our children; we are both siblings and spouses, employers and employees, friends and enemies, neighbours and strangers, and so on. Yet still we persist in seeing these as *roles* beneath which there is a real 'me'. We persist in seeing the self as a *thing* when in fact it is an *activity* – when I'm being a daughter or an employee I have no self apart from these. The exception occurs only when I stop in the middle of a role and reflect on myself. The self produces itself by reflecting on itself. It is this self-reflection which gives us the absolute sense of individuality, a sense that tribal people perhaps lack.

I've always assumed that individuality was a good thing, but now I'm not so sure. It must have been extraordinarily bracing when it first arrived in Western Europe around the time of the Renaissance, when the medieval order began to disintegrate. Indeed the Renaissance was a celebration of the individual, newly freed from his ties with both Nature and the collective. The centre of the universe shifted from God to Man. This was the time, too, when alchemy began to loosen its ties with practical chemistry and to become more speculative, more 'spiritual'. At the same time, it seems that only the alchemists strove to maintain the bridge back to Nature, as if they foresaw the dangerous estrangement to which, almost immediately after the initial exhilaration, the sense of individuality would lead us.

Feelings of alienation from Nature and society are as much a cause of individuality as an effect. Once committed to the importance of the individual we quickly fall prey to an insufferable self-importance, a collective inflated egoism which resents and punishes Nature for the unbreakable grip she exerts on us through our bodily life, which regards all societies who maintain a kind relation to her as 'savage'.

The Ancients admired the exceptional men, the individuals, who aspired to the condition of gods; but they knew, too, what fate awaited them, awaited all of us who succumb to hubris, the spiritual pride of forgetting we are creatures of God and believing we are self-derived.

I wouldn't be surprised if the flowering of English drama in the late sixteenth century had something to do with alchemy. The histrionic death and rebirth of kings, like Lear; their marriages with queens; their serpent-toothed daughters and Machiavellian, trickster-like, mercurial sons – all these were transferred directly from the private cucurbit to the public stage. Jacobean drama was prepared in the vessels of the alchemists long before it broke free, fully fledged, into the conscious minds of the playwrights. In fact, it may be that alchemy, deprived of its dramas, fell into desuetude on that account.

The idea of individuality in our culture owes a great deal, if not everything, to the Christian notion of the *soul*. In other parts of the world a person is often deemed to have more than one soul – usually two, but sometimes three or more. The single soul, unique in the eyes of God, is peculiarly our own; and, although it is responsible for many of our cultural failings, rightly treated it is also responsible for our greatest triumphs. We are uniquely able, for instance, to conceive of an individual who is not merely subordinate to the collective as a part is to the whole, but also can embody the collective – either in his works (as does the Renaissance artist) or in his life (as does the Christian mystic).

If we think of the soul at all, we tend to think of it erroneously as a *thing*, like a glassy essence. It may well choose to represent itself as such, just as it may choose any image (although it prefers only a few – a whiteness, a woman, a full moon, a star . . .); but alchemy has shown me that in itself it is a kind of empty nexus where the constituents of the world interact. In other words it is, to all intents and purposes, Mercurius.

If it is objected that Mercurius is Spirit, I can only say 'yes, that too'; for soul and spirit are the same Mercurius manifesting himself in his individual and collective aspects respectively.

If I now think about my own mind – a word I prefer to Jung's consciousness (in fact I prefer all Smith's terms) – I find I can't think about it at all without that sense of 'I' which presupposes the act of thinking. Where does the sense of 'I' come from? It comes from the soul which determines individuality and so pre-exists the 'I'. But it is equally true to say that the collective Spirit only becomes individual through the 'I', and this individuality is the soul. Thus the soul both determines and is determined by the 'I'; they presuppose each other.

This paradoxical, confusing (but rather beautiful) relationship is embodied in the Opus and, more particularly, in the process of reflux distillation:

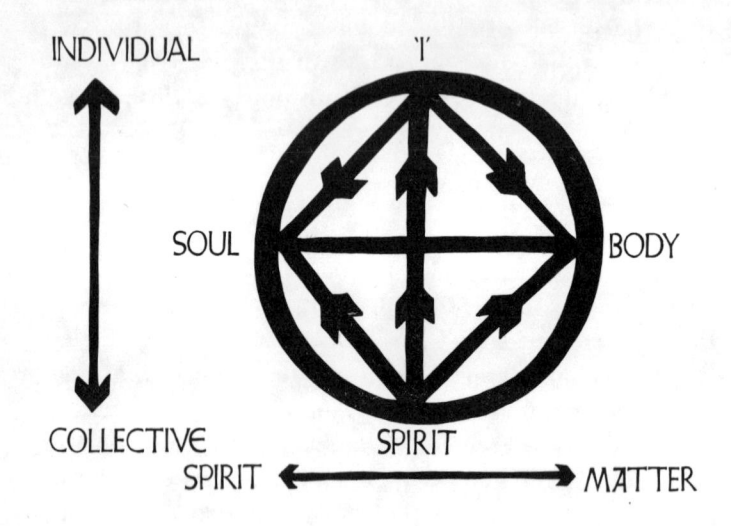

Here, the 'I' is 'distilled' out of the Spirit and, having 'condensed', returns to separate Spirit into soul and body. Conversely, the 'I' can be seen as a distillation of the soul separate from the body, returning to unite soul and body in the Spirit – it's a matter of reversing the arrows:

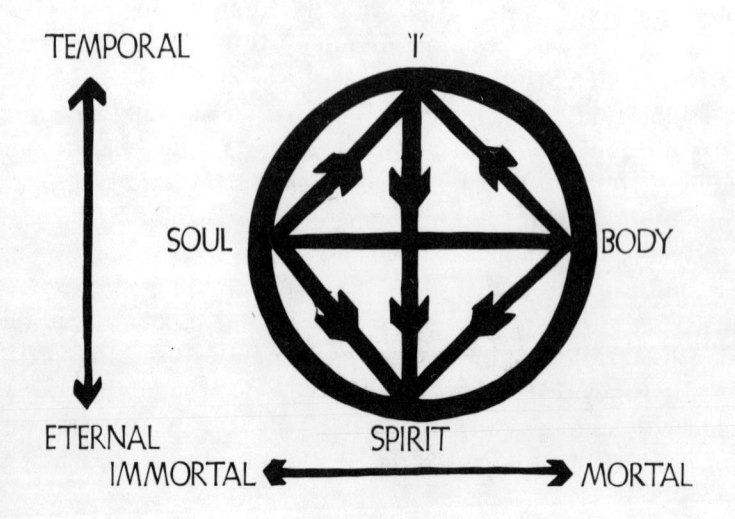

Reflux distillation provides a model – perhaps the only model – for the dynamic interrelationship of the elements within the human unity, and especially for the origins of self-consciousness. Moreover it is itself a product of the self-reflective process for which it is the model. Its equivalent in myth can be found in tales of a mother (notably a virgin mother) who gives birth to a son who is also her father.

Mercurius teaches us that at the root of things, in the spiritual realm as in the natural, there is a twoness, often but not always characterised by opposition, which has been neglected by our Judaeo-Christian tradition with its monotheistic emphasis on Oneness.

The alchemical metaphor of *marriage*, as the way of reuniting the Two in the One, emphasises the sanctity of the operation and the pre-eminence of the dyad masculine/feminine, which serves to classify all other dyads up and down the scale of Being. Also, and above all perhaps, marriage is not impersonal in the way that words such as 'union' or 'conjunction' might imply – it expresses the coming together of impersonal principles (masculine/feminine) in actual individuals.

My anger at Dad has been intense but short-lived. It wasn't directed at his repulsive little vice, but at his fundamental lack of love. I already suspected, but could not face, the fact that he is a husk whom any casual breeze can blow away. If he has a kernel, it is outside himself, in his work. (But what does his work amount to? He has not fulfilled the promise of his early brilliance.)

There are some for whom academic life is a temptation stoutly to be resisted. Dad is one of these. Sheltered all his life by university stud farms, bred for cerebration alone, he is – despite his worldly appearance – a clever little boy who has remained exactly that. He is stunted, loveless, selfish and unutterably sad. He is a good scientist – objective at all times, especially towards other people, but never towards himself. Smith, at whom Dad would laugh, is the exact contrary: subjective towards others (and even towards the matter for which he feels such compassion) while always striving to be objective about himself. This is what a man and a father should be.

Coming towards the great slab of the standing stone, I saw someone detach themselves from its shadow and face me, as if waiting. It was Pluto. He was not the first person I wished to see. However, since I couldn't very well ignore him in all that space – and since the stone provides a natural stop in the landscape – I leaned against it and bid him good morning, before turning away to survey the view.

He remained standing a few feet behind me. He had seen me leave the Vicarage on my walk, he explained, and had deliberately set out to intercept me. Well, that was honest, at least. I said a quick prayer that he shouldn't want to resume (though I feared that it was precisely what was in his mind) our conversation in the pub on Christmas Eve.

He was silent for so long that I thought I might be let off. And, when he did speak, it was irrelevantly, nothing to do with Mrs Z. He asked me if I knew what the stone was called. I didn't. He said it was 'the Blind Dancer'. Nobody knew why that was its name, unless it referred to the legend that the stone used to move about of its own accord, such that no map of the area exists with the megalith in exactly the right place.

'In the olden days,' he went on, 'the girls from all the villages for miles around used to come here during May and walk nine times around the stone, and rub themselves against it, up and down, because it made them fertile.'

I felt a trifle uneasy, propped against the stone; but Bradley didn't seem to notice. He continued talking in the same musing tone:

'I used never to believe in the old legends. But, I don't know, there may be something in them. Nora's always been a great one for them. She gets it from her grandmother. Oh yes, Mrs Maltravers was a rare old bird . . . what the country people used to call a "wise woman". Well known for cures of all kinds, she was. Better than the doctor, some said. It's fashionable now, isn't it? Herbalism and so on? Anyway, Nora was devoted to her – inherited the second sight from her, I've been told. Nora wouldn't discuss that sort of thing with *me*.'

This is more or less how he rambled on. I only repeat it here because of what he said next. I was beginning to grow cold and restless. The day was overcast, the view drab. Politeness alone prevented me from cutting him short.

'Mrs Maltravers had some fairly outlandish ideas. Nora has recently passed some of them on.' He gave a short apologetic laugh. 'Severe diseases, she believed, needed severe cures. What she called "canker" was a severe disease. She recommended the application of fresh animal blood to the afflicted part.' A premonitory shock passed down my spine. 'Now, if you had cancer of the stomach and there was really not much that could be done about it, wouldn't you be tempted to try anything? Eileen?' He spoke my name gently for the first time. I nodded my head. 'Especially,' he added, 'if you were very frightened of dying. You might try any old wives' tale. For example, you might first of all try bathing in water which has an ancient reputation for healing.' I nodded again. 'And if that failed, you might try something – anything – more . . . extreme. Mightn't you. I'm sorry you had to find out about the hens before I did. I guessed from the look on your face.'

I had the distinct sensation of something *clearing* in my head. I looked into his shrivelled face and I said something very stupid:

'You're John Smith, aren't you? That's why you hate my cellar. It's where you were burnt. It's where your Great Work ended. It's why you left the Church. I understand!'

He didn't laugh. He shook his head sadly. Then he introduced himself as Bradley Caldwell.

One thing that dreams, myths, literature, etc. have in common is a disposition to evade the limitations of time, space and causality. They suggest that beneath the orderly constructs of culture there is another, highly coloured realm which, although it has laws of its own, does not obey the laws on which our scientific world-view depends. Occasionally we find the laws of this other realm disrupting the normal laws of our consensus-reality. For example, Jung exercised himself mightily over one such disruption in the law of cause and effect on which so much of the scientific edifice – including the theory of Evolution – is built. He was referring to the phenomenon of *meaningful coincidence*, and he often tells this story:

A patient of his was in the middle of recounting a crucial dream in which she had been given a golden scarab. Suddenly she was interrupted by a tapping at the window, caused by a flying insect. When Jung let the insect in, it turned out to be a rose-chafer, the nearest local equivalent to a golden scarab. Contrary to its usual habits it had wanted to enter the darkened room at that particular moment.

Jung saw this as an example of a phenomenon familiar to everybody – the 'simultaneous occurrence of two meaningful but not causally connected events'. He proposed the existence of an 'acausal connecting principle' which he called *synchronicity*, that is, 'happening together in time'.* He avoided the more usual word 'synchronous' because he wanted his principle to include related coincidences of psychic state and physical event, such as Swedenborg's vision of the great fire in Stockholm,[1] and dreams which prefigure the future – coincidence, that is, where the events are as yet too distant in space or time to be immediately verified.

The principle could be extended to include systems of divination: astrology and the Chinese 'oracle', the *I Ching*, recognised a synchronistic equivalence between inner and outer worlds whereby the first can be 'read' in the second. In other words our psychic states are synchronistic with Nature at all times so that they can potentially be 'read' anywhere, even, presumably, in tea-leaves, flights of birds and ox's entrails – all traditional means of focussing a seer's attention.

None of this can be explained by recourse to cause and effect. At best we can hypothesise a principle – Jung's 'unconscious' – which underlies both the psychic and the physical realms and manifests itself simultaneously in both. The separate manifestations, perceived as coincidence, are connected only by the intuition of meaning.

Jung was mindful of the application of synchronicity to alchemy. He couldn't rule out the possibility that what took place in the soul of the alchemist was synchronistically reflected in the material he was working on (or vice versa, of course):

---

* Jung's essay on the subject is in volume eight of the Collected Works, p. 419.

'While the adept had always looked for the effects of his stone outside, for instance as the panacea or golden tincture or life-prolonging elixir, and only during the sixteenth century pointed with unmistakable clarity to an inner effect,[2] psychological experience emphasises above all the subjective reaction to the formation of images, and – with a free and open mind – still reserves judgement in regard to possible objective effects.'*

The correlation of contradictions (such as matter and spirit) is always transcendental. We have to climb higher, like mountaineers who only see the view on one side or other of the mountain until they reach the top, when they can see both sides at once. In our three-dimensional world, the function of climbing is taken on by the fourth dimension, time. Our souls do not *change* in time; they reveal more and different and opposite views of themselves, just as the prima materia does in the course of its transformation into the Stone.

Larva, pupa, imago (caterpillar, chrysalis, butterfly).
I want to say that this sequence is a natural image of the Opus (nigredo, albedo, rubedo), but since there is really no actual image for the result of rubedo, I have to say that the imago corresponds to the albedo, the White Stone (not for nothing did the Greeks call a butterfly, *psyche*). The White Stone can no more be inferred from the prima materia than a butterfly can from a caterpillar. To include the Red Stone in a sequence of natural transformation one has to resort to the absurd:

prima materia	nigredo	albedo	rubedo
spawn	tadpole	frog	prince.

---

* *Myst. Conj.*, p. 533. The passage occurs during an analysis of the work of the late sixteenth-century Belgian alchemist Gerard Dorn who especially endeared himself to Jung by showing himself aware of alchemy's 'inner effects' – that is, its psychological components.

If you told a tadpole he'd become a frog, he'd laugh in your face. Just as inconceivable is the albedo to one who is sunk in the waters of the nigredo – yet the transformation will take place; the frog will emerge to meet the white princess who, with a slow fiery kiss, will transform it into the red prince.

SIX

Congelation

SMITH

At noon I brought Nora home. It was Tim who decided me to risk the revulsion she must feel for me – he felt that she was lonely and unhappy. This idea was intolerable. My fears turn out to be unfounded. She said:

'I'm glad you're here. I wanted you to come so badly. Things have been a bit . . . desperate.' She tilted up her chin and attempted a wry smile; but she was gulping back lumps in her throat. I was aghast. Why, I asked, had she not come back to the vicarage *immediately*? She shrugged and pointed to her abdomen. I asked her how she could think for one minute that I'd abandon her because she was going to have a baby. But I needed no reply. I saw with great clarity and a kind of creeping self-disgust how stiff-necked I'd been. How could dear Nora think otherwise when she had seen how harshly I had judged Jenny Stebbins – how I'd *collaborated* with Caldwell in sending her away.

I assured Nora as best I could of my fidelity. She has no need to worry on any score. I'll take care of her, of everything. Her face, white and strained with dark circles around her eyes, relaxed. All at once she succumbed to a great tiredness. It was all she could do to climb the stairs to her room. On the landing, between yawns, she told me what I already knew: that Bradley had proposed. 'I was so desperate that I was tempted for a second,' she said. 'He's been very kind.' *Kind*. However, this was no time to remonstrate with her.

I fetched her two hot-water bottles. It seemed insensitive to enter her room in the light of our last, shall I say, encounter, which we had apparently – and tacitly – agreed not to mention. I laid them down by the door and called out to her. An hour later they were still where I'd left them.

*

Congelation is that stage of the Magnum Opus in which the Albedo, begun in secret, in darkness, is completed and made manifest. What was hidden is revealed. It is the fruition of the Regimen of Luna by which the Above is united with the Below to form the White Stone of the Philosophers. *Id est aut Plenilunium aut Astrum.* [That is either the Full Moon or the Star.]

My master spoke several times of the great and learned Dr Dee whose *Monas Hieroglyphica* I believe he knew by heart.[1] Most of what he said passed over my head, of course; but I remember the wistful note in his voice as he conjured up a portrait of the tall black-clad Elizabethan Philosopher moving gravely through his house in Mortlake which contained the greatest library in England. Here he was visited by most of the English Renaissance's leading lights,[2] as well as some of the continent's most famous scholars. Queen Elizabeth I called on him or, more often, summoned him to Court for consultations on such matters as a suitable astrological date for her coronation.

My master spoke with admiration of Dee's many talents – as mathematician, astronomer, astrologer, antiquarian, engineer, expert on optics, navigation and cartography. But, above all, he was passionately dedicated to the study and practice of the three occult philosophies: the Hermetic, the Kabbalistic and the Chemical [i.e. the alchemical].

As the sixteenth century drew to a close, Dee's star fell from its ascendancy. So far above the common herd was he that, with his influential friends mostly dead or out of favour, no one understood his lofty philosophy. There were allegations of sorcery and diabolism which grew stronger when James I – who had himself written a book against witchcraft [*Daemonologie*, 1587] – replaced Elizabeth on the throne. A mob burned the great library. Dee died in penury in 1608.

My master dated his decline from the day, in March 1582, Dee being then fifty-five years old, when a former apothecary's apprentice called Edward Kelley knocked at his door. He became one of the most notorious men in Europe; and, if history has done a grave injustice to John Dee by reviling and ridiculing him, the same is even truer of Kelley who has subsequently been condemned as a charlatan, an imposter, a scoundrel and a sinister, almost devilish figure.

Personally I've always entertained a sneaking liking for Kelley. There's something picaresque and appealing about the way he boldly offered his services as scryer [i.e. spirit medium] to the famous doctor; and, instantly successful, became overnight the great man's companion, confidant and teacher. Primarily he assisted Dee in his chemistry and in that branch of natural magic which invokes angels. I myself have read with great interest Casaubon's *True and Faithful Relation*... in which are recorded Dee's conversations with the angel Uriel who was contacted by Kelley through Dee's 'shew stone' and also his 'magic mirror'.*

My master drew a vivid picture of the pious Doctor being gulled by the small, demonic Kelley who had formerly been accused of fraud and necromancy and whose ears had been cropped for coining. However, I do not see how Kelley could, or would wish to, dupe Dee for six years or more – besides which, the latter was shrewd enough to have detected any imposture in Kelley, who remains for me an intriguing, ambiguous, mercurial figure, emerging from obscurity and returning to it after flashing to brilliance at the Court of Rudolf II of Bohemia. I certainly see less reason to impugn his honesty than my master. (I've found no convincing evidence for this business of the ears; I suspect it is largely a slander, unexamined and compounded down the centuries by those who have an interest, whether out of malice, fear or intellectual laziness, in defaming Kelley's character.) After all, even though Dee acclaimed him in his diary [for 10 May 1588] as the man who opened the Great Secret to him, Kelley himself never claimed to have made the Philosophers' Stone. What he did claim was that he had been led by a revelation to Glastonbury – the most sacred site in Europe – where he found a quantity of the wonderful red transmuting powder, hidden there by St Dunstan some six centuries earlier.

---

* Meric Casaubon, ed. *A True and Faithful Relation of what passed for many years Between Dr John Dee ... and Some Spirits* (London, 1659). The 'shew stone' which seems to have acted like a crystal ball is a round, smoky piece of quartz. The 'magic mirror' is a disc of polished obsidian, thought to be of Aztec origin. Both are in the British Museum. For further details of these angel-conjuring sessions, see James O. Halliwell, ed. *The Private Diary of Dr John Dee* (London, 1842).

With this powder Kelley performed numerous transmutations,[3] especially during his four-year stay along with Dee in Bohemia, at both Prague and Trebon – and he continued to perform them after he and Dee had quarrelled, and the latter had returned to England. He was so successful that Lord Burghley, Elizabeth's Chief Counsellor, begged him to return to England as well; or, failing that, to send a portion of the transmuting tincture to the Queen – enough to help defray the expense of building up her navy to withstand the might of Spain.

By 1591 Sir Edward Kelley (as he now was) had fallen from the Emperor Rudolf's favour and was imprisoned, probably for heresy. I'm not sure what happened thereafter. My master said that he was certainly tortured, perhaps released and then reimprisoned. He is believed to have fallen from a window while trying to escape in 1595, and to have died as a result.*

Is there no end to blackness? Every day I bathe our sulphur in the marvellous mercurial water which falls like dew from Heaven; yet he shows no sign of growing whiter. Uncleanness clings to the body, preventing the ascension of Sol and his union with the blessed Luna who by her descent accomplishes all her phases and embraces Sol in her full circle. It is this conjunction of the risen sun and the full moon which we call our Star.

At first I put it down to Nora's condition. After all, she is entitled to be a little absent-minded and besides, what's a window left open here and something trivial missing there? What if she does choose to clump about at night? It was only when I found my papers in disarray and the inkpot, mercifully unspilt, on the floor that I drew the line.

However, when I taxed her with these irritating misdemeanours she not only denied them but also attributed them to me. We ceased accusing each other. She decided at first that the vicarage itself must be responsible. She confessed that it had been getting on her nerves

---

* However, in *Rudolf II and His World* (Oxford, 1973), R. J. W. Evans suggests that Kelley was still alive in 1597, at the castle of Most, where the Paracelsian doctor Oswald Croll appears to have visited him.

for some time, as if it were charged with static electricity and subject to sudden fits of unsocial behaviour. I put these fancies down to her sensitive condition but I, too, had to admit to a certain uneasiness about the place, a faint strain in the fabric of the house.

Then, with sudden insight, Nora attributed these effects to my 'experiments'. I'm forced to agree: elementary poltergeist manifestations are not wholly unexpected even if they are exasperating. The Opus cannot but make itself felt. The wind of the Holy Spirit bloweth where it listeth. I asked her to be patient, saying that things will settle down in a day or two; she was content.

In the struggle to take up my pastoral duties once more, I've instructed Nora to call me if anyone pays a visit no matter how trivial their business. It's both a relief and a sorrow that such visits rarely occur.

However, today Nora summoned me with three knocks on the laboratory door and I hurried up to find Janet in the study. I was surprised by a sudden rush of pleasure. She, too, was lit up for a moment by the fleeting dazzle of her old smile. Then her face faded away again behind its drawn lacklustre mask.

We drank tea. There were flashes of our former rapport; but my preoccupation and her sad renunciation made our muted exchanges a far cry from the merry conversation we used to have. I said that we should see more of each other; there's no reason for us to become estranged. She agreed, but listlessly. Then, quickly, lest I should think that she was still hankering after Robert, she explained that there are certain domestic difficulties: her husband's partners have more or less forced a leave of absence on him which, rather than curing his indolence and drinking, has made it worse. His doctor has warned that the drink does no good to his dicky heart, but any attempt by Janet to regulate his habits meets with fits of temper followed by sullen obduracy. Poor old Farrar – it's the fate of the absolute bore, perhaps, to wish in the end to escape from himself. I offered to speak to him, to help in any way. She shook her head and smiled. It'll sort itself out, she said. Besides, she did not come to talk about herself or Farrar.

She fidgeted nervously while I coaxed her to tell me the real purpose of her visit. It was as follows: village opinion has it that it was I who got Nora with child. The source of this opinion, Janet thinks, is Bradley Caldwell; its dissemination lies in the capable hands of Mrs Beattie and her circle of tale-bearers.

I received this intelligence without surprise. I asked Janet if she believed it. She fixed her level grey eyes on mine.

'Nora has told me everything,' she said.

As she was leaving she kissed Nora goodbye. I had no idea they were on such good terms. Nora tells me that Janet was kind to her and came to offer assistance at the time when her condition became known.

I can't raise any indignation, or even interest, let alone anger over Bradley's slander. It seems a paltry thing, mere hysteria on his part. He has his way with Nora; in a momentary aberration he decides to 'do the honourable thing'; he proposes marriage; she turns him down. In the heat of his resentment at being scorned he denounces me as the culprit. He is widely believed (who doesn't relish a scandal attached to a vicar?).

He is probably somewhat worried at this very moment that Nora will stand up and deny his allegations, or that I will challenge them. As it happens he need not worry on either score. I have made it clear to Nora that she is not required to say a single word on the subject. Just to see her humming about the house again, busy and carefree, with that dreamy, contented, rather secret look on her sweet face is a great joy to me. I will not have her bothered – least of all to defend my honour which she doesn't even realise has been impugned. Nor will I demean myself by answering Bradley's demented charge. Once its absurdity is generally recognised, as it will be as soon as the early desire for sensation has blown over, young Caldwell will be laughed to scorn.

The recent heavy rains have waterlogged the ground at the church's east end. From my window it resembles a beached ship. You can almost see the damp spreading up the walls and loosening the masonry.

I can hear the water rising in my well. It has a melancholy resonance. When I look down the shaft the water is high enough to catch a glimmer of light. It reminds me of the one-eyed serpent in cahoots with the rainclouds above, and ascending inexorably towards the cellar. I drink a cup of the water and savour its steel-cold slither down my gullet.

I see no way to advance. No matter how much impurity is removed, there always seems to be more. Whereas in Putrefaction all my care was to coax the soul from the refractory body, now it is impossible to bring about their reunion.

Luna bends over Sol; her salt tears daily saturate him, daily growing more salty in the hope of washing away the dross that holds him in sulphurous decay. To no avail. I feel the tears start up in my own eyes at the thought that the Work should come to this. For without the union of Above and Below, the wedding of Heaven and Earth will never come to pass.

I never had any virtue, at most the appearance of it. Now I haven't even that. I neglect my parish; I perform services like a robot. I'm nothing. Less than nothing. Dross fit only for the rubbish-heap.

Caldwell senior has been to see me. It crossed my mind that he was going to try and buy off Nora to protect his son. In fact he came about Nightingale Wood.

He sat in my chair on one side of the fire while I sat opposite in Nora's. We sipped sherry. All very civilised. I was somewhat abstracted after a particularly intense period of contemplation of the Opus. I found it hard to concentrate on the issue of the wood. The date set for its destruction is only weeks away; but although I tried to muster some of my former indignation, I felt detached from the whole matter. There is too much else afoot, enough to overwhelm me unless I give it all my attention, and so I have no ardour to spare for events in the outside world.

Caldwell was clearly surprised at my subdued tone. We have scarcely exchanged a word since the spring. He, too, seemed prepared to conciliate. Gone was the bullying stance and the ill-concealed condescension; instead he employed a charming air of confidentiality: he didn't *want* to cut down the wood – he *had* to cut it down because he urgently needed the cash that the timber would bring in.

However his argument from necessity rather than wilfulness lost much of its force when I gathered that the general tenor of the parish council was against him. He appears to think that I have somehow architected the rebelliousness, whereas, in fact, I have done nothing for months. He did not expect me to condone the destruction, merely to leave well alone until after the event. Actually I hadn't thought of doing otherwise. I'd like to forget the whole business. But, more out of habit than conviction, I refused to co-operate with him. I wearily repeated that while no one disputes his ownership of the wood, his right to chop it down is outweighed by his obligation to maintain it, regardless of economics.

He licked his lips a bit nastily. 'Well,' he remarked, 'I don't see that you're in any position to take such a high moral tone.' He let his gaze wander pointedly towards the door. I wasn't slow to realise that he was referring to my alleged sexual relations with Nora. I was tempted to counter them with allegations of my own – after all, it is Bradley, not I, whose proclivities have been firmly established, as the Stebbinses will testify. However, I held my peace. 'Your private life is your own affair,' he was saying, 'but others might not take the same view. Things could become very unpleasant for you, Vicar.' This, presumably, was a threat to tell the Powers-That-Be in the Close about Nora and me. 'I have also heard that you're up to something rather . . . *irregular* in that cellar of yours. You're not up to anything, are you, Vicar?'

I couldn't help laughing. His whole carry-on was so absurd. He was plainly nettled by my amusement; in fact I doubt whether he believed any of his own insinuations. As attempts at blackmail go, it was not a success. We bid each other a very *civil* goodnight.

There's nothing to be done. Mercurius is in charge of the Work. *I* can only wait for the miraculous return of the Spirit which in its re-descent also raises up the matter – to perform the true union of Above and Below. For, in the dark heart of the Opus, the seed of incandescent whiteness was laid and I can only wait for it to grow; wait and watch for the sun to rise out of the dark earth and the moon to attain her plenitude.

To this end I bear witness to the dissolution and coagulation, the endless purifications which, I pray, will at last prove decisive. I can't leave it, yet I can't bear to stay. The awful stillness of the Opus holds me in suspension – as if to move or speak were to snap.

The Magnum Opus is not *Christian* (it's not sanctioned by the Church); but never was work more Christian *in spirit*. Ever since my ordination I have been like an officer who reads out the instruction manual while his men lie dying around him. The letter kills, the spirit gives life. My dog-collar has been just that.

Tim came to see me in the study. Since, he said, I'd trusted him with my secret 'cooking experiment', he'd like to entrust me with *his* secret. It was to do with the 'flying saucer'.

I pulled up a chair closer to the fire (which I've taken to lighting for cosiness as much as warmth now that the evenings are drawing in) and poured him a cup of tea.

'When Michael and his dad ran away from the light I stayed behind,' he said. He looked anxious. He was afraid that I was not going to listen to him or believe him. I indicated that I was paying full attention. 'I had the idea that the light was meant for me,' he went on. 'It sort of looked *right into* me. It was hovering over the graveyard. I went up to it. I wasn't afraid. It wobbled a bit like a bubble, then it sank to the ground. A woman was standing in the light. She might've been making it – I couldn't tell. She was smiling at me like Mum used to. Well, actually, like I *think* Mum used to. I can't really remember. Anyway she was nice. *Very* nice. She said, "Hello. Don't be afraid." I said, "Hello. I'm not afraid." How would I be afraid? She was the opposite of frightening. I s'pose she was what you'd call a beauty.' He paused for quite a long time, thinking. Then he said quickly: 'That's all really. We had some conversation and then she disappeared inside the light. I didn't actually see it go; but I think it went off at a great speed. I'm not sure why I didn't see it. Perhaps it just disappeared. I'm not sure.' What sort of conversation did they have, I wanted to know. Tim went red and stuttered:

'I'm sorry, sir. I . . . I . . . can't say. I *promised* her I wouldn't.' I said that was fair enough. 'But she said she'd come back,' he added eagerly. 'Said she'd show me some wizard places. She didn't use those words exactly.' When would she come? 'Oh, soon, I think. Very soon. I don't think she's from another planet, do you?'

I said I didn't know. Probably not. He wasn't looking for an explanation from me. He just wanted to tell me about it. It was the 'most important event of my life', he said in a clipped, rather pompous way. He sounded so like Monty that I nearly smiled.*

What does one make of this? First of all I told him that he was a lucky chap and that he'd probably be wise not to tell too many people about it because special experiences such as his sometimes get lost over a period of time, especially if they're sort of 'talked away'. Tim was indignant; he wasn't even going to tell Nora. We toasted each other in lukewarm tea.

Tim knows the legend of the Virgin Mary's appearance to the old dyer woman. It's possible that his *imagination* seized upon the story in order to clothe the person as a beautiful woman, who (I suspect) is his soul-image. But some external stimulus may also have been present. The location of the event suggests that the sphere of light and the woman are spiritual counterparts of the geographical site – sort of *genii loci* [spirits of the place] linked to the spring, the well, the church, the graveyard; in fact, the whole of the immediate vicinity whose sanctity is attested in the folklore associated with it. More disturbingly – but I can't rule this out – the apparition may have been to do with the Opus. It has been called *ludus puerorum* [the game of boys] and, to Mercurius, it is child's play. (It's *wrong* of me not to have faced up to the possible effects of the Magnum Opus on the 'outside world'. I've always known that it's folly to suppose that it can remain a *personal* matter – *nothing* which takes place in the Hermetic Egg is without its correspondence in the macrocosm.)

I realise that Tim has not worn (at least to my knowledge) a single article of women's clothing since I forbade the silk stockings. He obviously took my disapproval to heart. I ought to be glad, but somehow, secretly, I'm not. In his grey shorts and jacket or brown jersey he looks like any other boy. Convention has taken something

---

* Presumably Field-Marshal Montgomery.

away from him. Whereas before he was so expressive, flamboyant, devil-may-care in his bright scarves and dashing earrings, now he is crestfallen.

I can't take my eyes off the obdurate blackness. I can't act or pray, but sit merely, willing each drop of Luna's tears to turn the matter, like the sudden thickening of whipped cream, into whiteness. The darkness is, strictly, unimaginable – no matter how I hurl myself against it, no image can exist there. But it is certain that without such efforts the blackness will not break into the radiance it contains.

With every circulation I sense that such an extremity of darkness will be reached that Nature cannot help but invert herself, with a sudden convulsion, into light. Thus, as the bright sun must blind us, so must this dazzling eclipse enable me to *see*.

Nora tells me she has seen the White Lady. I demanded at once to know what she looks like – but Nora couldn't say. It was more of a fleeting impression. The face was in profile, obscured by her hair. She was sitting *at my desk*, apparently reading and dressed in a white shift or nightgown. Interestingly, Nora felt no fear and no curiosity. She merely glanced through the open doorway of the study, noted the presence of the Lady, and passed on. It was an hour later before she began to tremble – and to register fully what she had seen. 'I wasn't surprised to see her,' she said. 'It was just like she belonged there. It was no more of a surprise than if *you*'d been sitting there.' Whatever next.

A peculiar thing has just come to light as I sat at the kitchen table with Tim and Nora, eating poached eggs. They fell into a mild argument as to how long their father had been at sea this time; and how long his leave had been. Nora was able to calculate exactly when her father's leave had begun because she remembered the day so well – she had taken the lunch-time bus into town to meet him and he'd splashed out on a taxicab to bring them home. She particularly remembered being distressed at having to leave the vicarage without telling me – I'd been 'down there' for a long time –

and so having to leave a note. The note was the one I'd found the following day and assumed had been left the same morning when in fact it had been left *the day before*.

I felt a physical gripe of anxiety in my abdomen as I realised the truth. I questioned her sharply to make sure that she couldn't be mistaken. My heart beat far too fast. Thinking back, I have to say that some part of me had known it all along: at no time during the night of Conjunction had Nora been within a mile of the vicarage. Whatever had been in her bed was certainly not her.

De Anima Mundi

Why should it be necessary to expound the existence of the world-soul? She has been celebrated since time immemorial – until the onset of this barbaric modern age when we are so estranged from our own souls that we no longer experience our innate grounding in the Soul of the World. For inasmuch as we are natural (though self-transcending) creatures, the Soul of the World is also the collective soul of mankind; and only through us can groaning, travailing Nature achieve her goal – which is, to *know herself*.

However, nowadays we are asked to believe that the World-Soul was a mere doctrine which lingered on in ever cruder, more material forms, from ether to electro-magnetism, until she died like a superstition, suffocated by the hand of dead mechanical matter.

But she is not dead, only buried. Her dim cries can be discerned in the faint twitchings of the dowser's rod when he divines more than water. Then is his soul bathed in intolerable nostalgia for that Golden Age when the World-Soul sent her lenient silver streams shooting among us, bringing refreshment and vitality to mankind and his lands alike.

Our Philosophy doesn't distinguish between *Anima Mundi* and *Spiritus Mundi* [the Spirit of the World][4] except in so far as they are male and female respectively, as their Latin genders suggest.* (At root, before the One became Two and again when the Four becomes

---

* *Anima* is feminine and *spiritus* is masculine. The latter was sometimes translated 'breath' after the Greek *pneuma*; *anima*, of course, corresponds to the Greek *psyche*, 'soul'.

One, even distinctions of gender no longer obtain.) For John Dee, this Spirit or Soul was simply 'our mercury' which drew down the 'power of heaven' into special objects (such as sigils), places or moments, uniting the separate realms of Heaven and Earth. (As the powers or astral influences were drawn down, so the Philosopher himself was raised up – a notion most congenial to the Renaissance with its emphasis on the divinity of man.)

In his *Twelve Keys*, Basil Valentine identified the Soul or Spirit of the World with *an earth-spirit which is life itself*, endowing all created things with strength, yet itself as intangible and invisible (he says) as the reflection in a mirror. It is of course found in 'our earth' – the prima materia – and is the 'root of all bodies', or substances, necessary to the Art.

When I was a better churchman I used to think of it as the Holy Ghost; now I think of him as Mercurius. But I also think of her – especially when I lean my back against the Blind Dancer and watch the spring perform her annual transformations – as the Imagination of Nature.

There are many more images floating in the wellspring of the World-Soul than we can see. We used to see them in the old days when she lay basking on the Earth's surface and Heaven bent down to her. In those days dragons roamed the world; now, like moth-eaten yetis, they've all gone to sleep in remote caves, waiting for the time when they are reawoken.

Understand the Soul of the World and you will understand *gravity* whose mystery will never be unravelled by Science's mechanical explanations but by a true perception of the kindly inclination one heavenly body has for another.[5]

Robert has given me hope and courage! The world is full of meaning, people utter great truths, all the time, if we did but know it, if we only had *ears* . . .

I didn't expect him to be in, but he was. He said, gruffly, that he'd been 'away'. His great hall of a room was like a furnace – fire roaring, kiln going full-blast, lamps blazing, stove cooking. The paintings hanging from the roof-beam revolved in the fierce thermals.

Robert looked like a madman: filthy, ragged, smelly, his dark face burnished like copper in the heat, his staring eyes showing too much white. He took a long swig from a green bottle and asked me rudely what I wanted. I didn't want anything in particular.

I sat near the kiln while he went on with his work, savagely grinding and mixing his glass ingredients. Now and then he'd throw out a remark, like a cry of pain, into the sizzling air.

'I s'pose you think I'm about ready for God, eh? I s'pose you've come to drag me off to Jesus?' Nothing was farther from my mind so I remained silent. The bitter questions were, in any case, not really addressed to me.

'If you ask me, it's bloody Jesus who's caused all the misery in the first place.' And so on. His words were somehow dissipated in the heat or, rather, their meaning was, so that by the time they reached me they were stripped down to his simple enormous hurt. I let it lodge in me like a stone. No reply was required so I said nothing.

He was quiet after a while, merely remarking that it was cold. He threw another log on the fire. A profound drowsiness overtook me. Sparks flew up the chimney. Flame-shadows patterned his shiny face. Another person making his own little hell.

I must've nodded off. The fire had died down; the light had moved away from the high windows. Robert sat opposite to me. When I opened my eyes he put a mug in my hand. There was raw gin in it. I took a sip. He said softly:

'I've made a nonsense of things, padre. Going away was no good. Had to come back. It's all such a bloody *waste*.' I couldn't disagree. He sighed and said, more briskly, 'How's Tim? How's your Nora? I miss her, you know. Miss them both. She was a help to me, you know. She was the only one who— ' He broke off to lean forward and look at me. He seemed to see me for the first time, as if through a haze. 'What's up, padre? Trouble?' I didn't know what to say. I shrugged. He may have said 'Oh padre' under his breath. He stroked the twin white scars on his neck.

Then, in a single surge forward, he put his hands under my armpits, lifted me out of the chair and, holding me very tightly, whirled me around the room with a savage long-drawn-out 'Ar-r-r-r-r'. I was like a rag doll in his grip. It was not unpleasant being whirled around, knocking into obstacles, crashing into the swinging pictures. When he stopped for breath, I rested my heavy head for a bit on his shoulder. It was not cold but warm.

'This will cheer you up.' He put a piece of dark thick oval-shaped glass into my hand. I held it up to the fire. It was blue, of course – an intense heart-breaking blue that gathered in and held the light before letting it go again. I gave him a questioning look.

'No. That's not *it*. But it's near, isn't it? It's *near*. I've been working hard at it. Nothing else to do.' He took the glass from me and pointed to some tiny bubbles and striations in its depths. 'You see? Imperfections. They're caused by impurities in the melt.' I didn't see; but I desperately wanted to.

'I'm too bloody good at glass-making,' he explained. 'I'd forgotten that it's the idiot third son – stumbling blindly on, talking to animals, trusting to luck – who marries the princess. I've been trying to recreate the conditions of medieval glass-making, but I've been too careful to allow any impurities to creep in. Last week, in a blind rage, I mixed up a batch any old how. I was careless. I dropped ash in the melt and God knows what else. Out comes this blue glass! You see? The imperfections *help* to give it its opaque, jewel-like quality. You see the irony – part of the key to the Chartres blue lies in the impurities which I tried so painstakingly to keep out!'

I saw the irony all right. I saw the irony so clearly that I wanted to hug my friend.

'All I need now,' he went on, 'is the secret ingredient to make *the* blue . . .'

I thought of my own Work. I said:

'Perhaps you're trying too hard. Perhaps it's like the impurities – the missing ingredient could be something so obvious, so *close* to you that you think it's worthless. It could be in this room, under your nose, but you can't see it.'

When I went outside, rain was falling in drops the size of half-crowns. I didn't mind. I knew that Robert had inadvertently revealed to me the way forward.

EILEEN

The struggle to interpret the alchemical enigma, the battle with its paradoxes, seems only to deepen its mystery. I'm farther away from an understanding of it than when I started. Every time I wrestle it to the ground it surges up again more strongly, like Antaeus who drew strength from every contact with his mother Earth. Must I, like Hercules, hold the entire mystery aloft, in my mind, before it can be strangled and laid to rest?

I'm frightened. Sometimes I'm flooded with more ideas than I can handle. Odd hypnagogic images come screaming towards me on the edge of sleep. Lately they come, or threaten to come, when I'm fully awake. Areas of myself I didn't know I had suddenly open up like parts of a secret nervous system. Electrical flashes light up my solar plexus and spine. It spooks me to think about Smith; it's weird to imagine him in this house, harbouring the Great Work. Yet I can't help thinking and imagining – it's like gazing into the night sky and forgetting yourself and finding your gaze returning to observe itself, like light turning full circle through curved space.

Among the Gnostic writings found at Nag Hammadi in about 1945 was the Gospel of St Thomas which contains many uncanonical sayings of Jesus. My favourite is:

> Jesus said to them:
> 'When you make the two one,
> and make the inside like the outside,
> and the outside like the inside,
> and the upper side like the under side,
> and (in such a way) that you make the man
>   (with) the woman a single one,

> in order that the man is not the man and the
> woman is not the woman . . .
> then you will go into [the Kingdom].'*

Doesn't the transformation at the Rubedo include the adept himself, who is united with that other unknown part of himself, the hidden female foreshadowed by the White Stone? And doesn't this union also represent his union with the absolute otherness of matter as manifested in the Hermetic vessel – matter which is now transformed into a resurrected body, both individual to him and yet androgynously co-extensive with all that he once thought of as Nature? A body through which the Spirit has broken, like stigmata, turning male and female, soul and flesh, inside out?

She was dozing on the sofa, which seems to have become more or less her permanent position. She had deteriorated. Cheeks caved in; eyes rimmed with darkness like an Arab woman. Sleeping, her face lost its hard outline, its bitter fire. She was reduced to her surface, like a softer, more vulnerable self.

I hadn't really meant to come. Too much weirdness still attaches to Mrs Zetterberg – and, besides, I hate and fear illness. But I had been beavering away at the Art, brooding over its strange heart-wrenching paradoxes and, being over-full of turbulent thoughts about the Reverend Smith, I had wandered out on to the Green to breathe and stretch my legs. From there, my feet had carried me to the Manor gates and I thought, 'Why not?' Mrs Z., after all, is a link with Smith. I have hopes that she will throw some light on him. It's no longer a matter of mere curiosity – day and night I can't get him out of my mind.

I sat on a stool near her head, lost in reverie. She fidgeted in her sleep and uttered a small throaty cry. A moment later her eyes snapped open. They swivelled wildly, making no sense of their surroundings. Then they rested on me and at once wrinkled into the most friendly smile, a thing I never expected to see.

---

* I have corrected a couple of inaccuracies in this quotation, which can be found in Robert M. Grant with David Noel Freedman, *The Secret Sayings of Jesus according to the Gospel of Thomas* (London, 1960).

'You're in love,' she said. I thought fleetingly, almost guiltily, of P. Was he ever more than a figleaf of my imagination? I'm changing so fast I hardly know.

'Not any more,' I said.

'You had that look about you. Oh well.' It was the sort of remark that might once have given me the creeps. Perhaps I'm simply getting acclimatised to the old bat.

At her insistence I made tea, of which she only took two token sips. She was pleased to see me. Touching really. I wouldn't say that her illness has rendered her helpless, but it has caused one or two cracks to appear in the brittle façade. Her abrupt bouts of craziness, I'm beginning to think, are only a mask, like the violent smears of coloured clay tribesmen apply to frighten their neighbours or to hide from querulous spirits.

We were quite cosy together, near the fire, with the hot tea and a crumpet for me. She was drowsy but, in the face of my eagerness to listen, inclined to reminisce.

She met Mr Zetterberg – Al (!) – on a cruise (!!). He was (and is) Canadian. She was young and attractive, but socially handicapped by an illegitimate child, a son. She had no desire to leave England – she'd never been abroad – but needed a father for her child. Al had none of the English compunction about tangling with a fallen woman. She had an odd way of expressing the upshot:

'Fortunately, I was able to secure him.' Mindful of the faded opulence of my surroundings, I commented that it was also fortunate that he should be wealthy as well as liberal-minded. Mrs Z. surprised me:

'Oh, it was *I* who had money. It had been left to me, along with ... items of value. I had my attractions no doubt; but money was not the least of them. Al did his best to spend it, and rather foolishly, too. Luckily, he was not an imaginative spender. And, besides, I kept him on a short rein. I also became quite handy at investment. We were comfortable ... a new house in the suburbs of Toronto and so on. Not ideal, but as good as I could have hoped. Al was a nice man – weak, but well-meaning. He was a good father to Timothy, without ever really understanding him. I don't understand him myself.' She sighed. 'Tim always had his own ideas, even as a child. He's a very ... *high-minded* individual. Has his own way of doing things. You don't interfere.' She looked a little puzzled and depressed after this, so I asked her why she had split up with Al. It was her turn to look surprised:

'Because Tim had grown up, of course. I wanted him to come back to England with me. But, you know, he was quite the Canadian by then. He did very well in the law, you know, until he wandered off.' She sounded a shade peevish. 'I had a letter from him eight months ago. It took three months to reach me. He spoke of hardship and hunting and beauty. I believe God cropped up as well. He ought to be marrying at his age, not spouting about beauty and God.' In her irritation, her voice lost its veneer of refinement and its touch of mid-Atlantic twang. It became pure West Country, as if that were the accent of her heart.

'So you had no further use for your husband,' I said, 'once Tim no longer needed a father.' It came out priggish. *God*, I *am* a prig. Mrs Z. raised her eyebrows and then gave a laugh that was coarser than it needed to be, I thought. My old fear of her prickled my skin. What if these confidences were a way of manipulating me? What if she were lying? What if, beneath these droplets of sentiment, there was a heart as hard as jade?

'My dear . . . Why don't we say that Al and I needed each other? You haven't yet experienced the great passion of your life. When you do . . . if you do . . . if it is unrequited . . . you will take, as I did, whatever measures are necessary to plod on.' She suddenly looked very tired. I was unaccountably moved by her old-fashioned words. 'The great passion of my life.' 'Unrequited.' And the way she called me 'my dear' like that, out of the blue, almost tenderly. It made me want to cry. Her eyes closed.

'I was away for seventeen years,' she murmured. 'I counted the days until I could return here. But of course it's never quite the same as you dream it will be. Bye, bye, dear. Come again soon.'

Jung was pleased to notice that the alchemical Opus is an inversion of the Christian myth: whereas Christ descended from the Above to the Below (the Incarnation) and then ascended from the Below to the Above (the Ascension), the Opus represents an ascent of Spirit followed by a descent, a return to matter. The Emerald Table describes how the sun-moon child 'ascends from the earth into the heaven, and again descends into the earth, and receives the power of the superiors and inferiors. So thus you will have the glory of the whole world'.

One has the impression, comments Jung, of a mirror world, 'as if the God-man coming down from above – as in the Gnostic legend – were reflected in the dark waters of Physis [i.e. matter]'.

This is not the whole story. Jung himself cites alchemical texts which appear to be structured in a similar way to the Christian myth. For example, Sol or Rex sometimes descends to rescue Luna or Regina from the depths; or the King himself is drowned or devoured by the subterranean ddragon like Jonah swallowed by the whale. These 'descents' take place before the subsequent 'ascents', as when the King is rescued by his son.

I'm not surprised that the alchemical myths contain symmetrical inversions of each other. Since alchemy prides itself on its self-regulating processes – 'no fixing without a complementary volatilising' and vice versa – I would be surprised if the many versions of the Opus didn't contain all permutations, just as my own text contains a significant set of reversals – the diagram for Congelation, for instance, is the same, though transformed, as that for Solution. The undifferentiated unity represented by the dragon is restored at a higher level in the marriage of Above and Below represented by the full moon, the union of Sol and Luna or the star.

Actually, it wouldn't surprise me if the Christian myth wasn't so much separate from the whole alchemical-Hermetic-Gnostic mythology as itself part of the mythology. I think Jung was getting at this idea when he suggested that alchemy was compensating for an incompleteness in the Christian myth, that it was Christianity's chthonic counterpart – maintaining those links with the dark feminine material side of human nature which the Christian emphasis on spirit, the Above, Heaven, etc. had neglected. By implying that the Christian myth was prior to the alchemical he avoided having to confront the possibility that they are both variations on a still greater, more inclusive, more fundamental theme, a kind of hypothetical Ur-myth out of which the Christian and Gnostic-alchemical myths sprang simultaneously. (Not that we Lévi-Straussians really subscribe to such an Ur-myth! There is no final mythological solution to the problem of discontinuity between Nature and Culture or between Heaven and Earth; there is only the interplay among a finite set of elements, like the play of mirrors in a kaleidoscope. But this doesn't rule out an *existential* solution – the creation of some Being, like the Stone, in which the opposition continuity/discontinuity can be marvellously overcome along with all the other impossible contradictions . . .)

To return to the idea of descent and ascent, it occurs to me on second thoughts that even when the Christian and the alchemical movements seem to be the same, there is in fact an important difference. Christ's descent from Above to Below was a descent from Heaven to Earth; but, in alchemical texts, Above and Below represent (at least in the first instance) the surface of the earth as opposed to the 'underworld' – either the depths of the sea or of the earth. Thus alchemy adheres to the threefold cosmology which is more widespread than the Christian opposition. In common with mythologies as far apart in time as the ancient Greek and the South American tribes', it places earth in a middle position between sky/heaven and a subterranean realm. And this is why my alchemical text distinguishes between the union of Above and Below at Conjunction and at Congelation. The first is the dark union of the 'earth's surface' with the subterranean, the ego with the shadow, the personal with the impersonal; the second is the light union of the 'sky' with the surface, consciousness with the unconscious, the individual with the collective. This second union is called Heaven. Formed by a double ascent it must now descend to be reunited with Earth.

Christianity can't of course ignore the threefold scheme altogether. It adds hell to heaven and earth and hints that it's located in some underworld of fire and brimstone ruled by the Devil. This notion was probably derived from Near Eastern myths whose underworlds, however, though they contained the dead and were ruled by gods, were free of the connotations of punishment and evil which characterised hell. The fact that Christ descended into hell to redeem the damned after his crucifixion means that Jung's description of the Christian myth has to be modified: Christ executed a double descent, from Heaven to earth and from earth to hell. This was followed by a double ascent – from hell to earth (the Resurrection) and from earth to Heaven (the Ascension). Alchemy's inversion of these movements holds good, as we have seen, as regards the double ascent; but the corresponding double descent is unnecessary because the subterranean realm has already been 'redeemed', that is, raised up into the Above. If a true symmetry is to be preserved, we would have to cut out Christ's Ascension and have him remain on 'middle-earth'.

This afternoon I spent a lot of time burrowing among the boxes in the manuscript room, looking for bits and pieces, tracking down clues. It was dark by the time I popped into the drawing-room. Bradley sprang up from her bedside. 'Sofa-side' I should say. He appeared relieved to see me. I'd had no intention of staying but he looked so badly in need of a break that I settled down near Mrs Zetterberg – or 'Nora' as I'm to call her – while he left the room, returning a minute later with a large whisky and soda for me. Nora has lost the desire or the capacity for strong drink.

'Find what you're looking for, dear?' she asked. She was awake and alert, but had that frightening, hollow, feverishly intense look in her eyes that you see in famine victims. I shook my head. The drawing-room, though spacious, is beginning to pong with that sweet queasy-making smell which chronic invalids exude.

(I don't think I've realised till now that Nora is going to die. Since she refused all medical treatment and opted for her own peculiar methods of cure, I suppose I half-thought that the cancer wasn't too serious – an evasion on my part, but one that wasn't challenged as long as she was mobile and apparently fit. Bradley is more depressed than he allows himself to show. He told me on Thursday – his voice cracked; I was mortified – how he had begged her to have proper treatment. But she won't be 'mucked about with'. Her fierce, even desperate self-sufficiency – bordering on hubris, in my opinion – won't allow her to seek the help of doctors who, she claims, will dispense a cure that's not only more pernicious and painful than the disease, but will ultimately be ineffective. She may be right. Who knows? At any rate, this is something she's *sure* of and won't negotiate. Death-with-Dignity is what she's going for – a notion she can apparently reconcile with pagan rites and drinking hens' blood. But, then again, who knows what expedient, fervently believed in, might not do the trick?)

As soon as Bradley had left, she said:

'Try and cheer the poor old bugger up if you have a moment, will you? He gets very attached to people, like an old dog.' She made a noise in her throat like a chuckle. 'He came with the house, you know. I bought it off his father. Old man Caldwell fancied himself as a farmer, but his heart wasn't in it. He and his wife went back up North. Pluto and I came to an arrangement. I've been glad of it – there may be only half of him left, but he's still worth two of most men.'

'You knew him before Canada, then?'
'We were at school together as children.'
'His injury . . . he was burnt, wasn't he?'
'Yes.'
'In the fire in my cellar. Your cellar.'
'So you know about that.'
'I know that John Smith died in it.'
'Did he? You'd have to ask Pluto about that. But it won't do any good. He never talks about it. Not even to me. Between ourselves, dear, I think he never got over having failed to save the vicar's life. But, as I keep telling him, if the vicar had wanted to live he would've saved his own life, wouldn't he? Anyway that's what I tell myself.'

'Perhaps he couldn't save his own life.'
'Don't you believe it, dear. He didn't need Pluto to save him. He could've walked on water if he'd wanted to. Not that he did want to.'

I never know what she's going to come out with next. I was dying to know more about John Smith, but Nora had had enough for one day. I think she knew John less well than she pretends; I think she enjoys tormenting me.

The Secret . . . Let's say certain religious disciplines have certain secrets – yogic techniques, for example. These can confer power on the adept. But the catch-22 is that the adept can't abuse this power because he can't attain the goal that gives him the power if he abuses it, that is if he's a bad person. He is so changed in the course of his spiritual training that any misuse of the power he acquires on the way will set him back.

This is also true of alchemy. But the trouble is that the Work is not a purely inward, spiritual development (although it is also that). It involves the manipulation – like magic – of powers which are to all intents and purposes *outside* the alchemist. Powers which he attributes to the 'earth spirit'. And these can very easily be used for evil ends, without much 'spiritual' development on the part of the adept, simply by using knowledge of the secret to raise forces which, because of their origins, are even more dangerous and powerful than those traditionally raised by ordinary ritual magic.

Collected the Fulcanelli book today.* An amusing if unimpressive read. So much of this mysterious French alchemist's history depends on the sparse testimony of his alleged disciple, the reclusive Eugène Canseliet – who, I gather, is still alive and still working at the Opus, though he must be in his eighties by now.

Fulcanelli's identity remains unknown. The name, meaning 'little volcano' in Italian, is an alchemical pseudonym. He wrote two books in the 1920s, *Les Demeures Philosophales* and *Le Mystère des Cathédrales*, which were published through the agency of M. Canseliet, who never revealed the author's real name. The latter is on record (in a communication to Walter Lang who wrote the introduction to the English translation of *Le Mystère*) as saying that he performed a transmutation in September 1922, using a minute quantity of Fulcanelli's Powder of Projection. It took place at a gasworks laboratory at Sarcelles, in the presence of the chemist Gaston Sauvage and the artist Jean-Julien Champagne. The result was one hundred grammes of gold.

It crossed my mind that Fulcanelli might have been Smith's 'master', but this is unlikely since the latter was still working in Paris in the early thirties while the former disappeared well before then, never to be seen again except once, by Canseliet, thirty years later.[6]

Apparently Canseliet was summoned to Spain by Fulcanelli in 1954. (The author of my book was told what happened there by 'sources close to Canseliet' . . .) He was met at Seville and taken to a castle somewhere in the mountains where he was greeted by his master who still looked about fifty years old, that is about

---

* Almost certainly *The Fulcanelli Phenomenon* by Kenneth Raynor Johnson (Jersey, 1980).

Canseliet's age at the time. He was shown to his quarters in one of the castle's turrets. Looking down on the courtyard, he watched a group of children playing there. There was something unusual about them which, he suddenly realised, was their costumes – they looked as if they had come straight out of the sixteenth century.

During his stay, Canseliet was allowed to work and experiment in a laboratory placed at his disposal where Fulcanelli would occasionally come to visit, speaking to him briefly or checking on his progress. Canseliet had the impression that the castle was a 'secret refuge for a whole colony of advanced alchemists – possibly even Adepts like his master – and owned by Fulcanelli himself'.

One morning, Canseliet was taking the air at the foot of his turret's staircase, in an archway that opened on to the courtyard, when he heard voices. Three women, chattering among themselves, were coming across the courtyard; like the children, they wore 'long, flowing dresses of the sixteenth-century style'. As they passed, one of the women turned, looked at him and smiled. It was only for an instant, but Canseliet was amazed: he swears that the face of the woman was Fulcanelli's.

Another intriguing anecdote in the Fulcanelli book is apparently taken from *Journey through Asia Minor* (Amsterdam, 1714) by the eighteenth-century French traveller and writer Paul Lucas.

While at 'Bronosa, in Natolia', Lucas was introduced to four learned Dervishes – presumably Sufis – one of whom, an Usbec, seemed more accomplished than the others, speaking every language Lucas could think of. This man looked about thirty years old but claimed to have lived a century. He was, in fact, 'a sage' who was happy to discuss religion, natural philosophy, chemistry, alchemy and the Cabala.

The conversation turned to death. The Usbec remarked that a sage does indeed die, for death is inevitable, 'but he does not die before the utmost limits of his mortal existence. Hereditary disease and weakness reduce the life of man, but the sage, by the use of the true medicine, can ward off whatever may hinder or impair the animal functions for a thousand years.'

Lucas cited Nicholas Flamel as an example of one who had certainly possessed the Philosophers' Stone, and yet was dead.

The sage 'smiled at [his] simplicity', and remarked that Flamel was still living: '... neither he nor his wife are dead. It is not above three years since I left both the one and the other in the Indies; he is one of my best friends.'

What happened, the Usbec sage said, was that Flamel had seen how dangerous his position was when Charles VI sent one of his agents to enquire as to the origin of his riches. Realising that he was about to be arrested under suspicion of having the Philosophers' Stone, he avoided persecution by faking his wife's death, and then his own. While she fled to Switzerland to wait for him, he had a log buried in her stead; and later, by bribing doctors and clerks, Flamel brought off the same deception as regards his own 'body'. Since then, the two of them have roamed the world as Adepts of 'our Philosophy'.

A lorry pulled on to the Green while I was drinking my morning tea, curled up on the deep window-seat. It made an ugly noise, offensive to my ears which were still sensitised by sleep. It had been a late night. I watched as the lorry scattered the kids who had been playing their usual Sunday morning game of football. I was annoyed. I'd been enjoying the game.

The driver parked the lorry in the middle of the Green. At the back it had some sort of diesel generator which the driver started up. It made an irritating, insistent putt-putt-putt. The children gathered at a distance to see what he was up to. I was curious myself, and stood up in the window to get a better look. The generator was attached to a cumbersome machine from which there protruded a wide flexible pipe, like a giant proboscis. Stuff began to pour out of it. Several children ran off like mad things towards their homes on the estate. I went to get dressed and then stepped out for a closer look.

By the time I arrived, other people were coming out of their houses from all directions. The children had returned with brothers and sisters and friends. Pretty soon most of the village was encircling the lorry, which went on pouring out its stuff, more and more of it, until it spread over the grass all around and mounted up higher and higher until it was as high as a cottage.

The stuff was foam. It sat there in a vast shuddering creamy pile like a giant's bubble-bath. And still it poured out in a fabulous gush from the pipe attached to the foam-making machine. It was so weird and so white that no one knew what to do, except laugh.

Suddenly three tots broke away from the awed respectful circle of villagers and headed at full tilt for the foam which the breeze was now sculpting into fantastic crenellated shapes like a fairy-tale castle. Two of them were caught and hauled back by parents who obviously thought there was danger of suffocating or drowning; but the third disappeared through the towering white wall, chased by an older sister. Seconds later they emerged on the other side of the pile, reeling, disorientated, smothered in suds, screaming with glee.

A cheer went up. There was a general surge forward, in which I was caught up. We charged into the muffled twilight world of bubbles, shot through with tiny jewelled rainbows, where we carved great caverns with a sweep of the arm, where we frolicked and rolled and flung boulders of foam at each other in a riot of soapy ecstasy. No one could resist it. Dour old buggers came out of the pub and, looking about self-consciously, marched through the shifting shivering portals of foam. It was as much fun to watch the antics as it was to join in. The noise of the engine was drowned by screams and laughter. It was like waking up as a child to find that thick snow has fallen – but more so, because the miracle was unlike anything in Nature. For forty minutes or more, whatever divisions existed among the villagers, young and old, man and woman, were annihilated as the foam, like an act of grace, gathered them in.

I spotted Bradley on the sidelines and, bouncing up to him, bombed him with suds – urged him to disport himself. He smiled thinly. He didn't think he would. 'I wouldn't want to frighten the children.' I felt thick-skinned and tactless, and went on talking to cover it up. Whose idea was it? Who paid for the machine? As soon as I asked, I knew. Bradley rolled his Cyclopean eye towards the Manor. I could just make out Nora at an upstairs window, both palms pressed like a prisoner against the glass, looking out over the fun and games. 'Not like her to splash out like this,' said Bradley, as if the foam were five-pound notes.

A wind got up and began to blow the bubbles all over the place. The machine had stopped some time before and they were already subsiding. There was a sudden gust which scooped up fat slabs of the stuff and sent them sailing over the rooftops. More gusts followed. For a while the air was crazy with swirling chunks of bubble – and then there was nothing left. A light rain began to smatter down and, presently, to fall in a steady dispiriting curtain. People turned towards their separate homes. Some of the smaller kids, over-tired, began to grizzle.

SMITH

Robert's inadvertent words are a clear sign of how to proceed! Without delay but gently, gently, I dismantled the alembic and restored the matter to my pelican wherein I began at once to circulate our mercury.

I realise that I have been *obsessed* with removing the dross and scoria that can in fact only be washed away up to a point – beyond which there must always remain a residue of impurity. It is the glory of the Work that *its dross also can be raised up*. The Albedo can not only succeed *in spite of* the remaining stain, but *because* of it. It is in the nature of Sol, may he rise never so high, always to bear with him a reminder of the sulphurous darkness where he died and decayed! (Only in the final accounting, perhaps, when the body is exalted and made volatile can the last dark vestige of fleshliness be wiped out and the corporeal spirit descend into its spiritual body.)

'Wherefore the Wisemen', says Philalethes,* 'did at length know and consider that in [mercury] the watery crudities, and the earthly faeces, did hinder it from being digested; which being fixed in the roots thereof, *cannot be rooted out, but by turning the whole compound in and out* [Smith's italics].'

A gleam of light in the darkness! No more than a gleam – like the palest reflection of moonlight – but it presages, *surely*, the advent of beautiful Luna, who will cast off her old black wrinkled chrysalis and take to her wings, yes, even bearing aloft that core of scoria St Paul knew as the 'thorn in the flesh',** the original stain

---

* In chapter 11 of the *Introitus*.
** See II Corinthians 12, v. 7: 'And by reason of the exceeding greatness of the revelations – wherefore, that I should not be exalted overmuch, there was given to me a thorn in the flesh, a messenger of Satan to buffet me, that I should not be exalted overmuch.'

that brands us like the mark of Cain and which, irremovable, can only be accommodated by the grace of God.

Nature fell along with Adam and Eve. As her guardians we perform the Great Work to lift her up again – to free the *Anima Mundi* from her incarceration in matter.

Transmutation is only the healing, through the medicinal Stone, of patient Nature in imperfect and unhealthy metals. It is the restoration of homesick matter, aching for Eden, to its original state.

De microcosmo

'Understand that thou art a second world in miniature', says Origen, 'and that the sun and the moon are within you, and also the stars.'

This profound truth has been almost wholly ignored by Western civilisation since it parted company with what I shall boldly call reality. There is a vital correspondence between the world and the 'little world of man', the macrocosm and the microcosm. In earlier times the microcosm was identified with the body which, as an unknown realm, was open to all manner of fantastical imaginings concerning its nature. However, when the body was opened up, literally, in the new anatomical schools of Padua (at about the same time – history is full of these little symmetries – that new lands were being opened up by geographical exploration), the microcosm was firmly identified – as it always had been by the cognoscenti – with the soul.

I've set down elsewhere [see p. 348] the soul's ability, as *imago Dei*, to mirror all the world's images contained in the universal storehouse of the Spirit. This is the sense in which it reflects the macrocosm. One might say that the soul is Janus-faced, both subjective and objective, gazing in one direction towards the universal Spirit and, in the other, towards the particular individual. (It is, in some ways, absurd to talk of *my* soul when 'I' am as much a part of 'it' as it is of me.) Again, one might say that the soul is like the human face: in its plan it is universal, with a regulation number and arrangement of features, yet in actuality no two individual faces are identical – each proclaims the uniqueness of its owner.

The Hermetic egg is also a microcosm since it contains what I've called the objective aspect of the soul – that is, the operation of Mercurius in the microcosm. He demonstrates, in the course of the Opus, that *the microcosm is arranged in the same way as the macrocosm.*

These days we are largely insensible – except in unusual and probably mystical 'states of mind' – that we are entire 'little worlds'. The injunction to 'know ourselves' means that we must know our own souls: and, knowing them, we know the world.

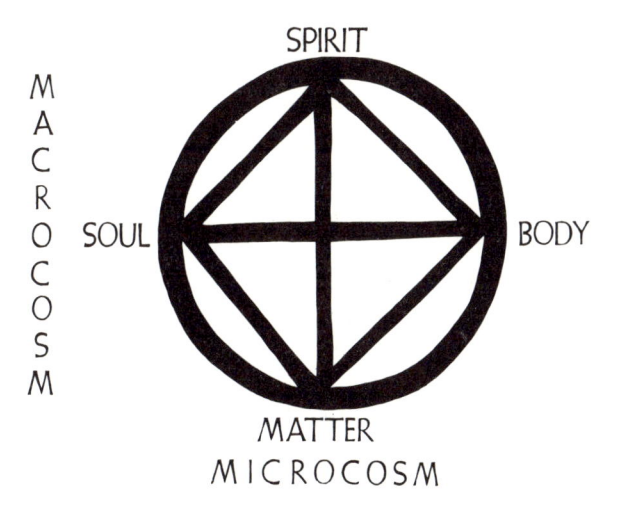

MACROCOSM

SPIRIT — SOUL — BODY — MATTER

MICROCOSM

I have always taken a pride in being honest with myself. Pride is, once again, the operative word. I am rigorously selective about those events of my inner life which I subject to scrutiny. It is easy to be honest about events that barely scratch the carefully lacquered veneer of my self-esteem. The others – the *real* events – are simply left off the agenda.

I told myself, for example, that I would not demean myself by challenging Bradley's accusation that I was the father of Nora's child. What I omitted to mention to myself was that the accusation is true: I was guilty of violating Nora. It doesn't matter two hoots that I'm not guilty of the actual crime. I ravished her in thought (and very nearly in deed). I can't simply blame it on the Worm.

Guilt rots us to the core. It's the skin in which the human

condition is parcelled up. It's merely sentimental to imagine otherwise. We expend a great deal of energy inventing lesser guilts for ourselves – guilts over our parents or children, work or sex, or whatever – in order, firstly, to cover up our single primal guilt and, secondly, to rid ourselves of these guilts and so attain the illusion of freedom and regained innocence. Authentic guilt can't be got rid of by ourselves. The best we can do is to strip naked before Our Saviour and beg him to flay the guilt from us. The nakedness itself is often mistaken for a return to innocence but it is not – even if we expiate the guilt accumulated in our personal lives, we have not come to the bottom of it. It extends beyond our past into the history of our race, the history of human life. That is what the myth of the Fall is about.

To strip ourselves down is to repent. If Our Saviour consents to flay us, in truth the pain is only the pain of love and atonement by which we are gathered up, together with our guilt, into the Spirit who makes all things new and spotless.

It's possible that Bradley believes me guilty of violating Nora. Might not his own guilt compel him to attribute to *me* that which he can't face in *himself*? I know this *is* possible because I have done exactly the same thing. It seems a long time ago, and yet I relive that moment far more vividly now than when it happened. For then, swathed about in clouds of confusion and anger, it was like a dream:

I took three strides across the room and hit him in the mouth. I hit him because he had hit on the truth – that, yes, *I wanted Nora for myself.*

I watched her sunbathing from her bedroom window. I picked up her petticoat from where it lay languidly on the floor and pressed the cool fabric against my hot face. I watched her move her long legs in the long grass as she read her book. There was a red blur of desire in front of my eyes. When I went down to her she had gone. I fell down into the imprint her body had left in the grass. I stroked the book she had been reading. I gave in to my foul imaginings, heedless of the effect their intensity would have on her, on me, on the Work, on the world. The book shifted under my caress to reveal another naked book beneath, as lewd and unexpected as my own hidden thoughts. I wanted to cry. I buried my face in the silky aromatic grass as if it grew between her legs.

*

Each time I go down into the cellar my anticipation increases, my weary leadenness is dispelled; I feel lighter and able to breathe more easily in the change of air. The outside world recedes into the misty distance; everyday events seem mere foam on the simple sea-swell of my circulations. Exertion is a delight since the Work provides the energy for it. As each new change unfolds in the wonderful Egg, I rejoice with it and, rejoicing, feel myself elevated to a place where my lost youth, my sinful past, seems not too far away, not perhaps irrevocable.

Not so long ago, to return upstairs was to step out on to a planet with stronger gravity where every movement requires muscular effort, where one plods instead of gliding. I slipped back into my old anxieties like one who plunges into a denser, more opaque element. Lately, however, my habitual stiffness and chronic preoccupations have begun to lose a little of their power over me. I carry back some of the lightness and joy of the laboratory. Sometimes when I ascend the steps and throw open the door I half-expect to see in the grey half-light of dawn a strange new world arrayed in unknown colours where She is waiting for me, open-armed among rare and beautiful denizens.

Whenever I return to that night of Conjunction, to the weird chiaroscuro of Nora's room, I return to the head turning on the pillow.

I can't write those simple words without my head swimming, my heart racing, my skin breaking out in points of fire – without the feverish weakness of my legs carrying me back to her bedside.

The thing I remember, what *occurred* to me with a certainty as palpable as the Worm-driven desire, was that there'd be *no fear* on that immaculate face when it turned like an unknown world towards me. It was as if I were *expected*. For the briefest of moments the prospect of the expectant innocent face – how shall I say? – *disarmed* the Worm. Like Milton's Satan, when he first laid eyes on Eve's heavenly nakedness, his malice was overawed; for a space he stood abstracted from his own evil and remained stupidly good. Then, as a flame gutters and dies down in a sudden draught, 'the hot hell that always in him burns' flared up again more strongly.

Yes, but not immediately – and not in the same way. The fractional doubt, the tiny hesitation somehow broke the circuit of self-accumulating lust. The Worm and I were divided for an instant in our brute collision. At once the faint swish of the body under the sheet, the whisper of hair on the pillow, told me that the sight of that face would be unendurable. The craving to look upon it was matched in intensity only by the fear of seeing it. Even as the intolerable Worm of fire urged me on, it recoiled in dread from the forbidden countenance. Madness was only a whisper away.

Needless to say, it wasn't I who wrenched my body out of the room. Maybe it was the Worm, unable to risk the sight of itself reflected in that dispassionate Sphinx-like face; maybe it was some other, unknown power, greater than the Worm's power, which rolled over it as the head turned on the pillow. I know now that the head did not belong to Nora. To whom then, or to what? To some transfigured image of Nora conjured out of the Worm's hallucinatory fever? To the phantom White Lady (I'm only half-joking) clothed in the colour and substance of desire? I know this much: *she is real and absolutely to do with me.*

It may be, it *may* be that she is the one I've been looking for all my life. The one whom the Annabelles and the Noras of this world simply prefigured. I had rather assumed, I suppose – ah, ye of little faith! – that she was not to be found in this world. What if – oh God, are all things really possible with you? – what if she *exists*? What if she is palely waiting like an epiphany in the whiteness – turning her head slowly around to bestow her shattering glance? It may be that I *will* be able to look upon her because of what happened later that dreadful night – how much later I can't say (hours? Hours that seemed like weeks) – when I had been returned below. Maybe then I paid the price when He or She or It appeared (there is no gender, not even an inhuman neuter, where it comes from). To look upon the one-eyed Horned One was to touch the bottom of the world. It was death, of a kind. There are no words.

Who knows the inscrutable ways of Mercurius? And might it not be that her face is light as that other's was dark – that the two faces are but different phases of the one, like the new moon and the full?

*

I preached today on the text 'I have been crucified with Christ; yet I live; and yet no longer I, but Christ liveth in me'.* The sermon was greeted with apathy by a sparse congregation. Afterwards Lydia Simmons hissed: 'You must do something, Vicar. She's poisoning everyone against you.' She swivelled her eyes to indicate my old friend Mrs Beattie. What do I care – except that Lydia has to live with poor unhappy horse-faced Mrs B.?

As the dark moon gives birth to the full, so today I have seen the first fleck of white, like a condensation of moonlight. No more than a snowflake it *shines*, as a remote star shines at the bottom of an unfathomable shaft.

I'm not deceived! The fleck of white expands like the pupil of an eye, *watching me as I watch it*.

I increase the heat to the fifth degree, as it's written. The black earth must be incinerated. The whiteness of ashes is the snowy robe of the soul. What is not washed by our water must be purged by our fire. Virgin's milk and old man's cinders.

Wonders will never cease. I'll set down what Robert said, in order, more or less in his words. I found him in the hall on returning from a ramble. (It was a surprise in itself – Robert has called on me, I think, but once before.) First of all he exclaimed, 'You're a bloody genius, padre!' I said that this was unlikely. He pulled out of his pocket several pieces of coloured glass, from yellowish to brownish, from purply to, finally, a wonderful blue.
'Is this *it*?'
'No. But it's close. Thanks to you. Do you remember saying that the secret ingredient could be something like the impurities – something so obvious I'd overlooked it?' I didn't remember. 'Well anyway, I sat down and rethought the whole process. I thought about the huge amounts of wood the medieval glass-makers used to fire their kilns. I thought of the beech forests that used to surround

---

* St Paul's letter to the Galatians, chapter 2, verse 20.

Chartres. I imagined a glass-maker stoking his fire with beechwood. I saw him take a handful of ash and toss it in the melt. It came to me that maybe I was wrong in using a soda flux . . . maybe I should try potash, from beechwood. It makes a perfectly good flux. So I burnt some beech logs and tried the same trick. Lo and behold! All the colours you're holding were made by the same ingredients. All that's needed to change their colour is to vary the temperature, ventilation and so on. I haven't tried all the combinations yet. But the *main thing* is, I'm certain my blue glass – *the* blue glass – was coloured just like this, by trace elements *in the flux itself*[7] – the beechwood ash!'

I congratulated him warmly. He refused my offer of sherry; he had been on his way out when I arrived.

'You didn't come to see me?' I asked.

'No. I came to see Nora. I've only just heard about . . . her condition. I'm so happy that you don't judge her. To tell the truth, I had no hope that you'd understand.'

I admitted that I had perhaps judged her, when I first heard, but not for long. Of Bradley, I said nothing. As for understanding, I think I understand Nora as well as anyone. I was rather put out by Robert's presumption; however, I was touched by his concern for Nora – and more than touched when he said he'd make provision for her. I thanked him saying that I could manage. He seemed on the point of leaving and then he changed his mind.

'I *would* like to explain. Not to try and justify it, only to explain.' He was so earnest that he made me smile. I said there was no need; as far as I'm concerned, Nora requires no defending. It's bitter to recall one's obtuseness. Robert insisted.

'You see, padre, I was out of my mind with missing Janet. I'd been drinking a lot. Not that I blame it on that. I knew what I was doing. Nora came because she'd had some sort of row with her father over Tim. She'd been looking forward to seeing him on leave; she'd gone to meet him and then there'd been this row, so she'd walked out. You were busy, or away, or something so she came to me. I could see that this thing with her father wasn't serious. She had some private sorrow. She wouldn't confide in me, but I could tell it was a love problem. Unhappiness in love is a great leveller. We understood each other so well. She tried to put aside her misery to rouse me from mine. She was an angel. . . .

'It got rather late. She didn't want to go home. I can't really explain, padre. A man like you could never understand. It just happened. She just sort of . . . took me in. I'm not ashamed, padre. I'm sorry about the consequences, for Nora's sake. Everything I do is a disaster. I've just told her that in all honesty I can't marry her – although I'll do everything I can for her.' He gave a short laugh. 'It's funny but she was shocked that I should even *think* of marriage. She said: "Janet would never forgive us if we got *married*." She said she'd already told Janet about . . . the other thing. She said it was "all right". Anyway, Nora wants to stay here if that suits you— ' He stopped talking as he saw the look on my face. 'Oh bloody hell,' he said quietly. 'You didn't know about me and Nora.' I shook my head. 'I'm sorry. Try not to think too badly of me, padre. I don't want to, well, lose you too.' I shook my head again. Who was I to think badly of him?

After Robert had left, I stayed standing in the hall. In a little while Nora came through from the kitchen with her arms full of clean sheets. She didn't notice me until she was half way up the stairs, when she suddenly looked over her shoulder and let out a little exclamation. She turned around and said:

'He's told you, hasn't he? I was afraid to . . . ' She sat down abruptly on the ninth stair. 'I'm so sorry, sir.' She craned her neck forward for a moment and then, as she began to cry, dropped her face forward into the pile of snowy linen in her lap.

I went up and squeezed myself in beside her and took her warm dry little hand in my hand. It's the first time I've touched her. 'Never mind, never mind,' I said, for want of anything better. After a while she stopped crying. With difficulty I said:

'That you love him is all that matters. Love is all that matters.' Love. It can so easily get left out. The Philosophers have so little to say about it. Nora raised her head.

'We did it out of pity,' she said. 'Pity for each other and ourselves. It's not *him* I love. It never was.'

Her hand in mine was perfectly still. We sat on, silent, cramped on the narrow stair as the house grew dark. I thought of all that had happened. Feeling her hand, I thought how different Nora was from the one I believed I knew. How much more mysterious, unpredictable, wonderful, the real Nora was.

At length she went up to bed and I went outside to look at the stars. The night was cloudy, so I came in and wrote this.

I've so many thoughts, so many ideas. They crowd in on me from the past – and the future; they run amok – No! that's not it – they're perfectly lucid, profoundly clear, but they whirl through me and around me with such breathtaking speed that I'm half-afraid they can't be stopped. They surge and swell, mounting up above me, breaking over me while I hang on to myself as a surfer clings to his board and rides the crests of wave after wave. If I were to try and call a halt I'd be annihilated in the thundercrash of some cataclysmic eucatastrophe!

At times there is a lull and I can contemplate my Work with equanimity. Then, without warning, I am swept up and hurled down on the huge rotating wheels of my own mind until they seem not wheels but great coloured planets turning on their axes and, turning, appear as cogs in the wheel of some greater rotation yet, sweeping through space on immeasurable orbits around the sun – no sooner pictured, but that it swings about my brain's black vastness, turning in a stately cosmic dance around other suns that circle each other in galaxies that wheel and spiral around greater galaxies . . . !

I am stretched across the infinite darkness while my bright thoughts approach the speed of light and I fear that they will surpass that absolute speed and, breaking free from their hub, go wildly spinning away – to dissipate like a child's sparkler in the abyss of space.

I was afraid. I was afraid of Annabelle from the first moment I saw her on the sofa behind the teacups, shimmering in her dove-grey dress. That vision of her impaled me; I spent years struggling to free myself. The thing I could not bear was that, in the light of the vision, she turned out to be ordinary. I had seen her in a moment of perfect repose when her soul was transparent to her body as her white body was transparent to the dove-grey dress. I never got over the sight of her sitting there as gracious as an angel haloed in light.

I began to remake her in my chosen image as soon as I

had ascertained how unexceptional she was (except in the sense that everyone is exceptional – as an immortal soul). In this there was not only dishonesty but also vanity: I could not admit that I, the exception, had fallen in love with the banal. I did not deny my desire for her; I denied the *nature* of that desire. I wanted a goddess, not a lover. I certainly denied *her* desire. I did not allow her any sensuality. When our first kiss threatened to smash with its passion her pristine image I was badly frightened and pulled away, pretending that I'd lose control of my desire, pretending that her kiss had been innocent. It wasn't true. I was afraid that she would reveal to me the depths of *her* desire, already intimated in that feral smile.

I had to possess her. That is, I had to possess the girl in the pure vision – possess her soul. To possess her body would have been to compromise the vision and to accept the unacceptable – that she and I were both sexual beings like everybody else. I went to Cornwall to protect myself from my own wild desire. When I returned I had no choice but to propose. I had no thought of the implications of such an action. I simply had to test my power over her, to bind her to me, body and soul.

If it had been a mistake to kiss her, it was a catastrophe to propose marriage. My image of her could not withstand a second of married life. It already took an enormous imaginative effort every time I saw her, to recapture even a fragment of that mysterious Being behind the teacups. Was my love for her entirely an illusion then? It had become a lie. My vision was not an illusion. One does not mistake the shattering intrusion of Reality into a room. I was in love all right; but I was in love with Reality and not with Annabelle. Or should I say I was in love with that portion of Reality which found its expression uniquely through Annabelle? In this sense I did love *her* and that's why I could never shake the feeling that she was play-acting at being ordinary and that at any moment she might tear off the mask to reveal the white immortal woman beneath.

My sin was a *lack of faith*. I did not have enough faith to leap the gulf between the loved one as I would have her be, and the girl she *was*. It is faith alone which can discern the vision in the everyday and reconcile the ordinary with the extraordinary. I lacked faith; I was afraid. I must have known even then that marriage was impossible. For a wedding is the public statement of that very act of faith, and marriage is its willed renewal on a daily basis.

I fled back to Paris. I told my master everything. It's not true that he said nothing. He said, *'Marry her.'* Of course, I had not returned to hear *those* words. I had to learn to despise him, the truest man I've ever met; I had to learn to despise the Great Work itself. All this to protect myself from the truth. It is difficult to write without tears. It is difficult to admit that a sin compounds itself like an addiction and casts an ugly shadow over the world until we block our ears to truth and curse everything that reminds us of our deafness. I should have married Annabelle; instead I became a Pharisee.

There was an element of spite in seeking ordination: I wanted to *pay Annabelle out* for the obsession I was suffering on her account; to revenge myself on her for having such power over my physical desire. I also wanted to spite my master for not collaborating with my self-deception. Of course I only spited my own face.

I went farther: I wanted to play the martyr. I revelled in the idea of a harsh joyless life, an endless round of duty and jumble-sales. Because the Great Work had been delightful to me, I supposed I'd been taken in by its glamour. (In fact, if that had been the case I would not have lasted a week. The Work was as hard as anything I've known – harder even – but I engaged in it gladly because it was my vocation. I believe in the forgiveness of sins because I have, against all the odds, been *given a second chance*.) In reality I was seduced into the priesthood by the false glamour of my perverse need for spiteful self-martyrdom.

However, these sins were venial compared to the thing which cut across all my actions: pride. I wanted God *all to myself*. I was determined to be 'spiritual' all by myself. Alone I would climb the Mount of Sorrows until, high up in an air so rarefied that other men cannot breathe it, I'd be swept away in the avalanche of God's love.

Meanwhile, instead of breaking off my engagement immediately, I maintained the fiction of our marriage – perhaps I vaguely let myself believe that one day it would 'happen'. God knows what it did to Annabelle, poor baffled anxious guilty trusting Annabelle. I should have married her. She wore herself out waiting without understanding, her warmth turning to ashes, her desire rotting like overripe fruit – all because of my cowardice, my faithlessness, my unforgivable pride. (To think that until now *I* could not forgive *her* in my heart for marrying the general practitioner from Leigh-on-Solent. No, I can't think of it.)

It's impossible to describe this *tremendum album* [tremendous white thing; or perhaps, white trembling]. A shoal of tiny silver fish rise out of the depths and riddle me with light. They are like eyes that pierce the deepest recesses of my flesh. They pierce and yet they heal the wounds they open. How clearly I now see that impurity is but the grit in the oyster which produces the pale Queen like a pearl of great price.

The more my burden is lifted, the more I feel pain for Janet and Robert. They should be recovering now; instead I see her spirit slowly breaking in a loveless marriage to a drunken bore and I see him torturing himself alone in that remote little chapel. I'm not so sure that, were I free, I wouldn't retract everything I said. I'm so tired of dogma and duty. I want to be on the side of the angels – Good Lord, of *love* – for once.

The harsh roar of a motorcycle and the honking of frightened ducks broke into my cogitations on the *Brevis Manductio*.* (How lucid he seems to me now, when he says, 'Our Stone is produced from one thing, and four mercurial substances, of which one is mature; the others pure but crude, two of them being extracted in a wonderful manner from their ore by means of the third. The four are amalgamated by the intervention of a gentle fire, and there subjected to coction [cooking] day by day, until all become one by natural, and not manual conjunction.' It's necessary only to undertake the Art for the truth of these plain helpful words to become apparent!)

I leapt up. I could see one of Bradley's cronies riding the machine experimentally around the pond on the Green. Bradley

---

* The abbreviated title of Philalethes' treatise *A short guide to the Celestial Ruby*.

himself was watching, with a cold eye on his bike's performance, from outside the Manor gates. It was the occasion I'd been waiting for, all the better for being done in public, with witnesses, to make the necessary humiliation complete.

He stood as still as a stone as I came up to him. His friend, doubtless anticipating a reopening of hostilities, rode his machine to within a few feet of us and revved the engine provocatively. Bradley waved a hand at him and he switched off the ignition. Three or four passers-by stopped nearby to look curiously at us. Perhaps they hoped to see me reprimand the young men for disturbing the peace; more likely, they hoped to see me add some fresh cause for scandal to my already shredded reputation. None of this was any concern of mine. Despite the stony look on his shut face, I was intent solely on stating the case to Bradley. I said:

'Bradley, I've completely misjudged you. I've been dishonest, stupid and bigoted. I'm deeply sorry. I can't undo the injustice I've done you, I can only offer you any form of redress you like. To begin with you could punch me in the face. Above all I beg you to forgive me.'

As I spoke, I felt with renewed force how essentially honest Bradley is compared to me. Even in the case of Jenny Stebbins he was guilty of little more than a straightforward youthful appetite for sex – something far less damaging than the refined perverse emotional flaying I practised on Annabelle. And, in Nora's case, his love for her – as his marriage proposal in spite of her pregnancy proves – is far above my own. My horror and fear of him was but the menacing mirror-image of my own weakness and jealousy and self-disgust.

Bradley didn't answer me. The look on his face changed from dislike and apprehension to something very like contempt. I suppose that as long as I was capable of smacking him in the mouth he was able to harbour a sneaking respect for me. Now I had shown myself in my true craven colours. He walked away without a word. The motorcycle roared into life and nearly sheared my legs off as it bucked past.

The last time I saw Annabelle, on that snowy January morning, beneath a huge leaden sky – why do I go on about it? There's no end to remorse as it is. Yet I can't get our last meeting *clear*. She broke off our engagement because of it. But wasn't that because she saw sense at last? Or was it because of something specific I said to push her over the brink? I don't want to remember. But I *do* recall something: she said, 'If you don't marry me now, you *never* will . . . '

She was right. She should have said it sooner, forced me to consummate our love or to break it off – at least to face the responsibility of it. By then it was too late. I'd already built the pedestal on which I'd imprison her for years.

My desire for her that day was frightening – more frightening, I think, than the bitter self-defeat of desire's gratification. Annabelle had so far colluded with my image of her spotlessness that she had recently become as cold and statuesque as I could wish her. But with these words the blood rushed to her cheeks and her breath made urgent little smoke-signals in the freezing air. 'Marry me,' she said, 'marry me, marry me,' in a despairing chant to ward off my refusal or, worse still, my prevarication. I should have married her.

Patiently I explained that we would have to wait until I was ordained or maybe a little longer, until I was strong enough and certain enough of God's will to risk the hazard of marriage – she didn't want, did she, to marry a man who was weak and dependent on her and easily overrun by base concupiscence?

The snowflakes on her long eyelashes made her starry-eyed. I sensed something ghastly was about to happen. I have dreamt of that moment but I can only remember running away down the avenue of black trees outlined in white, their branches closing above me like an iron cage until the sky, the snow, everything is blotted out and the temperature drops to absolute zero and my legs move more and more slowly as the ice cakes about them. At last I am immobile in the complete darkness; and the cold is so intense that I am frozen into a brittleness that the slightest tap can break.

'*Marry me,*' she said. 'Maarry me or I'll never see you again. I can't go on like this.' She was crying. She was crying, yes. But then she stopped crying. I can see her face, blotchy and determined. She seized my cold ungloved hand and tugged it towards her. She was taking quick little breaths that made a 'huh-huh-huh' in her throat. She pushed my hand deep inside the front of her fur coat. My fingers encountered a more primitive layer beneath. It took me a second to understand that *she was wearing no skirt nor any underclothes*. She forced my rigid fingers farther in, into a hot moist cranny which contracted like a squid. A guttural noise like an animal's came out of her throat. A powerful convulsion passed through her. It was like an earthquake, a nightmare. I tore my hand out and ran down the avenue where the tall trees struck stiff hieratic poses like the inhuman gods of some forgotten civilisation, standing in judgement.

Naturally at first I thought it was Nora coming down the stairs. I was concerned – she would only be up at that unearthly hour if something was wrong, perhaps to do with the baby. I began to climb. It wasn't Nora. I stopped, held my breath, waited. She descended evenly, soundlessly. As she passed me she paused and cocked her head, listening. Then she slowly turned her head towards me as if it were the natural thing to do.

Her face, well, I'll not forget it. Ever. It was nothing like the one I had imagined yet I knew it better than my own. It contained a little expression of surprise. Her hand was suspended in mid-air. A small, hesitant gesture. I had nothing to give her, no token of love, except the piece of paper on which I had just written a short meditation. I handed it to her. For a fraction of a second I fancied that our fingers brushed each other across time, and then, without looking at me, she continued her pensive descent as softly as a breath of air and faded into the darkness below. As I stare into the hot heart of the Egg I pray that she will, if it pleases the Spirit, be mine, as I'll be hers, and all the riddles be answered, the longing quenched, as together we address the impossible Redness.*

The remaining darkness unfolds like the multicoloured petals of a metallic flower. Each jewel-like petal scintillates in a constellation of sapphires, opals, emeralds, amethysts, rubies, chalcedon and

---

* The abrupt change of scene suggests that the foregoing passage more likely describes a dream or a vision seen in the alchemical glass than, say, an encounter with a ghost. In other words I don't quite know what to make of it.

onyx. The colours shift and merge, wink and dissipate, like an incarnation of Iris [the goddess of the rainbow].

The colours irradiate from the centre like the rays of Sol contained within the circle of Luna. They are many eyes which yet form the iris of the single astral Eye. This we call the *Cauda pavonis* [peacock's tail]. It watches me as I sit in front of it, pausing between one word and another. I see my own face, thoughtful, slightly skewed, as in a mirror-image. The Eye sees into my heart and my heart goes out to it. I am no longer myself.

High winds. Torn clouds race across the sky. The gravestones moan; the trees seethe, flinging tattered rooks into the air; squalls of rain batter the window-panes. The Green is strewn with leaves and twigs.

Tim, Nora and I attempt a game of cards in the kitchen, but end up sitting in silence, watching the fire roar in answer to the tempest's sudden gusts.

Yesterday the peacock's tail filled the cellar with its rainbow, stretching like God's Covenant between Above and Below. There was a subtle perfume of lilies. The Hermetic glass is like a double prism that divides the world into its constituent hues and returns them to the single white light that is their source and goal. This is the mystery of multiplicity in unity and unity in multiplicity.

I went into town and had my will drawn up. I leave all (all!) my worldly goods to Tim and Nora except for some books and my chemical equipment which I leave to Robert. Fifteen pounds go to Bradley to help mend his motorcycle. I have nothing to leave Janet that wouldn't be an affront. The children can sell my books – one or two are quite rare, though rather unfashionable, I fear. Whatever the outcome I shan't need them any more. *Rumpite libros ne corda rumpantur!* [Rend the books lest your hearts be rent!] The cry of the Philosophers resounds down the centuries. Books are good and faithful friends and guides; but I am at that point beyond which books can only block my path. Besides, when Luna reaches her plenitude, no book can prevent a fellow from being cracked like a flawed retort.

The three of us stare into the fire. Truth like a salamander fixes me with a baleful eye. It's time. Tim and Nora know something's up. Their darling faces are anxious. It's fine to be in their company at this moment. If – when – I see them again, will they still know me, and I, them?

I say goodnight to them. Nora starts forward and clumsily kisses my cheek. I am very moved by this. Her swelling abdomen gives her a mother's authority. Following his sister's cue, Tim offers me his hand. At risk of compromising his dignity, I give him a kiss which he gravely accepts.

I go into my study to collect myself. In a minute I'll go down to where – I pray – she is waiting. The White Stone, our Mercury of the Wise. I feel as young as when I boarded the train that would take me home from school to the long summer holidays. This morning the last moistness was drawn down into the magnetic centre where Sol and Luna consummate the silver wedding of Above and Below. Tonight I will look into the single eye of the Star from whom nothing is hidden; and, if the Spirit is gracious, I'll see the shining WHITENESS.

EILEEN

How could I have been so thick??

The Prime Matter has been under my nose all along! I've just this minute dispatched a sample of it to Jim Walters, the sweet mineralogist I used to work with on that science-without-tears book whose name I forget. He'll analyse it for me and ... well, Bob's your uncle.

I went down to the cellar because – I don't know why. Because I hadn't been down for a while and I wanted to see how the whitewash was bearing up and whether the well-water was still at an OK level. Actually, it's excellent down there: slightly damp but not oppressive. More fresh than damp, in fact, with a faint whiff of the sea as if my underground spring were exhaling wholesome airs up through the well. Anyway, since I was there, I thought I may as well parcel up some of the rubble in a plastic sack and dump it later. Staring me in my fat blind face was the lump of rock (or whatever) which had originally wedged the wrapped-up manuscript into the nook in the well-shaft! *It can only be one thing, surely.*

John left it there for me to find. For anyone to find, I suppose. The rock – it's partly crystallised, I think – goes together with the manuscript: they are the basic alchemical kit. Once I know what the rock is, I'll *know what he used* – perhaps what *all* the alchemists used – as their Prime Matter (or, at least, as their Raw Stuff from which the prima materia is derived by calcination and solution).

A nurse comes at nights to the Manor nowadays. Going there is not something I relish; but I can't bear to think of Bradley coping alone all day. He has lost weight, looks ten years older. The halves of his face, livid and red, are accentuated. The effect is strangely disquieting, even beautiful, as if his head had been artistically crafted from different materials, part human, part non-human. He is profoundly grateful for any little effort I make. In truth, I do little enough, far less than I should. Besides, Nora's no trouble.

Her appearance, however, is troubling. Bradley is not struck by it, nor by the changes in her behaviour, because he's there all the time. But I can't help noticing, even on a daily basis, something new to make the heart sink – the veins suddenly visible in spidery networks beneath her skin; the loss of flesh on her nose; the coarsening effect of increasing doses of painkillers which – another defeat – she can no longer refuse. Then there are the erratic remarks and irritable outbursts brought on by pain, drugs and, above all, by the poison which spreads inexorably from her stomach throughout her body. She doesn't eat, of course. Bradley has to ease liquids into her, drop by drop, hour by hour. Her bid for Death and Dignity is wearing thin.

Nevertheless, she's putting up a fearful struggle; and, inside her disease, she's still intact. But for how long? Until recently she referred to her cancer as if it were an antagonist. Now, as it eats into her spirit, she talks as if it were a god whose power must be appeased. She is afraid of taking nourishment lest the cancer grows angry.

Still, for the most part, she's perfectly lucid. I usually see her at her best, in the early evening. She likes to be read to – poetry, surprisingly. The Romantics and especially Milton. Satan meets Sin and Death at the gates of Chaos. That cheers us up.

'I used to read it when I lived with *him*,' she told me. 'Your vicar.' I hadn't imagined John living with anyone. I was startled and, to my astonishment, jealous. 'I don't mean "lived with", my dear. I looked after him. He didn't treat me as a housekeeper. More like a daughter. More's the pity.' Her laugh is a bit grisly now. Sort of a crackle in her throat. ' "Beauty is but a flower which wrinkles will devour . . . tum-ti-tum . . . Lord have mercy on us," ' she quoted. 'The first time I spoke to him I had a poetry book in my hand. I wanted him, even then, to think well of me. I had no shame. I pretended to like it more than I did. He wanted so much that I should like it. He grew excited when I asked to borrow Keats or Milton or Shakespeare from him. He was proud of me. But I'd hide other books inside them and read those instead. He was easy to fool, bless him. He was so innocent.'

I was affronted at her talking about John in this way. I pictured her as a pert, pretty, calculating young thing, pulling the wool over the poor Vicar's eyes, knowing nothing of his courage and largeness of spirit.

'Did you enjoy fooling him?' I asked. She gave me a sharp look that made me regret the irony in my tone.

'Oh, I did worse things than fool him. I flaunted myself to make him . . . *look* at me. I flirted with Pluto to provoke him. Or I'd lie in the orchard in the sun. I could feel his eyes on me from the window. I tucked up my skirt to show off my legs . . . let my hair fall over the book I was pretending to read. He tried not to look, but I'd catch him at it while we sat together after supper, in front of the fire, with our books.'

I shut the book I had been reading to her. I wanted to say something but didn't know what. I just sat there like a lump, angry, embarrassed, hurt – for myself as well as for John. Of course he would have no defences against such a scheming adolescent bitch. My heart bled for him, and for the Work he was striving to perform under such circumstances.

Nora's pleasure at having provoked me quickly changed to regret. Uniquely, her eyes filled with tears:

'Don't be too hard on me, dear. I was ruthless, yes. But, like all silly young girls, I thought I'd die if I didn't have him. Well, I didn't have him and I didn't die. And here I am.'

My anger melted on the instant. We were quiet for a while. Then Nora closed her eyes and I slipped away.

I must have another look at this psychological business of *projection*, which has been nagging me. I feel that it's crucial and to do with the basic dynamics of the psyche – but I have trouble getting a real hold on it. It may be the word itself; it may be that I haven't understood what Jung meant by it.

I do understand that the act of projection does not involve conscious intention. The unconscious projects. Our task – which requires moral effort as well as psychological understanding – is to distinguish between projections and the object which receives them. We have to withdraw our projections from the world if we are to perceive it truly. For example, if I were suddenly to regard the boy-next-door with all the passion and reverence due to a hero or saint (when, to any impartial observer, he is obviously a perfectly ordinary bloke), then it's odds on that this boy-next-door is receiving an animus projection on my part. That is, the masculine archetype or soul-image in my feminine psyche, seeking to become conscious, has (for whatever reason) seized the opportunity presented by the boy-next-door to manifest itself. If I can realise this, withdraw the projection and assimilate it to consciousness, the boy will lose all his numinous overtones and I'll see him as he is. At the same time, my consciousness will be proportionately expanded. I will no longer be under the 'illusion' created by the projection.

And here, I think, is much of the trouble. The notion of projection has, rightly or wrongly, pejorative associations – as if all projections were illusory.

However, my feelings toward the boy-next-door were not illusory. They were real, as all encounters with the animus are real. My 'mistake' was simply to identify the soul-image with something less than itself. In other words, the pristine *impersonal* archetype of the animus was distorted by the image of the boy-next-door and further blurred by the intervention of *personal* considerations – conscious expectations about the opposite sex, for example, as well as unconscious desires, past experiences, etc.

The idea that projections are somehow synonymous with illusions has sometimes given (even to Jung) a false impression of the Opus – as if the alchemist didn't know what was 'really there' in his vessels, but suffered from a series of quasi-hallucinations. This is patently untrue. The astonishing conformity of the images encountered in the Opus, regardless of culture or historical period, shows that they belong to some deep impersonal – or transpersonal – stratum of the unconscious.

At the same time, it would be misleading to speak of the Opus as if it were entirely unblurred and undistorted by the contents of the alchemist's personal unconscious. No alchemical text exactly agrees with another on the nature and order of the Great Work. Thus, although there *is* a common underlying structure, and indeed certain common images – dragon, sol, luna, mercury, blackness, redness, green lion, etc. – each Work was a unique variation on that structure and on those images.

In Jung's terms, therefore, we have to say that there are inevitably many contents of the personal unconscious – that psychic area full of repressed desires, memories, etc. – which are projected on to matter and which have to be withdrawn. Since matter is the unknown, impersonal realm of the inorganic, the projections which it evokes (unlike those evoked by a particular thing or person, such as the boy-next-door) are the correspondingly unknown, impersonal images of the unconscious – the archetypal images. However contaminated these may be by the personal unconscious, they are still clearly discernible. In fact, the first part of the Opus is devoted to withdrawing – 'dissolving' or 'separating' – the personal projections from the impersonal (archetypal) images – that is, those images which are common to all individuals regardless of their personal history and temperament, and which represent the journey of the soul towards that point where the individual is united with the collective.

Since the Opus is not an abstracted psychological process, it is better described as a progressive uncovering – a revelation – of the collective spirit. Personal contents are encountered and assimilated as the matter is dissolved and coagulated, volatilised and fixed, in a vigorous purging of dross and impurity. During the Nigredo – and more especially at Conjunction – the alchemist has to withstand the fires of his personal desires and weakness before descending into the darkness of the unconscious where his ego is all but extinguished and his personality realigned through a union with his own dark, feminine, lunar soul or *anima*. Thereafter he begins the ascent towards light – the Albedo – where his individuality, purged of its personal accretions, attains the status of the collective spirit which, as it were, had been present from the beginning in the undifferentiated unconscious unity of the dragon, only to rise up through the strata of personal attributes, taking on at each stage different theriomorphic guises (dragon, lion, crow, peacock) before appearing as itself, the full moon that embraces the sun of transformed ego-consciousness to form the Star.

The duration of the Work depends on the amount of personal stuff to be worked through. (One might say: the amount of sin to be expiated.) Presumably the Nigredo lasts as long as the personal unconscious casts its shadow on the matter. Self-purgation becomes identical with the purification of the Egg's contents. Only when our sins are 'washed white as snow' can the Albedo appear. It may be that there's a level at which sin is no longer personal and can therefore not be purged. It would be the equivalent of Original Sin. I find it difficult to attach any meaning to this – unless Original Sin is a kind of expression of the fact that we exist at all, the fact that we are incarnate in time and subject to death. It's in this sense, perhaps, that Smith's rejoicing is to be understood when he discovers that the Work can not only succeed *in spite of* a certain residue of impurity but *because* of it. This is the mystery of the *felix culpa*.

There's no pretence now that the Manor drawing-room is anything other than a sickroom. The sofa has been replaced by a bed Bradley has had brought down. Nora slumps back on fat pillows surrounded by the paraphernalia of illness, including vases of flowers sent by local well-wishers. Some of them have called in person, Bradley tells me, but Nora won't see anyone other than us. She has a fixed idea that they are only visiting because they want a share of her money when she's dead.

'But it's gone, dear,' she confided to me. 'All my life I've eked out what was left me and now it has all but trickled away . . . '

She returned to one of the semi-conscious states which occur more frequently these days. Occasionally she rouses herself to a rage, the reasons for which are obscure. Bradley usually bears the brunt of them. By the time I sit with her she is mostly dozing and, each day, slipping away a little more.

As I was about to leave today she turned to me and, seeming to resume her earlier theme, said sternly:

'Don't *hoard*, dear. That's my trouble. I hoard. It doesn't begin with money. It begins with memories. . . . I hoarded my past, you see . . . hated change . . . never really grew up. I suppose, at heart, I hoped he'd come back.' She rocked her head from side to side. 'I had faith in him. I felt safe. It was a mistake. One shouldn't have faith *in* anyone or anything. One should just have faith. Otherwise we are tied to what we have faith in. I wanted to be free in the world, but I always harked back to him ... hoarding him up like all the books and boxes upstairs, keeping him alive. Time to give him up, I suppose ... hand him over to you, dear.'

This is the sort of thing – a haunting mixture of sense and nonsense. Yet I've grown inordinately fond of Nora, almost by osmosis, simply by sitting near her, listening to her breathing, watching her body fall away from her soul.

It's probably better to regard the archetypal images that the alchemist encountered in his Work as *visions* rather than *projections*. Nevertheless, Jung still writes occasionally as if he would have the alchemists 'withdraw' the contents of the collective, as well as the personal, unconscious into themselves – that is, to internalise the archetypal images such as king, queen, fire, water, moon, etc. This would change the Opus into an entirely inner psychological process not unlike Jung's own technique of 'active imagination' [see p. 466] where the images 'projected' by the collective unconscious appear inwardly, before the mind's eye, instead of outside, on the dark 'screen' of the alchemical matter. However, the benefits of encountering the images internally – in dreams, waking dreams, inner visions or whatever – seem dubious. Why not continue to encounter them in the Egg where they can be clearly seen in their true colours? Why does Jung insist that the alchemical drama should be shifted from 'out there' to 'in here' leaving the stage of matter empty, grey and inanimate?

The answer is that a lot of the time Jung clung to the modern belief that we are wholly separate from matter, which can never be anything but a dead realm passively obeying mechanical laws. But at other times he began to doubt. Why, for instance, did the alchemists bother to develop such sophisticated and practical laboratory equipment if their Work was only a 'projection on to matter'? Wouldn't any old chemical substance and process have served to receive the projections? And why were they so fussy about their work and so intensely empirical in their observation of it, even if the observations they chose to make were different from the ones we'd choose now? And how come some of the finest minds in Europe went on struggling century after century with a chemistry that never produced anything (unless, horrors, it *did* produce something)?

Jung bit the bullet, bravely concluding that 'it may well be a prejudice to restrict the psyche to being "inside the body" '. In fact, there may be a 'psychic "outside the body", a region so utterly different from "my" psychic space that one has to get outside oneself ... in order to get there'.* He recognises that it's an historically recent and culturally limited prejudice to separate 'inner' and 'outer'. (At best we can say that the distinction is simply a contemporary spatial metaphor, analogous to Above and Below.) He can no longer, for example, call the *Anima Mundi* or world-soul a projection of the collective unconscious on to the world. He might just as well say that the collective unconscious is an *introjection* of the *Anima Mundi*. Actually, the two realms – inner and outer, psychic and hylic [i.e. physical] – are mutually dependent and may even be 'identical somewhere beyond our present experience'.**

Deeply embedded as we are in our twentieth-century model of the world, it's almost impossible to credit that at some point in the depths of our own soul (or, conversely, in the depths of matter), the psychic and the hylic are identical. Yet it is so: the outer world of Nature and the inner world of the collective unconscious mirror each other. In saying even this I betray my own intransigent dualism. Smith is right – as he has been all along – when he intimates that spirit and matter are simply complementary manifestations of the paradoxical Spirit who is Mercurius. We *ought* to be able to grasp such a contradiction if only because it has a parallel in the long history of theological debate as to whether Christ was God or man. It was the peculiar triumph of the Church to decide that, impossibly, He was both.

On the whole I'd prefer to do away with the idea of projection. It belongs with an inadequate mechanistic model of the psyche. For 'the unconscious projects', read '*the soul imagines*' throughout.

It is as if its light is diffracted through layers of stained glass which colour its images according to the personal, cultural, even racial constituents of the soul. One has only to dissolve the colours

---

* See *Myst. Conj.*, p. 300.
** ibid., p. 537.

and make the glass clear in order to transmit the pure universal light of the sun.

In writing these reflections, no matter how clumsy and ill-expressed they are, I feel – no, it is beyond emotion – I am sensible of having *passed out of* the cosy personal realm into a vast new landscape, like a desert, where I am nothing and alone and yet, and yet . . . I am more than ever before *myself,* sensing the presence of the other, the *truth*, who approaches from afar in a cold burning blast of solar wind.

I meant only to have a quick nap but it was already dark when I woke on my bed. Descending, half-asleep, the unlit stairs, I was arrested by a smell of lilies so poignant, so pregnant with undefined memories, that I was instantly lost in a dark swirl of profound associations.

I was so entranced that I barely noticed, until it was too late, the opening of my soul's remote sluice-gate. He came up on me, not in his suffocating rush, but gently, stealthily, as a lover might. I surrendered to his strange unwinding impalement, his upward expansion. I was pressed out of myself like a long exhalation until there was nothing left except his warm blissful irradiation, bleaching me of all thought, lining my domed mind with gold leaf. A patch of whiteness floated past the corner of my eye; my head turned but, rapt as I was, it escaped me.

What is left of Nora now is no longer in this world. She conducts faint murmured conversations with unseen people, sometimes weeping, sometimes smiling, but always oblivious of us whom she is leaving behind.

The piece of paper I discovered on my return was lying, where I must have mislaid it, on the staircase. It belongs to John, of course, to judge by the handwriting. It's curious only in that I have no memory of seeing it before. If I had, I would have remembered because it awakes in me an extraordinary feeling of mingled turbulence and expectation. It reads as follows:

De imaginatione
Imaginatio is not included as a stage in the Work because it is intrinsic to the whole.

'Let thy imagination be guided wholly by nature' advises the *Rosarium*. 'And observe according to nature, through whom the substances regenerate themselves in the bowels of the earth. And imagine this with true and not with fantastic imagination.'

So, first of all let it be clear that our Philosophy disdains what commonly passes for imagination: mere fantasy which is no more than the fleeting passage of dim involuntary images through the mind. True imagination belongs to the Spirit.[8] That small portion of our totality which we have ignorantly come to think of as ourselves can only passively look on as the Spirit creates its images for our delectation or terror.

The most important and the highest image in the Spirit's cornucopia of images is the human image, *imago Dei*, the soul. Uniquely, the soul is of the same *kind* as the Spirit, differing only in *degree*, as the individual differs from the collective, the particular from the universal, the microcosm from the macrocosm. As such, the soul shares the imaginative power of Spirit to create.

The *telos* or purpose of the individual soul, its peculiar glory, is to be the means by which the collective Spirit represents and realises itself – actually bodies itself forth – in the world. Whenever we intervene in the soul's imagining we define it in (or confine it by) some image that's less than itself – almost any image will serve: a country, a house, a loved one, even a decanter of wine or a bundle of money or a favourite teddy-bear. Wherever our deepest feelings of selfhood are found, there is the object in which we have invested our soul-image.

But if the soul is suffered to expand untrammelled, to realise its own ideal and to represent the collective spirit without personal encumbrance, then the images by which it represents itself are both limited and universal: the moon, for example, fire, a goddess, a sphere of light, a star.

In our Philosophy, this star is called the White Stone or, sometimes, the Mercury of the Wise, signifying the marriage of soul and spirit, the individual with the collective.

However, the White Stone is more volatile than fixed. That's to say, although it is *real*, it is not yet *actual*. It is the *potential* Red Stone of the Philosophers, and the sign that the soul's yearning for union with the Spirit has encountered in its fulfilment the Spirit's reciprocal longing to be embodied in matter and time. This is the task to which the Rubedo addresses itself.

The Art, then, while always remaining one, consists of this superb double movement: firstly, the soul's ascent in which it rises out of material darkness and impurity to put on the silver robes of the Spirit above. This brings the soul's self-imagining into union with the spirit's primal imagination and thereby raises the particular up into the universal. Secondly, despite the temptations of remaining in this exalted condition of whiteness, the soul-spirit must redescend into the fixity of a body (which is reciprocally raised up), thereby returning the universal to the particular. There are even fewer images for this miraculous action than for the Albedo – they include Christ, a resurrected body, an hermaphrodite, the Philosophers' Stone and the elixir of Life. The first has been historically realised by the incarnation of God's fullness (Christ) in a particular individual (Jesus); the others have been realised by those Philosophers who have run the perilous course of the Magnum Opus to its end, and whom the Fire Master describes as:

'Immortal mortals, mortal immortals, living their death and dying their life.'[9]

So much of this meditation of John's is obscure to me – but at the same time it stirs me up with an incredible excitement as if I'd been given a vital clue to the Work's solution. I can *physically feel* pieces of the alchemical jigsaw meshing together in my mind to form an altogether new world-view. When he says that alchemy requires us to 'see with the eyes of the spirit' I can no longer glide over this as if it were a rhetorical flourish. It's literally true: our eyesight must be transformed by the spiritual operation of the Art. It's like my experience of the *other* who looks out through my eyes and, as he does so, changes my ordinary seeing to a deeper perceiving.

To gaze steadily and with absolute *attention* for long hours and days into the Hermetic vessel – forgetful of food or sleep or self – is to bring the true imagination into play; and this imagination not only perceives the Work's meaning but also – like a beam of soul particles streaming laser-like out of the eyes – creates changes in the Work just as the Work reciprocally works its wonders in the Philosopher's soul.

If we can only *abolish* ourselves, root out our egoism, burn up the buried rubbish of the past – then there will be nothing to stand between the soul and the clear imaginative starlight it casts upon the world, which, with the shadow lifted, the doors of perception cleansed, is remade in the Spirit's image.

Thus the Work is truly an Art which, far from imitating Nature, draws on the source of all creation – the Spirit – to recreate Nature in the Hermetic Egg.

The word 'image' has come to mean something less than real. The reverse is true: an authentic image is the thing itself, an *imago*, as the soul is *imago Dei*, as a work of art is more real than the natural object which suggested it. The Work is not art in this sense, but the Art that bodies forth the soul itself, purified of all personal taint, so that Art and Artist are One Thing.

SEVEN

Sublimation

SMITH

[The following entry is a draft of part, or all, of the sermon which Smith delivered at Nightingale Wood. It's hardly surprising that it was not favourably received. Whether it is actually heretical, I'm not qualified to tell.]

Friends,

The time for talking about Heaven and God is past. I want to talk to you about Earth – and the Devil. Stand very still for a moment. Close your eyes. Feel the ground beneath your feet. Feel beneath the ground. Feel downwards with your whole being. Your souls are rooted in the Earth just as the trees in this wood are. Send down tendrils towards the bedrock. Listen with the soles of your feet. Can you hear him? The Devil? He groans and travails, breathing fire and beating his black scaly wings.

Beware of the Devil. He haunts this place. He broods beneath the flagstone of the Earth, beneath fields and cities, land and sea. He is the serpent under the tree, the worm under the rock. He lives beneath you. Beware of him.

Make no mistake: God exists, but at a distance. He has withdrawn with Our Saviour into his remote Heaven, and given over the Earth to his other son, Christ's dark twin, the Prince of this world who lives below, where the light of Heaven has never penetrated. Beware of the Devil. He is the Spirit of imitation who has a thousand shapes. He is the panic god of the wilderness, the shudder in our hearts at dead of night. He dwells in our darkest desires and torments our sleep. Beware of the Devil. He comes like a thief in the night. Shutter and bolt your doors – he's already stirring like an earthquake in the house's foundations, already tiptoeing across your attic with an axe. Beware of the Devil. His is the fleeting face at the window, the black shape in the sunny hedge, the distorted form in the dressing-gown on the back of the bedroom door.

Friends, be aware of the Devil. Let him rise up from the warm earth. For in his rising up he draws down the light of heaven like a golden crown for your heads. Welcome him and he'll be your friend. Deny him and he will possess you like madness. I say this not to frighten you but to warn you. Be aware of the Devil. He is the poison that heals. His is the face of Chaos you're afraid to see. Look at it and you will delight in the light of his countenance. For he is Lucifer, bringer of light and leader of souls, who wears a dark mask. Tear it off. We've lived too long with our heads in the clouds, hankering after some heaven made in our own image. We must come down to Earth and delve into the dark realm of the Devil, if we want to be raised up. For Heaven in our century is only come by via the infernal regions of Earth.

So, stop heaving your souls up to Heaven. Be aware of the Devil instead. Look around you at Creation. As Christ ransomed us with His Blood so we must ransom the Devil where he is interred in the Earth. Raise him up; feel him throb beneath your feet, flow like sap in your blood, sing in your head like a nightingale. He is the spirit in and through and by whom you have your natural being. He's nearer to you than you to yourself. He is life. Praise him.*

Everything about the Work up to the Albedo can be called natural for, in essence, it was a marriage of like and like – Above and Below – which took place within and through the Spirit. As Petrus Bonus of Ferrara says in his beautiful *Margarita*,** 'this art is partly natural and partly divine or supernatural. At the end of the sublimation (i.e.

---

* It must be obvious to us, as it couldn't have been to his congregation, that, by the Devil, Smith understands Mercurius. Cf. Jung: 'Alchemy... is the herald of a still unconscious drive for maximal integration which seems to be reserved for a distant future, even though it originated with Origen's doubt concerning the ultimate fate of the devil' (*Myst. Conj.*, p. 188).

** i.e. *Pretiosa Margarita Novella* (*c.* 1330), usually translated as 'the New Pearl of Great Price'. Jung cites this text as the oldest to treat specifically of the Stone's connection with Christ. He was keen to show that the Philosophers' Stone was, more or less consciously, seen as a kind of chthonic counterpart of Christ, with a parallel symbolism. He finds examples throughout the alchemical literature from Lull to the *Golden Tractate*, from Ripley to the speculative alchemists of the seventeenth century (see *Psychology and Alchemy*, pp. 332ff).

congelation), there germinates, through the mediation of the spirit, a shining white soul which flies up to heaven with the spirit. This is manifestly the (white) stone. So far the procedure is indeed rather marvellous, yet it is still within the framework of nature.'

The Rubedo is a work *against nature*, for it requires the volatilising and fixing of like with unlike – that is, of matter with spirit. Only one power in the universe can perform this reconciliation of incommensurables: Mercurius.

'The fixation and permanence of the soul and spirit', says Petrus, 'takes place when the secret stone is added, which cannot be grasped by the senses, but only by the intellect.' This secret stone 'is the heart and tincture of the gold, regarding which Hermes says: "it is needful that at the end of the world heaven and earth be united: which is the philosophic word."' The 'secret stone' is the fixing agent or body which receives the union of soul and spirit in Heaven and, in fixing them, is itself volatilised into Earth or, as Petrus calls it, the 'original body' to which the soul is restored at the Work's end. This new 'original body' is 'completely glorified, incorruptible, and almost incredibly subtilised, and it will penetrate all solids. Its nature will be as much spiritual as corporeal. When the stone (that is, the original body or Earth) decomposes to a powder like a man in his grave, God restores to it soul and spirit, and takes away all imperfection; then is that thing strengthened and improved, as after the resurrection man becomes stronger and younger than he was before'.

I walked as far as the Blind Dancer and back along Grimm's Down. Autumn is my favourite season; its colours and its watery sun, on the cusp of Sagittarius,* are suited to the melancholy temperament. The hills, bare of corn and beasts, huddle closer around the valley's cottage fires. The wind has a polished cutting edge. I met three men in the lane; they hurried past without meeting my eye. Only one of them returned my greeting with a grunt. May God grant me the means to do some small service to this parish before I leave it.

It was dark by the time I reached the church. Thus I was able to glimpse the flare of a struck match through the half-open door.

---

* i.e. 21–22 November.

It was, of all people, Robert. He was sitting in the front pew. He looked tired and ill. He looked beaten. He didn't mince his words.

'*Is* there a God?' He gazed around vaguely for somewhere to dispose of his cigarette, as if it mattered, and failing to find anywhere, stuck it back in his mouth. I sat down next to him.

'Yes.' I wanted to impress upon him that God need not be a dead monosyllable, but I didn't know how – didn't know how to will the living Spirit across the space between us.

'I've been admiring your glass,' he said with a gesture that took in all the windows. As if *that* were the reason he was sitting alone in the dark, smoking. I wondered from the slight slur of his words whether he was drunk. I hoped for his sake he was. But he was only tired and, I knew only too well, suffering.

'I'm glad you approve. How's *your* glass?'

He didn't answer the question. Instead, he remarked:

'I think some places are holy in spite of the Church's efforts, don't you? For some reason people are drawn to them. Ordinary humble people like in the legends – an old woman who dyed cloth, an unhappily married woman who ran away from her husband – what was her name? Saint Uncumber. Yes. And then the monks came, didn't they, and put up a great heavy monastery. And then a church. And so the legends and visions died out. But people still came, even to church, and their hopes and fears and prayers added to the place, leaving an imprint in the ground and stones. It's all that, not God, that I can feel in the atmosphere here.'

He stood up and walked restlessly to and fro for a minute before resuming his seat. I couldn't see his face; he was a shape in the darkness. His voice had a hollow ring in the empty church. I let him go on.

'You *can* feel history here. It's a scientific law, isn't it, that no two events can occupy the same place? But suppose that's not true. Suppose there's someone sitting where I am now. Someone from another time. It's possible. I mean, the opposite happens. Coincidences. You can think the same thought as the one you love, at the same time. Once I was staying in London and thinking of her' – I had no need to ask whom – 'so I picked up the telephone to call her. She was on the other end. She had phoned me at the same time, even though we were miles apart. So I don't see why two people or events can't coincide in space while being distant in time. It's no more unlikely than coincidences in time separated by space. There ought to be a scientific word for it. Something Greek; from *topos*, "a place", perhaps.'

'Syntopicity?' I said quickly. I could see he was growing tired of talking, as he obviously was, for the sake of it. I didn't want him to leave, not like this.

'Yes. Why not?' Losing interest, he made a movement as if to leave. Immediately I began to speak, saying the first thing that occurred to me.

'What you say about the special aura certain places have is true. But I'm convinced it doesn't stem only from past associations. I believe the places we used to call sacred each have a *genius*, a presiding spirit. I think these are local manifestations of a general Spirit which runs through the Earth's veins like blood, concentrating in places for which it has a predilection. In these spots the Spirit is more likely to show itself – psychically, perhaps, in the vision of a dryad or the Virgin Mary; or maybe physically as in an act of healing. We don't pay much attention to the Spirit these days. It's a mistake. The Ancients knew how to divine its currents and to regulate its flow with artificial landmarks,[1] like the Blind Dancer, and so bring the landscape into harmony and spiritual equilibrium. We might still "dress" a holy well, make a pilgrimage up a hill, picnic at a stone circle, carve our names on a special tree, even visit a church – but we don't really know why we're drawn to such places. We tell ourselves we like the view or put it down to some quaint custom. But willy-nilly the Spirit flows on, exerting its hidden influence over us for better or worse . . .'

Robert was getting restless. I wanted so much to – what? Save him, I suppose. But my presence was doing no good. 'You'd rather be alone,' I said.

'Yes. But thanks for talking to me, padre. I *was* listening. You're a bit of a pagan on the quiet, eh? It's just that I'm . . . I'm not interested in anything any more. Sorry.'

'Take her away,' I found myself saying. 'She'll go with you anywhere. Take her and *go*. It's your only chance. Her only chance.' He bent forward and covered his face with his hands.

'I thought you were against it. Against us,' he said without resentment.

'Forgive me. I was wrong. I've had a change of heart.'

'No. You were right. I know she'd come if I asked her, but she'd never forgive me in the long run for dragging her into "mortal sin". She'd end up hating me. Besides, it would destroy that poor miserable sod Farrar. I don't wish him any harm. I've done him enough already, whether he knows it or not. Janet and I belong together, but she can't come so there's no use going on about it. So be a good fellow, padre, and bugger off.'

I got up and said:

'I know you don't pray. Especially to God. But try listening. You might hear something. You never know. Others have seen and heard things in a place like this. You could think of Saint Uncumber – her problem was solved by a thing as simple as growing a beard.' Then I buggered off.

The demolition of Nightingale Wood is arranged for a fortnight's time. I have called on virtually all the villagers but they are unwilling to speak to me on this (or any other) matter. Thus I've written letters to every household, stating why it should not be allowed to happen. I make no personal attack on Caldwell. He more than anyone will suffer the consequences of his destruction. The difficulty lies in persuading people to *see* that they are connected to the trees by more than simple tradition – that every axe-blow will be visited on their, and their children's, heads. They must realise what the desecration will entail *before* it happens, not after, when it'll be too late. I'm sure that as soon as the reality of the proposed demolition sinks in, the people will lay aside personal considerations – including their disapproval of me – and act as one against Caldwell and for the common good.

My little alfresco service has made an impression. I didn't expect such a good turn-out. I suppose that the notice posted on the church door, saying that matins would be held at Nightingale Wood, aroused a measure of curiosity.

Afterwards, Out-of-Sorts Simmons was the first to make a concrete response. With his narrow face going white and red by turns he resigned his position as verger. He wouldn't say why. Mrs B. is behind it, as ever. To her credit she is the only one who has said anything to my face. As I passed the bus-stop she stepped forth like a prophet from her huddle of disciples and boldly announced that she won't be going to church any more because she can't 'in all conscience consort (*sic*) with a vicar who worships the Devil'. (Nods from her companions.) What's more, it Shouldn't Be Allowed.

All very disappointing.

The marriage of Above and Below was, is, all it should be and more. It beggars the imagination, its whiteness palpably enlightening. The Regimen of Luna is complete. (I never dared think that I might write those words!) Every day I contemplate lovingly the inconceivable Star which burns my soul like ice, riddling me with light.

Reading St Paul . . . The Greek language distinguishes intelligently between the correct time (as told by the clock) and the right time (as told by the heart). The former, in other words, is the quantitative aspect of time (*chronos*); the latter is time's qualitative aspect (*kairos*).

The Opus transforms *chronos* into *kairos*. Or, I could say, it is like *time cutting into itself* in order that the timeless may enter through the incision. Eternity is *more* than half in love with time. It expresses itself through *kairos*, the ripeness – *the fullness* – of time, when the Moment becomes the doorway into Eternity.

St Paul does not speak of the world as cosmos but as Creation. Cosmos is the self-contained rational universe which Science inherited from Greek philosophy. Creation is God's handiwork and we, as creatures, are part of it. Much confusion can be avoided by distinguishing between these two words. We are perfectly entitled to regard the world as cosmos, that is, as an object of cognition and theoretical understanding. We are not entitled to confuse cosmos with Creation, which cannot be an object of cognition. Creation can only be understood by *gnosis* which properly means 'knowledge', not in the sense of objective, cognitive, 'scientific' knowledge, but an experiencing, participatory knowledge. Notably, it signifies the knowledge men and women have of each other in the Biblical sense; and the knowledge that men and women have of God. Cognitive knowledge is secondary to *gnosis* as cosmos is secondary to Creation.

The Magnum Opus is a work of *gnosis*, naturally. The Philosopher, it is true, begins – like any good scientist – with a cosmos (in his case, a *microcosmos* in the Hermetic egg). Like every cosmos from Aristarchus of Samos to Einstein, his is an imaginative attempt to represent Creation. Unlike the scientist, however, who too often thinks of his secondary cosmos as an accurate representation of Creation's primary reality, the Philosopher is content to set his cosmos in motion and allow it *to conform itself* to Creation. It does this through the operation of Mercurius who is present, though hidden, in every cosmos, and only revealed in Creation; and, of course, like Creation he can't be known cognitively but only by *gnosis*. (Thus the Work presupposes that the very cognitive knowledge to which the modern scientist clings – indeed, which defines him as a 'scientist' – must annihilate itself in proportion as the cosmos more and more corresponds to Creation.) In fact, it is not we who know Mercurius but he who knows himself through and in us. We participate in his knowledge of himself. We only know Creation by participating in the process of Creation.

At about 3 a.m., as I sat at this rickety card-table, not writing or thinking or feeling, but simply sitting in the sphere of the Egg's gloriole, I heard the low dry cough of a man who has spent too long in the company of cucurbits, crucibles and stills with all their attendant spirits of fume and vapour; a cough I hadn't heard for twenty years or more, a cough which caused my heart to lurch. I sprang up. It was indeed my dear master.[2]

There's so much I want to say to him.

I began to blurt things out but he silenced me with a wave of his dismissive bony hand. He peered into the Egg and smiled his thin smile. He hasn't changed really. He looks a bit more worn, a bit more brittle perhaps; his beard is stragglier and streaked with all the colours of the metals and chemicals he has tried out over the years. His eyes are set farther back in their sockets; they burn with unsatisfied hunger like bears glaring out of the backs of caves. At last he turned to me and, after a long appraising double-barrelled look, said:

'I see you're a minister now. You've chosen to marry others rather than marry yourself.'

'You were right. I should have married Annabelle. I was dishonest, faithless, afraid. Forgive me.'

He waved dismissively again. 'Forgive yourself,' he said. 'You were right not to marry her – for all the wrong reasons. When I found you and saw how unafraid of fire you were, how much in your element, I knew your life belonged to another, and your desire to another fulfilment, which only the Opus could obtain.' He looked at me with something very like affection. 'The Spirit uses us inscrutably, against our will, without our knowledge, so that even sin can become the means to salvation. He plays us like fish. The farther away we run from him, the more line he gives us, the greater our illusion of freedom, the more inevitably will he reel us in and land us, gasping, on the shores of another element. Your past actions, freely chosen, including those that wilfully sinned against faith and love, were nevertheless ordained by his Providence, pulling you back full circle into the fold of yourself where, I wouldn't be surprised, you'll find her – as she promised – waiting from all eternity.'

I remembered again the words of the chimera I encountered towards the end of Solution – that scaly-legged Annabelle who had said softly, 'I'm still waiting.' I knew that my master was right: it wasn't Annabelle who was waiting but *she* – she who had taken on Annabelle's shape because my eyes couldn't then withstand the sight of her raw self. A dead weight was raised from me.

'And you, master – did you find what you were looking for?' He shook his head.

'The Albedo, yes. But not the holy marriage of Heaven and Earth. My time ran out before I could attain the immortal Red Tincture. That's why I'm here. The Albedo, as you know, gives wisdom; but it's a solitary volatile thing. It longs for the last descent into fixity. I'm weary of wandering between worlds. I need you to complete what I left unfinished, for your Work and mine were bound together from the first . . .

'I've come to warn you not to repeat my mistake – not to be seduced by the delights of the White Stone. If one doesn't keep one's shoulder to the wheel it grows increasingly unstable with time . . .

'The Work is incomplete without that impossible geometry, that wholly new configuration of infinite spirit and finite body which turns time and space inside out within the glass, making the squared circle of here and forever, now and everywhere.'

He lowered himself wearily into my battered old armchair and combed his beard with restless fingers. We stayed for a long time in silence, each of us lost in our own thoughts. Thoughts of the past perhaps, of what we had done and what we had failed to do, what lost and what gained, weighing them in the balance, scruple by scruple, grain by grain.

'How shall I go on?' I asked.

'You already know. "As a lion is always born of a lion and a man of a man, so all things owe their birth to that which they are like. Thus the Stone which is to be the transformer of metal into gold must be sought in the precious metals, in which it is enclosed . . ." ' It was a characteristically ironic touch to quote Philalethes at me. I clapped my hands. 'Yes. You have it. When during the Rubedo we speak of Sol, common gold is to be understood. This is the only time that gold is used in the Work.'

I held up my father's gold fob watch. He squinted at it with his expert eye. 'There's a lot of copper there. Are you using copper?' I shook my head. 'Then make sure you rid the gold of superfluities before subliming it. As for the rest, that's up to the secret fire which brings everything to perfection, the gross with the subtle and the subtle with the gross.'

I noted down everything he said. There was so much more I wanted him to say. So much to say to him. Twenty years' worth of things I could say to no one else. I closed my eyes for a moment to order my thoughts. I must have dozed off because when I opened them again, he was gone.

My master corresponded at one time, he told me, with a Neapolitan Philosopher who decided to dispense altogether with chemistry and devote himself to the purely mental cultivation of *astrum* [star].[3]

He began by concentrating, to the exclusion of all else, on a decanter of wine. He described this exercise in terms of detaching his 'star body' and, by a supreme effort of will, transmitting it into the decanter until he knew what it was to *be* that decanter, and the wine it contained. When after a long time he could perform this exercise at will, he practised it without the actual decanter, using instead an image of it which he held before his inner eye. As he transformed the star body into the image of the decanter, the latter daily gained greater substance, more reality. (My master explained that in fact the star body was *simply materialising itself*, but in the shape of the decanter which the Philosopher had chosen.)

Day after day he imagined the decanter in every detail, down to the last play of light across its glass surface and the different intensity of glow emitted by the wine within. One day he returned to his house to find the decanter sitting on the table where he had imagined it. His surprise at the sight of it caused it to dissolve into thin air; but, emboldened by this success, he renewed his efforts to visualise and, ultimately, materialise the object. At last the day came when a visiting friend, sitting down at the table, helped himself to a glass of wine from the decanter. He pronounced it a bit on the young side but otherwise very palatable.

My master disdained such 'tricks', which he called frivolous magic. All magical rituals and spells are techniques for evoking and concentrating the star body. This is the imaginative power in man which produces those apparent contradictions of natural law that we call magic. Objects or people, for example, can be affected for good or ill at a distance simply by visualising them together with the appropriate intention. This power of imagination can be augmented by the vital spirits inherent in plants, animals and even humans, and more especially in the blood of the two latter. However, this vitality is short-lived and moreover casts a lurid glow over the magician's intention. (Conversely, the intention is invariably base and unwholesome that needs the aid of blood to become effective.) In short, blood sacrifices cannot begin to compare with the enduring efficiency of our metallic sacrifices which, being seminal to the Art rather than supplementary, are correspondingly laborious to achieve. The primitive magician is unwilling to undertake the lengthy and arduous study, work and prayer the Work requires; he wants quick results. He may get them, but only by a perversion of the Spirit for which he will pay the price (he usually wrecks himself with ever larger doses of stimulants, such as sex and drugs, in an ever more desperate effort to coerce his failing imagination).

Of course there *is* a magical element in our Philosophy, as there is in all religion – witness the Transubstantiation [i.e. the changing of bread and wine into the Body and Blood of Christ in the Catholic Mass]. Equally there is a religious element in all magic. The decisive difference between magic and our Philosophy is that the magician imposes his private will on the imagining Spirit, compelling it to shape itself according to his chosen, often inferior, visualisations. Because he seeks power (I should say, force) instead of illumination, he dictates to the Spirit instead of surrendering himself to *its* will.

The Philosopher, on the other hand, has no wish to intervene in the operation of the Spirit. He wants only to raise it up, to extract it from the metals and let it shine forth according to its own lights, not his. If he is successful he will be rewarded by the manifestation of the star body – which is, so to speak, *the unadulterated image of the imagination itself*.

Napoleon Buonaparte was essentially a magician. It is said that he was under the protection and guidance of a daemon or familiar spirit which at times took on the shape of a shining sphere which he called his 'star'. At other times it visited him in the form of a dwarf clothed in red who warned him.

The 'star' and the 'dwarf' were different images of his own soul, which took on whatever guise was appropriate to its function of either guiding or warning. Rightly perceiving this star as the guiding light of his destiny, he mistook its nature and purpose: instead of interpreting it correctly as the command to conquer (that is, to realise) himself, he chose to see it as an injunction to conquer the world.

Thus it is with all world-conquerors – they shrink from the difficulty of mastering the 'little world' of themselves and take the easier path of attempting to master the planet. And, even if they succeed, they come up against the annihilating world-weariness of Alexander the Great who had nowhere left to hide – from himself.

What is imagination but the eternal dreaming of the Spirit in whom all images, known or unknown, potentially exist? It is the self-delighting dance of Fire which we can't know except by becoming the dancer. This our souls yearn to do – yearn to grow co-extensive with the inconceivable fullness of the Spirit, just as the Spirit yearns to enter time where its images can become actual. (Many of them have already, as it were, woken up in time before sinking back again into the Creator's timeless dream, the unicorn no less than the dinosaur; others have yet to appear.)

*

The congregation at Holy Communion has halved since my open-air service. I can't blame them for staying away. My conduct smacked of the very religious 'enthusiasm' I normally avoid like the plague. Matins is about the same as Communion, evensong a little better. I can't tell whether the Caldwells are officially boycotting me or not because their presence at any service has been intermittent for some weeks – and then, I suspect, only because Caldwell likes to keep an eye on me for signs of insurrection. I wouldn't be surprised if my extracurricular activity in the cellar didn't account for one or two apostates. Would they be reassured if I threw my laboratory open to the public? I doubt it. I'm truly sorry that I do not conform to the general notion of a pastor, but I can't do much about it, least of all worry. I'll do my rounds until every door is closed to me; I'll hold regular services until the last parishioner has had enough. I have to follow where the Spirit leads, and the village, in its own way, will do likewise.

It isn't necessary physically to 'rend the books'; it's necessary only to read them in a different way. For example, whereas before the Albedo I might have devoured this passage written by the noble millennarian Artephius,[4] scanning it for the Great Secret, I can now contemplate it with unalloyed pleasure for its beauty and truth alone. I cannot improve upon this description of the Rubedo from *The Secret Book*, which is among the plainest possible accounts of the Magnum Opus – so much so that Artephius was obliged to put the stages of the Work in the wrong sequence in order to protect it from the profane:

> Hear now this secret; keep the body in our mercurial water, till it ascends with the white soul, and the earthy part descends to the bottom, which is called the residing earth. Then you shall see the water to coagulate itself with the body, and be assured the art is true; because the body coagulates the moisture into dryness, like as the rennet of a lamb or calf turns milk to cheese. In the same manner the spirit penetrates the body, and is perfectly commixed with it in its smallest atoms, and *the body draws to itself his moisture,*

to wit, its white soul, like as the lodestone draws iron, because of the nearness and likeness of its nature; and then one contains the other. And this is the sublimation and coagulation, which retaineth every volatile thing, making it fixed for ever.

This compositum then is not a mechanical thing, or a work of the hands, but as I said, a changing of natures; and a wonderful connexion of their cold with hot, and the moist with the dry ... by this means is made the mixture and conjunction of body and spirit, which is called a conversion of contrary spirits and natures, because ... the spirit is converted into a body and body into a spirit. *So that the natures being mingled together, and reduced into one, do change one another* ...

And when you see the true whiteness appear, which shineth like a bright sword, or polished silver, know that in that whiteness there is redness hidden. But then beware that you take not that whiteness out of the vessel, but only digest it to the end, that with heat and dryness, it may assume a citron colour, and a most beautiful redness. Which when you see, render praises and thanksgiving to the most great and good God, who gives wisdom and riches to whomsoever He pleases ...

De Lapide Philosophorum

I have already said too little and too much about the Stone of the Philosophers. Why should I not speak more plainly still? Why shouldn't I, too, prise open a small door in the King's shut palace?* In our century the danger doesn't lie with being misinterpreted, misunderstood and misused. Our Philosophy is not interpreted, understood or used at all! The adept no longer has to hide from persecution and envy – he can shout the truth from the rooftops and, if he is heard at all, the most he can expect is a spell in the lunatic asylum. History has a delightful sense of irony.

Michael Sendivogius risked a great deal when he said of the Stone that 'the sages call it the phoenix and the salamander. Its generation is a resurrection rather than a birth and for this

---

* A reference to Philalethes' *An Open Entrance to the shut Palace of the King.*

reason it is immortal and indestructible'.* It's important to notice his distinction between 'resurrection' and 'birth' — what is often nowadays called 'rebirth'. There's a lot of loose talk about rebirth, as if it were a metaphor. I have heard clergymen, and not only they, speak of 'dying to themselves' in order that they may participate in true life, the life of the spirit; but I see precious little evidence of it beyond giving up cigarettes for Lent. How much the less, then, can they even begin to understand what the wise Sendivogius meant by resurrection! To her credit, the Church stubbornly and embarrassingly insists on the literal ascent of the physical body to Heaven; and having insisted, lets the matter drop, rather in the way that it has dropped the Athanasian Creed which explicitly requires us to believe that 'all men shall rise again with their bodies and shall give account for their own works'.

This shouldn't be read as some comical revivification on some Day of Judgement; nor as some clumsy metaphor for the immortality of the soul. It is a command to resurrect ourselves. This can only realistically be achieved by the Stone which transforms us into whole — and therefore androgynous — resurrected bodies.

The Great Work consists of a stupendous double movement. The first of these, the Regimen of Luna, effects the descent (or death) of the body and the ascent (or rebirth) of the soul; this simultaneous event corresponds to the raising up of the Spirit, celebrated in the union of Above and Below. The second — the Regimen of Sol — effects the fixing of the soul and the volatilising of the body, which correspond to the drawing down of the Spirit, celebrated in the marriage of Heaven and Earth. The Work is One Thing: if it separates soul and body, spirit and matter, it is only that they may be more joyfully and completely reunited, making the heavenly spirit corporeal and, ah!, the earthly body spiritual and glorified. In the instant that Heaven embraces Earth we are transmuted into rare new beings — mermaids! hermaphrodites! — for whom a single step takes us through the quicksilver waterfall of Time — into Eternity.

---

* *Novum Lumen Chemicum*, or *A New Chemical Light* (1604).

'And the son of God is dead, which is worthy of belief because it is absurd. And when buried he rose again, which is certain because it is impossible.'*

It's not possible to attempt the Rubedo, or even to talk about it, without the knowledge that the Albedo bestows. The White Stone instructs the Philosopher how to proceed; in truth, *she enables that which she teaches* by virtue of her unique properties.

I no longer need either the remainder of my Heaven-sent raw matter or my trusty manuscript. Lacking a disciple to whom I can pass them on, I have wrapped them securely and hidden them in an appropriate place within my laboratory. Doubtless they will be unearthed one day by someone who will throw them out in the rubbish; or (since there is often a providence in these things) by someone who will know, as I did, what a secret they contain.

Christ, Christ, Tim, dear Tim is dead.

---

* Tertullian, *De Carne Christi* (*c.* AD 208).

EILEEN

I have tried, during my vigils with Nora, to make myself useful. That is, I have tried to exercise compassion. It came about last Saturday when she suddenly broke through her stupor and began to thrash about, plucking at herself and moaning, 'Get them off, get them *off*... These bloody clothes are too *heavy*. I'm burning up. Oh, oh. For God's sake *get them off me*,' etc.

I stripped back her bedclothes. She lay there, tossing and turning, in only the thinnest of nightdresses – but still she wouldn't stop. 'Get them *off*.' Her distress at these imaginary clothes was very great. She paid no attention to my assurances that there were, in fact, no heavy clothes on her. In despair, I even removed her nightdress, but still she plucked at her skin in a vain attempt to unburden herself. For a moment my distress, enhanced by helplessness, was almost as great as hers. However, I managed, after some false starts, to expel mere emotion and to apply myself to practical compassion. What is it, after all, if not 'co-suffering'? Therefore I began to concentrate and, with effort, to enter her pain.

I have since developed quite a creditable technique. It's a matter of sitting absolutely still, of breathing slowly and of visualising the cancer. It took about three days' work to attain any reasonable success at the latter, which presents itself as a sticky, brown, spider-like entity. A certain amount of revulsion has to be overcome before I can pass through it to Nora: there must be no trace of natural horror and disgust in the space I clear in my mind to receive her suffering. At first, it exercised my powers to the limit and only now has it become easier. Even so, I can only reach the necessary state of mind more quickly; and by no means can I identify myself with all her pain. Inexperienced as I am at this, and impure, there's a point beyond which her suffering would crush me.

Nevertheless, I enter the pain as best I can – or, perhaps more precisely, draw the pain into myself and hold it, endure it, there in the clear space, where it exists hurtfully but also, so to speak, harmlessly because in me it is free of the additional tentacles of personal rage, resentment, fear, bitterness and sheer physical weakness which cling to the original bearer of it. I'm unable as yet to put myself exactly in Nora's place. Perhaps I never will (as it is, I don't recover quickly or easily from the experience). But human goodwill is limitless, and it's possible to go a long way towards substitution. At any rate, Nora ceased that first time to pluck and fret; and since then she sometimes seems less ravaged and more relaxed.

What about Carl's archetypes then?* Where've I got to with them? I'm tempted to say – no, I *do* say – that they aren't really *necessary*.

There's no getting away from the fact that a number of archetypal *images* – my primary elements – exist; but I can't see them any longer as manifestations of a number of separate archetypal forms. There's *only one* 'archetype': the Spirit Mercurius, who appears in a number of guises.

The so-called archetypal images are just the signs of our developing relationship with the Spirit. As we individuate, working through the chaotic images of our personal unconscious, we begin to encounter the collective images that look as though they've walked straight out of some myth – the Trickster, the Animus (or Anima), the Maiden or the Boy Hero, the Great Mother or the Wise Old Man, or whatever. Jung struggled to interpret them as symbols but never quite recognised that their meaning couldn't be derived from themselves, but only from their relations with other terms. He lacked the principle of analogy, by which the archetypes could (so to speak) be broken down into more basic components. We can't say that the 'Mother archetype' has any consistent meaning behind her many images; we can say that:

Mother : son :: female : male :: older : younger :: bigger : smaller. Similarly,

---

* i.e. Jung's.

Shadow : Anima :: male : female :: dark : light :: personal : impersonal.

Rightly or wrongly, the notion of 'archetypes' suggests to me a set of *things* when really they are dynamic patterns in an imaginative 'field'.

To be fair, Jung was not altogether unaware of his description's shortcomings. He laments the tendency of his archetypes, if left to themselves in the unconscious, to collapse in on one another and return to their original undifferentiated unity. Where he scores is in his repeated emphasis on the need to separate out these images, to differentiate and assimilate them consciously in order to reunite them at a higher level and so create that transcendental reconciling entity, the Self. (In a sense his 'Self' is the equivalent of the one 'archetype' – Mercurius – although we also have to say:

Self : collective unconscious :: Philosophers' Stone : prima materia :: differentiated : undifferentiated :: end : beginning.) This process, he insists, is the strategy of the Spirit. If we don't conform to it, it will go hard with us. 'Make of yourselves living philosophical stones!' The alchemist's cry is both a command and the exultation of one who has pierced illusion to perceive in an instant of ineffable vision the oneness of spirit and matter in the inchoate Raw Stuff, the primeval soup of some great original Monad which must be worked upon by the imagination, both scientific and artistic, to dissolve it and recongeal it until we, at one with ourselves and with the world, are returned to that mysterious mercurial unity. No matter how far we stray, or must stray, from the centre, our estrangement is only apparent – we cannot stray beyond recall from the source by whose virtue we have form, substance, being – life – at all.

Mercurius is One and Three – like the Trinity! He is therefore the earthly counterbalance of the purely 'heavenly' three-personed Godhead. He is God's dark mirror-image.

But since he contains as many opposites as I can think of he also has an equally bright 'light' side. It seems that because this was more or less taken care of in conventional exoteric religion the alchemists concentrated on his dark side – the serpent or dragon.

Another way of looking at him, then, is (as the Gnostics might elegantly put it) as that part of God which, when He imagined the

World into existence, was left behind and buried in His creation. Mercurius is the snaky earth-spirit whom Jung compares to a 'fragment of primeval psyche into which no consciousness has yet penetrated to create division and order . . . '

Thus Mercurius represents the collective unconscious which alone has all the ambiguities and paradoxical qualities associated with him.

'He's always at his papers,' said Nora abruptly, with her eyes still closed. 'Just like you. You're made for each other. Haven't you met him yet?' Her eyes opened.

'Who?' I asked automatically. I don't always give her words my full attention. They make no sense to me half the time.

'Don't play silly buggers, dear. John, of course. I never called him that, you know. I called him "sir".' Crackle of laughter.

I gently reminded her that John Smith had died a long time ago. She appeared to absorb this information for a while. Then:

'You remember the rabbits in the Russian rocket? They sent up some baby rabbits and killed them one by one. On the ground they wired up the mother to a machine. Every time they killed a baby in space the machine went "blip" . . . like a teardrop . . . as the mother rabbit felt the loss in her body. That's what it's like. When a man has touched you at a . . . certain depth, you always know what's happening to him. I never felt any blip, dear.'

She drifted away for a minute or two, uttering random sentences and moving her eyes in concert with the patterns of firelight on the ceiling. It was freezing outside, but the drawing-room was stuffy and airless.

'I've seen him in town,' she said distinctly. 'He's ahead of me in a crowd . . . coming out of the cinema. He looks over his shoulder . . . looked right at me.' She moved her eyes to and fro. 'I fought past the people but when I get to the spot . . . he's gone.' Crackle. 'Slippery fellow. Doesn't look a day older.'

Poor Nora; she recedes daily, like one touched with senility, into a timeless world of her own.

The distinction between the personal and impersonal aspects of Spirit is particularly hard for us to understand, I think. The reason is that we belong to a tradition (regardless of whether we are religious or not) which emphasises a personal deity: a warm loving Father who is in Heaven.

Jung criticised this image of the deity on the grounds that it valued spiritual *perfection* at the expense of that *wholeness* which incorporates the neglected feminine side of human nature. In practice, we have to add a feminine principle to the masculine Godhead, as (Jung thinks) the Roman Catholics have unconsciously done by raising the status of the Virgin Mary. He also thought that alchemy was just such an unconscious attempt to counterbalance a paternal religion by concentrating on dark, material, feminine Nature below, rather than light, spiritual, masculine God above. This is a congenial idea, comparatively easy to grasp and even agree with, because it only requires a transformation of gender – a personal goddess, as it were, is added to a personal God.

Our trouble begins when we have to incorporate *impersonal* aspects of God into religion – aspects which are neither masculine nor feminine, neither warm nor loving (not even unjust and wrathful like Jehovah). Unfortunately the Great Work demonstrates that this is exactly what we have to do – the Spirit can be as cold and as indifferent as a stone. In other words it can, and will, appear as something the complete opposite of what we have come to expect of it. Something monstrous, for instance, or diabolical. Eastern religions are perhaps wise in relegating their pantheon of personal deities to a level lower than the final void. In our culture an atheist may be someone who can only respond to the impersonal aspect of Spirit.

It is appalling, frightening, to think that we've not only lost the concept of Spirit but, more especially, the concept of Mercurius, without which the divisions in ourselves, and between ourselves and Nature, can never be healed. For it is he alone who, as the principle of opposition itself, can lead us back through all the lesser conjunctions to the grand reunion of male and female, Heaven and Earth.

If we lose the concept of Mercurius, his reality can no longer find a natural outlet of expression such as the Opus provided. This puts us in mortal danger. How long can we damp down his fires or poison his vivifying springs? Or, worse still, appropriate his power for our own ends? Not much longer. The more we deny him, the more Mercurius will insist on recognition, if necessary by floods and holocausts and monsters. Failing these, he will, reluctantly, shrug us off the planet.

A month ago she barely tolerated a single visit from the doctor. Now she barely notices his daily calls. She shouldn't really be alive at all. Toxins, or whatever, have spread throughout her body. It is their effect on the brain, as much as the absence of nourishment, which threatens her coherence.

There was half an hour of rambling today, plus a spot of incontinence. I'm handy with the bedpan, but if Nora doesn't signal in time, and messes her bed, I'm equally adept at changing her nightie and sheet. Bradley and I have agreed that, apart from a plastic undersheet, there are to be no special concessions to incontinence. Nora is to be treated as an adult, no matter what. We are mindful of her dignity. We conspire against the night nurse, who is less scrupulous. Bradley has found it necessary to intimidate her. We are determined to change Nora as often as it takes. Naturally, although I come in the mornings now as well as the evenings, I still only have to attend to her for a fraction of the time. The saintly Bradley is rarely seen without clean linen in the crook of his arm.

It continually surprises me how unconcerned I am by Nora's incontinence. I am generally nauseated by bodily excretions of most sorts. Hers, however, are as inoffensive as a baby's. When I pick her up, she is hot and she trembles like a fledgling, light as a feather. Yet there's also something of the dowager duchess about her – a haughty nobility, as if she were simply too grand to be bothered with the usual lavatorial channels. Her murmured conversation doesn't falter as I lift, wipe, wash, dry, apply cream to the bed sores on her shrivelled shanks. She moves in and out of lucidity like a sleeper drifting in and out of a dream. It is perhaps wrong to call her incoherent; rather, I don't understand how to put together her fragments of speech.

For example, today she was chanting (rather aptly):

'I am sick . . . I must die . . . Lord have mercy on us!'

I took no notice. I didn't realise she was quoting until she snapped at me:

'Come along! It goes:

> Queens have died young and fair,
> Dust hath closed Helen's eye.
>   I am sick, I must die
>   Lord have mercy on us!

But what comes before that? What's the bloody line *before* that? For God's sake what is it?' and so on. She grew miserable and restless, her fingers clawing at the sheet, her mouth working. I dimly recognised the poem. I looked among John's books, but I couldn't find it. It was hopeless, even with anthologies of poetry, without the title or first line. I wanted so badly to find the missing bit for her. I looked for ages, but I couldn't *find* it.

The peculiar intensity of the alchemist's attention to the Work, his concentrated ritual operations, his isolation, his prolonged study, fasting, prayer and toil – all this helps to evoke the visionary images of Spirit. If the Work were a conventional ascetic discipline, it would take place 'within' the adept and produce that visionary pattern of self-realisation whose culmination in Oriental philosophico-religions is variously named *samadhi*, *satori* or *Nirvana* ('freedom from opposites'). These are the equivalent of the Albedo.

The orthodox mystic withdraws from the world – both the world of society and the world of Nature. The alchemist likewise withdraws from society but, so to speak, takes Nature with him in the form of his First Matter. He performs the Art in a kind of twilight, working hand in hand with Nature, not in her plural organic aspect, but in her single inorganic aspect.

The religious ascetic may well return to the world after the illuminative experience (I think of St Teresa of Avila bursting out of her enclosed Order to found a string of convents and to issue down-to-earth advice); but the alchemist does not return to the world after his Albedo because in a sense he never left it. His task is to reunite himself with it in order to bring about a union of which the conventional mystic knows very little: the marriage of Heaven and Earth. (He doesn't concern himself with the social world at all. He'd probably see St Teresa's activity as an extension of Christ's redemptive purpose towards mankind. He, on the other hand, is concerned to redeem that part of the world which he sees as having been overlooked by Christianity, viz: the world of Nature.)

The analogy here is not with religious mysticism but with art, as the Philosophers understood. They began by orchestrating the drama of transformation and ended, like the audience of a Passion play, by participating. Matter was their raw material. They shaped it in the fire of the imagination, according to the pattern set down in their sacred texts, just as the First Philosopher moulded man himself out of clay and fired him in the furnace of Creation. In return, they were reciprocally remade by the same imaginative power – Mercurius the shape-changer, who changed their minds as only he can do, dwelling as he does beneath both man and matter, remaking the one into his other immortal Self and the other into the one Stone.

The true saint, like the true philosopher, can (if God wishes it) work directly with Nature at their common level of Spirit; and, through their mutual imagination, create the spontaneous alteration of water into wine, lead into gold. Miracles are only the mystic's works of art.

Isn't there something redemptive about all great Art?

Social anthropology tells me that there's a structure common to both the individual and the collective: the economy of the human psyche is reflected in social organisation. Alchemy goes further. It says that the structure of both individual and social organisms is *au fond* also shared by the natural world, even down to the remotest constituents of matter.

This Piscean sky, lit by a watery sun, is a light, almost hallucinatory blue. Gusts of wind come at you like icicles, probing the thickest clothes for weaknesses. I totter to the village shop, preferring to pay over the odds for grub rather than freeze on the way to the supermarket in a car whose performance is uncertain – probably only points or plugs, but not something I want to go into now. I struggle back to the fug I've worked up in John's library and work as the sky turns green and the fox-coloured sun slinks behind the hill. I brave the draughty hall in a dash to the kitchen where I heat my vat of bacon and vegetable stew, enough to last three days, or four if I eke it out with bread, cheese and Toblerone. As soon as the lights come on in the Manor, I set out for my evening shift.

Nora is, to put it mildly, skin and bone. It is gruesome and marvellous to see with what ferocity – whether through fear of death or love of life – she hangs on to her tattered body. Having built up a certain resistance to pain-killers she suffers agonies, especially late at night. I practise at a distance my inadequate visualisations of her pain before I turn in for the night. I can't be sure that they do any good, but they do no harm; and, if they do not help her, they help me because I could not stand it if I weren't with her in spirit at this time.

More and more, as I picture the cancer in her stricken flesh, her pain is for me a sickening substance to be drawn out of her, like pus. But then, more and more, I am not alone in my endeavour: in the same clear space where I receive the pain, I see the radiance of him who rises like a sun through the unravelling labyrinth.

I asked Bradley where my dear John is buried.

We were sitting at the corner table in the Green Man where we sometimes come by mutual accord as soon as the night nurse arrives. The days are long for Bradley. We buy each other pints of the powerful beer and then have a round – a whisky chaser, say – out of the Manor's housekeeping. 'We'll have one on Nora,' says Bradley. 'She can afford it.' Usually we are silent while we drink whatever Nora has bought us by proxy. Bradley's customary reticence might be mistaken for calm; but, underneath, he's distraught. He tends to speak only as much as politeness demands; and he's so tired that he's liable to nod off into his drink. But then, as if it were a sin to relax for a second, he jerks awake at once with a wild look in his shiny eye. In some ways I am more concerned about him than about Nora, who is pretty much past human care.

People hush their voices as we pass them in the bar, as

though we were already the bereaved. Even the irreverent Brendan creases his brow in concern and ceases to press me for marks on his outfit. He might ostentatiously look the other way and casually loosen his jacket to reveal the backing on his new velvet waistcoat. Whereupon, whether or not I'm in a mood to humour him, I praise its beauty. He struggles to hold his expression of sincere concern, but the brow soon smoothes out in a smirk of pleasure which never fails to amuse me. He is in awe of Bradley whom he calls 'sir' without irony. To me, Bradley is always 'yer Man' – 'How's yer Man doing up at the ould house?' or, with solicitude, 'Yer Man looks a bit on the knackered side.'

The Reverend John Smith, said Bradley, is not buried anywhere. His body was not found after the fire. He sounded angry. Pedantically I insisted that there are always *some* remains after a fire. Teeth etc. He winced. 'Oh, leave it alone, can't you?' he said.

I explained that I could not leave it alone; that I was caught up in this – that it was, after all, I who had to live over the bloody cellar where John Smith, vicar and Philosopher, had been incinerated thirty years ago.

Bradley was very still, except for his chest which rose and fell rapidly. His knuckles were white where they grasped his pint glass. He was both angry and (as I realised to my mortification) close to tears.

'The man went down the well. What else?' he said at last. It sounded laughable, like 'Ding Dong Bell, Pussy's in the Well'. On second thoughts, it sounded horrible.

Surely, I continued ruthlessly, he would've floated to the top? Gases in the corpse and so on? I rather think Bradley hated me then. God forgive me, but I was driven to go on: was the well dragged or searched or whatever? If not, the body may still be down there? Unless, of course, as Nora sometimes seems to imagine, John Smith escaped the fire altogether . . . ? I put it to Bradley that he had saved John from the fire.

Bradley had had enough. He drained his glass and smacked it down on the table. He said, slowly and emphatically, as if I were hard of hearing:

'I didn't save him. I killed him. No one . . . no human being could have survived that inferno. I *know*. I was *there*.' He jabbed a finger at his own rased face.

'And you survived it,' I reminded him. But Bradley didn't hear me. He had risen from his chair and was striding out of the pub.

The lid was off the well, as I had left it. The cellar was suffused with an indefinable scent, as delicate as petals. Would a man who was in imminent danger of burning clamp his arms to his side and step into the round manhole? Would he choose to drown in that narrow shaft rather than roast?

I reached in and removed the grating which had been added to prevent anything from inadvertently falling in. The water had dropped. It glimmered dimly, two man's lengths down. Its surface rippled slightly. The well-shaft is where the underground spring stands up. What if this spring is not a miserable seeping thing, but a lusty stream – as its power to swell and flood suggests? What if a man, dropping like an arrow into the well, were to rocket down to the bottom – there to be grabbed and swept away by the stream? And if the stream had worn away a tunnel, as local lore has it, might not a man find his head suddenly in the clear, breathing in the darkness? Mightn't he follow the tunnel like a potholer, hour after hour, half-dead with cold, wet fatigue, until he saw a chink in the blackness, a tiny overgrown hole in some hillside a mile or two from here through which he might heave himself out to collapse beneath the stars; and then, with a backward glance at the smoke which still billowed from the cellar of his distant home, to set his face forward and begin a new life?

Or did he drown at once, and sink, never to rise again? Has his flesh been long distributed by the meandering spring throughout the earth's cracks and fissures? Are his bones now being tugged apart by tiny eddies, enriching the well's water with their sweet deposits of calcium?

As I entertained these vivid images, wondering and wondering whether my dear John had truly exchanged ordeal by fire for death by water, wondering if by some remote chance he had escaped ('*His body was not found . . .* '), wondering if he had died ('*No one . . . could have survived that inferno . . .* '), asking myself whether his soul lingered in the cold dark streams below or whether, his body vapourised by a sudden blast of flame, his essence had gone sailing up like a spark through the ceiling, the roof, up through to the other side of the sky itself – as I pictured all this and wondered and was troubled, I felt the stone floor lurch under me as if I were on a raft and the raft was being shaken by the premonition of a tidal wave thrown up by some volcanic cataclysm an ocean away.

One of Lévi-Strauss's most famous remarks is central to his conception of the collective unconscious:

> '*Nous ne prétendons donc pas montrer comment les hommes pensent dans les mythes mais comment les mythes se pensent dans les hommes, et à leur insu.*'

Unfortunately the expressive French reflexive is pretty much untranslatable into English; but in my edition of *The Raw and the Cooked* (London, 1970) it runs like this:

> 'I therefore claim to show, not how men think in myths but how myths operate in men's minds without their being aware of the fact.'*

Literally, Lévi-Strauss is interested in *how myths think themselves in men without their knowledge.*

It's the idea of *thinking* that bothers me. I mean it's wonderful to discover that so-called pre-logical tribal people have a logic which is equal in sophistication to our own – a logic that's constructed out of contrasts in the sensory qualities of concrete objects such as raw/cooked, wet/dry, male/female, etc. It's a mode of thought which has been said to differ from our 'scientific' way of thinking as an abacus differs from mental arithmetic.

But is Lévi-Strauss right to emphasise *thinking*? In his keenness to show that 'primitive' people are as intellectual in their own way as he is, he seems to forget that intellectuality of his kind is rare enough in any society, including ours. It's not, surely, the *intellect*

---

* Compare the translation in *Yale French Studies* (1966; subsequently published New York, 1970): 'We are not therefore claiming to show how men think the myths, but rather how the myths think themselves out in men and without men's knowledge.'

which in the first instance grasps and orders the world; it is, as Smith says, the *imagination*.

When tribes use natural species as a model of social organisation, it's not because plants and animals are 'good to think' (*bonnes à penser*) but because they are '*good to imagine*'. When the alchemist uses metals, animals, plants, etc. as a model of psychic organisation it's because they are similarly 'good to imagine'.

When Lévi-Strauss tells us that myths 'think themselves in men without their knowledge' he knows that this happens through the spontaneous activity of the autonomous human mind. Is 'thinking' really the best word to describe this activity? Of course not. Myths are spontaneous images arising out of the collective imagination; they are the way the Spirit represents itself to itself. (Lévi-Strauss's 'human mind' is the approved translation of '*l'esprit humain*'. When did the French *esprit* cease to be 'spirit' and become 'mind'?)

Both psychology and anthropology require us to translate the *other* into terms of ourselves, and vice versa: I put myself in his place as he is put by me in my place. This substitution is primarily an imaginative act. It's the basis of all fellow-feeling – of all compassion.

Alchemy requires the ultimate translation: that of the *absolutely* other, the non-human (inorganic matter) into terms of ourselves. But it recognises too that, at the limits of imagination, translation becomes transformation – the imaginative act becomes a mutual substitution and exchange: I put myself in his place as he puts himself in mine. Compassion is converted into reciprocal love, notably marriage. (The Redemption was Christ's act of putting himself in the place of all men; to become Christians we have to put ourselves in His place. This is the meaning of 'Take up thy cross ...' This is the meaning of St Paul's piercing cry of understanding: '*I have been crucified with Christ; yet I live, and yet no longer I, but Christ liveth in me.*')

I can't help wondering about Helvetius' story.[5] He obviously didn't make it up, since it has the ring of authenticity – and besides, as a professed disbeliever in alchemy he had a lot to lose. Might it have been a kind of vision? The details, the timescale, his wife's involvement, suggest not. Also, actual gold was produced and assayed.

It *is* temptingly romantic to believe that his description of the stranger with the stone is a portrait of Philalethes, who we know was in Holland in the same year, 1666, to deliver his manuscript to his Amsterdam publishers.

Nora quiet. I brushed her thin hair and forehead with my fingertips, which she likes. A vein or artery pulsed feebly in her temple. Her face is impersonal in repose, like an anatomical diagram of bone structure. When she opened her eyes, they scintillated dangerously. She seemed to focus on some point the other side of me and said loudly:

'Brightness falls from the air. Of course.' Then she gave a little laugh, as nearly normal a laugh as I've heard from her in weeks – so normal that I panicked and ran for Bradley. By the time we returned she was sleeping.

It was such an odd thing to say, but also beautiful and sad, and strangely familiar to me.

SMITH

Sleet on the empty village streets. Cold uneaten food. An ash-filled grate. Nora's hot tears on my cold cheek. The creak of the graveyard yew. A draught on the back of my neck. The pity of it.

Why couldn't it have been me instead of him?

Why not me? Because that's never the way. It's never the sinful who die. They have to go on living with their guilt.

Detachment, yes. The end of personal suffering, yes. That's what the whiteness bestows. At the same time the beneficiaries are no longer protected by crassness from reality. The deaths of others are no longer unimaginable. At the moment when he described his extravagant parabola through the empty air, I was the tree that shook him loose, I was the helpless onlooker, I was the iron ground he struck. The surprised cry that laid me open like a scalpel was my own.

Why didn't I foresee it? If I had, I might have – *why, if*: the eternal wail of the damned.

Christ have mercy on Tim's soul.

Nightingale Wood had to be saved, therefore it would be. As I set out across the Green, I had no doubts. Never, in fact, have I felt so sure. My step was quick and springy; my back was straight. I left dark prints in the light powdering of frost which was beginning to fade under the clear eye of the sun. I carried the heavy chain and padlock proudly, like a medal of office. I spared a thought for Caldwell who didn't know he couldn't prevail.

People came out of houses and cottages as I passed and began to follow me. I paid them no mind, being inwardly set on the task ahead. They were welcome, all of them, but my strength and our success did not depend on their numbers. My course of action was sanctioned by its justice.

At the edge of the wood I counted thirteen men with axes and saws, Caldwell among them looking as calm as I was. I didn't recognise any of them. They were mercenaries hired for the occasion and little more amenable to personal appeal than the spanking new bulldozer around which they gathered like acolytes. It had caterpillar tracks at the back and, in front, long arms of iron joined at their ends by a heavy steel sheet, slightly concave and half as high as a man. It would easily sweep through the five skinny pines of the wood's front line, laying open the heart to the men's implements.

I marched forward with my army at my back. I saw no reason why the right words shouldn't pierce the hearts of these men like arrows and bring them to their senses. I bid Caldwell a brisk good-morning. He said:

'Go home, Vicar. This will do no good.'

'We can't let you do it.' He looked slightly puzzled. I realised why when, walking to the higher ground between the bulldozer and the trees, I turned around – my 'army' had transformed itself into a sizeable crowd, well over a hundred souls, of onlookers. Some had the grace to look sheepish; most looked curious; a few, like Mrs Beattie who stood well forward, were gleeful. Still I had no doubts.

I raised the chain above my head and began in a loud voice to make the final decisive plea for the life of Nightingale Wood. Caldwell made a signal and my words were drowned by the racket of the bulldozer's engine starting up. It roared and puffed out smoke like a mechanical dragon.

I slung my chain around the nearest of the five pines. It was then that I realised I couldn't attach myself, suffragette-like, to the trunk without help. I scanned the crowd, wishing I hadn't forbidden Nora to come with me, hoping that Robert had providentially come out of retreat. The bulldozer clanked into gear.

A figure detached itself from the mass and, almost bent double, ploughed up the slope towards me. Janet. Without a word she pushed me back against the tree and wound the chain tightly around me, from neck to ankles, clipping the padlock neatly on at the end. My arms and legs were pinioned, my head could only move a fraction to left and right. She looked frightened. I smiled at her; indeed, I almost laughed – it was such a melodramatic little pantomime! She clapped me on the shoulder and retreated with a helpless gesture which, in sudden anger, she changed into a shake of both fists at Caldwell. He looked exasperated; but, according to some well rehearsed plan, he signalled again to the driver whose face was hidden by light reflected off the windscreen. The bulldozer began to jerk towards me.

At this point a doubt entered me. With a curious sensation of incredulity and amusement I thought it might just mow me down. However, at the last moment it veered to my left. I pictured myself quite clearly: a ludicrous cleric tethered to a solitary standing tree, while all about me, its brothers and sisters lay flattened over acres of ground.

I craned my neck to watch the adjacent pine go down. As the machine waved its lethal steel shunter experimentally and edged towards it, I glimpsed a huge exotic red bird perched in the thickest branches at the top. The biting wind made my eyes smart. The pine tree at my back swayed slightly. The view over the down was extraordinarily beautiful on that crisp clear morning. Over the heads of the people the cathedral spire rose like a stalagmite in the distance. I screamed as loudly as I could but it was a paltry noise against the rattling roaring engine. I fought to free my hands; I exerted every muscle in my body, but the chain seemed only to bite into me more deeply. No one would meet my rolling eyes to read there the terrible realisation.

The bulldozer hit the tree a jarring blow. Its trunk slewed sideways. The crimson bird sailed out of the branches, his skirts billowing, his jewellery sparkling in the sunlight. What caused him to hide in the tree? Some misplaced loyalty, perhaps; or some quirk of his own dramatic nature? I don't know. He took a long time to fall, in a smooth, heart-stopping arc. He gave a little surprised cry, like the cry of a bird. He hit the iron-hard hill in a sickening scarlet heap. I slid to the ground, my padlock still intact, the chain inexplicably falling loosely at my feet.

His back and neck were broken, I think. I supported his head for a minute or two while he still lived. His face was perfectly made up in a gay mask. His eyes were open but unseeing. He made a little sound in his throat once or twice. Then gradually his eyes acquired a tremulous film, like a premonition of ice on a winter pond. Then they froze over.

I have no stomach for a lengthy description of the Rubedo, but I will briefly finish what I've begun. (In any case, the Opus is in sole charge of itself and I, a simple onlooker – at best a menial servant for raising the temperature.)

There's no reason why the Regimen of the Sun can't be completed in a very short time, thanks to the grace of God who enabled me to attain the Mercury of the Wise, that is, the perfect Star of Whiteness. Strictly speaking there are two parts to the Rubedo: Sublimation and Exaltation. The first takes the Work up to the Citrinitas [yellowness] which, however, I do not recognise as a distinct division in the way of the other three colours because it is continuous with White and Red, merely marking the transition between them. Similarly, Exaltation is but an extension of Sublimation whose purpose is solely to make the spirit corporeal and the body spiritual – that is, to perform the final fixing of the volatile and volatilising of the fixed.

To this end I've taken three parts of Sol and nine of Luna and digested them together in order to rid Sol of grossness and to draw out our subtle red sulphur. It is this which is thenceforth sublimed with our white mercury which it tinges through and through until it reddens.

In short, and to speak plainly, the whole secret of the Art is to prepare our double mercury – by which I mean Mercurius – so that it turns inside out. We will remember that Mercurius was originally four-fold, or a double twin. However, once Above and Below are conjoined to form the White Stone, he becomes double only – volatile on the one hand, and fixed on the other; on the one hand spirit, on the other matter. These are as unlike as man and woman. And yet by the miraculous marriage of Red and White they become one thing, the Stone. Thus, in another sense, it is necessary only – through the mediation of Mercurius – *to change the gender of masculine spirit and feminine matter.* This were impossible, were it not that each already contains a portion of the other, just as each human, being a four-fold unity of body, soul, spirit and mind, is more or less three parts one gender and nine of the other. As a man, for example, I am masculine as regards body, spirit and mind and feminine as regards soul. For a woman the reverse is the case. It's always the soul which has the opposite sex to that of the body.

I took a spade and climbed the hill to Nightingale Wood. Tim once said: 'If I could be a tree I'd be a copper beech. They like to grow in pairs, you know, for company.' He was buried today. I had Jones come over and do it.* Hadn't the heart myself; and, besides, they blame me. No more than I blame myself.

A large turn-out in thin mizzling rain. My presence clearly thought to be a presumption. I stood at the back of the crowd, an exile in my own churchyard. The grave is next to his mother's. Thomas wept openly as the coffin went down. It looked so *small* to contain so much life. Nora, round with child, stood very straight and stony-faced. She stayed behind when the others had gone. She held my hand tightly for a while, shivering. I wiped the rain from her face and told her to go. She seemed relieved to hear a clear directive. She wanted me to return with her to her father's. I couldn't. Later, she came back to the vicarage and went immediately to bed. I took some Ovaltine up to her. I heard her crying behind the door. The time for talking hasn't yet come, so I tipped the Ovaltine down the sink and went back out to the grave. My legs did not support me. I had to kneel in the fresh drenched earth. I have no doubt of the soul's immortality, no doubt that Tim's in Heaven, cheering up the gloomy saints, no doubt of Our Lord's Providence, no doubt no doubt no doubt.

I took the spade and climbed the hill. At the western edge of the wood I found what I was looking for – a copper beech sapling almost choked by undergrowth and overshadowed by its parent. I looked up into its bare branches which but a short while ago had been a green-gold-scarlet blaze, and suddenly I saw the ancient copper beech as our mercurial fountain, distilling itself out of the

---

* Presumably a neighbouring clergyman.

ground. Just so does the Work grow: rooted in the prima materia the Spirit draws its own seed up out of the black earth, shoots up its own silver bole, breaks into the leafy redness that disperses the Spirit into a million dewy droplets which, falling again to earth, are absorbed and coagulated until the chemical tree bears its golden fruit.[6]

As Paracelsus tells us: 'Gold, through industry and skill of an expert Alchymist may bee so far exalted, that it may grow in a glasse like a tree,[7] with many wonderfull boughs, and leaves, which indeed is pleasant to behold, and most wonderfull' [*De rerum natura*]. I've heard that Sir Isaac Newton grew such a tree of philosophical gold, but I doubt the truth of it.

I dug up the sapling and replanted it twenty paces away where it can grow and thrive and be a companionable child to its parent. It took longer than I thought in the dark and wet. While I dug and planted, I held Tim in my mind. Then I let him go.

A curious evensong. My flock is down to five. I sensed Nora's reluctance to come any more, partly because of her condition, partly because of Tim — I don't really know why. She says she feels closer to God than before, well, everything. I forbade her to come to church on *my* account, naturally.

So I'm left with the two widows, Berkitt and Turner; the two Lyddons; and old man Roach. I don't think any of them have heard that I'm no longer *persona grata* here; and if they have they don't understand. Old Roach took no more part in the service than usual, moving his lips during the creed and moaning vaguely during the hymns. Mrs Lyddon, clearly bewildered and embarrassed by such little 'cover', sang out bravely and flatly. Her husband's stentorian tones echoed in the rafters. I didn't expect him to turn up — he's an erratic churchgoer at the best of times. He's not popular in the village for no other reason that I can see except that he wears rather 'sharp' clothes and owns a garage on the outskirts of town. I hardly know him. As for his wife, whenever I've called on her, the sight of me seemed to panic her and so I stopped. (Now I think of it, she began to attend services as soon as I ceased visiting — out of gratitude, perhaps.) Mrs Berkitt is a closed book. I visit her regularly but she has never once addressed a word to me except through the mediumship of her innumerable cats who are named after members of the Royal family, except for a stray she took in called Wallis: 'Would the vicar like another cup of tea, Georgie? Would he? You go and ask him. Show the vicar your ringworm, Mary. Go on, show him how much better it is.' Etc. Sometimes we sit in comfortable silence while the room purrs like a many-headed engine. I find her company restful and that of the cats congenial. She made a valiant effort to find the right hymn and gave up only two short. Mrs Turner was the revelation: she has a beautiful voice, usually drowned by the collective drone, but today gaining in confidence with every verse until it was she, not I, who led the singing.

I didn't preach but gave a short impromptu address on the Good Samaritan. I made no collection even though Lyddon jingled the coins willingly in his pocket during the last hymn.

There was, of course, a sixth member of the congregation: Lydia Simmons. She is a rock. Without her tactfully muted harmonium it would be difficult to keep up the illusion of a proper service. As it was, we all made quite a decent fist of it, considering.

There's no more talk of chopping down Nightingale Wood. Caldwell is defeated. The trees are Tim's monument.

Exaltation! It may be expressed by this conceit:

The lunar disc slowly turns and, turning, reveals that it is a sphere whose hitherto hidden side is not as we imagined – dark – but as bright as the sun. It is the white Star, in which Luna and Sol were married, made corporeal and red, red.

In the post this morning, a sad little note which read:

YOUR AN EVIL CURSE ON THIS PLACE YOU AND YOUR HORE CAN CLEAR OUT OR ELSE.

I burnt it lest Nora should see it.

*

Cycled into Town. Fixed my will (Nora, of course, gets Tim's share). Arranged for her confinement. It's a long way off but best to make sure etc.

Supper in front of the study fire. A perfectly poached egg, a piece of hot buttered toast with Marmite, and weak tea. Exquisite. I have trouble convincing Nora, except on the evidence of my fitness, that I really don't need much food and certainly not a cooked dinner. However, I eat a little, for the joy of it, and enjoy watching her 'eating for two'. We don't speak much these days, not since she talked away some of her grief over Tim, but we know something of each other's state of mind none the less. I sense the smallest agitation on her part through two brick walls. It must be a little how a married couple of fifty years' standing feel. At her request I read a few *Songs of Innocence* to her.* She seems content; and I am free, at least, of anxiety.

She invites me to feel the baby. I lay my hand on her swollen tummy. There are the strangest little ripples under her taut skin. They give me a pang of intense happiness. When the child is quiet again, we discuss names for him or her. I suggest Obadiah and Rapunzel, Galahad and Fifi, just to hear her giggle. Nora decides on Florence, after her grandmother, or Timothy. It's dark in the room. She says she can see my head glowing 'like an American pumpkin on Hallowe'en'. I make suitable grimaces. We laugh, lingering on by the fire, past her bedtime and my time to go down to the Work.

At about a quarter past ten our idyll is interrupted by the sound of breaking glass in the dining-room across the hall. A brick has been thrown through the window. Nora is not frightened except for her baby. I make light of it and nail wood over the broken pane. What are things coming to? Who'd do this? Nora could have been hit by flying glass, for God's sake.

For the first time since my arrival, I lock the front door. It's a kind of defeat.

---

* By William Blake.

SUBLIMATION

There were people moving about in the dark outside my window a moment ago. Six shadowy figures, or maybe four, moving about. I tiptoed to the front door and threw it open. 'Come in! Come in!' But there was only the rapid patter as of rats' feet and the flash of a white face. I think it might have belonged to one of Bradley's chums.

I don't want Nora getting hurt on account of animosity towards me. I told her: 'Go home for a while till this nastiness blows over.' She pursed her lips and gave her blonde mop a little shake. Then, blinking rapidly, she said in a rush: 'I'm not leaving you. You're worth the lot of them put together.'

To Janet's. To do – to do what? To do what I should've done before, I suppose. We sat whispering in the kitchen in order not to wake Farrar who is apparently cantankerous if woken before noon. He goes to bed late, I gather, after a skinful of drink. He no longer makes any pretence of going to work. The situation is dire.

Janet is also, well, run down, for want of a better description. Unhappiness hangs in the kitchen like the smell of old boiled cabbage. She had no desire to see me, of course, since I'm a reminder of happier times and unhappy decisions. However, once I was there, she wanted news of Robert. Wanted it yet didn't want it, unable to help herself, unable to stop herself from asking, unable to prevent herself from listening. I told her what little I knew.

She needs love like light and air. She has to get up and walk out of her house and carry her love like a trophy to Robert. She has to forget the rules and regulations, forget Farrar who's killing her, and take the plunge (as I did not take it with Annabelle because like Janet I was religiously afraid), take the leap into happiness. Happiness can't begin until we leap from thirty thousand feet into the unknown. It's only then we discover that the fall doesn't kill but, being our own parachutes, we float gently as thistledown to earth. I said as much.

'I can't,' she said. 'I can't. It's too late. It was too good to be true.' She began to cry with awful gobbling dry sobs as if she had no tears left. I couldn't leave her alone. I had to try and undo some of the bad I had in my righteousness foisted on people in the past. If I could just break through the ice-pack around her heart, break the vials of her tears... While I spoke in a forceful stage-whisper she made feeble warding-off gestures and flung her head from side to side. I had to be ruthless to withstand her hatred of me for carving her up and opening the wounds. Yet she wanted to hear more, to bleed, weep, shout, break away from the table and run, run to where she belonged. I ordered her to leave at once for Robert's house.

In an instant she was calm. Tears squeezed out of her eyes. 'I must, mustn't I,' she said.

'You must.'

She looked at me curiously. 'You're not the same man you were when we first met, are you?'

'No. I'm not.'

She rose from her chair slowly like Venus out of the sea. She blinked as if waking up. The door opened and her husband was standing there. He belched. Janet went very small and grey. 'The vicar's just leaving,' she said. 'I'll put the kettle on.'

The citrinitas [yellowness] deepens to a lustrous orange colour – and then lightens again. The circulations take place with extraordinary rapidity. The Egg strains to contain the great slab of heat which threatens to blow it apart. At every rise and fall there's a slight faltering as if some final impurity, some last ineradicable thorn in the flesh, were preventing the Spirit from becoming fixed. I'm not uneasy but I can't help trembling as I move more deeply towards the Mystery. Watching, meditating, praying are a single movement of gratitude and love. All is in readiness. The beautiful Luna is present, here, behind the trembling veil, preparing herself for the bridal bed – and yet still she will not turn and turn into the refulgent Sol.

I sense that this is the premonitory shock which the eternal must feel before entering time.

She hesitates modestly on the threshold because of her concern for the body's finitude. It's as if she wished solicitously to tempt the body – but tempt him *back*, not tempt him *on*, because she is jealous of her own immortality. And so also matter, at its furthermost limits before it is volatilised into Spirit – matter must also shudder like a bridegroom before his little death in the act of love.

The Egg burns and burns but is not consumed. Our matter is dazzling, charged with lightning. Have mercy upon me. I think of Annabelle, Nora, Tim, Janet, Robert, Lydia, Farrar, Mrs Beattie, Out-of-Sorts . . . they are threaded like beads on the golden rosary of the Holy Ghost. Sin cannot plumb the abyss of forgiveness. Forgive me. Forgive them who will not see the resurrected monster gambolling across the sunlit, the redeemed fields.

Tomorrow is Christmas Eve. I dug up the tree in the garden and set it up in the study in a bucket which Nora covered with red paper. It will be just the two of us. Thomas wrote to say he'll be in Lisbon.

There's an infernal row going on at the Manor. The Caldwell parents, it seems, are visiting relatives up North, leaving their house to their son's tender mercies. He has lost no time in throwing a party. There are lights in every window, loud discordant music, incoherent shouts. Nora has (bravely) been over to tick them off. She talks scornfully of the villagers 'cowering in their homes', too frightened of Bradley to interfere with his merrymaking. Let him have his fun. It'll come to no good. I know this as I know so many things, including the gender of Nora's child. (It will be a boy. I can't yet think of him as Timothy.)

We sang hymns together – 'While shepherds wash their socks by night' – as the potatoes boiled. After supper Nora urged me to return to the cellar. She knows I have to be there.

Well, it's all over. My career in the Church has been brought to its ignominious close. It's for the best, I know, but, on Christmas Eve, well, they picked a hell of a time.

I tolled the bell. Lydia wheezed away on the old harmonium. Nobody came. I went on pulling the bellrope until a quarter past eleven. Still nobody came. I pulled until the single clang became too funereal and then I crossed the Green to the Green Man.

The pub looked as though it hadn't closed at all the previous night. You could cut the smoke and beer fumes with a knife, not to mention the silence that fell as I pushed in.

'Anyone coming to church?' You have to make sure, give them every chance. No reply. I took a good look around. All the smudged faces closed down one by one. 'Fair enough.'

Lydia was still sitting at her silent instrument. I said:

'I'll just close the church down now.' She nodded. We switched off lights. I stashed my kit in the vestry. Lydia remarked:

'God's above all . . . all *this*.' She waved a hand that might have included the church, the village, possibly the world. I wanted to say, 'Come and live with Nora and me at the vicarage.' But I didn't. That isn't her way.

Outside it was bitterly cold. A few enormous snowflakes swirled down from the dirty grey sky. I turned the heavy key and rattled the doors to make sure they were locked. Anything I might have said to Lydia would not have been enough, so I simply said; 'I'd never have kept it up this long but for you.' She smiled and, turning away, replied:

'It has been a pleasure and an education. It is not often one meets a man of God.' She gave a little self-conscious bob and walked away, home to her husband and sister.

I hurried back to my laboratory.

It was almost dark when I came up again, red-hot, for air. Later than I thought – time for a late tea in the study's snugness. Sensitive as a bat to my preoccupation, Nora insisted that I return to my Work. I told her it could wait until we had trimmed the tree. (I wasn't sure about this.) It looked magical with its new decorations. I've always associated Christmas trees with old decorations – last year's candle stubs, tatty tinsel, chipped glass balls, a mutton-dressed-as-lamb fairy for the top. They're lovable, old decorations. Every year you swear to get new ones but when it comes to the point you can't bear to part with the rich associations of the old. New decorations, on the other hand, are like a new beginning.

We lit the candles and put our presents under the tree to be opened tomorrow. There were three exciting-looking packages for me, two from Nora and one from Robert with a big sign on it saying NOT TO BE OPENED UNTIL CHRISTMAS DAY. My presents to Nora are: some packets of seeds, a novel I think she'll enjoy – Mary Webb's *Precious Bane* – a kaleidoscope, a diary (a big one for writing proper entries in), a large slab of chocolate, a box of fireworks (I bought these for Tim in November but forgot to give them to him), a cheap chemistry set, and a pinchbeck locket. I hesitated over the childish presents but thought in the end that she is old enough for them. You're never too old for a kaleidoscope and a chemistry set; and, besides, she can always keep them for her son. I gave him, incidentally, a post office savings account with £50 in it, about all I've got left.

I suggested we toast the tree. No drink in the house bar the dregs of a dry sherry. I said I'd nip over to the pub. Nora began to cry softly.

'They've been outside, shouting your name. They've been drinking in the graveyard and . . . and other things.'

'Who?'

'People from the Manor. From the pub too, I think. Boys. And girls. Motorbikes. I don't think Pluto was there. I'm sure he wasn't. He's not like *that*, not really.'

'You should've called me.'

'I didn't like to. I thought they'd go away. They did in the end. Mostly I was worried that they might upset Tim . . . Tim's grave.'

As soon as she was able to laugh about it, I went out and checked Tim's grave. It was all right. There were empty bottles in the graveyard and some pools of sick, but nothing else. The weather was the same as last night, except the sky was lower and more leaden, dropping bigger snowflakes yet still unable to dump its full load.

Shadowy figures moved to and fro across the Green between Manor and pub. Both these places were brightly lit, all other buildings were quiet and dark. There were a lot of arhythmical percussive sounds from the drunken Manor tribe who were obviously amalgamating with the Green Man crowd to prolong yesterday's party well into Christmas.

As I crossed the Green a small black motor-car drove towards me at speed, bumping violently over the hillocks in the grass. There were human hoots as it swerved past me at the last minute. Other vehicle-owners among Bradley's guests took up the game. Motorbikes and small cars circled me, their drivers calling out to each other above the clatter of engines. It was hard to see how I was to proceed without damage to myself or them. As the driving grew more foolhardy and the circle tighter

I had to jump aside twice to avoid knocking into a bike. Luckily Bradley had the presence of mind to intervene, striding out from the Manor and waving the vehicles away. I signalled my thanks but he didn't reply. He just hunched his shoulders and thrust his hands into his coat pockets and stood there, swaying slightly and (I thought) staring coldly at me while the fat snowflakes blew like moths around his sleek head.

The situation at the pub had deteriorated since this morning. Nice Michael Crowther, not yet sixteen, Tim's pal, was outside the door. He looked up at me with unseeing eyes as I passed and then returned to his vomiting. Inside, men were face down in the ashtrays and women were singing songs the wrong side of bawdy in a joyless mechanical raucous slur. I was grateful that no one paid me much attention except young Sarah Buxton (who is certainly under age for alcohol). She greeted me with an insistent 'Coo-ee, Vicar, coo-*ee*, coo-*ee*'. I nodded civilly. She half-struggled up from her seat, spilling a large dollop of her red drink into her lap and then subsided again with a last forlorn 'Coo-ee'.

Farrar was at the bar buying rounds like a robot. Men were taking drinks off him without comment, turning away. Unintelligible utterances ejaculated out of him, accompanied by the uncontrollable jerky self-justifying gestures of the desperate; his eyes sloshed about in his head. Donovan the landlord stared at me defiantly from behind the bar. I asked him for a bottle of champagne. He thought at first I was making fun of him but he sullenly set off to root one out of his cellar.

Suddenly animated by the mention of champagne, Farrar battened on to my left lapel.

'Champagne, eh, Vicar? Cham-*pagne*?' he shouted. The refrain was taken up by others and punctuated by witty remarks in la-di-da voices: 'We only evah drink champers at the vicarage', 'Milady has expensive tastes now, don't she,' etc. Sensing that the wind was behind him for once, Farrar got carried away:

'Is that what you give to women, eh? Is that what you used to give my wife? Eh? She used to talk about you all the time. She doesn't now. Got tired of you, did she? Well, I don't bloody care either way, I'm bloody tired of her, she's a bloody useless wife.'

It was a bad business, a sad business. I disentangled his fingers from my coat. His outspokenness had caused a hiatus in the hubbub. Gradually an unpleasant rhubarbing grew up, getting more menacing as it got louder. Alex Peck, a man of few words, opined that my best bet was to bugger off. Others agreed. They weren't to know that Peck, poor fellow, finding himself short after his wife's operation, had borrowed a fiver off me in May and has yet to pay it back. It's terrible for him to be beholden.

The brays of outrage multiplied. A kind of sluggish slavering violence circulated the bar like a hyena looking for a point of weakness and focus. Am I responsible for bringing them to this? I put money into the returning Donovan's hand and retreated with the champagne, out into the clear freezing air, before anyone did anything they'd regret.

I skirted around the Green where I could hear curses and breaking glass. I thought I could see, on the far side, a tall hunched figure following me with his eyes – but of course I couldn't; it was too dark. I quickened my pace, being suddenly afraid for Nora.

At the bus-stop, waiting for the last bus before Christmas, a valise at her feet, stood Mrs Beattie.

'All this,' she remarked cosmically, 'all this is your doing.'

'Good evening, Mrs Beattie.'

'You've brought nothing but trouble. Trouble and evil. *Evil.*'

'It's true I haven't been much good. I'm sorry for it.'

'You and your dark doings. Well, I hope you're satisfied, setting families against each other.' (My heart gave a small leap.) 'You were always thick as thieves, you and that hard woman calls herself my sister. Well, I won't stay where I'm not wanted. I'm off to my friend's in Bognor. Good riddance, I say.'

I picked up the sad bewildered old baggage in a bear hug and twirled her around in the air.

'Goodbye, Mrs B.'

So. The worm has turned. Lydia has done it. I am *very cheered.*

'Sin is behovely,' says Mother Julian,* 'but all shall be well and

---

* Julian of Norwich was a medieval English mystic whose sixteen 'shewings' or visions, received in May 1373, can be found in her book *Revelations of Divine Love.*

all shall be well and all manner of thing shall be well.' Well, *yes*. The Work turns; the Marriage begins. Praise, praise to Mercurius who has it all in hand and always has. The unspeakable Stone, the ineffable Elixir forms from the union of Heaven and Earth. At last *I can live* yet *no longer I* but she who *lives in me*. Her white face turns towards me, suffused with love, *reddening*, the spirit fixed, the body volatile. *Yes*. 'In the self point that our Soul is made sensual, in the self point is the City of God ordained to him without beginning.' Ah yes.

EILEEN

According to the 'rules' of my diagrammatical sequence, the scheme for the Philosophers' Stone should mirror that of Conjunction, but with all the reversals complete and the whole work resolved like a squared circle, e.g:

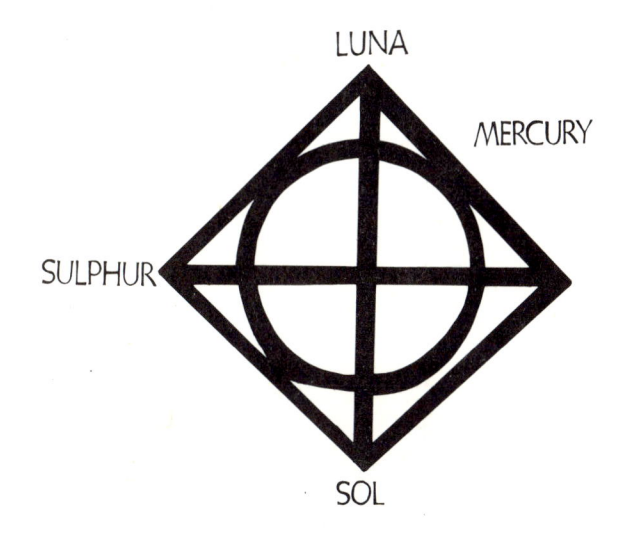

[Diagram: a square (rotated as diamond) with LUNA at top, MERCURY at right, SOL at bottom, SULPHUR at left; inscribed circle with cross.]

Jim Walters sent back the analysis of my sample at last. The Great Work's raw material is stibnite (antimony trisulphide, Sb_2S_3). The antimony content in my sample is unusually high at 78%. Apart from the sulphur which comprises the remainder of it, he found traces of lead, gold, copper and iron. I don't know whether these are significant or not.

(The dictionary tells me that, as kohl, antimony has been used for millennia as an Oriental cosmetic, e.g. hair dye and eye-shadow. Although most forms of antimony are poisonous, it is still used in certain modern medicines.)

*

Mercurius! He is the Spirit who informs us to our very fingertips but we never see him – except as he appears as something or some*one* else. To know him we must be *like* him: airy, fluid, invisible, shape-shifting, flickering like fire.

Cursory research reveals that the standard method of preparing antimony was (and still is, I guess) to heat stibnite with some small pieces of iron and a flux. The iron combines with the stibnite's sulphur to form a slag of iron sulphide which floats to the top, while the metallic antimony sinks to the bottom. The flux helps to separate the layers so that, when the whole lot has cooled, the upper slag can be easily removed. Underneath, the antimony has a metallic lustre; and, if the purification has been done correctly, it will have formed into long thin crystals.

Occasionally these crystals arrange themselves so as to resemble slender, fern-like branches on a central stem. In very exceptional circumstances – the metal has to be purified and cooled under exacting conditions – the silvery crystals may radiate from a central point to form the 'star of antimony'.

Antimony has a special affinity with gold, which can be refined or 'exalted' by heating it with antimony ore. Any impurities in the gold combine with the sulphur in the stibnite and rise to the top. The gold sinks to the bottom, along with the metallic antimony. From there, the gold can be recovered in a very pure condition.

Bradley arrived on the doorstep this morning just as I was about to set out for the Manor. He said:

'It's all over.'

We embraced, without constraint. Our quarrel over the fate of John Smith was forgotten. I kissed his purple cheek. There were tears trapped in its wrinkles. He smiled.

'Thanks for visiting her so late. She was glad. She died an hour after you left,' he said. I told him that I hadn't called last night. 'Oh. Well, she thought you had. That's what counts. She was glad. I was there at the end. She didn't say anything.'

God rest her soul.

In the Green Man the landlord told me that Brendan had done a runner, with £61.57p from the till. Well, pluck me G-string. That kind of money won't buy him much of an outfit. The landlord isn't bothering to prosecute. He offered his condolences and a drink on the house. However, I had to leave because I found that I was crying.

Somewhere in his 'notes', towards the end of Solution, John mentions the 'triumphal car' of Sol rising into the Above. If I had been more attentive I would have seen that this must be an allusion to Basil Valentine's *Triumphant Chariot of Antimony* (1604) which claims that 'in Antimony also there is a spirit which is its strength, which also pervades it invisibly, as the magnetic property pervades the magnet'. Like a magnet, then, the spirit of antimony draws out the essences of metals and draws down the celestial influences.

Artephius begins his *Secret Book* thus:

> Antimony is a mineral participating of saturnine parts, and has in all respects the nature thereof. This saturnine antimony agrees with Sol, and contains in itself argent vive [mercury], in which no metal is swallowed up, except gold . . . Without this argent vive no metal whatsoever can be whitened; it whitens laton, i.e. gold; reduceth a perfect body into its prima materia, or first matter, viz:- into sulphur and argent vive, of a white colour, and outshining a looking glass . . .

The sun enters Aries today. Time for all good Philosophers to begin the Great Work . . .

To do the Work is to enter into that spiritual unfolding which is natural to Western man and, perhaps, to all men. Its expressions and images, which once seemed so alien to me, are the fertile subsoil out of which our modern selves have grown. Its Secret can never be entirely lost, no matter how it is overlaid by baseness and dross, because our souls need it for salvation, and nothing is finally hidden from the ardent truth-seeking soul.

I shall not be taking up mortar and pestle. The Work has already done its healing work in me. What I have said concerning it has not been said well; what more there is to say cannot be said by me. I know that the Art is divine, for it recapitulates the original work of Creation, making that which the One was pleased to divide, indivisible again.

To do the Work is to enter into the myth of the individual, and to make of that myth, history – by bringing time to bear on eternal being.

It is clear how the alchemical terms – Sol, Luna, etc. – might act as a changing code for the actual substances. For example, Luna might designate stibnite until the latter is separated into its component antimony and sulphur. These might then be called mercury and (not inappropriately) sulphur respectively.

Alternatively, mercury might refer to the stibnite, and sulphur to the iron which is added to it. Iron and stibnite are the 'Red man' and 'white wife' to which Philalethes refers and which are 'married' in the proportion of one to three at the start of Solution. Smith tellingly refers to them as Mars and Venus – that is, not iron and copper, as the conventional interpretation suggests, but iron and antimony (stibnite) – which he mixes in the proportion of four to nine.

As the substances change their form or combine in different ways, they are reassigned different names from the common stock of alchemical terms.

What the prescription for the simple preparation of antimony omits is mention of the powerful vapour it gives off. 'No process can finally fail,' says the wise Philosopher Jacob Boehme [1575–1624], 'where the invisible universal mercury, or spiritual air of antimony is present.'

Thus, at the start of the Work proper, Sol is the spirit of antimony which flies into the top part of the glass, returning to 'open up the metals'. Below, his solid metallic counterpart shines like the moon beneath a surface layer of still unseparated 'mercury' and 'sulphur' . . .

If anyone would begin the Art, they must remember that the mercurial spirit of antimony is easily lost or destroyed. The purification of the ore may take months rather than minutes – no matter: any ignorant or crude attack on the antimonic ore will cast out the spirit, leaving him to wander homeless and unrecognised about the world.

Bradley has arranged for Nora to be buried in our graveyard. Despite the closure of the church, it is still consecrated. She is to be interred next to her mother, who died when Nora was a slip of a girl, and her brother Timothy who died as a boy.

This morning I was up in the beautiful wood which is known locally by his name. Two magnificent beeches, like father and son, act as portals through which it seems one passes over the threshold of spring. Dead leaves steam in the warm sun. Trees bud. Tiny leaves, exquisite as a baby's fingernails, burgeon. Plucky little flowers push up in the clearings. Birds' voices rejoice like peals of bells. It does the old heart good.

On the track at the crest of the down I was greeted by the sight of a young couple, one of whom was chasing the other around the Blind Dancer. The girl broke away, making a dash for it, hotly pursued by her boyfriend. He quickly caught her and together they tumbled down the steep slope, their laughter sounding strangely in the grassy depression. My happiness for them was tinged with the sadness peculiar to spring when, loveless, one is pierced by the happiness of lovers.

They were too absorbed in each other to notice me wandering above them. But as I looked down I was shaken out of my reverie: they were not young lovers at all. They were Mr and Mrs Hawkes, Michael's elderly – but obviously sprightly – parents. I had seen them but once, through the Manor window on that memorable Christmas Day, yet they were unmistakable. They must have come, of course, for their old friend's funeral. Under the circumstances, I should have been more surprised – even a trifle scandalised – at their levity. As it was, I felt like laughing aloud.

Suddenly it's possible to see, to *see* how small yet how integral a part of the great totality I am! How mighty Mercurius surrounds and enfolds me! How he dances over land and sea, through air and fire, and everywhere he pauses some image out of his superabundance takes shape and springs to life! All my life he has waited like a patient lover for me to return to him. It's impossible to express the joy I feel at knowing I *cannot* fall without falling into his arms. I'll turn inside out and wear my red heart on my white sleeve! I'll sprout wings and fly deep into the glittering desert places where, eternal as stone, the images of the Spirit lazily lift their huge heads like grazing beasts, and watch dispassionately as I plough into the Ground of all Being . . .

Can Mercurius ever be known in himself? No. He is the grand Image-Maker of a thousand names who never appears as himself because he is the empty Power who takes on the coloration of his surroundings. His face can only be guessed at behind his many masks, inferred from his images and especially those images which are common to the souls of all mankind.

But I believe, I believe he can be *experienced*. I believe, I *know* it's possible to transform one's self – to allow him to transform one's self – so that we may enter intact into his nature as he enters into ours, for our natures are alike. He can be fixed in our bodies as they can be made volatile in his Spirit.

Like death, the experience of Mercurius can't be an event in our lives; unlike death, we can live to experience him by virtue of his power to resurrect.

At the graveside Bradley beckoned me forward from the back of the surprisingly large crowd of mourners. Quite a lot of the 'new' villagers turned up as well as the old. Everyone arranged themselves instinctively at the distance from the grave which corresponded to their distance from Nora in life. Sweet Mr Salmon was there in an immaculate black suit and his best pink cheeks.

I took my place beside Bradley, conscious of one or two curious stares at my hatlessness. The vicar from Upper D— did his best to disfigure the ceremony with his affected and nasal intonation. But even he could not in the end mar the stirring words of the burial service.

Nora's death has left a great vacuum, not only in my life but also in that of the village. As I ascertained during our recent increased intimacy, Bradley will prevent the winds of change from rushing immediately into this sealed corner of the world – the Green will not, if he can help it, sprout streetlights, nor will the Vicarage be turned into a weekender's dream house complete with granny flat. But it's only a matter of time. Meanwhile he has said there's no need for me to leave. Indeed, he asked me to stay. I will – for a week or so until I'm sure he can cope (not that I have any illusions about being of any real use to him) and then I'll move on. I don't know where I'll go or what I'll do. It doesn't seem of any consequence. I am free of care, thanks to John. All I know is, that this short intense period of my life is over, and another more truthful one is beginning.

As the coffin was lowered into the shallow grave – a deep one would invite disaster from the watery ground – I thought of how, strictly speaking, it is impossible to die. We move from matter to spirit and – who knows? – back again from spirit to matter. Yet it's fitting to mourn because this lovely world will never be looked on again in quite the same way after the departure of Nora's vexed and indomitable soul. As he bent down to toss a ritual handful of earth on to the coffin, Bradley swayed dangerously and had to be steadied.

The crowd melted respectfully away. The only people at the funeral tea were Mike Bruford and his wife, Mr and Mrs Hawkes, Michael and myself. Bradley had gone off on his own somewhere. Michael, unusually silent, soon left. His parents are staying on at the Manor for a day or two to help Bradley. Mrs Hawkes told me how Nora had made Bradley promise not to send for her son. She was unwilling that her death should interrupt his life. (Her wish was bound to be respected in any case since no one seems to know Timothy's exact whereabouts.)

The Manor, which was such an intense focus of reality compared to my former existence, now seemed like a dream from which Nora's death had woken me. I left as soon as I could and returned here, to my proper home, where I can sit at this desk and commune with myself about events, and with John, whose absence, acutely felt, grows daily more like a presence.

*

This morning, Bradley tapped at the window. I invited him in. He stood stiffly in the study, refusing my offer of a chair like a child for whom any distraction might cause him to forget the message he had to deliver. If a man can be said to have aged overnight, that man was Bradley. He was still wearing his funeral suit, as if he hadn't yet been to bed, and it looked to be the only thing holding him together, like a scarecrow.

'Nora wanted you to have these,' he said formally – and handed me three folders of papers. 'They are the remainder of the Reverend Smith's personal papers. Before she died she asked me to say that he is yours now and that perhaps he always was.'

I asked him what she meant. 'I don't know,' he said quickly. It was obvious that he didn't relish this duty. 'She also instructed me to give you this.' He took from his pocket a small wooden box with a carved lid. It might have been the sort of box you keep on the dressing-table for hairpins and so on. I thought it might contain a piece of jewellery. As I fumbled with the little brass catch on the box, Bradley said sharply: 'Don't open it now!'

I looked at him in surprise. He shifted from his good leg on to his bad, and back again. His eye was fixed glassily on some distant object outside the window. The box was much heavier in my hands than it should have been for its size.

It was a tremendous moment. The certainty made my legs go weak. The birds sang very loudly outside. I could hear the shouts of children on the Green. A ray of sunlight lay like a trail of honey over the back of the sofa. The air in the study gathered itself up and settled itself down again like dust. Bradley's voice sounded curiously muffled:

'She said it was what she foolishly made her fortune with. She said you'd know how to use it more wisely.'

'John gave it to her . . . ?'

'No. She saved it from . . . down there' – he pointed to the floor – '. . . from the hot ashes . . . the broken glass. God forgive me.'

'You know what it is?'

He shook his head. 'I don't know anything. I only know what Nora told me . . . what she believed. And what I saw with my own eyes.' He lifted his right arm helplessly and let it drop by his side. 'It wasn't like anything I'd ever seen. And it was alive.' Abruptly he sank down on to the sofa.

'Won't you tell me about it?' I asked. He looked at me with his weary eye.

'There's not much to tell.'

All the same, he told me; and every word was branded on my memory.

Mercurius! I have you at last...

'*There is nothing*, says the Philosopher, *save a double mercury*. I say that no other matter has been named. Blessed is he who understands it: seek therein and be not weary.' Thus speaks Basil Valentine.

Our mercury is the spirit incarcerated in the blackness of matter, *spiritus et anima mundi*, both earth-spirit and Soul of the World who ascends in the vessel as an airy vapour and descends as a heavenly water, drawing down the powers of Heaven to Earth.

The other half of this *Mercurius duplex* is more sinister. It's the devouring dragon whose poison is fiery and corrosive:

'I am the poison-dripping dragon, who is everywhere and can be cheaply had,' announces the *Aurelia Occulta*.* 'My water and fire destroy and put together; from my body you may extract the green lion and the red. But if you do not have exact knowledge of me, you will destroy your five senses with my fire... I bestow on you the powers of the male and the female, and also those of heaven and earth... By the philosophers I am named Mercurius; my spouse is the gold; I am the old dragon found everywhere on the globe of the earth, father and mother, young and old, very strong and very weak, death and resurrection...'

The dragon performs the dissolution of the raw matter and produces the spirit. But the dragon is itself the matter which it dissolves with its poison; and its poison is the spirit which both dissolves and is the product of dissolution. Dragon, poison, spirit are one circular process as pictured in the self-devouring ouroboros.

Mercurius stands at the beginning and end of the Work. He is prima materia and stone, poison and healing Elixir, dragon and hermaphrodite. But he is also the Spirit by which the transformation takes place: Mercurius is the *Magnum Opus*

---

* In *Theatrum Chemicum*, vol. IV.

itself. THERE IS NOTHING SAVE A DOUBLE MERCURY. (Or as Paracelsus reminds us, a *doubly* double Mercurius: 'In respect of its nature, mercury is dual; that is, our mercury is fixed and volatile. In regard to its motion, it is also dual, for it has a motion of ascent and descent . . . ')

SMITH

My dear Robert,

It's Christmas Day. Just. I have your kind letter in front of me. A moment ago I went to the tree which Nora and I trimmed earlier (you should see it! There's something magical, otherworldly almost, about candles and tinsel on natural greenery. It reminds me of Tim) and I brought your present over to my desk and carefully unwrapped it. It's truly *beautiful*. The best of all presents. I shall treasure it.

Well, it has been a momentous evening for us both. Certainly the most important of your life and, I dare say, when in a while I go down to my Work for the last time, the most important of mine. That's why, with the short time remaining, I thought I'd write this to you. After this I shan't be writing again. There won't be any more words.

Anyway. I'll tell you about my evening:

10.20 p.m.: Nora bangs on the cellar door. She is upset and shaken. There is a crowd gathering around the vicarage. It's in danger of becoming a mob, she tells me. I ask her to come down. I stand her in front of the Rubedo. She is a little overwhelmed at the rising of Sol, but she is soon calm. She sways gently in front of it, pushing out her pelvis slightly as if showing the baby. The trouble above is forgotten.

She wants to know everything. I tell her what I can. She understands the imminence of the Elixir Vitae. I explain projection to her – how a crumb of the stone, concealed in wax to prevent its instantaneous combustion, is cast into a crucible of molten metal; which, if it is changed into gold, proves the Elixir.

Nora nods, speechless, her eyelids fluttering. However, presently her fears return. She finds it hard to breathe in the laboratory. She feels as though she is very high up, in some airless vertiginous place.

She finds the Egg uncanny, too much. Even I make her nervous in this new context.

I draw her a cup of water from the well. The cold crystal water refreshes her – but a moment later she is disquieted again. The water 'has something in it', some intoxicant. She shivers. She says, 'I feel like an intruder. I'm not wanted here. There's someone else in here. Something dreadful is going to happen. It's *haunted* in here. Isn't it?'

I put my arm around her and help her up the stairs. She is frightened by the hollow sound of her own feet on the wooden steps. As we emerge on to the ground floor I am struck by the noise from outside.

Of course Nora can't understand or sympathise with the Great Work in the way you might have. But really one does have to be chosen for it. I used to think I was. It exacts a price. It is costly. To a large extent (in retrospect, perhaps too large) you have to seal yourself off from life in order to cultivate the Art, to bring an end to all the groaning and travailing. Meanwhile, life has a way of coming like a thief in the night to steal from under your nose everything of value. The Work, one way or another, exacts blood. It must be innocent; it must be shed. That's the pattern. No one knows why.

Shall I tell you the Secret of our Philosophy, Robert? The secret of the Secret Fire? You'd laugh. You wouldn't believe it. You'd think it of such little account that you'd probably forget it at once. It's so close to us, Robert. Nearer than we are to each other (we're very near each other now). Nearer than we are to ourselves. Anyone who cares to can find it in my writings. It's safe. No one will care to. There's a certain irony in this, even a kind of gallows humour. Philalethes knew this: I sometimes detect a recklessness in his writing, even a kind of despair, as if he knew he marked the end of an era, like the last beacon before our new Dark Age. The Secret's only the beginning. We learn the secret of the Secret the hard way – by embarking on the Magnum Opus.

You'd be surprised if you knew how, for want of a better word, lucky I've been. How blessed. It may be that once in a while – what else can I think? – Mercurius likes to choose a really choice example of stupid confused sinful humanity just to show that it doesn't matter a jot through whom he does his works and displays the perfect laws which look like accidents to us. His power is such that he can use a stone as well as a saint. It may be that *that's* why he chose me. I say 'he'; I mean something else.

Nora runs across the hall, sits down on the stairs and covers her ears. The din is savage – saucepans banged together, sticks beating out rhythms on every sort of utensil, whistles, rattles, shouts and a weird high-pitched wailing chant. It goes on and on, now approaching, now receding; it seems to be outside one window but, as soon as I arrive there, it is at another. Now the awful clashing charivari is again outside the front door which begins to resound under heavy blows. A piece of brown paper drops through the letterbox. The hammer blows grow louder, the tinny drumming faster, the wailing wilder. On the brown paper there's a browner mess. Someone has seen fit to post a fat sausage of dog's muck.

As soon as I draw back the bolt, the knocking and riot stops. By the time I unlock the door and fling it open there's not a soul to be seen. I call out:

'If you'd care to come in, all of you, come in. If not, go away.'

There is a silence so charged that my voice cuts it like a cleaver. I scoop up the brown paper and carry it to the edge of the hall light's semicircle. I lay it beneath the laurel bush by the front gate, which is swinging open. I can hear the scurry of feet, then silence again except for a bell ringing in the distance, insistent, slightly hysterical, like a fire-alarm. I walk slowly back to the house. I hear the missile clearly before it strikes me but I make no attempt to avoid it. It's only a clod of earth, which hits me on the side of the head. A stone inside it causes a slight cut. I turn around to scan the darkness but I can't see anyone, not even a misty breath in the sullen freezing air. I pray that there will be no more trouble because, with Nora in my care, I can't be certain that I won't damage someone.

After a minute or so I return to where Nora is waiting, with her coat on, just inside the front door. Someone comes hurtling through the open gate, out of the blackness, breathing hard.

You're wondering how I can sit here so calmly, describing a calamity that's barely an hour old. It must seem inhuman to you, dear Robert, to whom suffering grew so intense in the end that you could not get your head free of its poisonous cloud to breathe. I am human, Robert. I feel, I suffer, I bleed; yet no longer I, but someone, something – he, she, it – feels, suffers, bleeds in me, Robert, and it is worse. Mercurius, Robert. *Mercurius.*

It wouldn't mean anything to you, perhaps to anyone. Not now.

'Who were those *people*? What're they *doing* here?' Janet asked, running up to us, breathless. She glances over her shoulder at the encroaching darkness. There is a new silence, an empty silence. The rout seems to have been dispersed as much by Janet's charge from the rear as anything else. She does look unstoppable. There is force in every angle of her face.

'Nobody,' I tell her. 'Just nuisances.' She turns her scorching face on me. She is still gasping.

'I went to Robert. He wasn't there. I found this. It's for you. Oh God. Oh Jesus. His glass. His lovely glass. It's all broken.'

We stand in the doorway, the three of us, with the big damned snowflakes settling like confetti on our heads, as I read the letter she has given me.

'It's all right,' I say. 'I know where he is. I'll go at once.' Janet's arm is already linked with Nora's. The women have an understanding. 'She'll come home with me,' Janet says. There's fear in Nora's eyes. Not for herself, but for me. She knows me so well. She has read the letter in my eyes. I walk briskly to the gate before I break into my mad run.

Dear Robert, I'm not going to come out with any big statements. We both know there aren't the words. Besides, it's not our way, is it? It was always the wary respectful distance we kept between us that kept us close. We never probed into each other's privacy, did we? I never even found out how you came by those two white scars. But you knew your work. The double pelican alone is testimony. You knew when to pick me up and whirl me bodily around that chapel of yours. I would like to have done the same for you, yes, to save you as you saved me. It's this failure that pains me most. I won't be able to make up for it now; the time is past.

Don't get me wrong. We can, we do recover the past. Once out of time it returns to us whence it has been hiding in all the nooks and crannies of our lives – returns in all its fullness to be enjoyed or endured. But never again can we get any purchase on the past: recovery is not redemption. The temporal act or omission stands for all time – unless we become the immortals we are, renouncing eternity and returning to time. But that's another matter.

I reached the fork in the track in no time at all. My feet wanted to carry me on up, to Nightingale Wood. Instead I went down to Beard's Pond. I didn't get far. The ambulance and the police car were there before me, blocking my path. A heavy sergeant relaxed when he saw my dog-collar. 'They're bringing him up now.' There was nothing for me to do. The sergeant suggested that I might tell the next of kin, seeing as how etc. I said I would.

I trailed up to the wood and lay down next to Tim's tree. There was nothing, no stars, no moon, nothing except the heavy snowflakes which fell unmelting on my face. I thought I heard a nightingale, but it was only the distant urgent bell of one emergency service or another.

From my study window I can see nothing. All the Manor lights are out at last. The heart-beat of my former parish has slowed to accommodate the long winter. When it's light I'll go to Janet and tell her that the man she was about to leave her husband for, and Nora that the father of her baby – my friend – is dead. Then I will get them through it because with God all things are possible.

As for me, dear Robert, well, I'll learn to live as you at least tried to live. Without consolation, without home. Without her. Without.

I'd like to have set eyes on it, the Stone; but that's a small thing. Perhaps the sight is, after all, too much for us mortals. It's waiting on me now; I can hear movement in the cellar. It won't wait for long. In any case I won't be going down now, will I. It's the price Mercurius has to pay for putting himself, the most powerful thing in the world, in our weak tremulous hands. The pattern is always the same [Smith's journal ends abruptly here in mid-sentence.]

[From its content it's clear that the following is the letter which Janet gave to Smith.]

Dear Padre,

I'm so sorry to trouble you with this. If there were anybody else I wouldn't.

In a little while I'm going down to join the big pike. There won't be any mistakes. I have some pills and booze to help me. I'd prefer to be left there but I tell you this in case you think it's appropriate to send the authorities along. I won't bore you with the reasons. You already know them.

My will is in the drawer of the table beside my bed. I leave my property to Nora and the baby, plus some money to Janet in case she wants to be independent at any time.

You will have opened my present to you by now. It's my best piece of blue. As near as I'll ever get it. Since you have been kind enough to take an interest I'll tell you the secret: copper. Actually it's no secret. Everyone knows that the medieval glaziers used copper to make reds and blues. The trick is to go on combining it with the beechwood ash under different conditions until you come up with the blue you want – in this case the kind that transmits the longer, redder wavelengths of light as well, giving it that extra warmth and glow. The rest of my glass I've broken because it's no good.

And now the difficult part of the note. You must at all costs *in no way* blame yourself or imagine that somehow you've let me down. I believe that, really, you know you haven't. It is my freely taken decision, being of sound mind etc. The only thing that has stopped me from killing myself before now is the thought that Janet will believe she has something to do with my death. *Make her understand*, John, please, that she has kept me alive. I would have done it long ago but for her. She is the best thing in my life, and loving her has opened up an *entirely different* world to me. I have no need to believe in an afterlife because I have seen heaven and it's here on earth. So don't be unhappy and so on because I myself am happy at the thought of an end to all the muddle, fatigue and so forth I've brought on myself.

My apologies once again, old chap, for being such a burden, and my thanks.

Robert.

EIGHT

Projection

EILEEN

I have read John's journals. (The poor lamb.) I see how they overlap and fit with the fragmentary lab notes that Nora gave me so long ago. I understand them – and, I dare say, *him* – as well as if they had been addressed to me alone. So much is illuminated! They are as precious to me as the treasure in Nora's little box. Indeed, they are part and parcel of that treasure. Everything is clear. I see my way now and marvel only that I ever thought it could be otherwise.

And so, my decision is taken. It was not so much difficult to take (although it was also that) as inevitable. I was, of course, free to act differently; but that would have been a poor way of acting, less like freedom than caprice. If nothing else, I have learnt that freedom does not consist in one's own will but in submitting to the will of the Spirit, discernible in the world as Providence. So, let his will be done.

Above the crippled church, ripples of white cloud have been left by the ebbing tide of pale blue sky. The gravestones are as bright and hard as facts against the deep-green undulations of grass. A light breeze ruffles the black rags of rooks circling the treetops. I may as well finish as I began – by writing down whatever is or isn't happening. What do I expect? Death? Not exactly.

New light has been thrown on the harrowing tale that Bradley pushed out painfully as if the sparse words, the memories of that barbarous Christmas Eve, were packed down tight with guilt, real or imagined I can't say, at having caused the Reverend Smith's death. It comes from Mr and Mrs Hawkes, denizens of the village at that time, both of whom *knew my dear John personally*.

With a kindness that is, I guess, characteristic, they invited me out for a drink yesterday evening. In the absence of Bradley who prefers solitude I lost no time in interrogating them about

John. There was a thoughtful silence, an exchanged look. Mrs H. tentatively remarked that, although she for one had the highest regard for him, he had managed to antagonise most of the village. They were, at the end, up in arms against him. But it was a *mistake*, wasn't it? – she appealed to her husband – all a mistake: the vicar was an exceptional, a good man. Mr H. nodded. Those last days, he said, were like a bad dream. Looking back, it seemed that the village was overshadowed by something. The sort of unhinging that can turn a crowd into a mob. 'It crept up on them . . . on us all. No one was immune, except the vicar. Perhaps Nora. That's why, I suppose, he was made the scapegoat. An evil influence, they called him. That was pure nonsense.' Did they know, I asked, that he was practising alchemy?

Mrs H. smiled, and then, seeing that I was not joking, looked puzzled. Her husband, on the other hand, was struck: 'Alchemy! Good Lord. *Alchemy*.' He couldn't get over it.

The rustling sound has grown very loud. No, not loud. It has not increased in volume but in magnitude. It is as if the single insect sound in my ear were really a myriad insects, at a distance, crepitating against the earth for miles around. A sound sensed as much as heard: a million moths' wings beneath the surface, fluttering to be let out.

To say that I had reservations is to put it mildly. There was certainly an instant of what I can only describe as stark terror. Yet beyond all that, beyond the mere shrinking of flesh and the horror which the natural part of oneself must feel when faced with its extinction, there was a sense of buoyancy and calm. The moment I took it, all doubt was dissipated. A thrill of the most tremendous happiness passed through the length of me. I cannot claim the serenity of a Socrates as he sipped his hemlock, and yet there is a certain tranquillity at having taken an irrevocable step and put oneself wholly in another's hands. My hand hovered at my mouth for a minute, an eternity, like the hand of one who holds their first love-letter in the mouth of a letter-box. Then I popped it in and swallowed.

*

Mrs Hawkes saw someone being taken away on a stretcher from the vicarage. It was, she realised, the same ambulance as the one which contained the drowned man. She had it in mind to step forward and look at the drowned man, but the screams of the burnt body on the stretcher distracted her. A woman in the crowd told her it was not the Reverend Smith, but ought to be. Mrs H. slapped the woman's face. Wisps of smoke floated out of the front door. Nobody seemed to know, or wanted to know, what had occurred. As soon as it was evident that the brief furious fire – if fire it had been – had consumed itself in the relatively airless cellar, the remaining onlookers melted away.

Mrs H. was prevented from entering by a policeman. The house was infected with dangerous fumes from the broken bottles of noxious chemicals. The whole cellar was still unstable, he said. The nature of the fire puzzled him. He said as much at the inquest. It was intense enough in one part of the cellar to fuse glass and vitrify stone; yet in another part, it had done no more than burn the furniture. A scientist supported his assessment of the anomaly, saying that, had the vicar been at the heart of such an explosion of heat, there would not necessarily be any identifiable remains. Depositions stated that the vicar had been seen away from the house shortly before the fire – running across the Green, at Beard's Pond. One even claimed that he was in the crowd watching the injured Bradley being brought out. Bradley's own deposition, dictated hysterically at the hospital and maintaining that he had killed the vicar, was sympathetically dismissed. If anything, he was the injured party. The well was plumbed. Nothing was found. The verdict was left open. Mr H. believes that he was vaporised by his own experiment; Mrs H. believed for a while, until she adopted her husband's view, that John would reappear, perhaps in a state of shock or amnesia. He didn't. The ill-omened vicarage was shut up. A new vicar arrived with a young family two years later. He had no success in the parish and was withdrawn. The church was left to expire in its own time.

Bradley was at pains to point out to me that he was not sober when he crept into the vicarage that Christmas Eve. He discounts himself as a reliable witness, even to those events which left him half-dead.

The study door was open as it is now. I see him gliding past it, his dark glossy hair swept back in a defiant quiff above his set, resentful face. The remembered exhortations of his cronies egg him on. He is tired, a trifle bewildered, but full of drink and reckless bravado.

He sees the Vicar seated at this desk, as I am now, his head between his fists; his black clothes damp and creased like rook's feathers. He is vivid before me, even more vivid than when Bradley described him, yet I do not see his face because of the fists clamped to his head full of Philosophy and memories and images of death.

Bradley moves like a ghost to the door by the stairs. The darkness in the narrow back passage is charged by a crack of light under the cellar door. He turns the handle. The door is unlocked.

I see him at the head of the wooden steps as I see the gravestones fade into the darkness. The sun's last afterglow dies behind Grimm's Down. My little tilted church settles deeper into the earth. The colour drains from the trees and the rooks bed down in their stork nests.

The night air blows steadily through my open window. It has no power to chill me because I offer it no resistance. It passes harmlessly through me. My amazed hand continues to write, but there's no medicine to help me express the scent on the breeze or the deep-down rustle and flutter which sounds more loudly now in rhythmic bursts like the swish of distant surf on a pebbled beach.

He is dumbfounded. There are none of the shabby accoutrements of sorcery he imagined; there's only laboratory apparatus. He stands at the head of the steps, unmanned by the stillness of the stone room. The oil lamps' viscous yellow light is held by the oddly shaped glass containers. It glistens in the drops of water on the flagstones by the black mouth of the open well. He feels dizzy, as if he were high up in the rarefied air of a mountain, closes his eyes – as I do, the better to feel his appalled heart accelerate, to hear the nervous stair creak under his swaying feet.

After Bradley had finished his story and wiped away his tears and left to withdraw into his private grief, I opened Nora's small carved box. I expected from its weight to find a greater amount than there was. Only a fragment remained – enough, however, to do such things to the light that my eyes hurt to look at it. It was indeed reddish in colour, deepening to ruby in the shade and lightening to burnt orange rimmed with icy yellow when I held it up to the window. Its glassiness gave the appearance of brittleness, but in reality it gave under pressure from my fingers. Yes, I would use it wisely, as Nora had hoped.

I brushed my hair out and put on my comfortable long white nightdress and took a last look at the world – the sudden swerve of starlings like shoals of tiny fish in the limpid azure air, the circling of the tattered rooks, the exquisite rippled clouds, the green luxury of grass. I lay down on the sofa, swallowed the Elixir in a teaspoonful of honey and waited for something to happen.

At first there was a warmth, real or imagined, in the pit of my stomach. It seemed to spread outwards, increasing in heat, making my arms and legs tingle. Then, nothing. I watched the rippled clouds disperse as a mauve bank of rain-bearers moved up from the west, outlined in gold by the sun sinking behind the curve of the down. The headstones cast grave-long shadows. Brightness fell from the air. The earth drew up its covers over the church, over Nora in her box, over the last steely glints of water in the shining meadows beyond the holy spring. Never had England looked more lovely.

I closed my eyes. The last shouts of the children leaving the Green for their tea lingered in the dusk like an echo, which by and by did not diminish but continued to reverberate like an insect's rustle in my ear. Then, nothing. And so I rose and, feeling nothing if not foolish, took up my pen again to record this nothing that is happening.

The sound expands. I see it now as the dim music the world makes, turning through space; now, behind the surf-like swish on the cold rattling beach of time, I hear the knock, like footsteps, of thirty years worn smooth by the Spirit's thundercrash. Scarcely breathing, I wait. Through the subterranean maze the thrilling surge ushers in His presence. It's only a matter of time.

On the dark night of the fire (Mrs Hawkes is speaking), the

vicar is called out on a pastoral errand: one of his parishioners has threatened suicide; a desperate, forlorn, drunken man. While the oblivious village is distracted by noise and drink, he walks into the black legendary water of Beard's Pond.

By luck or chance (she gestures towards her silent husband), Mr Hawkes is in the vicinity of the pond that night. He sees the awful pale thing floating in the water, plunges in, battles to land it and to apply artificial respiration. He's not to know that the shock of the icy black water stopped the man's heart before he could drown.

'I did my best to save him.' (Mr Hawkes interrupts.) 'I might perhaps have done more. I wonder sometimes. I think I did my best. I'm pretty sure I did. When I saw I was having no effect, I ran like the devil for the ambulance. I tried to save him.' I am taken aback by his obsessive fervour.

'Of *course* you did,' says Mrs Hawkes in a voice that suggests she has reassured him many times before. 'No one could have done more.' Visibly upset, her husband runs his hand through his hair and plucks nervily at the parallel white scars which run up his neck and over his jaw. Mrs H. confides: 'The man who died in Beard's Pond was, you see, my first husband. Robert was almost more distressed than I was. He arrived at my house frantic and, having broken the news, passed out. Curiously, my first thought was not for poor Arthur – he'd been killing himself one way or another for years – but for the Vicar. I left Robert with Nora and went to the vicarage . . . to tell him that Robert was all right, that it was Arthur who . . . Anyway, I never found him. I never saw him again.'

I watch Bradley tensing his muscles, quickly descending the creaking stairs, half-expecting to hear his steps echoed by those of the Vicar. He glances behind him, once, twice, and – there! At the far end of the cellar, sitting in its own red glow, the rotund glass vessel pulses – like a living thing, he said. Like the Sacred Heart. He is afraid.

The purple clouds bruise black; the breeze suspends its motion and settles gently on my shoulders like a velvet stole. It's night. No moon. Myself, I have no need of one. My skin is pale, transparent to the blood that circulates thinly and very fast, singing in my veins.

Earth sounds its great bass gong. Walls tingle like spines; arteries trill like telegraph wires. He's very close. (A gold flash, a trail of lightning, He snakes through the world's labyrinthine nerves.)

The young man stands aghast before the Stone. It's not a stone, he can't describe it, his eyes are seared. He averts his head from that convulsion of love – there's too much beauty and terror in the red invagination of matter, the white extrusion of spirit. Blindly he lifts the iron pestle that lies to hand. He hears, but doesn't heed, the cry from the stairs above. He swings the pestle into the redness. (But I am being unravelled. The dim conduits, all the meandering passages, light up – unloop at His approach; red as blood He suffuses my pale skin, tinges my white bones.)

For a second the cellar is drawn in on itself, an eerie vacuum. Then the glass groans, blows out. (He flows in a gold tide up the stone shaft, strikes the air, breaks into incandescence.) A clawed ball of solid flame leaps across the room with a muffled roar, halving him in one blast. His hair stands up in a clown's frizz of sparks; he flails in the jelly of his own skin. Pain and flames are a single howling envelope. He blacks out, comes round, like blinking; the cellar's a series of snapshots. There's a smell of burnt meat. Someone in black is at his side, raising him, shoving him up the stairs ahead, shielding him from the blaze behind. He hauls himself right-handed through the doorway as the stairs combust into ash. Sight and mind fail. He can barely take in the intolerable image below – the black figure frozen in white heat, niched between arcs of dancing fire, unconsumed, burnished by beating wings of flame, red streamers flying from his shining head – before it evaporates behind his eyelids. But I see Him ascend in stately splendour, scorching the rungs, lighting the narrow passage like a torch, shaking the ground with his tread. I am no longer I. His golden face rises over the dark horizon. He stands up, a red-gold rod in my body, in my head a crown of bursting stars, I AM

the one MERCURIUS, the fiery water, the cold fire, who shines in the air above, burns in the earth below. I run through the world yet no one sees me; I work wonders by the powers of sun and moon. Rejoice; for I am the red wedding of Heaven and Earth from whom I rise new-born.[1]

NOTES

Calcination

1. *'Maier says . . . '*
   Count Michael Maier was an influential alchemist who wrote, like so many other great Philosophers, around the turn of the seventeenth century. The idea cited by Smith is to be found in *De circulo physico quadrato* (Oppenheim, 1616). His best-known work, accompanied by a series of telling engravings, is probably *Atalanta fugiens, hoc est, emblemata nova de secretis naturae chymica* (Oppenheim, 1618), i.e. 'Atalanta fleeing' as a new emblem of alchemy. Maier's name has been linked with that strange 'theosophical' movement whose members called themselves Rosicrucians. In that excellent introduction to alchemy, *Prelude to Chemistry* (London, 1936), John Read describes Maier's introduction of music into alchemy and reproduces one of his compositions.

2. *' . . . the works of the mighty Basil Valentine.'*
   Basil Valentine, or Basilius Valentinus, was the pseudonym of an outstanding alchemist who was supposed to have been a medieval Benedictine monk of St Peter's, Erfurt. According to the *Last Will and Testament of Basil Valentine* (Strasbourg, 1645; London, 1671) his writings were hidden under 'a table of marble, behind the High-Altar of the Cathedral Church, in the imperial city of Erford', only to be miraculously discovered after his death.

   However, even a casual reading of his works indicates that this cannot be true – they were obviously written much later as the clear Paracelsist influence shows (see J. M. Stillman, *The story of alchemy and early chemistry*, New York, 1924).

[425]

In his book *The Chemical Theatre* (London, 1980) which, incidentally, apart from giving a brilliant alchemical 'reading' of Shakespeare's *King Lear*, is one of the best introductions to alchemy I've come across, Charles Nicoll is surely right when he says that Basil's works were likely to have been 'written by their "editor" and publisher Johann Thölde, a chemist and salt manufacturer from Frankenhausen, and the reputed secretary of the Rosicrucian fraternity'.

Nevertheless, as both Sir Isaac Newton, for example, as well as Smith, attest, Basil's treatise known as *The Twelve Keys* – published in 1599 – is among the most illuminating alchemical texts. (*The Twelve Keys – Duodecim Clavibus* in Latin, *Zwölf Schlüssel* in German – is probably a direct reference to Sir George Ripley's 'Twelve Gates'.)

According to a note written on the 1624 edition, the author's name is an anagram of *albus intus latens* ('The white one hiding within'). I don't see it myself: the rules of anagrams allow them to be one letter out; but with no 'v' and no second 'i' for a start, this is surely stretching it a bit.

3. '*As so often, it is Sir George Ripley who is most explicit . . .* '
Sir George Ripley was the most influential adept of the fifteenth century, especially on the Continent where his works were held in high esteem for over two hundred years. His date of birth is unknown but likely to have been around 1415. He was certainly writing about alchemy between 1450 and 1476. He died in 1490.

Ripley was canon regular of the Augustinian Priory of Bridlington in Yorkshire. In his *Compound of Alchemy* (which contains the famous *Twelve Gates*) he tells us that he travelled to far countries to study alchemy, including Louvain and Rome. Elias Ashmole (see Introduction) says that Ripley visited the island of Rhodes where he stayed with the Knights of the Order of St John of Jerusalem. (Another eminent fourteenth-century Philosopher, Bernard of Treves, is supposed to have learnt the secret of the Art while staying on Rhodes for eight years.) Ashmole also says that Ripley 'gave yearely to those Knights of Rhodes £100,000 towards maintaining the war (then on foot) against the Turks'.

This sounds an enormous sum; he doesn't mention whether or not it was paid in gold!

The *Compound*, dedicated to Edward IV, was published in 1591. His collected works, *Omnia Opera Chemica*, appeared some years later. Jung has written an extensive commentary on Ripley's alchemical poem 'Cantilena' (*Mysterium Coniunctionis* pp. 274ff).

At the end of his life Ripley became a Carmelite and lived as a hermit for the last two years before his death at St Botolph's, near Boston in Lincolnshire. He is of particular interest for the present work because of his seminal influence on Philalethes, who wrote five illuminating and profound 'expositions' of Ripley's works in *Ripley Reviv'd*.

4. '... *I recollected the Exposition upon the vision by Philalethes, sanest of men* ...'

Nothing much is known for certain about Eirenaeus Philalethes, who is clearly Smith's favourite Philosopher, and one of the greatest of them all. (It's customary now to point out that he is not to be confused, as he formerly was, with his contemporary, Thomas Vaughan – brother of the mystical poet Henry – whose alchemical pseudonym was *Eugenius* Philalethes.)

In his treatise *Secrets Reveal'd: or, An Open Entrance to the Shut Palace of the King* ...,* Philalethes claims to have attained the Philosophers' Stone in 1645, at the age of thirty-three. Other editions say he was twenty-three. (It may be that his publishers added on ten years because a twenty-three-year-old might seem too young to have made the Stone.) Jacques Sadoul (*Alchemists and Gold*, Jersey, 1972) suggests that both figures may be symbolical: twenty-three years might stand for the length of time it took to complete the Great Work; while thirty-three might be a mystical number associated with the age of Christ at his death.

However that may be, George Starkey reports that he was in America in 1650 (see *The oil of sulphur*, London, 1665). Starkey has been implausibly identified with Philalethes himself. He was certainly an alchemist, and studied for a time with John

---

* In Latin, *Introitus apertus ad occlusum regis palatium* ... Smith abbreviates the title throughout to *An Open Entrance* ... or *Introitus* ...

Winthrop jun. whose interest in medicine, mining and metallurgy is well known, but not his passion for alchemy, concerning which his famous library contained many works.

Starkey relates that his father took in a lodger at his apothecary's shop. The lodger, who spoke with an English accent and gave his name as 'John Smith', asked if he might use the dispensary behind the shop. Starkey senior said that he could, and detailed George to keep an eye on him. Through a chink in the wall, the young man saw the lodger melt some lead in a crucible and drop in some reddish powder. After fifteen minutes the molten mass was poured into a mould. George saw that it was gold.

At this moment the lodger, without turning round, called out to George, saying that since he was so interested he may as well come in. The shamefaced George went in and was instructed in the rudiments of the alchemical Art. The Starkeys naturally begged Smith – who confessed that he was also known as Philalethes (i.e. 'lover of truth') – to teach them the secret. He didn't. Instead he simply left one day, never to return. George wrote about these events when he returned to England from America in 1664.

The only other detail of Philalethes' whereabouts we have is that he was probably in Amsterdam in 1666 where he gave *An Open Entrance*... to a publisher called Jean (or Jan) Lange to be translated into Latin. This was the year in which Helvetius entertained the mysterious stranger who gave him a fragment of the Stone (see p. 474). Might Philalethes have popped over to the Hague...?

5. '... *as the fair Perrenelle helped her husband, the peerless Nicholas Flamel.*' Nicholas Flamel (*c.* 1330–*c.* 1418) was possibly the greatest and certainly the most famous alchemist of medieval times. His story is found in almost every book about alchemy. He tells it himself in a tract called *Nicholas Flamel, His Exposition of the Hieroglyphicall Figures, which he caused to be painted upon an arch in St Innocent's Churchyard in Paris*. My summary is from the 1624 translation from the French by one Eirenaeus Orandus:

Flamel was a notary by trade. He had a booth in the street of Notaries close to the chapel of St James of the Boucherie in

Paris. One day he bought for the sum of two florins a 'gilded book, very old and large' which was not made 'of paper or parchment . . . but was only made of delicate rinds (as it seemed to me) of tender young trees'. The book was by 'Abraham the Jew'. It contained twenty-one pages engraved with Latin characters except for five pages which were illustrated with the seven 'hieroglyphicall figures'. These symbolic alchemical pictures, four of which were said to represent the prima materia, included a scene showing a king with a great sword having babies killed by soldiers in front of their weeping mothers. Since this recalled Herod's Slaughter of the Innocents, Flamel had all the figures set in an archway in St Innocent's churchyard. (The archway survived until the eighteenth century. A drawing of the symbols was reproduced in many editions of Flamel's book and is still a popular illustration today.)

He laboured for twenty-one years to decipher the book, and especially the pictures which hid the secret of the First Matter. Together with his wife Perrenelle, who was as eager as he was, he tried 'a thousand broileries' but with no success. In despair he embarked on a pilgrimage to 'St James of Gallicia' (i.e. Santiago de Compostela, the famous shrine of St James which seems to have been held in special reverence by alchemists). He took with him an 'extract of the pictures' so as 'to demand the interpretation of them at some Jewish priest, in some synagogue of Spain'.

On the way back, he met in Leon a Christianised Jew called Master Canches to whom he showed the pictures. Canches fell on them with delight, saying that he had believed the book to be lost but was now overjoyed to hear that it was safe in Flamel's possession. Together they set out for France, with Canches interpreting 'the greatest parts of my figures' on the way. Unfortunately he fell ill at Orleans and died.

Flamel returned to his beloved Perrenelle and, knowing 'the first principles, yet not their first preparation', with her help worked for three years – years filled with error, study, labour and prayer.

'Finally I found that which I desired, which I also soon knew by the strong scent and odour thereof. Having this, I easily accomplished the mastery, for knowing the preparation of the first agents, and after following my book according to the letter I could not have missed it, though I would. Then the first time that I made projection was upon mercury whereof I turned half a pound, or thereabouts, into pure silver, better than that of the mine, as I myself assayed ... This was upon a Monday, the 17th. of January, about noon, in my house, Perrenelle only being present, in the year of the restoring of mankind, 1382.

'And afterwards, following always my book, from word to word, I made projection of the red stone upon the like quantity of mercury, in the presence likewise of Perrenelle only, in the same house the five and twentieth day of April following, the same year, about five o'clock in the evening, which I transmuted truly into almost as much pure gold, better assuredly than common gold, more soft and pliable ... '

By the time of Perrenelle's death in about 1413 (Flamel was devastated by the death of a wife he calls chaste, sage, discreet, devout and a blessing to him) they had 'founded, and endowed with revenues fourteen hospitals in this city of Paris ... built from the ground three chapels ... enriched with great gifts and good rents, seven churches ... besides that which we have done at Boulogne, which is not much less than we have done here'.

Flamel's account repays reading in full. It strikes the reader as having been written by a good, honest, loving man. His story is impossible to substantiate in full. However, it seems certain that there was a Nicholas Flamel living in the house mentioned in the story; that he gave considerable sums of money to various charitable concerns; that he was at the very least interested in alchemy. A marble tablet from his tomb, now in the Musée de Cluny, recounts that Flamel, formerly a scrivener (a trade that was unlikely to make him a fortune), left to the church of St-Jacques-la-Boucherie where he was buried – it was demolished at the end of the eighteenth century – rents and houses bought in his lifetime and that he also made gifts to various churches and hospitals in Paris.

6. '*Sort of* womanly. *Arms akimbo.*'
This remark of Robert's suggests that Smith's double pelican looked something like this:

Any vessel which had a tube at the top connecting back into the main body was often called a pelican because it resembled the shape of that bird when it bends its long neck over in order, as was thought, to peck its own breast. (In fact, this action signifies that it is regurgitating the food in its pouch.) In Smith's case, the pelican is 'double' because it has a 'neck' on each side through which vapours that have condensed on the vessel's cold upper surface can trickle back into the main 'body'.

The pelican was more sophisticated than a simple retort – usually a glass or ceramic globe with a spout – but less efficient for distillation than an alembic which had a long spout (and, later, a 'worm condenser', or coil, made of glass or copper) connected to a separate receiver.

The breast-pecking behaviour of the bird led to the belief that it was feeding its young on its own blood. Thus the pelican had a deeper significance in alchemy than as a simple emblem of the vessel: it was a symbol of the Stone whose 'blood' feeds its offspring metals so that they can grow; and, because of its self-sacrificial shedding of blood, it was also a common symbol of Christ.

The 'womanly' appearance of the vessel was probably chosen for aesthetic as well as practical reasons – alchemists were more or less aware of the sexual element ('sublimated' or otherwise) inherent in the Great Work.

7. *'The Smaragdine Table . . . '*
This is a literal translation of *Tabula Smaragdina*, usually known as the Emerald Table (or Tablet). One legend says that Alexander the Great found it, engraved in Phoenician characters, in Hermes' tomb. Another claims that Abraham's wife Sarah came across it by chance in a cave near Hebron where she prised it out of Hermes' stiff long-dead fingers. The Arabic writer Ibn Arfa Ras (d. 1197) asserts that Hermes, the son of Adam, was born in China, travelled to India and settled in Ceylon where he discovered a cave full of treasure, including a portrait of his father and, among the gems, a single enormous one, the Emerald Tablet. [See E. O. von Lippmann, 'Some remarks on Hermes and Hermetics', *Ambix*,* II–III, (1938–9).]

In fact, the Emerald Tablet probably derives from a Greek original, dating back to the first two centuries of the Christian era, which makes it one of the earliest alchemical texts. The sort of Latin version available to the first European alchemists, such as Albertus Magnus, can be found in Julius Ruska's *Tabula Smaragdina* (Heidelberg, 1926). Because of its huge influence on later alchemists it's worth quoting in full; and the translation I give here, only one of many, is from F. Sherwood Taylor's *The Alchemists* (Paladin edition, 1976, pp. 77–8):

1. True, without deceit, certain and most true.
2. What is below, is like what is above, and what is above is like that which is below, for the performing of the marvels of the one thing.
3. And as all things were from one thing, by the mediation of one thing: so all things were born of this one thing, by adaptation.
4. Its father is the Sun, its mother is the Moon; the wind carried it in its belly; its nurse is the Earth.
5. This is the father of all the perfection of the whole world.

---

* The Journal of the Society for the Study of Alchemy and Early Chemistry.

6. Its power is integral, if it be turned into earth.
7. You shall separate the earth from the fire, the subtle from the gross, smoothly and with great cleverness.
8. It ascends from the earth into the heaven, and again descends into the earth and receives the power of the superiors and inferiors. So thus you will have the glory of the whole world. So shall all obscurity flee from thee.
9. This is the strong fortitude of all fortitude: because it will overcome every subtle thing and penetrate every solid.
10. Thus was the earth created.
11. Hence will there be marvellous adaptations, of which this is the means.
12. And so I am called Hermes Trismegistus, having three parts of the Philosophy of the whole world.
13. What I have said concerning the operation of the Sun is finished.

Solution

1. '... *it has been the fashion to follow the Mutus Liber which depicts in dumb show the gathering of spring dew* ...'
The *Mutus Liber*, or Silent Book, by 'Altus' is a series of fifteen alchemical engravings first published at La Rochelle in 1677. Nothing more seems to be known about it. Although it appeared in the first volume of Manget's *Bibliotheca Chemica Curiosa* (Geneva, 1702), it is not mentioned in the text nor does it carry any description beyond the title. The twentieth-century Philosopher Armand Barbault (see p. 274) swore by it, especially the plate which depicts the gathering of dew to 'burn' the First Matter – sheets of canvas are dragged over a dewy field and then wrung out. The penultimate plate, which I find curiously affecting, shows the adept and his wife taking a vow of silence having completed the Work. Between them appears the legend: *Ora lege lege lege relege Labora et Invenies* (Pray read read read reread toil and you shall find).

2. '... *All hail to the three wise Marys – Prophetissa, Sidney and South!*'
This curious cry of tribute to women alchemists refers to Maria Prophetissa whom Smith has just been discussing; to Mary Herbert née Sidney, sister of Sir Philip Sidney who was the leading light of the English Renaissance under Elizabeth I; and to Mary Anne Atwood née South, a Victorian writer on alchemy.

Mary Herbert, second Countess of Pembroke, was a powerful patroness not only of many leading writers but of many 'chymists' as well, and she is on record as having spent a great deal of money annually on the Art. John Dee certainly visited her at Wilton as did his former pupil the Earl of Leicester (her uncle), and such alchemists as Edward Dyer and Sir Walter Raleigh whose half-brother Adrian Gilbert – another colleague of Dee's – was her 'laborator'. (See Nicholl, op. cit.)

Mary Anne Atwood née South (1817–1910) lived with her father Thomas South in Gosport, Hampshire. They shared an intense intellectual life and a passion for mythology and mysticism. Their profound study of esoterica, and of Hermeticism in particular, led them to the notion that alchemy was not simply primitive chemistry but a code concealing the secrets of the ancient Greek and Egyptian Mystery religions. While Thomas decided to write an epic poem on the ancient wisdom, Mary Anne tackled it from another angle in a large prose work entitled *A Suggestive Inquiry into the Hermetic Mystery with a Dissertation on the More Celebrated of the Alchemical Philosophers*. Her father did not bother to read the finished work, which was published in 1850, and a hundred copies or so were sent out to libraries and reviewers.

Then Thomas read the book. With Mary Anne's consent he promptly recalled as many copies of it as he could and burnt them on the lawn of his house, together with his own unfinished poem. (A few copies did survive and the book was reissued in Belfast, in 1918.)

The reason for this odd retraction, according to their biographer Walter Leslie Wilmshurst, was that they 'had upon their consciences the responsibility of publicly displaying a subject of extraordinary and – to them at least – sacred moment'.

Thomas died soon after and Mary Anne married the Reverend Alban Atwood in 1859. When he died in 1883, she lived on, increasingly reclusive, until her death at the age of ninety-two. She always maintained a keen interest in occult and mystical circles, but never wrote anything more beyond letters to her friends.

3. ' . . . *Jabir was born in . . . Tus . . .* '

Unfortunately, the biographical details which Smith gives us about Jabir belong to legend. In fact, scholars tell us, Jabir may not have been an individual at all. His writings may be the work of a whole group of people – a mystical sect, perhaps, like the Sufis. However, it *is* certain that they contain plans for new refined stills, recipes for the preparation of new salts and (for the first time) of nitric acid. The later Latin texts attributed to Geber were probably written by yet another author or authors: his *Summa Perfectionis*, for instance, a seminal work for the medieval chemist, might have been written as late as the second half of the thirteenth century.

4. '*You gave me* [Jung's] *last great book* . . . Mysterium Coniunctionis.' Since Eileen draws a great deal on the work of the Swiss psychologist C. G. Jung (1875–1961), I ought to say a brief word about him here.

Jung was the favourite pupil of Sigmund Freud until his views on the psyche began to diverge dramatically from those of his master. To begin with, he noticed that some of his dreams contained symbolic material which could not be explained by reference to his subjective experience alone. His intuition that the psyche might contain a deeper, impersonal level was confirmed by his patients. For, whereas Freud's patients were neurotics whose psychological problems could largely be traced to forgotten or repressed events in their early experience, Jung's patients were more seriously deranged psychotics; and it became evident that they often displayed dreams and fantasies whose contents could not be explained by recourse to their personal history alone.

In some cases, they spontaneously expressed symbols and myths of which they could not have been aware in their ordinary conscious lives. Jung realised that beneath the *personal* unconscious – Freud's subconscious filled with repressed memories, desires, etc. – there was a larger and wider *collective* unconscious. Here dwell the archetypes, forms common to all mankind, which unconsciously influence every aspect of our lives in as real and as powerful a way as the classical gods and goddesses (who are themselves, Jung says, manifestations of the archetypes). Jung also deviated from Freudian doctrine when he denied that sexuality was the sole motivating factor in the personality. He held that sexuality played an essential, but not the only, part in the psyche's overall drive towards wholeness or self-realisation. He rejected the idea of a mechanistic subconscious and proposed instead an unconscious which was dynamic, purposeful and intent on reconciling the oppositions in the psyche. This process, which he called the central concept in his psychology, was termed *individuation*. If successfully allowed to take place, it integrated consciousness with the unconscious to produce the Self.

When he first came across alchemical material, Jung found it rather silly. However, in 1928 his friend Richard Wilhelm sent him a book of Chinese alchemy called *The Secret of the Golden Flower* which led him to take the subject more seriously. Eventually he realised that his analytical psychology coincided with alchemy in a curious and exact way. For example, the Great Work of alchemy seemed to be primarily concerned with uniting the opposites – just as the individuation process is. However, the problem with individual case-histories is that they are never complete, but provide only bits and pieces of individuation like a tantalising mosaic. The Great Work, on the other hand, a procedure built up over the centuries, displays a richness and consistency of symbolism that no single case-history can match. The Work, in other words, is a paradigm of individuation; or, as Jung puts it in his autobiography (*Memories, Dreams, Reflections*, London, 1963): 'the experiences of the alchemists were, in a sense, my experiences, and their world was my world. This was, of course, a momentous discovery: I had stumbled upon the historical counterpart of my psychology of the unconscious.'

Jung's most important early alchemical writings are collected in volume thirteen of his Collected Works, *Alchemical Studies* (1967), which includes studies of Zosimos, Paracelsus and the Spirit Mercurius. Through Paracelsus he was led to discuss alchemy as a form of religious philosophy in *Psychology and Alchemy* (1944). Subsequently, wishing to discover what special problems of psychotherapy were treated in the alchemists' works, he hit on the *coniunctio* (conjunction) – a concept which corresponded to the psychological problem of 'transference'. He dealt with this in an essay called 'Psychology of the Transference' (1946). Finally, Jung wrote his own *magnum opus* – on which Eileen bases much of her analysis – called *Mysterium Coniunctionis* (*The Mystery of*

Conjunction, 1955–6) and subtitled 'An inquiry into the separation and synthesis of psychic opposites in alchemy'. (I abbreviate this, where appropriate, to *Myst. Conj.*)

5. ' ... *the martyrdom of Ramón Lull signalled the end of the first wave of our Philosophy in Europe.*'
I don't know quite what to make of this cryptic statement of Smith's with which he abruptly ends his short dissertation on the beginnings of European alchemy. By all accounts Ramón Lull, or Raymond Lully, was a remarkable man. He was born in Majorca and died at the hands of the Saracens in 1315. In between, there are many legends about his life but few facts. He is variously described as a sage, magician, alchemist, philosopher, healer, kabbalist, etc. He exercised a mesmerising influence over the European imagination for more than three hundred years, yet curiously there's no evidence that he wrote a single one of the hundreds of alchemical treatises attributed to him. Rather like Jabir before him, his name seems to stand for a continuous philosophical movement or school of thought.

6. ' ... *the marriage of Sol and Luna, on which the whole of Hermetic philosophy rests.*'
Hermetic philosophy made an enormous impact on European culture as soon as Marsilio Ficino translated the *Corpus Hermeticum* in 1460. These writings were believed, like the Emerald Tablet, to be the work of Hermes Trismegistus who was identified with the Egyptian god Thoth, scribe of the gods and divinity of wisdom. As a forerunner of Pythagoras and Plato, his works were accorded the status of divine revelation and they formed a vital philosophical framework for alchemy. One of the Hermetic treatises, the *Asclepius*, purported to describe the religion of the Egyptians; and, typically, it details the procedures for drawing down the powers of the stars – in this case, into the statues of their gods. Others deal with astrology and the occult sciences, and with sympathetic magic based on secret knowledge of the virtues of plants and stones.

Through this ancient knowledge, this *prisca theologia* or pristine wisdom, it suddenly seemed possible at a time of great turmoil and uncertainty to recapture the magical Golden Age.

However, in 1614, disaster struck when Isaac Casaubon, a Swiss Protestant and outstanding Greek scholar, showed that the *Hermetica* were not of profound antiquity at all, but were written in the second to third centuries AD – and not by Egyptians but by Greeks. (Dame Frances Yates tells the full story brilliantly in *Giordano Bruno and the Hermetic Tradition*, London, 1964.)

Clearly, Smith feels that this discrediting of the Hermetic Philosophy's origins (of which he can't have been unaware) does not detract from their truth; and, indeed, the Hermetic writings are interesting in their own right, containing a complicated pre-Christian philosophical mixture of Platonism, Stoicism, Gnosticism, Jewish mysticism and astro-magic! Above all, they stress the importance of direct illumination through contemplation of the cosmos as reflected in the disciple's *mens* or *Nous* (i.e. the mystical or intuitive faculty in man) which alone can apprehend the divine meaning of the world and provide spiritual mastery over it.

Incidentally, Yates (following A.-J. Festugière) mentions that the writers of the *Hermetica* seem to fall into two camps: those who believe that matter is evil, asceticism is the only way to salvation, and that the soul must rise up through the spheres of the planets to attain a return to the Godhead; and those who believe that 'matter is impregnated with the divine, the earth lives, moves, with a divine life, the stars are living divine animals, the sun burns with a divine power, there is no part of Nature which is not good for all are parts of God' (Yates, ibid. p. 22). Thus, whereas both camps are united on the crucial importance of *gnosis*, or direct knowledge of God, the first camp clearly has more in common with what we usually associate with the Gnostics, and, later, with Manichaeism, while the second camp is obviously more congenial to alchemy. However it's doubtful whether both camps can ever be wholly divorced from each other, just as the traditional Christian mystic's *via negativa* contains some remnant of the *via affirmativa*, and vice versa. (At a lower level, we might say that Jung's 'introversion' is rarely, if ever, unadulterated with 'extraversion', and vice versa.) Alchemy is paradoxical in that the alchemist himself shares much of the solitude and asceticism associated with the Gnostics while at the same time affirming the positive values and images of matter through his Great Work.

7. *'So, all in all it won't be long before the soul is done away with for good.'*
The day after I read this, I was amused to read by chance an article in *The Times* newspaper (9 December 1985) by David Hart about 'the Archbishop of Canterbury's report on urban priority areas'. According to Hart, the authors of the report 'are clearly embarrassed to use the word soul. It always appears between inverted commas, as though it has become archaic and cannot offer any meaning to modern readers if left to stand alone'.

Later on, the report apparently speaks of the soul thus: 'Philosophy has moved far beyond Descartes and has finally exorcised the Ghost in the Machine: few philosophers now allow for a separate component, or "soul", with which religion can be uniquely concerned ... Everything tells against the notion that there is a "soul" independent of social and economic conditions, to which an entirely personal gospel may be addressed.'

Hart comments: 'If the existence of the soul as an entity in its own right is to be questioned, how is compassion to be offered?

'What is compassion if it is not a spiritual exchange where one who is not suffering offers to take into his soul some of the spiritual burden of one who is? How can it be complete if the soul is to be redefined as inescapably qualified by the material world?'

Hart ends by saying: ' ... because he has been given a soul by God, [every individual] has an inalienable right, as well as the means, to make his own relationship with God. This is the greatest right of the individual; for the faithful, the right from which all other rights derive their authority.'

8. *'Like the hexed African its soul is lost ... to lie down and die.'*
Case histories on death by hex, voodoo, etc. can be found in the *British Medical Journal* for 1965. There is never any obvious cause of death – the victims literally lie down and die. Post-mortems show that the adrenal glands are drained dry, pointing to a

massive release of adrenalin (through fear?) followed by a sudden and critical drop in blood pressure, followed by death.

9. '*I've always found it hard to grasp the archetypes.*'
So have I. However, since Jung found proof of their existence not only in our collective myths but also in the dreams, fantasies and visions of the individual unconscious, and since they are central to his analysis of alchemy, I ought to add a word about them here.

Jung insists that the archetypes are determined only as regards their form. They are, as it were, empty – a priori possibilities of representation. He draws an analogy between them and the axial systems of crystals, which seem to predetermine the crystalline structure in the saturated solution without themselves possessing material existence. So, although the axial system decides a crystal's underlying structure, its individual appearance will vary slightly from every other crystal.

Similarly, the archetype is pre-existent as a kind of psychic 'axial system'. Its 'solution' is the collective experience of humanity, images of which crystallise on the archetypal 'axial system'. An image is not 'produced' – it already *is*, but is, as it were, in the dark. Like a crystal it 'grows' – towards the light of consciousness where it becomes more and more sharply defined. (The analogy of archetypes with crystals is particularly apt in regard to alchemy; and, since the latter probably included crystallisations, it may be more than an analogy.)

Thus we can never encounter archetypes as such; we can only infer their presence from the image or symbol in which they are clothed. The universal distribution of certain images – the sacrificial hero, for example, or the witch, the Earth Mother or the Trickster – might tempt us to call them archetypes, as indeed Jung does on occasion. But, as Eileen rightly says, they are strictly speaking archetypal *images*, whose ultimate and underlying reality can't be known.

10. '*The shadow is our dark* alter ego.'
Eileen doesn't mention the 'persona', a concept which helps to explain the shadow. If I understand Jung correctly, the

persona is a kind of mask we interpose between ourselves and the environment in order to adapt to the world. It is a compromise we have to reach in order to reconcile the demands of the outer world and the needs of our inner constitution.

In someone who is well adjusted to both inner and outer worlds, the persona – though still a barrier between them – will be flexible enough to constantly mediate between inner needs and outer demands. However, the danger occurs when we use the persona to hide our real nature. We begin to identify with our persona – to think we *are* our persona. It becomes rigid, like a mask grown on to the face, while behind it our real selves wither away.

In fact, no matter how elastic our persona is, it cannot embody or express all our characteristics, some of which are always left unfulfilled, repressed or underdeveloped in the unconscious. And these traits will tend to be the ones we dislike or fear – they will be, in other words, the opposites of those which are freely expressed through the persona. So, while the persona merrily addresses itself to the outer world, the dark unwanted aspects of ourselves fester in the personal unconscious like Dorian Gray's picture in the attic. They constitute the archetype of the 'shadow'.

The shadow won't go away; it has eventually to be integrated into consciousness. Until then, it exerts its occult influence over us to the same degree, and with the same energy, that we repress it. As its name suggests, it casts a dark stain over the world we gaze on, without our being aware of the fact.

Ideally, the persona should, as it were, destroy the brilliant image it has of itself and, voluntarily dying – sinking down into the grave-black shadow – it will be born again as the true self. Once it has served its purpose, the persona has to be grown out of or dismantled – if only because, while we can send it to a cocktail party, we can't send it to meet our Maker.

Separation

1. *'After some eight or nine circulations . . .'*
F. Sherwood Taylor (op. cit.) tells us that 'circulations' were 'the main feature of the process based on the Lullian treatises and as practised by the English alchemists.'

Circulation means *reflux distillation* – the evaporation and condensation of a liquid in a still or in a vessel such as the pelican. Each stage of the Work comprised a number of circulations, during which the alchemist observed minutely all the changes. 'The combination of two bodies', says Taylor, 'he saw as a *marriage*, the loss of their characteristic activity as *death*, the production of something new, as a *birth*, the rising up of vapours, as a *spirit leaving the corpse*, the formation of a volatile solid, as *the making of a spiritual body* . . .'

It may also be that circulation is analogous to the kabbalistic practice of *gematria*, a key process in Lull's system, which involved the manipulation of numbers derived from the numerological value of words (in Jewish mysticism, notably the Torah). Numbers, like the alchemical elements, can be combined and recombined through all manner of permutations until something transcendental is produced, either in the mind of the manipulator, or in fact, or both.

2. *'Abbot Cremer . . . strove in vain for thirty years.'*
Abbot Cremer of Westminster was said to be one of the earliest English alchemists, operating in the first half of the fourteenth century. His *Testament* was first published in *Tripus Aureus* or *The Golden Tripod* (Frankfurt, 1618) which was edited by Michael Maier and also contained Basil Valentine's *Twelve Keys* and Norton's

Ordinall. In Ashmole's version of the *Testament* (taken from an ancient parchment copy not later than the early fifteenth century) Cremer describes how his thirty wasted years were vindicated when he went to Italy and met Raymond (i.e. Ramón Lull. See p. 438). The latter was persuaded to return to England where he stayed with Cremer for two years during which time the Abbot 'obtained all the work'. Moreover, he introduced Raymond to King Edward (evidently Edward III): '... and being there with many promises, covenants and agreements moved and persuaded by the King, he was contented by the sufferance of God with his art to enrich the King, upon this only condition that the King in his own person should fight against the Turk, the enemies of God...'

The amount of base metal transmuted by Raymond into gold was estimated at 22 tons. Unfortunately the King did not keep his promise to Raymond who 'sore afflicted in spirit... fled hence beyond the sea...'

There's a lot that's dubious about this story. For example, Lull's death in about 1315 took place some twenty years before the events in Cremer's account; Cremer is not listed among the Abbots of Westminster, nor was he mentioned by the famous fifteenth-century Philosophers Ripley and Norton. It's interesting to note, however, that Westminster Abbey – like Notre-Dame in Paris – was probably a centre of alchemical practice. Elias Ashmole published in 1652 an engraving of an alchemical painting which could still be seen on an arched wall in the Abbey. He attributed this hieroglyphic device to Cremer. He also describes a former window in St Margaret's, Westminster, which symbolised in full colour the whole process of the *Magnum Opus.*

3. '*What I do not know ... is* the secret of the secret...'
This enigmatic remark of Smith's reminded me of a passage I came across in *Mysterium Coniunctionis* (pp. 172–3) where Jung contends that alchemy represents a genuine mystery. It can be interpreted according to contemporary understanding which, in our case, happens to be psychological – but this does not mean that psychology has the last word to say on the subject. 'If it is a

mystery it must have still other aspects' says Jung. 'Certainly I believe that psychology can unravel the secrets of alchemy, but it will not lay bare the secret of these secrets.' He expects that some time in the future the psychological explanation will seem as 'metaphorical and symbolical' as alchemy now seems to us. Then the Stone, or the Self, will develop a wholly new aspect, which is dimly foreshadowed in the psychological interpretation as that was in the alchemists' formulations, so that 'the investigator of the future will ask himself, just as we do, whether we knew what we meant'.

4. *'As that old wind-bag, von Hohenheim, insists . . .'*
Philippus Aureolus Theophrastus Bombastus von Hohenheim (1493–1541) is better known as Paracelsus, a name he may have assumed to indicate that he was superior to the Greek physician Celsus. He was a controversial character all his life, a strange violent man whom his enemies accused of perpetual drunkenness and debauchery.

He studied first at the university of Basel, and then under Johannes Trithemius, Abbot of Sponheim and an authority on magico-mystical doctrines, whose *Steganographia* was widely read by Hermetic philosophers (John Dee dashed off his *Monas Hieroglyphica* in twelve days after reading it). Next, Paracelsus travelled around the Tyrol studying minerals, mining and the diseases of miners. In 1526 he became Basel's physician and a lecturer at the university where he arrogantly rejected all other medical theories. Throughout his life he continued to travel far and wide, always studying Nature, collecting remedies and picking quarrels.

Alchemy was central to Paracelsus' view of the world. Its chief importance, however, lay in its usefulness for healing: he was only interested in curing disease, not in making gold. It was alchemy which extracted the essences (or quintessences) of things that he called *arcana*. These contained the curative 'virtues' of plants and herbs. (Paracelsus dealt almost entirely with vegetable matter rather than metals; to this extent he worked in the Lullian tradition.)

The essences or *arcana* were, of course, spiritual in nature and thus able to carry the vital astral influences without which the medicine would be ineffective; for *astra* – the stars – ruled every action and substance, and every part of the human body. Each disease had its particular *astrum*, and so did every remedy. If disease and remedy shared the same star, there was an affinity between them. This notion, that 'like cures like' or 'as the disease, so also the physic', was the basis of Paracelsus' homoeopathic remedies.

He saw the main purpose of alchemy as freeing the pure from the impure, the spirit from the dross, the quintessence from the four elements. Ultimately it is God who makes the medicine, but not in its pure form – Man must refine it. An alchemist is a 'Vulcan' who directs everything to its final end, whether it is iron to a sickle or sword, wheat to bread, stone to statue. Paracelsus saw himself as only one kind of alchemist, 'who takes away from medicine what is not medicine'.

The new Paracelsist physician therefore emphasised a practical medicine. He did not indulge in vague Galenist theorising, but experimented, distilled and extracted to produce cornucopiae of balsams, salts, oils, waters and essences. He was not particularly interested in the mystical aspects of alchemy which tended to become a separate discipline associated with 'natural magicians' like John Dee or speculative 'Rosicrucian' philosophers such as Heinrich Khunrath, Gerard Dorn and Robert Fludd, or mystics such as Jacob Boehme. In short, 'philosophy' became separated from 'chemistry'; or as Jung puts it: 'Paracelsus and Boehme between them split alchemy into natural science and Protestant mysticism. The Stone returned to its former condition: *vilis vilissimus*, the vilest of the vile, *in via ejectus*, thrown out into the street.'

5. ' ... *the legend of Wei Po-yang* ... '
Smith is referring to the author (around AD 120) of a renowned alchemical treatise called *The Kingship of the Three*. I paraphrase the legend as told by Joseph Needham in volume five (which is full of fascinating stuff on Chinese alchemy) of *Science and Civilization in China* (Cambridge, 1956):

Wei Po-yang withdrew into the mountains to prepare a gold

elixir. He was accompanied by three disciples and a white dog. When the medicine was made Wei Po-yang suggested that they test it on the dog. If the dog lived and soared into the air then the medicine was safe for humans; if the dog died, well, it wasn't safe.

The dog died. The elixir was clearly not perfected. 'What shall we do?' the disciples asked Wei Po-yang. 'You wouldn't dare take it now, would you, sir?' The master replied: 'I have abandoned worldly ways and forsaken my family and friends to go up into the mountains. I should be ashamed to return without having attained the *hsien* [i.e. the immortal; Needham translates it 'the Tao of the Holy Immortals']. So, to die of the elixir would be no worse than living without it. I must take it.'

So he took it – and fell down dead. The disciple Yu said: 'Our teacher was no ordinary person; he must have done this with some special intention.' He too took the medicine – and died. The two remaining disciples said to each other: 'The point of making the elixir is to achieve immortality. But since this elixir has brought death, it would be better not to take it and live a few decades longer.' And they left the mountain to fetch burial supplies for the two dead men.

Shortly after they left, Wei Po-yang revived; and, placing some perfectly concocted medicine in the mouth of the dog and disciple, restored them to life. And the three of them went the way of the immortals. Wei Po-yang sent a letter of thanks to the two disciples via a wood-cutter. When they read the letter the two disciples were full of regret.

And so the moral is: without faith and trust, no man can discover the elixir.

6. '... *the Green Lion who in truth is the Babylonian Dragon*...'
This is a quotation from Philalethes' *Introitus Apertus*... where the 'Sophick Mercury' – 'our water' compounded of 'Fire'! – is discussed. The author says it is truly a 'Chaos' with which he knows how to extract all things, even gold and silver without the transmuting elixir. If the reader wishes to understand this sophic fiery watery chaotic Mercury, he should

obey the much-revered instructions provided by the full context of Smith's quotation, viz:

> 'Learn to know who the companions of Cadmus are; what the serpent is which devoured them; what the Doves of Diana are which conquer the Lion by caressing him; I say the Green Lion who in truth is the Babylonian Dragon, killing all things with his poison. Lastly, learn to know the Caduceus of Mercury, with which he works miracles, and what the nymphs which he holds by enchantment, if you would fulfil your wish . . . '

(Cadmus is the character from Greek myth who killed the dragon guarding a sacred pool and sowed its teeth; the crop was men – the Spartoi – without mothers. Mercury's Caduceus is his rod entwined with two serpents.)

7. ' . . . *the first five stages . . . correspond to those in Sir George Ripley's Twelve Gates . . .* '
i.e. the first six, including Calcination as the first. Ripley apparently thought his first six 'gates' or stages were the most important because the remaining six – taking us from the White Stone to the Red – occupy only 61 stanzas out of the alchemical poem's 212 in all. They are Cibation, 'a feeding of our matter'; Sublimation, 'to make the bodie spirituall . . . that the spirite may corporall bee' (Eileen adopts this name for the single stage which follows her Congelation); Fermentation, Exaltation and Multiplication – all obscure processes, although at some point the Red Stone has been made because Multiplication usually refers to the process of increasing its power, while the last stage of all, Projection, measures the efficacy of the Stone by transmuting base metal to gold.

Conjunction

1. '*Mercurius with brooding wings oversees the conjunction of Below and Above.*'
I'm indebted to Eileen for the insight that Above and Below do not refer exclusively to the top and bottom of the vessel respectively. This may have been the case when, in Separation, say, Sol condensed at the top of the glass and (himself a distillate of Luna) ran back down to the matter below, where his properties – now fierce and 'leonine' – divided it into our sulphur and our mercury, or 'body' and 'soul'. Here, however, the matter seems to have become more quiescent and less volatile so that the Above refers simply to the matter's *surface layer* of 'lunatic' blackness which lies over the clear 'solar' 'water' Below. This is the incestuous coitus between Sol and Luna which sows the 'chrysosperm' (gold-seed) of the *Filius*, or divine Son who is also the Stone. Eileen would no doubt add that Sol is the ego-consciousness which is swallowed up by, or sinks down into, the unconscious 'blackness' of Luna *qua* new moon or dragon's womb.

2. '*So says Thomas Norton whose* Ordinall of Alchemy, *copied by Smith from Ashmole . . .*'
Norton's Ordinall, written in 1477, was first published in Latin at Frankfurt in 1617. The original English version did not surface until 1652 – in Ashmole's *Theatrum Chemicum Britannicum*.

Norton came from a prominent Bristol family. He was a privy councillor and probably pretty well-off. He says he began to study Philosophy at an early age, riding over a hundred miles to meet his master who, it has been widely assumed, was Sir George Ripley. However, internal evidence militates against this, as does the testimony of his great-grandson Samuel Norton, also an alchemist. At any rate, he stayed with his master for forty days, during which time he claims to have learnt all the secrets of alchemy. He was only twenty-eight when he attained the Philosophers' Stone which was apparently stolen from him. It was composed of two materials, male and female in nature, he says: a 'White worke or chosen Markasite' and 'a second Stone called Magnetia'. No other materials are required except 'Sal Armoniak and the Sulphur of Mettals'.

More interesting than this information is his tale of Thomas Daulton who had a large store of the 'red medicine'.

Daulton is described as a good man, 'clerke' to a certain Sir John Delves, who was 'squire in confidence' to the King (Edward IV). Despite an oath of secrecy, Sir John told the King that Daulton had made him a thousand pounds' worth of gold in less than half a day. Meanwhile, another of the King's squires, Thomas Herbert, had brought Daulton from an abbey in Gloucestershire to the Court.

Daulton told the King that he'd thrown his medicine into a lake to be rid of the problems it had already caused him. The King let him go. But Thos. Herbert lay in wait for him and took him off to his seat in Troy, Monmouthshire. He kept Daulton there for four years, but Daulton refused, even under threat of execution, to reveal the secret of the medicine. He was eventually released, and died soon after.

Some of this can be substantiated. Sir John Delves and Lord Herbert of Troy, at least, were real people; and what Norton subsequently tells us about them is historical fact – i.e. that Delves died at the battle of Tewkesbury in 1471, and that Herbert died a little before, not long after the alleged death of Daulton.

3. '*Charnock . . . was given a second chance to learn the Great Secret . . .*'
In his amusing autobiographical poem, the 'Breviary of Alchemy', Thomas Charnock (*c.* 1524–81) tells us that he began to travel all over England in his early twenties looking for someone to teach him the secret of the Art. At the age of twenty-eight he was finally given it by a man he refers to as 'I.S.' or 'Sir James', who was a 'Priest of the close of Salisbury'. (Interestingly, Sir James

was not told the secret. It was 'put into his head' by God as he was lying in bed.) However, when Charnock's apparatus went up in flames one fateful New Year's Day, the secret went up with it – he'd failed to copy it down or to memorise it.

He could not proceed with the Great Work until years later, when he came across an old blind man at an inn who seemed to know a lot about the Art but who swore he would only reveal his knowledge to one Thomas Charnock, whose reputation for Philosophy made him worthy of the trust. Charnock eagerly made himself known to the old man and duly received the secret in 'three or four words'. The old blind man turned out to be a former Prior of Bath Abbey who had himself got the secret, via some unknown intermediary, from Sir George Ripley. His name was William Holloweye, sometimes known as Gibbs, and he was the first Prior of Bath Abbey before its dissolution in 1525, more than thirty years before. At that time he hid his Red Stone in a wall, but, returning to collect it a few days later, he found it gone. He immediately lost his wits and wandered about the countryside. Later, having also lost his sight, he presumably lost his ability to remake the Red Stone.

Charnock returned to the Work with renewed zeal. After many months, just as he was about to succeed, he was pressed into the army which was being sent over to defend Calais in 1557–8. In a rage of disappointment he took a hatchet to his equipment and smashed the whole lot to pieces!

On his return from the war, he *again* took up the Work – only to be foiled once again on the brink of success when his daughter carelessly allowed the fire to go out. He laboured on, suffering countless setbacks, until his death more than twenty years later.

He says very little about his actual operations – except that they consisted of 'circulations', each of which lasted a week. Since he performed 610 of these, he must have been at it for nearly twelve years.

F. Sherwood Taylor (op. cit.) tells us that Charnock made a note in 1574 to the effect that he believed he had made the White Stone. However, he was still at work two years later – trying for the Red Stone, perhaps – and in 1581 he died.

Ashmole adds some interesting corroboration of the Prior of

Bath Abbey's story about hiding his Red Stone in a wall. He cites a tale he received from a Mr Rich, 'Wakeman Towne Clearke of Bath', who in turn often heard it himself from a certain Old Anthony (who had died about twelve years before) and from two shoemakers of Bath called Belcher and Foster, who had died about twenty years before. These men had testified that, after the dissolution of Bath Abbey, during the pulling down of some of its walls, a 'Glasse' full of 'Red Tincture' was found. This Tincture 'being flung away to a dunghill, forthwith it coloured it exceeding red'. The dung was later taken away by boat and spread in 'Bathwicke field, and in the places where it was spread, for a long tyme after, the Corne grew wonderfully ranke, thick, and high: insomuch as it was there look'd upon as a wonder'.

This, then, was the fate of the Prior's 'Red Stone', which, incidentally, had been made with the help of the famous hot spring at Bath, which provided the gentle heat required by the Great Work.

In *Ambix*, vol. II, p. 153, F. Sherwood Taylor quotes the report of a clergyman named Pascal who, hearing that a manuscript had been found in a wall of Charnock's house at Combwich in Somerset, went down there to investigate. (This was about a century after Charnock's death in 1581.) Pascal saw the place where the manuscript was hidden, and also ' . . . saw a little roome, and contrivance he had for keeping his worke, and found it ingeniously ordered, so as to prevent a like accident to that which befell him New Years day 1555, and this pretty place joyning as a closet to his Chamber was to make a Servant needless, and the work of giving attendance more easy to himself. I have also a little iron instrument found there which he made use of about his Fire. I saw on the dore of his little Athanor-room (if I may so call it) drawne by his owne hand, with coarse colours and worke but ingeniously, an Embleme of the Worke, at which I gave some guesses, and soe about the walls in his Chamber, I think there was in all 5 panes of his works, all somewhat differing from each other, some very obscure and almost worne out.

They told me that people had been unwilling to dwell in that house, because reputed troublesome, I presume from some traditional stories, of this person, who was looked on by his Neighbours as no better than a Conjuror. As I was taking Horse to come home from this pleasant entertainment, I see a pretty antient man come forth of the next door ... He told me he had heard his Mother (who died about twelve or fourteen years since and was eighty years of age at her decease) often speak of him [i.e. Charnock]. That he kept a fire in, divers years; that his daughter lived with him, that once he was gon forth, and by her neglect (whome he trusted it with in his absence) the fire went out, and so all his work was lost'.

4. *'This is the last dispensation as Joachim of Fiore foretold.'*
The medieval theologian also known as Joachim of Flora or Floris renewed the idea of 'ages' of development in history – as against Augustine's idea that the last age was upon us and being enacted under the Church. Joachim reckoned that the ages of the Father and the Son were already over and that the age of the Holy Ghost had been inaugurated.* He believed that the ages overlapped so that one age is born out of another (in this way he was a forerunner of Marx and other utopianists).

5. *'Alexander Seton ... refused to say a word.'*
The story of Seton overlaps with that of another famous alchemist, Michal Sendivoj or Michael Sendivogius, a Pole who at this time was unsuccessful at the Art. Tradition claims that he rescued Seton who, out of gratitude, gave him some of the transmuting powder – but without telling him the secret of its manufacture. Seton, being poorly after all that torture, died a few months later, in 1604. Sendivogius married his widow in the hope of discovering the Great Secret, but to no avail.

Subsequently Sendivogius is supposed to have begun passing himself off as a true adept, performing numerous transmutations with Seton's powder and even publishing Seton's manuscripts as his own. When the powder ran out, he resorted to trickery to keep up his fraudulent claims. He died in his bed at the age of seventy.

---

* Smith overlooks the fact that this age was to end in AD 1260.

However, in *Alchemy: The Great Work* (Wellingborough, 1984), Cherry Gilchrist cites evidence to suggest that the story of Sendivogius' fraudulence was fabricated in the seventeenth century by a Frenchman, Pierre Des Noyers, who had a strong prejudice against Poles, and especially against Sendivogius.

It's probable that he was in fact a master of alchemy and the true author of *Novum Lumen Chemicum* (*A New Chemical Light*, Prague, 1604) by which contemporary Philosophers set such store. He may well have rescued Seton (whom he could have met at the University of Altdorf) from prison, but he never married his widow. Instead, Sendivogius rose high in the favour of the Emperor Rudolf II under whose rule Prague had become the great European centre of alchemy. This supports another often-repeated story, namely that Sendivogius instructed Rudolf in a successful transmutation (whether or not with Seton's 'powder', we don't know). The Emperor was himself an expert on alchemy and, having imprisoned any number of frauds, would not have been easily taken in by Sendivogius. Nor would Rudolf have given him a high appointment at Court if he weren't convinced of the Pole's genuineness.

At Rudolf's death, incidentally, his treasure was found to contain four tons of gold and three of silver, all in small ingots. Either his passion for alchemy paid off, or he had inherited the last spoils of the Habsburg plundering of Mexico and Peru!

6. '... *with the sudden rash of transmutations ... the alchemists were deliberately drawing attention to themselves.*'

There may be something in this insight of Eileen's. It was certainly fashionable in the seventeenth century for men of high standing to have coins struck from alchemical gold. Smith notes that King Gustavus Adolphus of Sweden – that military genius of the Thirty Years' War – ordered a coin to be struck from gold he had seen transmuted before his very eyes. His portrait is on one side and the signs for Mercury and Venus on the other.

Elsewhere I've read that Vienna's Kunsthistorisches Museum has one medal cast from alchemical gold before His Serene Highness Philip, Count Palatine of the Rhineland, on 31 December 1716;

and another, of alchemical silver, attributed to a transmutation in 1675 by Johann Joachim Becher.*

In 1647 the Emperor Ferdinand III witnessed a projection by an alchemist called J. P. Hofmann. The gold medal struck on this occasion included an elaborate design and an inscription which says that five drops of the 'tincture' transmuted 1 lb. of iron into gold. In 1648 Ferdinand himself performed a projection. After taking extraordinary precautions against fraud, the Emperor took a single grain of tincture (given to him by an alchemist called Richthausen) and, casting it on to 3 lb. of mercury, turned the whole lot to pure gold. The coin which commemorated this event was apparently worth 300 ducats.

---

* J. J. Becher (1635–82) was influential in forming the theory of phlogiston, by which combustion was explained throughout the eighteenth century.

Putrefaction

1. '... *Swedenborg's vision of the great fire in Stockholm* ...'
Emanuel Swedenborg (1688–1772), the Swedish scientist and visionary whose mystical ideas became the basis of a religious movement, was about to sit down to dinner in Gothenburg one day when he suddenly turned pale and went outside. When he returned he told the assembled company that a great fire had broken out in Stockholm, 300 miles away, and that his own house there was under threat. He paced up and down anxiously for about two hours until, at about eight o'clock, he said: 'Thank heavens, the fire is under control; it had almost reached my doorstep.' All this turned out to be correct, down to the last detail. This was only one of several well attested precognitions that Swedenborg had in the course of his long life.

2. '..."the adept had always looked for the effects of his stone outside... and only during the sixteenth century pointed... to an inner effect..."'
Jung was naturally keen to show that alchemists were aware of the psychic nature of the Great Work. He detects such an awareness in occasional references to the idea that the substance which harbours the divine secret can be found inside the human body as well as outside. For example, in *Sermo de transmutatione metallica* (an early work that can be found in *Artis Auriferae*, Basel, 1593), 'Morienus' (the author) says to King Kallid: 'For this substance is extracted from you, and you are its mineral' (i.e. raw material).

However, as I've already indicated in my footnote, it was Gerard Dorn who especially excited Jung with remarks such as 'out of other things thou wilt never make the One, until thou hast first become One thyself' (*Philosophia meditativa*) or 'Transmute yourselves from dead stones into living philosophical stones!' (*Speculativae Philosophiae, gradus septem vel decem continens*.) In this same treatise Dorn writes:

'Within the human body there is hidden a certain metaphysical substance, known to only the very few, whose essence it is to need no medicament, for it is itself uncorrupted medicament.' Dorn sometimes calls this substance – the secret fire – *caelum* (sky, heaven); at other times, as here, he calls it *veritas* (truth):

> As faith works miracles in man, so this power, the efficacious truth, brings them about in matter. This truth is the highest power and an impregnable fortress wherein the Philosophers' Stone lies safeguarded.

A number of Dorn's treatises can be found in *Theatrum Chemicum*, vol. 1 (Ursel, 1602; Strasbourg, 1613).

Congelation

1. '... *the great and learned Dr Dee whose* Monas Hieroglyphica *I believe he knew by heart.*'
It has been well established that Dr John Dee (1527–1608) was of central importance in the English Renaissance and the revival of Hermeticism which, together with the Jewish Kabbalah and alchemy, was to form a quasi-religious system of *magia naturalis,* or natural magic, that would fulfil the religious and mystical needs of those who were disillusioned by the schism between Catholicism and Protestantism. Dee was the very type of the Renaissance magus who, it has been suggested, inspired Shakespeare's King Lear and Prospero in *The Tempest.* (See Frances A. Yates, *Giordano Bruno and the Hermetic Tradition,* London, 1964, and *The Occult Philosophy in the Elizabethan Age,* London, 1979. Also, Peter J. French, *John Dee: the World of an Elizabethan Magus,* London, 1972.)

Dee was well versed in the complexities of alchemy long before he took up serious laboratory work with Edward Kelley – the largest number of manuscripts by any one author in his library were those of Ramón Lull (and the pseudo-Lullian authors), followed by those of Roger Bacon and his followers. *Monas Hieroglyphica,* or the Hieroglyphic Monad (Antwerp, 1564), was an early example of an esoteric, purely speculative alchemical work. Dee describes it in his dedication to Emperor Maximilian II (father of Rudolf II) as a 'magic parable' which emphasises the spiritual transformation of man over the chemical transformation of metals. The hieroglyph itself had a profound symbolic meaning for Dee who thought that contemplation of it could perform miraculous psychic changes. Peter French (ibid.) calls it 'a unified construction of significant astro-alchemical symbols that embodied the underlying unity, or *monas*, of the universe'. It looks like this:

The philosophy of the *Monas* is far too complex to go into. (Interested readers are referred to C. H. Josten's excellent translation and commentary on it in *Ambix*, vol. XII, 1964.) Suffice it to say, the *Monas* played a key part in attracting and controlling the supernatural forces from the celestial realm and effecting a corresponding elevation of the terrestrial realm – which resulted in a 'Gamaaeea', or marriage, performed through the mediation of 'our mercury'. This had its mystical counterpart in the person of the magus himself, such that 'he who fed [the monad] will first himself go away into a metamorphosis and will very rarely be held by mortal eye. This . . . is the true invisibility of the magi which has so often (and without sin) been spoken of, and which . . . has been granted to the theories of our monad'.

Smith, as well as his 'master', was obviously familiar with the *Monas* as can be seen in his reference to John Dee's 'mercury' in the meditation *De Anima Mundi*.

2. ' . . . [Dee] *was visited by most of the English Renaissance's leading lights* . . . '
At one time or another Dee taught the poet and diplomat Edward Dyer; Robert Dudley, Earl of Leicester; and, above all, that doyen of the English Renaissance, Sir Philip Sidney, who was a regular

visitor to Dee's house and library. (Smith has already extolled the virtue of his sister, Mary Herbert, Countess of Pembroke, who entertained many Philosophers at Wilton House, probably including such continental Hermeticists as Giordano Bruno.) Sir Walter Raleigh was also attached to this circle, along with the Earl of Northumberland, popularly known as the 'Wizard Earl'.

Raleigh's particular interest lay in medicinal distillation (see Nicholl, op. cit.). When James I's son Prince Henry lay dying in 1612, the Queen herself asked Raleigh to compound his 'great cordial' for him. This cordial passed into legend: Robert Boyle, the 'father of chemistry', was rumoured to have the recipe and, according to Aubrey, 'does great cures by it'. 'In 1662,' writes Charles Nicholl, 'the diarist John Evelyn recorded accompanying Charles II to "Monsieur Febure, his chemist" to see his "accurate preparation" of Sir Walter's cordial. Lefevre's version was a cocktail of distilled herbs, mixed with powders of pearl, red coral, deer's horn, ambergris, sugar, musk and antimony, but it has been plausibly suggested* that Raleigh's secret ingredient was some form of quinine from his South American expeditions.'

Raleigh spent most of his last thirteen years imprisoned in the Tower of London where he devoted himself to alchemy, setting up a still-house in the garden by converting 'a little Hen-house ... where he doth spend his time all the day in his distillations', as a new lieutenant wrote in 1605. He was soon joined by the 'Wizard Earl' who immediately set up a laboratory. We know from accounts preserved in Alnwick Castle (and quoted by Nicholl) that 'bricks, tyles and necessaries for makinge the furnace' cost 18s. 6d., two lead cisterns 15s. 10d., two stills 8s. 6d. and various glassware 31s. 6d.

3. *'With this powder Kelley performed numerous transmutations . . .'*
In his diary entry for 19 December 1586 Dee records that Kelley projected his powder 'in the proportion of one minim' upon an ounce and a quarter of crude mercury and produced nearly an ounce of best gold. This was witnessed by Edward and Francis Garland.

---

* By Robert Lacey in *Sir Walter Raleigh* (London, 1973).

The French chemist Nicolas Barnaud saw a drop of Kelley's tincture transmute a pound of mercury into gold at the house of Rudolf's chief alchemist, Tadeas Hajek.

Edward Dyer attended a transmutation in Prague in 1588, which he later described to John Whitgift, Archbishop of Canterbury:

> I am an eyewitness thereof, and if I had not seen it, I should not have believed it. I saw Master Kelley put of the base metal into the crucible, and after it was set a little upon the fire, and a very small quantity of the medicine put in, and stirred with a stick of wood, it came forth in great proportion perfect gold, to the touch, to the hammer, to the test. (Quoted in Ralph Sargent, *At the court of Queen Elizabeth: The life and lyrics of Sir Edward Dyer*, London, 1935.)

In his notes to his *Theatrum Chemicum Britannicum*, Elias Ashmole adduces this testimony:

> ...I have received it from a credible person, that one Broomfield and Alexander Roberts told him they had often seen Sir Ed. Kelly [*sic*] make projection, and in particular upon a piece of Metall cut out of a Warming pan, and without Sir Edwards touching or handling it, or melting the Metall (onely warming it in the fire) the Elixir being put thereon, it was transmuted into pure Silver.

Smith's unusually lenient view of Kelley seems to me to be worthy of further research.

4. '*Our Philosophy doesn't distinguish between* Anima Mundi *and* Spiritus Mundi . . . '
Plato described the *Anima Mundi* in detail in the *Timaeus*, after which the concept became a regular feature of neo-Platonic (and Hermetic) philosophy. Jung calls the *Anima Mundi* 'the feminine half of Mercurius'. He might just as well have called the *Spiritus Mundi* the masculine half. Smith is clearer on the subject: Mercurius is assigned either gender at different

times in the course of the Great Work; but, as prima materia and Philosophers' Stone, he or she represents respectively the unity of being before gender arises and the reunion of opposites where both genders are synthesised in the hermaphrodite. It's in this way, I realise, that he uses the capitalised Spirit – to signify the androgynous Mercurius who is both prior and subsequent to 'its' division into masculine and feminine aspects represented by Sol and Luna, King and Queen, Sulphur and Mercury, etc.

5. '... gravity *whose mystery will never be unravelled by Science's mechanistic explanations ...*'
I don't understand this remark but it is reminiscent of the neo-Platonist Henry More's brave attempt to modify the Cartesian world-view, of which he approved by and large, fearing only that the complete severance of spirit from matter would end in tears. He wrote to Descartes, but failed to convince the stubborn dualist that he should temper his extreme position.

In *The Immortality of the Soul* (1659) More advanced the idea of a 'universal spirit, or soul of the world, to compensate for the inadequacies of mechanism by the directing of natural mechanical motions'. However, More did not go so far as to allow the interconvertibility of spirit and matter – the principle fundamental to alchemy – but wanted spirit to be able to *act on* matter while remaining separate from it.

6. '... [Fulcanelli] *disappeared ... never to be seen again except once, by Canseliet, thirty years later.*'
This isn't necessarily true. The French scientist Jacques Bergier recounts a meeting with a strange character who he believes was Fulcanelli.

In their famous best-seller *Le Matin des Mages* (Paris, 1960) – first published in England as *The Dawn of Magic* (1963) – Bergier and his co-author Louis Pauwels state their belief that alchemy is the relic of a lost civilisation whose science and technology were highly advanced, though different from ours. The primary aim of their science was the 'transmutation' of the alchemist himself into a higher state of consciousness. Power over matter and energy was a secondary consideration.

Bergier relates how he was working alone one day in 1937, in a test laboratory at the Parisian Gas Board, when 'Fulcanelli' unexpectedly turned up. He seemed to know a great deal about Bergier's work in atomic research and he issued a warning about its dangers. Atomic explosives powerful enough to destroy whole cities, he asserted, can be produced from 'a few grammes of metal'. 'Certain geometrical arrangements of highly purified materials,' he explained, 'are enough to release atomic forces without recourse to either electricity or vacuum techniques.' The stranger went on to affirm that civilisations in the past destroyed themselves by the misuse of atomic energy. Certain techniques for producing it have survived among alchemists who, however, never divorce their technical researches from their moral and spiritual preoccupations – unlike modern science which he saw as heading for disaster.

Under Bergier's persistent questioning, the stranger would say only this much about the secret of alchemy: 'there is a way of manipulating matter and energy so as to produce what modern scientists call "a field of force". This field acts on the observer and puts him in a privileged position *vis-à-vis* the universe. From this position he has access to the realities which are ordinarily hidden by time and space, matter and energy. This is what is called the "Great Work".... The essential thing is not the transmutation of metals, but that of the experimenter himself.'

7. ' ... *the blue glass – was coloured just like this by trace elements in the flux itself* ... '
I was sceptical about this until a friend of mine drew my attention to an account of some experiments in medieval glass-making conducted at Erlangen University in 1977: a batch was mixed containing a particular proportion of iron to manganese; and, under various conditions, colours from blue and green to yellow, brown and purple were produced. The experimenters specifically mention that iron and manganese are found in beechwood ash which, moreover, is known to have been used as a flux.

See C. von Sellner, H. J. Oel, and B. Camera, 'Untersuchung alter Glaser (Waldglas) auf Zusammenhang von Zusammensetzung, Farbe und Schmalzatmosphare mit der Elektronen-spektroskopic und der Elektronenspinresonanz (ESR)', *Glastechnische Berichte*, vol. 52 (1979).

8. *'True imagination belongs to the Spirit.'*
Smith's intricate 'meditation' on imagination has a historical counterpart not just in alchemy but in the views of the Romantic poets (notably William Blake) who doubted the ability of Reason to apprehend reality and replaced it with Imagination as man's most important faculty. The most famous expression of this view can be found in the thirteenth chapter of Samuel Taylor Coleridge's *Biographia Literaria* (London, 1817). Here, in a passage which has several points in common with Smith's meditation, Coleridge dismisses what we are now accustomed to call imagination as mere 'fancy' that is 'no other than a mode of memory emancipated from the order of time and space'. Authentic imagination on the other hand is of two kinds – primary and secondary.

> The primary imagination I hold to be the living power and prime agent of all human perception, and as a repetition in the finite mind of the eternal act of creation in the infinite I AM.

The secondary imagination he considers to be an 'echo' of the primary, 'co-existing with the conscious will, yet still as identical with the primary in the kind of its agency, and differing only in degree, and in the mode of its operation. It dissolves, diffuses, dissipates, in order to recreate; or where this process is rendered impossible, yet still, at all events, it struggles to idealize and unify.'

In Smith's terms the primary imagination would seem to be the prerogative of Spirit, and the secondary, of the soul. However, I must admit that I have nearly as much trouble understanding Coleridge as Smith. A passage that I've found helpful occurs in 'Making, Knowing and Judging', one of the essays in a collection called *The Dyer's Hand* (London, 1963) by the poet W. H. Auden. He adopts, and adapts, Coleridge's distinctions for his own artistic credo:

The concern of the Primary Imagination, its only concern, is with sacred beings and sacred events. The sacred is that to which it is obliged to respond; the profane is that to which it cannot respond and therefore does not know . . . A sacred being cannot be anticipated; it must be encountered . . . All imaginations do not recognize the same sacred beings or events, but every imagination responds to those it recognizes in the same way. The impression made . . . by a sacred being is of an overwhelming but indefinable importance – an unchangeable quality, an Identity, as Keats said: I-am-that-I-am is what every sacred being seems to say . . . The response of the imagination to such a presence or significance is a passion of awe.

A sacred being can be beautiful or ugly, sublime or terrifying, good or evil, etc., but it must arouse awe. Some sacred beings, of course, are sacred only to a single imagination – it's in this sense, I think, that Smith speaks of an object 'in which we have invested our soul-image', whether it is a country, a house, or a teddy-bear etc. Some sacred beings are sacred only to members of a social group – for example, 'the Latin language among humanists', says Auden; some, like kings, are only sacred to people within a certain culture. Some are sacred to all imaginations at all times: 'The Moon', for example, 'Fire', 'Snakes' and those 'four important beings which can only be defined in terms of nonbeing: Darkness, Silence, Nothing, Death'.

(By these criteria, it looks as though alchemy falls into the last category. Yet it is noticeable that it seems not to be *continuously* sacred to all imaginations at all times. Rather, it is sacred to different cultures – Greek, Arabic, Chinese, German, say – at different periods of their history; and, where it is transmitted from one culture to another, e.g. from the Arabic to the European, the sacred beings do not so much change but accumulate – just as Europe took on the 'mercury' and 'sulphur' added by the Arabs, so it also added its own sacred beings such as, on the one hand, 'salt' and, on the other, 'soul' as defined by Christianity.)

The secondary imagination is of another character, according to Auden, and 'at another mental level'. It is 'active not passive, and its categories are not the sacred and the profane, but the beautiful and the ugly'. In other words it is the secondary imagination which the poet or artist brings to bear on the sacred beings of the primary in order to *evaluate* them and (Coleridge would say) to *recreate* them. (Interestingly, Auden says that our dreams 'are full of sacred beings and events – indeed, they may well contain nothing else, but we cannot distinguish in dreams – or so it seems to me, though I may be wrong – between the beautiful and the ugly. Beauty and ugliness pertain to Form not to Being'.)

Both degrees of imagination are essential to the health of the mind: 'without the inspiration of sacred awe, its beautiful forms would soon become banal, its rhythms mechanical; without the activity of the secondary imagination the passivity of the Primary would be the mind's undoing; sooner or later its sacred beings would possess it, it would come to think of itself as sacred, exclude the outer world as profane and so go mad.'

In Auden's terms, the Great Work is entirely peopled by sacred beings. They process with archetypal splendour through the Hermetic Egg in which the dark unknown realm of the inorganic, contemplatively entered by the alchemist, both activates, and acts as a backdrop for, the transforming images of the primary imagination.

In his own practice Jung attributed the highest importance to a technique of 'conscious dreaming' which he called 'active imagination.' He is nowhere very explicit about it, nor is it especially well named since its aim is to allow images from the unconscious to rise up into consciousness where they are *passively* observed, as if in a waking dream. At any rate it's clear that what Jung has in mind is a method of activating the deepest layers of the psyche in order to evoke its archetypal images or, as he says, symbols. The creative, healing effect of these is realised by consciously assimilating and integrating them into the personality by means of some quasi-artistic activity such as mandala painting. (This corresponds to the activity of the secondary imagination.)

Mandalas (a Sanskrit work meaning 'circle') are chiefly found in Hindu and Buddhist art. Although no two are alike they display the same regularity of structure based on the circle and square (or four-fold arrangement, such as the cross or the four cardinal points). They occur spontaneously, Jung discovered, in the fantasies or active imaginings of his patients. He saw them as symbols which unified the oppositions within the psyche, i.e. as a primordial image of that psychic totality which he called the self.* A mandala, then, is what Smith would designate a soul-image, analogous to that of the star. Both star and mandala signal the union of Above and Below, consciousness and the unconscious – the circle in the mandala signifies, as it were, the 'solar celestial masculine principle' while the square signifies the 'lunar terrestrial feminine principle'. This 'archetypal' arrangement corresponds to an image of Smith's Spirit, i.e. it is *universal*; the content of the mandala – that which makes it unlike any other – corresponds to the soul's *particular* contribution. However, both star and mandala are still only *images* at this stage – volatile but not yet fixed, as Smith would say. They are the *potential* Philosophers' Stone and Self respectively, which must become actual and concrete in that final and mutual transformation of matter and spirit about which nothing can be said with any certainty.

It's tempting to say that the poetical notion of the primary imagination is identical to the theological notion of Spirit, the psychological collective unconscious and the neo-Platonic *anima mundi*. But, of course, each system of thought must be kept distinct. The true relation between them, as Eileen would remind us, is not identity, but analogy. So, for example, we can say that soul : spirit :: secondary imagination : primary imagination; or, soul : spirit :: *anima* : collective unconscious :: individual : collective; or, Albedo : Rubedo :: White : Red :: 'star' : Philosophers' Stone :: symbol of totality (mandala) : Self.

To return to Coleridge's (and Auden's) imagination, we can see that the poet and the Jungian patient have this in common: that they both strive to bring the active secondary imagination to bear on the sacred beings presented to them by the primary imagination. The results will be the same in kind but will differ in degree – roughly speaking, we might guess that the purely therapeutic image shades into the 'work of art' at a point

---

* Eileen's hypothetical diagrams of the Hermetic Egg, which is also an image of the psyche, are obviously 'mandalas'.

where it ceases to have purely private, personal and individual significance, and takes on a public, impersonal and collective significance. Alchemy is analogous to artistic activity but it's more complex, having links with philosophy, chemistry and so on, but also with religious ritual. The alchemist *gives himself over* to the sacred beings of the primary imagination, and, as Auden rightly says, risks being possessed by them and going mad. He does not primarily seek to transform them into a work of art but to allow them to transform him into a work of the Art. If he survives this process (which can be seen as the inverse of the artistic process – the primary imagination is brought to bear on the secondary), then his transformed secondary imagination will simultaneously take on the creative power of the primary whose images can then be actualised, e.g. as the Philosophers' Stone.

9. '... *whom the Fire Master describes as: 'Immortal mortals, mortal immortals...*'
The 'Fire Master' is Heraclitus, the fifth-century BC Greek philosopher. Elsewhere, in an entry I've omitted from the main text, Smith says:

> No one has yet understood Heraclitus who affirmed that the soul is composed of fire *and is therefore related to the order of the world* which was not made by gods or men 'but always was and is and shall be: an everlasting fire kindling in measures and going out in measures'. He knew that 'all things are an equal exchange for fire and fire for all things, as goods are for gold and gold for goods'.

The quotation in the main text was preserved by Hippolytus and is described by G. J. Kirk and J. E. Raven (*The Presocratic Philosophers*, Cambridge, 1957) as 'very obscure' – a verdict with which I have no quarrel. They go on to say vaguely that it has 'some connexion with the doctrine of opposites, but also suggests the deification of some souls'. It can also be translated as 'mortal immortals, immortal mortals...' or 'immortals are mortal(s), mortals are immortal(s)...'

Sublimation

1. *'The Ancients knew how to divine its currents and to regulate its flow with artificial landmarks . . .'*

    I am grateful to a friend of mine for pointing out that notions of an 'earth-spirit' have lingered on, usually in less exalted forms than Smith's *Anima Mundi*, which he identifies with Mercurius. Examples are Mesmer's 'animal magnetism'; 'vril', a telluric energy which exercised the Nazi magicians; and Wilhelm Reich's 'orgone' energy.

    More recently, the most eloquent exponent of an 'earth-spirit' theory has been John Michell. In *The View over Atlantis* (1969; revised edition, London, 1983), he contends that knowledge of an earth-spirit, possibly related to the earth's magnetic field and responding to the phases of sun and moon, was a commonplace in neolithic times when mankind led a nomadic existence of perpetual pilgrimage between certain landmarks whose sanctity was activated, as it were, at particular times of the year according to the seasons and the position of the heavenly bodies.

    Michell goes on to argue convincingly that, subsequently, the subtle flow of serpent-like earth energy was artificially strengthened by the addition, for instance, of mounds, standing stones and stone circles. A standing stone acts on the earth in the way that an acupuncture needle acts on the human body, while a stone circle might act as a key point – a sacred place – where the terrestrial energy is gathered, as if in a reservoir, and brought into union with the celestial or solar energy. The 'lines of force' form an intricate geometrical web linking holy places and prehistoric sites.* In China they have long been known as *lung-mei*, the 'paths of the dragon', which it is the task of geomancers to divine and

---

* Many of which were later 'christianised' by having churches built on them.

maintain in spiritual harmony; in Britain they were called 'leys' by one Alfred Watkins who in 1921 had vision of them forming a great prehistoric network of energy lines, often coinciding with old but still-existing paths. (See *The Old Straight Track*, London, 1925; reprinted London, 1970.)

As Michell says, there is 'no principle openly recognized today which can explain for what purpose this great work was undertaken'; but Smith at least seems to believe that contact with the earth-spirit can promote both mental and physical well-being and perhaps, more generally, the harmonious inter-relationship between man and the world. It may be that he sees the ancient large-scale engineering of the earth-spirit as the social counterpart of the individual alchemical Work; or, to put it another way, that the macrocosmic science of geomancy mirrors the microcosmic Art of alchemy.

2. '*. . . It was indeed my dear master.*'
It's not easy to know what to make of this entry. Smith's 'master' could be any one of a number of things: hallucination, ghost, real person or product of the imagination, for example. Smith may be dramatising an imaginary conversation, as if extending his device of using 'meditations' which, at the start of the Work, he defines as 'dialogues with oneself'. Following Eileen's lead, it's worth noting that C. G. Jung conducted a number of conversations with a character called Philemon. Although the latter seemed quite 'real' to him, Jung decided that he was a manifestation of the collective unconscious, in fact the archetype of 'the Wise Old Man', who symbolises *meaning*. Smith's master shares similarities with him, including a long beard and a style of speech both stilted and cryptic. It is possible then that Smith's unconscious is projecting this archetype in the image of his master who, since he was already 'old' in the early 1930s, would by now either be considerably older or, more likely, dead. It's obvious that this man did not pay a call on Smith in the usual way so that I think it's safe to say he is not an actual person. Nor does the general tenor of the entry suggest that the master is of a ghostly or hallucinatory nature, even though Smith is clearly prone to 'seeing things'. However, it bothers me that even the least unsatisfactory 'explanation' – the Jungian – doesn't really

explain the phenomenon. We may just as easily say that this master *is* a ghost or, why not?, a man who walks through walls. To invoke psychology for this sort of thing seems almost to be in bad taste. It may be better to take the event at face value, as Smith does; after all, his master behaves in a perfectly lifelike manner, even imparting hard information when he tells Smith to use gold. His apparent presence is certainly not more extraordinary than the entire alchemical enterprise!

Smith's response to his master's appearance is so matter-of-fact that it occurs to me that I'm making too much of it. Just because it seems decidedly odd to *me*, that doesn't mean that it *is* odd. I'm thinking of a comparable description I read years ago in the autobiography of the yogi Paramahansa Yogananda who was the first 'oriental' guru to have an impact on the West. He met his own guru again some time after the latter's death and was treated to a description of the afterlife and some good advice. This would not surprise the average Hindu for whom death is no barrier to continued contact with a spiritual mentor. Indeed, when an initiate is talking of his guru, he sometimes forgets to mention that his teacher is not incarnate at that particular time. Nor would Smith's experience surprise a Taoist who will tell us that some men become immortals and so, presumably, are able to turn up at any time with valuable advice. And, while I think of it, the 'legend' of Christ's resurrection has it that he insisted he was not merely a phantasm (nor a psychological aberration) and invited Thomas to feel his wounds. Might it be that Jung's Philemon was *both* intimately connected to Jung's psychological make-up (i.e. to his personal spiritual development) *and* an actual historical person? Perhaps, too, since gurus can have more than one pupil or disciple, there are some who represent the archetype of 'meaning' or the 'higher self' to a whole group of people – perhaps even to the whole world. In this case, the Christians' claim that Jesus is a tangible living person to them, and potentially to everybody, is not a metaphor, but, as they would say, a fact.

3. '... *the purely mental cultivation of* astrum ...'
   Astrum is a Paracelsian term whose literal meaning is 'star' and which implies something like 'quintessence'. Martin Ruland's *Lexicon of Alchemy* (London, 1622) says:

Imagination is the star (*astrum*) in man, the celestial or supercelestial body.

In *Psychology and Alchemy* (p. 265ff.) Jung comments extensively on what he calls this 'astounding definition'. He abandons his former description of the Magnum Opus as a series of images 'projected' on to inanimate matter by the alchemist; and, instead, asserts that – in the light of this conception of the imagination as a 'star' or (as Smith says) 'star body' – the Opus is not a series of 'immaterial phantoms' but something corporeal, a 'subtle body'.

Imagination, he says, is 'perhaps the most important key to the understanding of the Opus', and, in the following definition, which is no less difficult and astounding than the alchemical one, he says it is 'a physical activity that can be fitted into the cycle of material changes, that brings these about and is brought about by them in its turn. In this way the alchemist related himself both to the unconscious and to the substance he hoped to transform through the power of imagination . . . Imagination [as 'quintessence'] is therefore a concentrated extract of the life forces, both physical and psychic . . . [The artist] works with and through his own quintessence and is himself the indispensable condition of his own experiment'.

We can't say therefore that the alchemical transformations were either material or spiritual, either physical or psychical – alchemy itself insists that there is no either-or in the Opus, but always a both-and. In other words we have to imagine the Work taking place in an intermediate realm between mind and matter, says Jung – a paradoxical realm of 'subtle bodies whose characteristic it is to manifest themselves in a mental as well as a material form . . . Obviously, the existence of this intermediate realm comes to a sudden stop the moment we try to investigate matter in and for itself, apart from all projection; and it remains non-existent as long as we believe we know anything conclusive about matter or the psyche'.

But as soon as physics and psychology reach their limits at impenetrable darkness, then the intermediate realm of subtle bodies takes on new life: 'the physical and the psychic are once more blended in an indissoluble unity. We have come very near to this turning-point today . . . '

4. '... *this passage written by the noble millennarian Artephius* ...'
Smith is jocularly referring to the author's claim that 'the space of a thousand years, or thereabouts ... has now passed over my head, since the time I was born to this day, through the alone goodness of God Almighty, by the use of this wonderful quintessence'.

Artephius continues, as is usual, to promise that he will 'declare all things truly and sincerely, that you may not want anything for the perfecting of this stone of the philosophers' – except, of course, 'one certain thing, which is not lawful for me to discover to any, because it is either revealed or made known by God Himself, or taught by some master, which notwithstanding he that can bend himself to the search thereof, by the help of a little experience, may easily learn in this book'.

The only version of *Artephius His Secret Book* I have come across was published, together with Flamel's *Exposition* and the *Epistle* of John Pontanus, in London 'by T.S. for Thomas Walkley' in 1624, and '... religiously done into English out of the French and Latin copies. By Eirenaeus Orandus'. It is likely that the author adopted the name of Artephius from the Artefius who wrote an early tract (possibly around the eighth century, according to Jung, and of Harranite origin) called *Clavis maioris sapientiae*, 'the Key of greater wisdom', which can be found in *Theatrum Chemicum*, vol. IV (1659 edition).

5. *'I can't help wondering about Helvetius' story.'*
Johann Friedrich Schweitzer, better known by his Latinised name, Helvetius, was a scientist of high standing in the seventeenth century, author of medical and botanical books, and physician to the Prince of Orange. In his book *The Golden Calf* (trans. W. Cooper, London, 1673) he gives us one of the most frequently quoted stories of transmutation.

On the 27 December 1666, a stranger visited him at his house in The Hague. He was about forty-three or forty-four years old, average height, clean-shaven, slightly pockmarked, dark-haired. He had come to take issue with Helvetius over his published scepticism of alchemy and asked him if he would know the philosophers' stone if he saw it. Helvetius said that he wouldn't, whereupon the man took out a neat ivory box and from it produced 'three ponderous pieces or small lumps of the stone, each about the bigness of a small walnut, transparent, of a pale brimstone colour' which Helvetius was allowed to examine. But when he begged to be given a tiny piece the stranger refused, saying that it was 'not lawful'. At the stranger's request Helvetius showed him into his best room at the back of the house, hoping that he would change his mind. But the man only showed him five inscribed medallions, made of alchemical gold, which he wore underneath his doublet. He then told his host various stories about his master's activities and transmutations, and concluded by promising to return in three weeks' time to demonstrate 'the manner of projection, provided it were then lawful without prohibition'.

The stranger returned at the appointed time and, under great persuasion from Helvetius, was finally prevailed upon to part with a tiny piece of his stone. The doctor confessed that he was disappointed at such a small crumb, no bigger than a turnip seed. The stranger immediately took it back and cut it in half with his fingernail, saying, 'It is yet sufficient for thee.' Then he promised to come back in the morning and show Helvetius how to project.

But he did not come; and was never seen again.

> Nevertheless [says Helvetius] late that night my wife (who was a most curious student and enquirer after the art, whereof that worthy man had discourst) came soliciting and vexing me to make experiment of that little spark of his bounty in that art . . . saying to me, unless this be done, I shall have no rest nor sleep all this night . . . I commanded a fire to be made (thinking alas) now is this man (though so divine in discourse) found guilty of falsehood . . . Nevertheless my wife wrapped the said matter in wax, and I cut half an ounce or six drams of old lead, and put it into a crucible in the fire, which being melted, my wife put in the said Medicine made up into a small pill or button, which presently made such a hissing and bubbling in its perfect operation, that within a quarter of an hour all the mass of lead was totally transmuted into the best and finest gold,

which made us all amazed as planet-struck . . .

. . . Truly I, and all standing about me, were exceedingly startled, and did run with this aurified lead (being yet hot) unto the goldsmith, who wondered at the fineness, and after a short trial of touch [i.e. with a touchstone], he judg'd it the most excellent gold in the whole world, and offered to give most willingly fifty florins for every ounce of it.

The next day, with rumours flying, many illustrious people visited and suggested that Helvetius submit the gold to more rigorous testing – which he was happy to do, if only to gratify his curiosity. The gold not only passed with flying colours but even, in the course of one test, changed a sample of silver into gold 'by reason of its great and excellent abounding tincture'.

(It might be worth mentioning that the philosopher Baruch Spinoza was in The Hague at the time, and he wrote to a friend, Jarrig Jellis, saying that he'd visited the silversmith Buectel who had assayed the alleged alchemical gold. He also visited Helvetius and was able to inspect the crucible in which the transmutation took place, and also the gold.)

6. ' . . . *until the chemical tree bears golden fruit.*'
This passage is confusing but it's possible to see what Smith is driving at. He sees the copper beech as an image both of reflux distillation in particular and of the Opus in general. We are also reminded of the organic, continuous nature of the Work which, in one sense, simply 'grows' imperfect metals into the perfection of gold. One of the *Rosarium* illustrations shows a tree hung with golden suns like fruit.

Jung says that the *arbor philosophica* (philosophical tree) – which he related back to the paradisal Tree of Knowledge and compares to the Sephirotic Tree of the Kabbalists – is the commonest alchemical symbol for the process of individuation. It is a form of mandala to which a third dimension, that of depth and growth, has been added. It is a symbol of the Self.

However, Smith's metaphor takes a surprising, literalistic turn when he ends with a quotation from Paracelsus, who asserts that

7. *"Gold ... may grow in a glasse like a tree ... "*

This opinion is similar to Nicholas Flamel's when he writes (in his *Exposition*) that 'our stone is turned into a true and pure tree, to bud abundantly, and afterwards to bring forth infinite little sprigs and branches'.

Naturally I shared Smith's scepticism over Sir Isaac Newton's alleged gold 'tree' – until I read B. J. T. Dobbs's *The Foundation of Newton's Alchemy* or 'The Hunting of the Greene Lyon' (Cambridge, 1975). Newton, it turns out, studied alchemy for more than a quarter of a century and conducted thousands of experiments. His alchemical manuscripts total some 650,000 words. Dobbs quotes his laboratory assistant, Humphrey Newton, who described his master as rarely going to bed before two or three o'clock, and sometimes not till five or six, especially in spring and autumn (i.e. astrologically significant times) 'at which time he used to employ about six weeks in his laboratory, the fire scarce going out either night or day, sitting up one night and I another, 'till he had finished his chemical experiments, in the performance of which he was most accurate, strict and exact. What his aim might be I was not able to penetrate into, but his pains, his diligence at these set times made me think he aimed at something beyond the reach of human art and industry ... '

And indeed, Newton was not entirely without success. In the *Clavis* (*Key*) he describes in detail the process for making philosophical mercury, and his own results:

> I know whereof I write, for I have in the fire manifold glasses with gold and this mercury. They grow in these glasses in the form of a tree [*arboris forma crescuent*], and by a continual circulation the trees are dissolved again with the work into new mercury. I have such a vessel in the fire with gold thus dissolved, where the gold was visibly not dissolved by a corrosive into atoms, but extrinsically and intrinsically into a new mercury as living and mobile as any mercury found in the world. For it makes gold begin to swell, to be swollen, and to putrefy, and to spring forth into sprouts and branches, changing colours daily, the appearances of which fascinate me every day. [*Tumescere enim facit (aurum)*

turgere et putrescere ac crescere in surculos et ramos, mutando indies colores quorum aspectus me quotidie tenent.]

It must be said that the *Clavis* might in fact have been written by Eirenaeus Philalethes. The latter, as Dobbs has shown, had a profound influence on Newton. *An Open Entrance . . .* was Newton's bedside reading for twenty years; his copy, annotated on every page, can be seen in the British Museum. In William Cooper's 1678 edition of *Ripley Reviv'd* – five tracts by Philalethes – a treatise called *Clavis*, now lost, is listed among Philalethes' works. Moreover, many of the concepts treated in the *Clavis* are shared by Philalethes; and, in one place, a phrase is repeated as if Newton had made a mistake while copying it out. However, that said, Dobbs thinks that on balance the *Clavis was* written by Newton. Is it too much to see in this short text a kind of watershed in the history of scientific thought where, for a brief moment, the last truly great alchemist is indistinguishable from the first truly great modern scientist?

Finally, to return to the question of 'gold growing like a tree', some mention must be made of Archibald Cockren. His personal credentials are impeccable, being held in high esteem by those who knew him as a man of courage, honesty and integrity. He served with distinction in the Great War as part of a medical team, and was one of the pioneers of electro-massage. He experimented in alchemy for forty years before he found the secret which would give him real hope of success; and his results are set down in *Alchemy Rediscovered and Restored* (London, 1940), a learned exposition of traditional alchemy as well as an account of practical experimentation. Unfortunately for us, like all great adepts before him he preserves the secret of his prima materia. He worked in Surrey and retired to Eastbourne where he died in the 1960s.

In *Heart of Scotland* (London, 1956), C. R. Cammell, FRSA, describes how he visited his friend Cockren over a six-month period in the 1950s; and, during that time, he watched a 'crystal' of gold grow like a plant from a black mass in a hermetically sealed vessel.

I confess that my half-hearted attempt to locate Cammell's book failed; but it's referred to and quoted in a popular book on alchemy by C. A. Burland called *The Arts of the Alchemists* (London, 1967). Here, incidentally, Burland describes a visit to the British Museum's Department of Coins and Medals where he was shown some 'fine reproductions of the alchemical medals of the eighteenth century, and a strange specimen of apparently unworked gold'. The latter looked like a twig with a crystal-shaped fracture at one end and at the other a small hole as if gas had blown through the metal when molten. Its weight showed it to be of the specific gravity of gold. The label on it – of a type used some eighty years before – said it was a specimen of so-called alchemical gold. Further information about it had been destroyed by fire during the Second World War when the old offices had been bombed.

Projection

1. '... the one MERCURIUS ... from whom I rise new-born.'
The final paragraph of Eileen's text (which I have italicised) looks as though it ought to be a continuation of the Regimen of Sol in Smith's original manuscript. In alchemical terms it is an unremarkable passage, except for one detail: it is written on Eileen's paper, but in Smith's handwriting. This, I admit, gave me something of a surprise. I was suddenly faced with the possibility that Eileen had invented all Smith's notes and journals, forging them in a different script. However, if that were so – if she had taken all that trouble – why would she give the game away at the last minute? My second thought, therefore, was that she may have begun by inventing Smith (who was no doubt suggested to her by a real former resident of the house she had rented), but that she had somehow been 'taken over' by the character and had ended by believing in him. The highly charged emotional state she was in on her arrival may have led to some sort of nervous breakdown – a hypothesis supported by the whole tenor of her final improbable entry. Moreover, I think it likely that the effect of her immersion in a study of alchemy was ambiguous: on the one hand it helped her to hold mental disorder at bay; on the other, it stimulated an already unstable condition, leading her to make a number of inadvertent fabrications – and, finally, to lose touch with reality. Be that as it may, we must nevertheless give Eileen credit for composing an extraordinary document whose description of, and insight into, alchemy is unparalleled in my research at least. It can truly be called her *magnum opus* – even if, sadly, it did all take place in her imagination. She can take comfort in the knowledge that she is by no means the first person (as many Philosophers have testified) to be driven out of their wits by the mystery of alchemy.